LIGHTNING CHILD

BOOK 3 IN THE CHILDREN OF THE MOUNTAIN SERIES

www.rahakok.com
@rahakok

By R.A. Hakok:

Cody Doyle

Viable

The Children Of The Mountain Series

Among Wolves
The Devil You Know
Lightning Child

Visit www.rahakok.com to download *The Shoebox* and *The Map*, the free companion ebooks to the *Children of the Mountain* series.

RECAP?

If it's been a while since you read *Among Wolves* or *The Devil You Know* you'll find a recap at the end of this book.

WE TAKE BENJAMIN'S ROUTE, south through the mountains. We have just the one pack between us and I've lightened it for the hike, but there's the rifles, and where the drifts run deep the kid needs carrying.

I count off the landmarks we pass. The barracks at Fort Narrows. The veterinarian's outside Ely, where I found Benjamin's body. The Susquehanna Bank in Boonsboro that sheltered us from the storms after we fled Eden. We don't stop at any of them. We have to make time now. Peck has a start on us.

The first day we make it almost to the state line before darkness and cold run us off the road. We crest a shallow rise and I spot a small church in the valley below, sitting right on the banks of the Potomac. It has little to recommend it, but we've passed nothing else for miles, and I can't see anything better on the stretch beyond the river. I catch Mags eyeing it, weighing the shelter it'll provide against the shrinking sliver of gray to the west that still separates earth from sky. She turns back to the road, like she means go on, but I pull the mask I wear down and call to her through chattering teeth. It'll do for the few hours we mean to be here. I wait while she considers what I've said, hoping she doesn't call me on the rest of it. Truth is we've pushed hard to get this far; I'm not sure how much more I have in me now. Eventually she nods, points her snowshoes in the direction of the chapel.

There's no need for the pry bar; the door's already hanging back on its one remaining hinge. She heads off with the kid in search of wood for a fire while I make my way inside. I shuck off my pack and start tending to our dinner. My fingers are numb from the cold; it takes longer than it ought to get the cartons open and our rations assembled. I'm still working on the last of them when she returns, dumps what she's gathered on the floor and sets to work, stacking firewood and kindling with practiced ease. I add water from my canteen to the MREs, spilling as much as I manage to get into the cartons, then I shuffle myself as close as I can to the smoldering branches and listen as the chemical heaters do their work, hissing away as they slowly thaw our food. As soon it's passable warm I tear the top off one of them and start wolfing down what's inside. Mags waits a little longer before she opens hers, then starts poking around half-heartedly at the contents. When I've had the last of mine I throw the empty pouch on the fire. The foil shrivels and for a second the flames flicker brighter as it's consumed. I hold my hands close for whatever heat they'll allow, but already they're dying down again.

The wind howls around the gable, rattling the door against its frame. I pull the parka tighter around me. I'm exhausted, bone weary, but it's been worth it. We've come farther than I thought possible when we first set out this morning; farther than I ever hiked in a day with Marv. At first light we'll cross the river and then we'll be back in Virginia, with no more than twenty miles between us and the Blue Ridge Mountain Road.

I wonder where Peck is tonight. Angus said he'd set out with Kurt and the other Guardians yesterday morning. We didn't run into him on the way up with Hicks, so he must have taken the Cacoctin Mountain Highway. That road is easier, but it's longer, and he's no reason to push hard. If we can maintain the pace we managed today there's a chance we might yet overhaul him, make it back to Mount Weather before he arrives. I glance over at the rifles, propped against the wall. If we can do that maybe we can hold the tunnel, keep him out. For a moment I allow myself that hope. Truth is I have no other plan.

I take a final swig from the canteen and announce I'm turning in. But when I go to stand the muscles in my legs have stiffened; I have to reach for one of the pews to haul myself upright. I glance over at Mags while I steady myself, but she's busy fixing herself a coffee and hasn't noticed. On the other side of the fire the kid's focused on a HOOAH! he's liberated from one of the MRE cartons. I watch as he pushes the candy bar up inside its wrapper, then takes to gnawing away at the end of it with those little teeth of his. I'd gotten into the habit of tethering him while we slept; it feels a little strange to have him roaming free now. He looks up at me for a moment, like maybe his thoughts have run that way too, then he turns his attention back to his meal.

I undress quick as I can and climb inside the sleeping bag, pulling the quilted material tight around me. Mags is still sitting by the fire, swirling her coffee as she stares into the flames. When we set off this morning I thought she looked better; that the shadows under her eyes had faded a little, that maybe the angles of her cheekbones were a little softer. But now I'm not so sure.

I tell myself it's just the firelight. Besides, it's early yet; barely a day since she came through the scanner.

She didn't get the time inside it it'd been set for, but there's no way she's still sick. I've seen firsthand what the virus does to a person. Marv had been strong, and by the end he hadn't been able to lift a boot from the snow. When she took her turns breaking trail earlier it was all I could do to keep up.

I hold on to that thought for a while. It should bring me comfort, but somehow it doesn't. My mind keeps returning to the image I have of her, bursting out of the pedestrian tunnel. The way she had moved had been...unnatural. She had dealt with the soldiers, each in turn, without so much as a break in her stride. Even Hicks; she'd been on him before he'd barely had time to twitch.

I lie there for a while, trying to work out what it might mean. But it's no use; sleep's already plucking at my thoughts, unraveling them before they have a chance to form. I feel my eyelids growing heavy. I reach up for the dog tags I lifted from Boots. It's too early to tell yet, I know. I run my fingers over them anyway, testing for imperfections that weren't there this morning. Other than the letters pressed into the metal the thin slivers of steel are still smooth.

I close my eyes.

I'll check hers later, when she's sleeping.

*

WE'RE ON THE ROAD AGAIN before dawn. Mags takes the pack and rifles while I follow behind, carrying the kid on my shoulders. If breaking trail tires her she doesn't show it; her pace doesn't slacken, not even on the inclines. My legs are longer, and I have years of pounding the snow to my name, but I feel like it's me who's holding us up now.

We make good time, but it's already stretching into the afternoon before we catch our first glimpse of the Harry Byrd Highway. I set the kid down at the top of the on-ramp and search the snow for signs anyone's passed while I get my breath back. But there's nothing, far as the eye can see. The wind's been squalling all morning, however; if they came by more than an hour ago it'd already have wiped their tracks clean.

Mags adjusts the straps on her pack and sets off again. I hoist the kid back onto my shoulders and follow. From here it's a long steady climb and for the next hour I focus on her boots as they rise and fall ahead of me, following a tireless, mechanical rhythm, like she could do this all day. At last the road levels and off in the distance I see it: a faded blue sign announcing the turnoff to the Blue Ridge Mountain Road.

I catch up to her by a stand of spruce-fir that still clings stubbornly to the embankment and pull the mask I wear down to gulp in air. The thin cotton's iced up where I've been breathing through it, and for some reason that sets spidey off. Mags asks if I'm ready. I don't have my wind back yet so I just nod and she takes off again.

I'm about to follow when I spot something out of the corner of my eye: a length of chain, tangled up in one of the branches that poke through the snow. The old steel crucifix I used to wear, the one I placed on Marv's grave. Mags is already halfway to the first crest, but I just stand there, staring at it. I don't know what waits for us ahead, but I get the strong sense that whatever it might be, I won't be passing this way again.

I hesitate a moment longer then reach down, pull it free. I shake the chain to clear the powder from it, then I slip it into my pocket and take off after her.

The mountain road climbs sharply from the highway and soon my thighs are burning. When we reach the ridgeline it flattens enough that I consider setting Johnny down, but ahead Mags has picked up the pace so I just tell him to hang on. We follow the road along the spine of the mountain range, picking our way through the lifeless trunks that push up through the snow on either side.

Somewhere far behind clouds the color of gunmetal the sun's already dipping towards the horizon, but we're close now. We round a bend and I see a familiar sign, its dead lights hooded under black metal cowls, announcing we're entering a restricted area. We continue upwards for another half-mile and then finally the road straightens and levels. The trees fall away and we find ourselves in a large clearing that straddles both sides of the ridge.

Ahead there's the chain-link fence, the coils of razor wire above held outwards on rust-streaked concrete pylons. I stop and search its length for signs of a breach, but there's nothing. Spidey doesn't care for it, all the same. He starts pinging a warning, but like earlier it's vague, non-directional. Mags has already found the section I opened with bolt cutters the day I arrived. She slips through, holding the wire back for the kid. I set him down and he follows her in. While he's putting his snowshoes back on I unsnap the throat of my parka and lower the hood to listen. But the only sound's the wind, rattling a faded *No Trespassing* sign against the bars of the gate.

Mags unslings one of the rifles and hands it to me. We leave the guardhouse behind us and make our way into the compound. I scan the perimeter, counting off the concrete cowls of the airshaft vents as we pass. The snow on top of each is undisturbed, but that means even less than the absence of tracks out on the highway. Kane had the codes to the blast door for each facility in the Federal Relocation Arc; Peck wouldn't have planned on making his entrance the way I got back into Eden.

The control tower rises from the highest point of the ridge, its roof bristling with antennae. Dark windows slant outwards from the observation deck, staring down at our approach. The Juvies were supposed to post a watch while we were gone; if anyone's up there they're bound to have spotted us by now. I keep my eyes on the doorway, waiting for it to open. But no one comes out to greet us.

On the far side the helicopter landing pad, the tattered windsock snapping and fluttering on its tether. Spidey dials it up a notch as we hurry past. The temperature's dropping fast now, but that's not what's quickening my stride. We're almost at the portal.

The path curves around then straightens and at last I see it.

In the lee of the tunnel where the wind hasn't yet had chance to smooth it the snow's all churned up, a wide confusion of snowshoe tracks. Beyond I can see the guillotine gate. It's been lowered, a last desperate attempt to keep them out.

It hasn't worked.

The gate hangs inward at a defeated angle. The metal's twisted, charred; on one side it's jumped its runners. The bars that remain grin back at me, spare steel teeth in a gaping maw.

Behind the tunnel stretches off into inky blackness.

*

MAGS PUSHES HER GOGGLES up onto her forehead. She unsnaps her snowshoes and makes for the gate. I reach for her wrist.

'Maybe you should wait out here, with the kid.'

She makes no move to withdraw her hand, but for a second the shadows around her eyes that yesterday I thought were fading seem to grow a fraction darker. She tilts her head.

'You have a plan you're not sharing with me, Gabriel?'

As it turns out, I don't. I've had the last two days to come up with something, to figure out what we might do if Peck beat us here. But I've got nothing. Whatever hopes I had rested on us making it here ahead of him, finding a way to keep him out.

I shake my head.

'Then you're going to need me in there.'

She doesn't say it like there's much else needs discussing but she waits anyway, letting me work it through for myself. And the truth of it is she's right. It wasn't me who saved us, back in Eden. She took care of the soldiers, single-handed. All I did was let them in and then stand back and watch, for the most part of it slack-jawed, while she went to work.

She holds my gaze a second longer, then she just says *Okay*, and slips her hand from mine.

We make our way into the mountain. The darkness closes around us, swallowing us whole; soon I can no longer make out Mags or the kid in front of me. If not being able to see is a hindrance to either of them they aren't showing it; their footfalls grow steadily softer until I can no longer hear them above the sound of my own breathing.

I reach in my pocket for the flashlight, but then stop; it'd only mark us out to whoever might be watching for our approach. Instead I shoulder the rifle and shuffle over to the elevated walkway, groping for the guardrail. My fingers close around it and I set off again, lengthening my stride, anxious not to slip any further behind. The tunnel runs true for a ways and then I feel the rail start to curve. When it straightens again I start the count. For a long time there's nothing but my footsteps and the occasional drip of melt water, rendered distant by the darkness. At last I think I catch a glimpse of something: the tiniest grain of light, and soon Mags' silhouette once again separates itself from the darkness. She's farther than I had imagined, but at least now I can see again. I relinquish my grip on the guardrail and take off after her.

With each step the light grows, the mote becoming a sliver, then a slender shaft, until at last I can make out the blast door ahead. It juts into the tunnel at an unfinished angle, as though it has come to an unexpected halt, its trajectory interrupted. A pale glow spills out from behind, casting soft brace-wire and rock-bolt shadows over the roughhewn granite.

Mags moves closer to the wall, leaning forward to peer around the massive steel frame. She stays like that for a long moment, then disappears inside without saying a word. I shuck off my mittens and unsling the rifle, whispering to the kid to wait. I guess he mustn't care much for that plan, however, because he squeezes past me and takes off after her.

I follow them through the series of antechambers that lead in from the tunnel. Mags stops at each doorway to listen, moving forward again only when she's satisfied there's nothing waiting behind. When we reach the entrance to the main cavern she suddenly holds up a hand and I freeze, my nerves jumping like bowstrings. For long seconds she just stays like that. Eventually she whispers back at me over her shoulder.

'Hear that?'

I close my eyes, trying to quiet the pounding of my heart while I strain for whatever it is she's heard. But it's no use; I can't make out a thing. I shake my head.

I watch as she slips silently into the cavern. I take a deep breath and scurry across the street after her, my eyes darting this way and that for any sign of Peck or the Guardians. When she reaches the first of the buildings she stops. The kid crouches next to her. He angles his head up, one mitten cupped to his brow against the glare of the arc lights. His mouth opens in wonder and for a second I see this place as he must, as I did when I first arrived here. The huge, domed roof, the high vaulted tunnels; how much bigger it is than what we had known before.

Mags sets off again, keeping tight to the buildings for the thin shadows they provide. We pass the mess and cross to the infirmary, and now for the first time I hear it, too: a soft sound, intermittent, like water splashing. It echoes faintly off the cavern walls, in and out of the tunnels, making the source hard to pinpoint. There's only one place it can be coming from, though.

As we get closer to the lake the sound gets louder, and now in the space between there's something else, almost too soft to hear, like a gasped breath. I tap Mags on the shoulder and point. She nods, like she's already had the same thought. Mount Weather's tallest building, *Command*, is right there. From up on the roof we'll be able to see everything in the cavern laid out beneath us.

We hurry over to the entrance. I sling the rifle onto my shoulder and gently press down on the handle, feeling for the mechanism's biting point. There's a soft click as the lock releases and then we're inside. A sliver of red light pulses intermittently from underneath a door at the end, but otherwise the corridor's dark. The air smells fusty, stale, like it hasn't been disturbed in months. Mags pushes by me, making for the stair. The kid follows, padding silently up the steps behind her.

I follow, my boots squeaking softly on the tread plate. When I get to the top floor she's standing on tiptoe under the access panel that leads to the roof, the fingers of one hand reaching up for it.

'Wait, let me.'

I rest my rifle against the wall and undo the latch. The hatch swings down with a groan and a narrow metal ladder slides out on rollers. She already has her foot on the bottom rung before it reaches the end of its travel; in a few quick steps she's disappeared through. The kid squints up after her, like he doesn't much care for the lights burning from the brace-wired roof. And for a second I think I catch a glimpse of something; something I thought I saw earlier, in Eden's cavern, when he came back to us from wherever the scanner had sent him: a flash of silver, there and then gone again, like a fish under water. I feel the breath catch in my throat, but when I look closer his pupils are dark. It was just my own eyes playing tricks with me after the gloom of the stair.

I whisper to him to wait on the landing and this time he nods, like he might do just that. I turn and follow Mags out onto the roof. As my head clears the hatch I see her, standing on the ledge, looking down. I start to make my way over to join her, but when I glance over again she's already headed back towards me. Her lips have hardened into a tight line, and above her eyes are blazing. I step into her path, mouth opening to ask what's wrong, but I'm far too slow; the fingers that were meant for her shoulder close on thin air. I turn around to call after her, but she's already disappearing through the hatch behind me.

IT MIGHT HAVE WORKED OUT differently if I'd gone after her, right then, although all things considered I doubt it. But I'm only a few feet from the edge now, and curiosity takes over, insisting I witness firsthand whatever it is she's just seen. I step over to the edge, look down into the cavern, and then I'm running back across the roof too. I know even as I lower myself through the hatch I have little hope of catching her; she's long gone, the echoes of her boots already dying on the stair. I lean over the rail and call out, loud as I dare, but if she hears she's past heeding me. She hasn't even bothered with her rifle; it leans against the wall where she left it to go up on the roof. I snatch mine from beside it, shouting over my shoulder at the kid to stay where he is. There's no time to check if he means to comply.

I take the steps two, three at a time, the weapon bouncing on its strap as I bound after her. At the bottom the door swings open and I burst onto Mount Weather's bright, wide streets. Ahead of me she's broken into a silent sprint, heading for the lake.

I slide the rifle off my shoulder and take off after her, fumbling with it as I go. It feels no more familiar to my hands than when I leveled it at Hicks in Eden's cavern, a couple of days ago; the time I've had with it since doesn't seem to have deepened the bond between us. I get a grip on the charging handle and yank it back to chamber the first round, desperately trying to remember everything he told me about shooting it. The only thing I can recall is the bit about getting my breathing under control and there's little chance of that happening, so instead I grip it tight and run as fast as I can, trying not to think about what might happen after.

14

Ahead of me Mags has already disappeared around the corner. I reach the end of the sidewalk and then I'm clear of the last building and out in the open, a wide strip of concrete the only thing now between me and the water. I raise the rifle, press the stock to my cheek. My mind registers what I see as a series of freeze-frame images, presenting each in turn.

Up ahead the Juvies, kneeling in short, uneven rows. Their heads are bowed; here and there shoulders shake with tears. To one side, Tyler and Eric, the two former Guardians who fled with us here, also on their knees, their hands bound behind their backs. A beefy, apple-cheeked man stands over them, shifting his weight from one foot to the other, like he might not care for his current station. Scudder. But he's of little concern to me right now.

Another group, right at the water's edge. Zack, Jason and Seth, the other three Guardians. They're bent over a fourth person, lying on his back between them. His face is covered by a rag, but there's only one person it can be; no one else in our group approaches that size. A final figure stands over him, a rifle slung over his shoulder. Kurt. He's pouring water from a jerry can onto the cloth, a smile playing across his lips as he does it. Now and then he flicks his head back, clearing strands of lank hair from his eyes. Jake struggles furiously as the water hits the rag; it's taking all three of the Guardians to hold him down.

My eyes return to Mags. She's almost on them, but miraculously no one's spotted her yet; they're all preoccupied with what they're doing to Jake. That won't last; any second now all hell's going to break loose. I look around, desperately scanning the cavern for the one person I haven't found.

'Alright, let him up. We'll see if he'll tell us now. Kurt, pick me out one of his favorites, just in case he's still not feeling co-operative.'

There.

I swing the rifle in the direction of the voice. He stands to one side, hands clasped behind his back. He's facing away from me, out onto the lake, but there's no mistaking that iron-heeled stance. I sprint towards him, bringing the barrel up as I run. A few more yards and he'll be close enough that I might even stand a chance of hitting him.

Kurt takes his time emptying the last of the water from the jerry can. When he's done he turns around, takes a step back towards the Juvies and reaches down, grabbing a fistful of blond hair I think belongs to Lauren. She squeals as he drags her to her feet.

Peck's the danger; I shouldn't take my eyes off him, not even for a second. But any moment now Kurt's going to spot Mags, and he has a weapon. Even as I think it he finally sees her, bearing down on him. His mouth opens and he starts to slip the rifle off his shoulder, but he's left it far too late. She grabs the barrel, wrests it from him with absurd ease, and in the same motion swings the stock around high. There's a crunch as it connects with his nose and he drops, so quickly he might as well have been shot.

He's no longer a threat, I know it even before he hits the ground. But there's something happening with Mags now, and for an instant I'm unable to look away. Kurt's lying at her feet, hands cupped around his busted nose. It looks like it's a gusher; fat drops of blood are already spilling from between his fingers, spattering the sidewalk. Peck's right there, no more than a handful of yards behind her, but if that's a concern she gives no sign of it. She just stares down at Kurt as though transfixed.

I finally tear my gaze from her and swing the rifle around. My thumb remembers the safety of its own accord; it flicks the selector even as my finger slips over the trigger. But Lauren's still on her feet and Mags is in the way now, too. I open my mouth to shout at her to get down, but the warning dies on my lips. Peck takes a step to the side, placing her squarely between us, and I sense whatever chance we had for this going our way evaporating. In the end I never even see where it comes from.

One second his hand's empty.

The next it's holding the unmistakable shape of a pistol to the back of her head.

*

I SKID TO A HALT among the Juvies.

Mags still grips the weapon she took from Kurt. Peck barks at her to drop it, but she pays him no mind; from the way she holds it it's unclear whether she's even aware she has it.

I start to inch forward, but Lauren's standing in front of me, blocking the way. Her eyes are wide, her hair a bird's nest of tangles where Kurt has used it to drag her to her feet. I hiss at her to sit down. She starts at my voice, like she didn't realize I was there, and then she bobs her head, once, a quick up and down that suggests there's nothing she'd like better than to oblige. She makes no move to sit, though, just keeps staring straight ahead, like the part of her brain that might be in charge of processing that instruction has flipped the sign from *Open* to *Out to Lunch* or possibly even *Gone Fishin'*. A few of the Juvies glance up in my direction, but for the most part they keep their heads bowed, their eyes fixed on the ground.

Mags continues to glare down at Kurt, seemingly unaware of the gun held to her head. Peck shifts his gaze from her to me then back again, as though he's assessing which of us is most likely to cause him trouble. He takes another half-step to the side. He needn't have bothered. Even if my hands were steady there's no way I'd risk that shot. He tells her to drop the rifle again, this time jabbing the pistol into the back of her neck for good measure.

That gets her attention.

Her eyes flick to the side and I see her tense. And for a second I think she might be about to try something very foolish. An image pops into my head, from a dream

I had, not three nights back, sleeping on the floor of the church in Devil's Backbone. And for a moment I'm not in Mount Weather's cavern. I'm stood between a pair of crumbling gateposts at the end of *The Greenbrier's* long driveway. I can see the blood welling up from the hole the bullet has made. It trickles slow down her scalp to drip into the snow. In the dream it was me who had pulled the trigger, but if she keeps this up the outcome will be no different.

I lower the rifle.

'Mags.'

Her eyes jump to me and I think I catch a flicker of recognition there, but the pistol Peck has pressed to her neck's not helping. I call her name again, louder this time. Her eyes close, stay that way for a long moment, and when they open again it's like she's come back from wherever it is she's been. The Secret Service agent shouts at her to drop the rifle she's holding. She glances at it then lets it slip from her fingers. It clatters uselessly to the ground.

Peck turns to look at me, his eyes gray as the snow outside and just as cold. He pushes the pistol forward, pressing the muzzle into the back of her head.

'Alright, you can lay yours down too, Gabriel. Nice and easy now.'

Mags looks at me and shakes her head, but the Secret Service agent just reaches for her parka and yanks her backwards towards him, jamming the gun into the nape of her neck. Her eyes narrow, like she's struggling to contain whatever it was I saw there only seconds ago. She closes her eyes again and I hold my breath, but when she speaks her voice is calm.

'I wouldn't do that if I were you.'

'Really? And why's that?'

'Because I'm infected.'

A few of the Juvies raise their heads and there's the

sound of fresh struggling from the water's edge. Peck doesn't seem impressed by any of it, however.

'Nice try, but Gabriel's already played that card, remember? I'm not falling for it again.'

She shrugs.

'Suit yourself.'

For a long moment his eyes don't leave me, but then without warning they flick to her, and when they return for the first time I think I see doubt there. He glances over again, allowing his gaze to linger a little longer this time. She's got her back to him, but even from behind he must see how thin she looks. He hesitates a moment longer, then shifts the gun back a fraction. His free hand reaches forward to spin her around, but then he thinks better of it. He takes a slow step backwards, barks another order.

'Hands behind your head. Interlace your fingers.'

She does exactly as he says.

'Alright, turn around. Nice and slow.'

His eyes move to her face and for a split second I see his expression change. Under the glare of the arc lights there's no mistaking it; this isn't some Halloween lampblack stunt, like the one I pulled in Eden. He takes another step back. The gun stays pointed at her, but his eyes drop to the barrel, betraying him. He's not wearing gloves. Would the few seconds he had it pressed to the back of her head have been enough?

'On the ground. Now.'

She lowers herself to her knees, her hands still behind her head.

'We didn't come back for you, Randall. And right now you shouldn't be wasting your time worrying about us, either. You'd do better to concern yourself with how you're going to save your boss.'

Peck's eyes narrow at the mention of Kane, but he doesn't say anything. He looks distracted, like he's trying to work out how long he has; how quickly the virus might move through the metal in his hands. Mags keeps talking.

'You came down the Catoctin Mountain Highway didn't you?'

She doesn't wait for a response.

'I know you did, because we've just come from Eden too. We left the President in the care of some men. Soldiers. Serious types. They've already killed Quartermaster. If you let me show you what I have in my pocket I can prove it.'

Peck appears to consider this for a while, but his thoughts seem elsewhere. The gun doesn't move from her head, but his eyes keep returning to it, like it's something he'd be mighty keen to be rid of. Eventually he tells her to go ahead.

Mags reaches inside her parka and pulls out Kane's reading glasses. She holds them out for him to see.

I start to inch forward again. Mags is finally out of the way, but Lauren's still on her feet, just waiting for the first bullet to find her. I whisper at her to get down, but she just hitches in a breath and stays right where she is.

Peck's staring at Kane's glasses. He gives an almost imperceptible shake of his head, like he might not believe it. I take another step, racking my brains for something to say that will convince him.

'They're planning to bring him to somebody you might know. Dr. Myra Gilbey.'

At the mention of Gilbey's name Peck's eyes flick back to me.

'She's the one who infected Mags. She didn't seem a big fan of the President. My guess is he can expect similar treatment, soon as they get him back to her. They'll be on their way by now. They left right after us.'

'Where are they headed?'

I shake my head.

'You'll get that information when we're outside.'

Peck looks at Mags again, then back at me. He brings the pistol closer to her forehead, but this time he makes sure not to touch her with it.

'You tell me where they're bringing Kane, Gabriel. You tell me right now, or so help me I'll end her.'

I take a deep breath, then shake my head.

'In a couple of days she'll be done for anyway, just like Marv. I've seen how that goes, and it's not pretty.' His eyes flick to the barrel again. ''Fact, you'd probably be doing her a favor.'

There's fresh commotion from out by the lake as the Guardians struggle to restrain Jake. Mags looks over her shoulder and I see her brow furrow, like she may not much care for how I'm playing the hand she's dealt me either. I take a step closer. Lauren's standing right in front of me, so close I could rest the rifle on her shoulder if I chose. Still she doesn't move.

'But then I'd shoot you.' I raise my voice, so those out by the water can hear. 'And Kurt here, and all the rest of you, too, for good measure. And the President would still be with those soldiers on his way to Dr. Gilbey.'

Lauren's mouth drops open and she turns and stares at me over her shoulder, wide-eyed. Peck doesn't seem as impressed, but I can see him working through his options. I summarize them for him, just in case he's having a slow day.

'Randall, you've nothing to lose. If we're lying you can just come back in a week and we can do this all again.'

THE LAST OF THE LIGHT'S already slipping from the sky as we make it out to the portal.

Kurt eases himself through the ruined guillotine gate, his hands still clutched to his nose. He shuffles over to where Scudder and the Guardians are waiting and then turns to glare back at Mags and me. I ignore him; right now I have a much bigger fish to fry. Peck still has a pistol held to her head, but he doesn't look any more content with that situation than I am. His eyes keep flicking to it like it's a grenade he's holding, and he's just noticed the pin's not where it ought to be.

'Alright, we're outside, like you wanted. Now where're they headed?'

'First I want the map Kane gave you, the one with the code to this place on it.'

'That wasn't part of the deal.'

'Well it is now. Think about it, Randall. If Kane's still in Eden you can get it from him again. We don't know how to change them. If we did we'd have done it already, wouldn't we?'

He hesitates, like he's considering. I don't want him to dwell on it too long, or he might think to wonder just why *I* want the map from him. He can't know it, but the last thing I did before we quit Eden was take a trip along Front Street, to the command building. I figured Kane had to have his own list of codes for the bunkers in the Federal Relocation Arc, and I couldn't risk that list falling into Hicks' hands. Finding it turned out to be easier than I had expected; it was sitting right there on top of a filing cabinet, like he'd just had it out and hadn't yet bothered to put it away, which I guess was probably just the way of it. I checked the drawers and there was

23

no other, but that doesn't mean he wouldn't have thought to stash a copy somewhere else. If he didn't, though, then whatever codes he gave his Secret Service agent when he was setting out for Mount Weather might be the only ones not in my possession.

I flick my eyes in Mags' direction.

'Hey Randall, how long do you think it's been since you jabbed her with that pistol?'

He waits a second longer then reaches inside his parka with his free hand and takes out a blue and red *Standard Oil* map, just like the one Marv gave me, and tosses it over. It lands in the snow at my feet.

'Now put the gun down and I'll tell you where they're headed.'

His eyes shift to the pistol, and for a second I think he might just do it, he wants rid of it that much. But instead he shakes his head.

'Yeah, that's not happening, Gabriel.'

'Let Mags go back inside, then. Once she's safe I'll tell you where they're taking him. You can keep your gun on me.'

'Gabe.'

'It's alright Mags, I know what I'm doing.'

I say it with way more confidence than I feel. But I've had the walk through the tunnel to think about how this might play out, and I figure this is as good an outcome as can be hoped for. Afterwards I'm not sure if I blinked and I missed it or if he was just that quick, but one moment the pistol he's holding is pointed at her head, and the next I'm staring down the business end of a Beretta just like Marv's. I was ready for it, of course, at least as much as you can be ready for something like that, but nevertheless I'm a little thrown by the speed with which it happens.

My finger's been resting on the M4's trigger all the way out through the tunnel, but as soon as Mags steps out of the way I tighten it, until there's nothing left in the mechanism. With my thumb I reach up and snick the selector to its final position, the one that Hicks said would empty the clip in a little over a second. I don't dare take my eyes off Peck, but I have one more instruction for Mags.

'When you get back to the cavern fetch the other rifle from the roof and wait by the blast door. If you see anyone other than me you let rip. Tunnel that straight, it won't matter whether you manage to shoot straight. Right, Randall?'

If Peck remembers that those were his words to me on the day we fled Eden, he gives no sign of it. His eyes drop to the pistol he's holding, then return to me.

Mags looks from one of us to the other, like she's unsure what to do.

'Mags, take the map and go, now.'

She hesitates a second longer then bends down to pick it up, and just like that she's gone.

Peck stares at me over the barrel of the Beretta.

'Alright Gabriel, she's safe. Now tell me, where are they taking the President?'

I don't answer; in my head I'm counting.

He pushes the gun closer, until the muzzle seems like it's only inches away.

'I mean it now, start talking.'

I keep up the count, trying to not to let my gaze get drawn into the barrel; from this distance it looks about as wide and as dark as the portal must from the other side of that guillotine gate. When I think Mags has had enough time to make it to the blast door I tell him the soldiers are headed for The Greenbrier.

'West Virginia?'

I nod.

He drops the pistol into the snow, scoops up a handful of powder and starts scrubbing his fingers with it, like that might somehow help. I keep the rifle trained on him while I explain the rest of it.

'There's five of them. I reckon they'll be somewhere along I-81 by now. Angus and Hamish are coming down the Catoctin Mountain Highway. They'll tell you everything I just did, save you going all the way back to check.' I nod in the direction of the gate. 'You'd best be on your way, now, before you lose any more of the light. There's a farmhouse almost at the end of the ridge road, maybe a quarter mile back from the highway. It's your best bet for shelter.'

He wipes his hand on the front of his parka and pulls on a mitten.

'That's twice I've underestimated you now, Gabriel. Best you don't count on there being a third.'

He squeezes through the gate and joins the others. I watch as they hike up towards the control tower, and then one by one disappear into the gathering darkness. I stay like that for a while, just staring after them. At last I lower the rifle, sling it over my shoulder. Without something to occupy them my hands take to shaking. I have to press them together to get them to stop.

'I'm not planning on ever seeing you again, Randall.'

*

'HAVE THEY GONE?'

I turn around to see Mags and the kid standing behind me. I guess my attention must have been elsewhere; I didn't hear either of them coming back through the tunnel.

'Yeah, I think so.'

She looks past me, out to the control tower. I bend down to pick up the pistol Peck discarded. I wipe the snow from it then thumb the button to eject the magazine and slip it into my parka. I rack the slide to clear the round in the chamber, just like Hicks showed me, and pocket that too. The gun's safe, but I spend a while longer fussing with it. There's a question that needs asking, I know it; I'm just not sure I'm ready for the answer. In the end I just blurt it out.

'Mags, what happened in there, with Kurt?'

The kid tilts his head to her, then back at me. She opens her mouth as if to respond, then stops and looks over my shoulder, back into the tunnel. For a long while there's nothing and I'm working up the courage to ask her again, but then I hear footsteps, drifting up out of the darkness. They grow steadily stronger until at last I see the beam from a flashlight, jittering around the curve of the tunnel.

She turns and makes her way over to the mangled gate, leaving my question unanswered. The kid looks up at me then scurries off after her, just as Jake's bulk separates itself from the darkness. He stops next to me, his chest heaving, like he's been running. His hair's still wet from the lake and blood trickles slowly from a cut above his eyebrow. More of it oozes from his lip.

'You okay?'

He keeps his eyes forward, on the gate, where Mags is standing with the kid.

'I'm fine.'

'You should head back inside, have someone take a look at those.'

'I said I'm fine, Gabriel.'

His voice is terse, like somehow what I've just said has annoyed him.

I slip Peck's pistol into the pocket of my parka.

'Alright, but turn that off if you mean to stay.' I point to the flashlight he's carrying. 'If anyone's still out there it'll give them something to aim at.'

Out at the gate the kid shakes his head.

'It's okay. The dangerous man's gone. They've all gone.'

Jake stares at him for a second, like this pronouncement hasn't eased his mind any. He kills the flashlight, returns it to his pocket. Mags turns to face us.

'Do you think they'll be back?'

I shake my head.

'No, at least not tonight. Did you see the look on Peck's face when he heard Gilbey's name? He knows her.' I turn to Jake. 'We should have someone stand watch, though, just in case.'

His eyes narrow at the suggestion.

'We *were* posting guards, Gabriel.'

I'm not sure what I've done to piss him off; I'm pretty sure I just saved everyone. But right now I have other things on my mind. I hold my hands up.

'Hey, I never said you weren't. There was nothing you could have done anyway. Peck had the code for the blast door, and they had guns.'

He looks down at the snow and grunts, but he doesn't seem mollified.

Mags makes her way back from the gate. She stops in front of Jake and looks up at the cuts on his face.

'Gabe's right, you should have someone take a look at those. We'll take first watch, right Gabe?'

'Sure.'

The truth is I'm exhausted, but my nerves are still jumping; I suspect it'll be a while before I've any chance of sleep. And I need some time alone with her now, to find out what just happened in the cavern.

'Are you sure you're okay?'

I open my mouth to tell him I'm good, but then realize the question wasn't meant for me.

She nods.

'I'm fine.'

'So you're not...?'

'Infected? No, not any more. I was, but Gabe got me back to Eden in time.'

He glances over at me, then goes back to staring at her. Eventually he says: *Okay, then* but makes no move to go back inside. I pull my parka tighter around me.

'Jake, can you send Tyler and Eric out to relieve us in an hour?'

He doesn't say anything and at first I'm not sure he's heard me. When at last he delivers his answer he does it without taking his eyes off Mags.

'We had a roster worked out. They pulled a shift earlier.'

'Well, get them to do another. Unless there's someone else in there you think can be trusted with a rifle?'

It comes out a little harsher than I intend, but it's not getting any warmer out here. And there's something about the way he's looking at Mags that's starting to piss me off now, too.

He looks at me like he means to argue some more, but then Mags steps between us, rests a hand on his arm.

'Please, Jake.'

His eyes drop to her hand and the fight seems to go

out of him. He nods once, says *Alright*, then turns and walks off into the tunnel.

*

THE CONTROL TOWER LOOMS over us as we make our way up to it from the portal. The door at the base is open; it creaks as it shifts back and forth in the wind. I step inside, digging in my pocket for the flashlight while Mags and the kid start up the narrow steps. I crank the handle, but as the bulb starts to glow it splits, swims in my vision. My head grows suddenly light and for a second it feels like whatever has been keeping me going since The Greenbrier, it might choose now to desert me. I reach for the handrail, hold it for a half-dozen breaths, then follow Mags and the kid up the stair.

The smell of smoke hits me as I climb the last steps and when I sweep the observation deck with the flashlight the beam finds the blackened remains of a fire in the center. Mags is already at work rebuilding it from wood that's been stacked nearby, so I make my way over to one of the large windows that lean outward from the consoles beneath.

I cup a hand to my brow and peer through the glass, already beginning to realize the futility of the task I've assigned us. In daylight from up here you'd be able to see every part of the compound, but now it's dark I can't even make out the tattered windsock by the helicopter landing pad, not twenty yards from the base of the tower.

The kid clambers up onto the workstation next to me. I catch his reflection in the darkened glass and for a moment I study him, just squatting there on his haunches. It doesn't mean anything, I know; I guess he just got used to sitting that way from all the time he spent in one of Gilbey's cages. But crouched like that, the pale skin stretched over his bare scalp, the deep shadows that still circle his eyes and darken his sunken

31

cheeks, he reminds me of the thing that attacked Ortiz, in the basement of the hospital, in Blacksburg. I shiver inside my parka, an involuntary action not entirely prompted by how cold it is up here. If the kid notices he doesn't let on. He presses his face closer to the glass.

'What are you looking for?'

'Any sign Peck's coming back.'

He looks up at me.

'Which way will he come?'

I point towards the far side of the compound, in the direction of the steel gate.

'That way, I think.'

He looks puzzled.

'You mean where we came in, earlier?'

I nod.

'It's over there.'

He raises an arm, one small mitten extending to a spot to the right of where I know the guardhouse to be. I open my mouth to correct him. I can't see the gate now, of course, but I've been here all winter and I know this place like the back of my hand. But then I remember tracking the soldiers as they took the Fairfax Pike off I-81, and how he had been able to follow Jax's prints in the snow, long after I had lost them.

I stare out into the featureless darkness.

'Johnny, what can you see out there?'

He looks up at me again, like he doesn't understand. Then he just says: 'Everything.'

Mags has a fire going, so I make my way over to it while the kid keeps watch from his perch up on the workstation. There's a crate of MREs sitting next to the firewood. I pick a couple from the top, open them up, shake out the contents. I get the chemical heaters working on the food pouches then I toss the kid a HOOAH! He doesn't seem fond of regular rations, but since he came through the scanner he seems to like the candy bars just fine. He snatches it from the air and busies himself with the wrapper. As soon as he's got it open he takes a bite and goes back to staring out of the window.

When the heaters are done hissing I tear the top off one of the pouches and start poking around at what's inside. The question I asked down by the portal went unanswered, and I haven't yet worked myself up to asking it again. I keep glancing over at Mags. She doesn't seem much interested in her food either. After a while she sets the MRE aside and reaches for the chain around her neck. She pulls out Truck's dog tags, turns them over in her fingers. The light from the fire plays over the metal. It's dull, tarnished by age, but otherwise fine, with no sign of the virus.

'You want to know what happened, back in the cavern.'

I nod.

'I don't know. It was weird. When I saw what they were doing to Jake, up on the roof, I got so mad. I ...' She pauses, like she's searching for the right words. 'Part of me knew what I was doing, and that it was stupid. But I was so angry.' She hesitates again. 'I just couldn't help myself.'

She looks at me for a moment and then away, and I get the feeling that whatever she's told me isn't the whole of it. I glance over at the kid. He's staring down from his perch on the workstation, like he's suddenly developed an interest in the conversation we're having. She slips the tags back inside her thermals.

'I'm sorry.'

'It's okay. It all worked out.'

She shakes her head.

'It's not, though. We need to be smarter than that. *I* need to be smarter than that.'

I'm not sure what to say, so I don't say anything. She picks up her mug, swirls the coffee.

'What do you think it means?'

Truth is I'm not sure. I tell myself her anger has always been a quick thing, long as I've known her. It can burn hot and high, like a gasoline fire, but it dies down after just as fast. There's a small, faithless voice inside my head that's not content with that explanation, however. It starts to whisper that this was different. I hush it and it goes quiet for a moment, but then it shows me an image: her standing over Kurt, like an animal over its kill, transfixed by the sight of the blood spilling from between his fingers.

She's looking at me, waiting for my answer. I reach for the empty MRE carton, feed it to the fire. The cardboard curls, blackens as it's consumed.

'I don't think it means anything. You're fine, the tags prove it.' I say it with confidence, like there could be no doubt. But I can already hear the voice inside my head, getting ready with its next objection. I have no interest in hearing it, so I keep talking.

'It's been two days now, more than enough time for the virus to show. If it's anything it's probably just an aftereffect of being infected. I suspect Gilbey could tell you.'

I realize I've started to babble so I stop.

She looks into the flames then raises the mug to her lips, drains the last of her coffee, sets it on the ground.

'Let's not go back and ask her.'

There's a silence that stretches on for longer than it ought, and then from somewhere below the groan of a door being opened, followed by the sound of boots climbing the stair. A few moments later Tyler and Eric appear, bundled up in their parkas, their breath smoking in the cold. Tyler steps into the observation deck, but Eric hangs back by the door.

I get to my feet. My legs have stiffened, sitting by the fire; they protest as I stretch them out.

'Sorry to make you guys pull another shift.'

Tyler holds up a hand. When he smiles his teeth are surprisingly white against his ebony skin.

'It's all good, Gabe. I reckon Eric and me were next in line for the treatment Jake was getting. We were glad you showed up when you did.'

His gaze shifts to the windows and for the first time he notices the kid, crouched on one of the consoles underneath. The smile falters.

'Not sure what you expect us to see out there, though.'

I step over to where Johnny's looking out through one of the large panes and tap him on the shoulder, tell him to shift over. He looks up at me, like he doesn't understand: there's windows on all sides; I could choose any of them to look out of. I want the Guardians to see I'm not nervous of him, though, so when he doesn't move I shoo him out of the way. He shuffles across to the next console, goes back to staring out. I lean closer to the glass, but all I can see is my own reflection there. I cup a mitten to it. It makes no difference. Beyond there's only impenetrable blackness.

'Yeah, I'm sorry. When I asked Jake to send you out I hadn't thought it through.'

Tyler keeps his eyes on the kid a moment longer, like he's still distracted by him, then they return to me.

'No worries, Gabe. Like I said, we were just happy to see you.'

I start to make my way back to the fire, but then an idea comes to me. I turn to the kid.

'Johnny, how're you feeling?'

He looks at me uncertainly.

'Okay.'

'Not too tired?'

He shakes his head.

'Want to keep Tyler and Eric company for a while?'

He hesitates for a moment and then nods, but I catch the two former Guardians exchanging a look. Eric steps away from the door.

'Nah, Gabe it's okay. Really. We can manage.'

Tyler turns to me.

'Gabe, seriously, we got this. Sounds like you guys have had a long day. I'm sure…Johnny…needs his rest.'

The kid stares at me with those solemn eyes, waiting for a decision. The Guardians really don't want to be left with him and I can't say as I blame them; I'd be nervous too if I'd just met him. At least Tyler used his name, which is more than he got from me on our first encounter. What Mags said earlier is right, though: we need to be smarter now, and having someone up here who can actually see would make a lot of sense. The wind picks up, gusts against the glass. Peck's not coming back tonight, however. I'll give it a couple of days, let them get used to him; maybe catch Tyler by himself, explain the situation. I beckon the kid down.

'C'mon Johnny, let's go back inside.'

He jumps off the console and hurries over to stand next to Mags.

I take one last look out into the darkness and then make my way towards the door.

MY LEGS HAVE SEIZED worse than I thought; I hobble down the control tower's stair, clutching the railing for support. Mags asks if I'm okay, but I tell her I'm fine; just a little sore from the hike. The truth is we pushed hard getting back here; hotfooting it all the way from Eden has taken more of a toll than I had figured.

She holds the door open for me at the bottom and I follow her back to the tunnel, jealous of her easy, loose-limbed gait. I watch as she slips effortlessly through the ruined guillotine gate. I squeeze myself between the charred, twisted bars, wincing as I stand on the other side. She holds an arm out, says I can lean on her, but I shake my head and tell her I'll be fine; the walk will do me good, stretch out the muscles in my legs a little. The truth is I just want to snap my fingers and be back in our apartment.

She sets off into the darkness, the kid trotting along beside her. I flick on the flashlight and limp after them. The tunnel seems to have lengthened since I walked it with Peck earlier, but at last we reach the blast door. I shuffle through, leaving her to close it up. Just a little further and then I'll be able to take off my boots, lie down in a bed, *an actual bed*, and sleep for as long as I care.

But as I step into the glare from the cavern's arc lights it's clear that's not going to happen. All the Juvies are there, like they've been waiting for us to return. As soon as they see me they rush forward. Only Jake hangs back. He's changed his bloodied t-shirt but there's a sullen bruise spreading across his cheek and his lip's already swelling up where Peck or one of the Guardians split it. He stares at me like these things, and whatever else might currently be ailing him, I'm the certain cause of it.

The Juvies crowd around, bombarding me with questions.

'Where's Peck?

'Is he gone?'

'Will he be coming back?'

I close my eyes for a moment, letting their questions wash over me. I'm a little overwhelmed; I don't know who to answer first. But then suddenly everyone goes quiet. I turn around. Mags is standing at the entrance to the cavern, and for a second I see her as they must: head shaved; cheeks sunken, hollowed; the shadows under her eyes, still dark enough to convince Peck she was carrying the virus. The kid appears beside her. He looks even worse; like a fury in miniature. He slips back behind her leg, clearly uncomfortable with the attention. She reaches for his hand and the Juvies part quickly to let them through. I catch her eye as she passes; their reaction hasn't gone unnoticed. She takes Johnny over to where Jake's standing by himself. There's a long pause and then the clamor starts up again.

'Where did you go?'

'Were you really back in Eden?'

'What's happened to Kane?'

'Is it true Quartermaster's dead?'

I hold my hand up for quiet and the chatter dies. Answering their questions piecemeal is going to take forever; it'll be quicker if I start at the beginning. I lower myself to the sidewalk. When the last of them have settled around me I take a deep breath and begin. I tell them about the soldiers following our tracks to the high school in Rockbridge, and how we went back with them to The Greenbrier and met Dr. Gilbey. There are a few gasps when I recount what Gilbey had been doing to survivors who'd had the misfortune to make their way

38

there, and when I get to the bit where she put Mags in a cage and infected her with the virus they all shift around and take to staring at her again.

I press on quickly, describing how we escaped and fled to Eden so she and Johnny could go through the scanner and be cured. I linger on that detail for a while, letting it sink in, but I notice more than one head turning in her direction, like they may not trust the work I've told them the machine's done. I finish with how Mags saved us from Hicks and the other soldiers, but in my version she spends a lot more time skulking around in tunnels and far less bursting out of them like Wonder Woman. When I'm done an uncomfortable silence settles, and for a long moment I'm not sure how to break it. In the end it's Lauren who does it for me. She stands up, offering me a broad smile.

'Well, we're just relieved you made it back safely, Gabe.'

Her voice is calm, assured; her eyes bright, clear. It looks like she may even have found time to run a brush through her hair. The Juvies all turn to look at her, and I realize I'm not the only one who's shocked, and not just by the transformation from the shell-shocked stupor I witnessed earlier. I think that might be more words than I've heard Lauren speak all in one go, long as I've known her. Eden wasn't exactly a social place, of course; between work, chapel and curfew there wasn't a lot of time left for just shooting the breeze. Not that you'd ever accuse Lauren of that. She always made a point of sitting apart in the mess, her head down over her food; as soon as she was done she'd hurry back to her cell, long before the buzzer had a chance to announce curfew. I can't remember her showing up for movie night either, except when it was her turn to be custodian of the disc, and even then often as not she'd just hand it over and disappear. I suppose I'd always assumed she

39

was a little like me; just not one of those kids who was, as Miss Kimble put it in what would turn out to be my last ever end-of-term report, *well integrated socially*.

She presses her hands together and turns to Mags.

'You too of course, Mags.'

I feel a sudden rush of gratitude to her for that. She looks down at Johnny, adopting the tone you'd use for a shy three-year-old.

'And what's your name?'

The kid just stares back solemnly.

'I don't know.'

Her smile doesn't falter, but I'm not sure she knows what to make of his answer. He looks at her for a moment and then he tilts his head and his nostrils flare, like he's scenting the air. And for an instant it puts me in mind of the fury that was waiting for me outside, in the tunnel, when I first came here. It's a subtle gesture, though, barely perceptible. I don't think anyone's noticed.

The kid studies her a moment longer.

'You needn't be scared. I won't hurt you.'

Lauren lets out a nervous laugh, like he's said something funny. I glance around at the Juvies. If the kid's intention was to put them at ease I'm not sure it's worked. I quickly add that we've been calling him Johnny.

Lauren studies him a moment longer. The smile remains, but it seems a shade less certain than it was a few moments before. Then she turns to me and her face suddenly grows serious.

'You warned us this would happen, Gabe. You said Kane would send Peck, but we didn't pay attention. I think we all might be more willing to listen now.' She looks around, gathering support from the faces assembled around her. To my surprise I see heads nodding, murmurs of agreement. 'So tell us, what should we do?'

Twenty-three young faces swivel in my direction, waiting for an answer. Even Jake seems keen to hear what I have to say. I'm a little taken aback. I wasn't expecting to be having this discussion, here, now, in front of everyone. Tell the truth I'm not sure what we should do. Before The Greenbrier I was pretty certain we needed to leave. But a lot has changed since then. I tell Lauren the only thing I can: I don't know.

It's obvious this isn't an answer the Juvies care much for. For the next few moments they're all talking over each other.

'But you've been out there.'

'You escaped from Gilbey and the soldiers.'

'And you got rid of Peck.'

'He'll be back.'

'Should we leave?'

'Where should we go?'

'Just tell us what to do.'

'Yes, tells us.'

I close my eyes. Right now I just want to lie down and sleep for as long as I can. It's Lauren who comes to my rescue once again. She holds her hand up for silence.

'We're being unfair. Gabe's obviously tired.' She looks around at the Juvies, and then back to me, offering another smile. 'Why don't we let you sleep on it? I'm sure you'll have thought of something by the morning.'

And just like that I hear myself saying that I will.

*

I SLEEP LATE for the first time in weeks. When I finally wake I lie there for a long while with my eyes closed, counting up all the places it hurts. At last I gather up the strength to lift my head and look around the tiny apartment. Mags is long gone; only the faintest aroma of the coffee she made earlier still lingers. I let my head fall back to the pillow. It feels like my entire body's been worked over with a hammer. I don't understand: we both made the same hike. How come she isn't she suffering like I am?

The low, faithless voice inside my head has an answer for that, but I hush it before it gets the chance to give it. I reach one hand up for the chain around my neck, follow it down to the tags I wear, run my fingers over the pressed metal. Still smooth, and this is the third day. If the scanner hadn't done its work it'd be showing by now.

I lie there a few minutes longer, then I drag myself out of bed and limp into the shower. For a long time I just stand under the steaming jets, letting the scalding water soothe my aching muscles. When I step out I feel a little better. I towel myself dry and grab a clean t-shirt and a set of overalls from the closet, the first fresh things I've had on in days.

I gather up the clothes I left strewn across the floor on my way to bed the night before. My parka feels heavier than it should. I lift the flap on the big outer pocket and take out the Beretta Peck dropped in the snow the night before. I turn it over in my hands. Ash has dried on the metal from where it fell in the snow. More will have found its way inside; it'll need to be stripped and cleaned. Hicks would have had me do it

42

soon as I got back last night, but there was no way that was happening; I barely made it to the bed before I passed out.

I reach for the backpack and lift out the pistol I took from him, still wrapped in the gun belt. I unravel it slowly. The leather's worn, stained dark from years of use. I draw the gun from the holster and run my fingers over the metal, dull with age, the dark carrion bird scrimshawed into the yellowing handle. The etching looks like it's been done by hand. I wonder if it was him who carved it, or someone before.

I turn it over in my hands. Compared to the Beretta it looks ancient; an antique. I asked him once why he'd chosen something so old for a weapon. His answer was simple: he said it was because when he needed it to, he knew it'd work. Bitter cold or blazing heat didn't matter much to a gun like that, he said. It'd been riding on somebody's hip for the best part of a hundred years, and if there was anyone left in another hundred it'd probably be doing the same. I slip the pistol into its holster, roll the belt around it, then return it to my pack.

The clock on the stove says it's noon. My stomach sends an audible reminder that I haven't yet had breakfast, and that needs tending to, as a matter of urgency. I check the cupboards but of course they're bare, so I head out into the cavern and make my way over to the mess.

It doesn't occur to me until after I've pulled the door back that this might have been a mistake; it's lunchtime, and most of the Juvies are here. They all look up as I enter. I remember too late the promise I gave: that I'd have an answer for them as to what we should do. I glance over my shoulder. I feel like turning tail, but it's already too late for that. So instead I step inside, making my way quickly between the tables to join the end of the food line.

43

Things have calmed down a little from last night, but still everywhere I look someone's smiling or saying hi. It's a little weird; I'm not used to this much attention. Back in Eden there were a few moments in the sun, figuratively speaking of course, like when I started going outside with Marv. Everyone wanted to know how that was, at least at first. And then later, when I brought us here. That brief burst of popularity didn't last very long either, though; I lost it not long after we arrived, trying to convince them we needed to run away again. But now it's like there's been a poll overnight and I've just been elected President.

I grab an MRE from the stack on the counter, then stand in line for one of the microwaves. Amy insists I go in front of her and won't take no for an answer, so I smile a thank you and then pop the food pouch in and twist the dial. It pings to let me know it's ready and then I beat a hasty retreat for the farthest table. I pick a spot at the end and sit down, hoping to be left alone. I've barely freed the plastic fork from its wrapper when I hear a screech as the chair opposite's pulled back.

'Hey, sleepyhead.'

I look up to see Lauren setting her food down. She flicks her hair over one shoulder and sits, offering me a smile, and once again I'm struck by how different she is, not just from the Lauren Kurt dragged to her feet last night, but from the Juvie I knew before. Back in Eden we all spent a lot of time discussing who our matches might be; it was pretty much the only game in town as far as conversations went, unless you wanted to hear how many brace bolts someone had tightened that day, or the state of the plastic skirting on the growing benches over at the farms. Everyone had a list, a top five, and who should or shouldn't be on it was the subject of near-continuous debate. Lauren never made mine, and I don't recall her ever featuring on anyone else's either. Looking

44

at her now, for the life of me I can't understand why, though. Somehow, whether by accident or design, she just managed to spend all those years in our collective blind spot.

I mumble hello and then turn my attention back to my Shredded BBQ Beef. She looks over at the carton and then holds hers up.

'Hey, snap!'

She opens the flap and starts arranging the packets neatly in front of her.

'So I stopped by this morning, but Mags said we should let you rest.'

I spear a strip of beef and say something about being pretty tired. Lauren murmurs sympathetically, but then her eyes shift up and down the table, as though she's checking whether anyone's in earshot. She leans forward, lowering her voice.

'Are you sure she's okay, Gabe? Mags, I mean. She doesn't look well.'

I nod.

'She was pretty sick, after Gilbey gave her the virus. That's why we had to go back to Eden, so she could go through the scanner. She's fine now.' Lauren stares at me across the table, doubtful. I feel the need to add something. 'The virus can't survive that.'

I say it with more certainty than I feel. Lauren doesn't seem convinced either.

'It's just that yesterday, that thing with Kurt. She seemed, well, a little strange.'

Crap. Most of the Juvies had been on their knees, their eyes fixed on the ground, and I had hoped that had gone unnoticed. Lauren had been on her feet, of course, but she'd seemed pretty out of it. I guess not as much as I'd thought.

'She was just mad about what they were doing to Jake. You know how Mags can be.'

She nods, but she still seems unsure.

'She's fine, Lauren. Trust me.'

Her eyes dart down the table again.

'But how can you be so certain?'

I put down the fork and reach inside my t-shirt for the dog tags. I hold them up for her to see.

'We each wear these. The metal shows the virus. I check hers every day. If she was sick I'd know it.'

She reaches across the table. Her fingers hover in the air for a second, like she's unsure, and then she runs them over the pressed steel.

'Who was Private...Kavanagh?' She pronounces it slow, one syllable at a time.

'One of the soldiers we ran into.'

She looks into my face and her eyes brighten.

'A soldier. And you took them from him.'

I doubt she'd be as impressed if she got a look at Boots, or if I told her it was all Mags' doing anyway, so I keep those bits of the story to myself. She stares at the tags a moment longer and then lets them go. I lift the chain and slip it back inside my t-shirt, feeling the metal settle against my chest. Her eyes linger there for a moment and then she looks up at me again.

'So have you had a chance to think about what we do now?'

Truth is I've still got no idea, but I find myself saying I've had a few thoughts.

'Great. After lunch I'll get everyone together so we can hear them.'

*

I FINISH EATING and set off in search of Mags.

I meet Leonard on the far side of the lake, coming out of one of the tunnels. He almost runs right into me, like something's got him spooked. I ask him if he's seen her. He glances over his shoulder, jabs a finger back in the direction he's just come, then hurries off towards Main Street, like he has urgent business there.

I find her over in the fire station, showing Johnny the tender. The kid sees me first. He gives me a wave then goes back to staring at his reflection in the fire engine's huge chromed wheels. She looks up, offers me a smile. The shadows around her eyes are still there, but they seem a little better than they were yesterday. The whispering voice inside my head isn't happy with that, however. It reminds me of what I saw by the lake. I remind myself what I told her, last night: whatever happened with Kurt, it wasn't important; just an aftereffect of being infected. But somehow that explanation doesn't seem to have gained traction in the hours since I first gave it; it seems no more plausible under the glare of the arc lights than it did up in the darkness of the control tower.

She slips her hands into the pockets of her overalls.

'I was beginning to wonder if we'd see you today.'

'Yeah, I was pretty beat. Weren't you tired?'

She shrugs.

'Not really. I got a couple of hours' sleep, then Johnny and I went out to relieve Tyler and Eric. Jake came out at first light and warmed up a couple of MREs for us.'

I guess I should be happy she's eating, but for some reason the news that it's Jake who's fixing her breakfast doesn't make me feel that way. I turn away before those unpleasant thoughts have a chance to show on my face.

'Everything okay?'

'Um, sure.' I can see she's not buying it, though, and I don't care to admit to her what's really bothering me, so I switch topic before she can figure it out.

'Hey, is it just me, or does everyone seem a little weird since we got back?'

'How so?'

'I dunno; it's like everyone suddenly wants to be my friend.'

Even as I say it I remember how the Juvies had looked at her last night, when she came back in; how quickly they had parted to let her through. We both take to staring at the kid while I search for something to say. He seems oblivious, still mesmerized by his own reflection. He reaches up to touch the chrome, but before his fingers can get there she takes hold of his hand.

'We're not going to touch things, remember? At least not for a few more days.'

He looks up at her and nods, then goes back to studying the hubcap.

'Lauren stopped by earlier, while you were sleeping.'

'I know. I just ran into her in the mess. She's going to organize a meeting this afternoon, so I can tell everyone what to do.'

Mags raises an eyebrow.

'Lauren? Organizing a meeting? With people?'

'I know, right? I guess she's got a point, though. Peck's not gone for good, and I doubt Gilbey's forgotten about us either.'

'So what are you going to say?'

I shake my head.

'I'm not sure. Hicks knows we're here, and now Peck does too. We have to assume that at some point one of them's going to be back for us.'

48

She doesn't say anything for a while, like she's thinking. Then she reaches into the pocket of her overalls and fishes out the map we took from Peck. She unfolds it, holding it up to the fire truck's flank. I take a step closer.

'What are you looking for?'

She points a finger at the sole location marked there – ours. Next to it a single twelve-digit code, the letters and numbers scrawled across highways and mountain ranges in Kane's spiky script. She turns to me like I should get the significance, but I don't.

'It looks like our President didn't trust his Secret Service agent with more than one code.' She looks up at me. 'And you've got his master list, the one with all the others written on it.'

I nod. The list I retrieved from the command building, just before we left Eden, is back in our apartment, sitting in the inside pocket of my parka, next to the map Marv gave me. And for a second I allow myself to believe it. We might be safe here. But then I shake my head. Truth is we've never been that lucky.

'He's bound to have made a copy.'

'Maybe.' She says it like she's not so sure.

'If he has we've got to assume he'll give it up, if he hasn't already.'

She folds the map and slides it back into her pocket.

'So where do we go? Fearrington?'

'It's the only place we know anything about.'

'But?'

'I don't know. I was all in favor of it before, when we thought it was only Kane we had to worry about. Now there's Gilbey, too. With all the questions I asked she'll have no problem figuring out that's where we'll go next. And if Kane gives her the codes we'll be no safer there than here.'

I stare at the dusty concrete. The Juvies are expecting

an answer from me, and I'm no closer to giving it to them.

She hesitates a moment, like she has something to say.

'What is it Mags? If you have any suggestions I'd be sure happy to hear them.'

THE JUVIES GATHER BY THE LAKE, in the same spot where the night before they had knelt and watched Jake being interrogated. They arrive in ones and twos, taking their places by the water's edge. There seems no order to it, and yet when they're done somehow Mags has ended up off to one side with the kid, separated by a wide stretch of concrete that does not seem of her choosing. The Juvies chat quietly among themselves, but every now and then I catch one of them cutting a nervous glance in her direction.

Jake's the last to arrive; I spot him on the far side of the lake, making his way back from the farms. There's a fresh bandage above his eye and the bruise that had begun on his cheek has sunken into the socket, lending him the appearance of a large, muscle-bound raccoon. He takes a seat next to Mags, close enough that it annoys me.

I give him a chance to settle and then I get to my feet. The last of the conversations die and an expectant silence takes their place. I let my gaze roam the familiar faces. We sure don't look like much, huddled beneath the massive granite expanse of the cavern's dome. But this is it; all of us except Tyler and Eric, who are outside standing watch. I went out to the control tower earlier and set out for them the choices I now plan to lay out for the rest of the Juvies, so they'd have the same say as everyone else. When I was done Tyler was quiet for a while, like he was considering everything I'd just told him. I was expecting questions, but all he said was he was fine with whatever I reckoned was for the best. Eric plumped for that option too, although I think that was mostly because it was what Tyler had just said. That wasn't how I meant it to go, but if nothing else it gave me a chance to rehearse what I plan to say now. I clear my throat and begin.

'Well, there's been no sign of Peck, so I guess it's safe to assume he's gone, at least for now.'

Murmurs of relief greet that news. I wait for a moment for things to go quiet again.

'I doubt it's the last we'll hear from him, though, so we need to work out what we do next. As I see it we have a couple of options. But before we get into that I think we need to agree on something. There's only twenty-four of us left.'

That earns me a bunch of confused looks. Reading might not be their strong suit, but there's so few of us we all know what our number is, and since we quit Eden it's been twenty-three. I hear someone whisper *the little fury*, but I don't catch who says it. Mags shoots a look in Ryan's direction, but if he notices he has the good sense not to return it. Everyone else turns to stare at the kid who promptly takes to studying the square of concrete between his feet.

I raise my voice and continue on.

'So whatever we choose, we have to agree that we all stick together.'

That was Mags' idea. She didn't think it should be up to me or anyone else to tell the Juvies what to do next, however much they might appear to want it. It was high time they got used to making decisions for themselves, she said, although it probably made sense to start with an easy one, on account of how little practice they'd had in recent years. That was smart; I see it now. All around me heads are nodding in agreement, like they're pleased with themselves. I pause to let that sink in before I go on.

'Okay, well, our choices are pretty simple: we can stay right here and see what happens, or try and find another home.'

'Shouldn't we just go, before they comes back?' Amy looks around plaintively, as though in spite what I said at the outset she expects Peck to reappear at any moment. Jake just shakes his head.

'That's what we're here to discuss, Amy.'

Lauren glances over in his direction and for a second I see her eyes narrow, like somehow what he's said has vexed her. But when she turns back to me her features have softened again.

'So where would we go, Gabe?'

'Well, Marv's map has the location of a half-dozen bunkers, but I think it comes down to just one: a place called Fearrington. It's the only one we know anything about, and besides, the rest are all much farther away.'

'So where is it?'

'North Carolina.'

A few vague glimmers of recognition greet that piece of information, but mostly all I get are blank stares. Kane never showed much interest in our education, and geography was certainly no exception to that; so long as we could find the farms and the chapel that was about as much as he cared for. Perhaps we should be grateful for small mercies. Who knows what he might have taught us otherwise? A man like that that, it's quite possible he believes the world's flat and dragons patrol Virginia's southern borders.

Ryan asks how far it is. I catch Amy glancing over at the entrance to the cavern, like depending on my answer she might be considering setting off right after we're done here. The map is in my pocket, but I don't need to take it out to give him an answer. I've already worked out the route we'd take. US15 would certainly be quickest - it's pretty much a straight shot. But that would bring us uncomfortably close to The Greenbrier. I have no idea how things will play out between Peck and

53

Hicks, but whichever of them prevail it won't be long before they come looking for us, and we certainly can't risk running into them on the road. So instead we'll head out east to hook up with I-95, which we can follow south as far as Richmond. From Richmond I-85 will take us almost all the way there. It's longer, and mostly interstate, so the pickings along the way will be slim, but it'll be safer. I tell Ryan the best part of three hundred miles.

I see the Juvies exchanging nervous glances. I guess that must sound like a distance. Probably because it is.

'How long would it take?'

I figure Mags and I could do it in ten days. Maybe less, if I could find a way to match the pace she's been showing since she came through the scanner. The Juvies won't travel anything like that fast, however, at least not judging by how long it took us to make it here from Eden.

'Three weeks, give or take.'

More uncertain looks. That's twice as long as it took us to get here, and none of them recall that journey with any affection. They all remember fleeing Eden, though, the fear they had felt stepping out into icy wind, snow that had stung like needles. And later, when the storms had chased us off the road, cowering in an abandoned gas station or trash-strewn bank lobby while the lightning split the sky outside. Most haven't set foot beyond the portal since we first arrived.

'Winter's over now, though. If we decide to leave it's as good a time as any to go.'

I say it with a reassuring smile, but it doesn't seem to work. I see Lauren casting her eye over the assembled faces, gauging their reactions.

'How long before Peck comes back, Gabe?'

I shrug.

'I can't say. I'm not even sure it'll be Peck who

comes back.'

She gets to her feet.

'But somebody will come for us, right? If not Peck then those soldiers.' She looks around at the faces now staring up at her. 'The ones who infected Mags with the virus, who put her in a cage?'

The Juvies all turn to Mags as she says it, but I keep my eye on Lauren. I see what she's doing. The Juvies are scared of the outside; no amount of comforting words is likely to overcome that, and she knows it. She plans to give them something else instead, something to be even more afraid of. She looks at me, waiting for an answer to her question.

'Yes, I believe so. Someone will be back.'

'Then we should leave. Soon, before they get here.'

Jake shoots her a disgruntled look.

'Sit down, Lauren. We haven't decided we're going anywhere yet.'

Even now, part of me expects her to retake her seat. The Lauren we all knew before would have done just that. But then that Lauren wouldn't ever have gotten to her feet in the first place.

She turns to face him, and for a second I almost feel sorry for Jake.

'Haven't you been paying attention, Jake? It's not safe here.'

'You think I don't know that?' He points to the spot by the water's edge where the Guardians had held him down. 'It was me there, last night, Lauren, not you.'

'Then you should know better than anyone we can't stay here. Peck could be back any time, or if not him then someone worse. Gabe's already warned us once.'

Jake glances over at me, his face darkening with anger. He looks at Mags, like he might have something to say, but then he checks himself.

'We've just got the farms set up. If we leave now

we'll be throwing away a harvest.'

Lauren throws her hands up in the air, like she can't believe what she's just heard. She lets out a bitter laugh.

'And *that's* what you care about? We don't even need the stupid harvest.'

Now Jake's on his feet as well.

'We thought we didn't need the harvest when we were back in Eden. But the food ran out there.'

Lauren just rolls her eyes and looks to me for support. The truth is she's sort of right. We don't need the harvest, at least not here; what's in the stores will last the few of us who are left several lifetimes, even if we're not careful with it. But that's also missing the point. The real question isn't whether we need the harvest *here*; it's whether we'll need it wherever we go next. Hicks said Fearrington was thirteen stories underground, which should be plenty big enough, but the truth is I have no idea how well provisioned it might be. Gilbey had planned to continue her work there, which I'm hoping means it was stocked for her arrival. But I have no idea for how many, or for how long.

From somewhere near the back Leonard slowly raises a hand, like we're back in Miss Kimble's class.

'What happens if we stay here and Peck comes back?'

Jake takes it on himself to answer.

'We'd have to defend this place.'

It's clear Lauren doesn't think much of this plan. She shakes her head.

'That didn't work well yesterday, did it?'

'We have guns now.'

'But none of us know how to use them.'

'Tyler and Eric do. So does Gabe.'

'And what chance do you think they would have against Peck? He's a Secret Service agent. He killed Benjamin, remember? And Marv. And they were soldiers.'

Jake's still on his feet.

'I'd rather face Peck than whatever else might be waiting for us out there.' He raises a finger and jabs it at me. 'Gabe took Mags out there and he almost got her killed.'

Some of the Juvies go back to staring at Mags, but most look at me. I feel my face redden. I don't have anything to say, because the truth of it is, Jake's right. Mags is looking out onto the lake, like she's trying to work something out. After a few seconds she turns back around and when she speaks again it's to me.

'Why don't you tell them what you know about Fearrington, Gabe? Maybe it'll help us all decide.'

'Yeah, what's it like?'

I clear my throat.

'Well, I've never been, obviously.'

That earns me a bunch of uncertain looks, and I realize it may not have been the best place to start. I press on quickly.

'We did learn a few things about it from the soldiers, though. It's an underground silo. It goes down a long way, but even so it'll be nowhere near as big as here. There aren't many of us, though, so it should be enough space.'

'And we can definitely get in?'

I nod.

'Yes, we can get in.'

Jake looks at me like he wouldn't take my word for it if I were to suggest the water in the lake behind him might be wet.

'You just said you've never been. You can't know that.'

I'm still stinging from his last comment, and now I feel myself growing angry. I take a deep breath, making an effort to keep it from showing in my voice.

'The codes on the map Marv gave me have worked everywhere else I've been. There's no reason they shouldn't work there too.'

Jake folds his arms across his chest, like he's not happy with that answer.

'But you don't know.'

Lauren shakes her head.

'What would you do, Gabe?'

The Juvies quiet down. I see the ones in the back leaning forward to listen.

'Well, we like it here; there's loads of space and more supplies than we need. I took Kane's codes with me from Eden, and we have the one he gave to Peck too, so maybe next time he comes he won't find it quite so easy to get in.' I look over at Mags, but her expression's hard to read. 'I wouldn't count on it, though. Kane might have made a copy, and even if he hasn't there's a chance Peck will remember the code.'

Jake snorts at that.

'That's nonsense. Those codes are way too long for anyone to remember.'

Afterwards I regret what I do next, but right then I can't help myself; it feels like I haven't been able to catch a break from him since we got back from The Greenbrier. I reach into the pocket of my overalls and take out the tattered roadmap with the *Standard Oil* logo on the cover.

'What's that?'

'It's Marv's map, the one with the entry codes for all the facilities in the Federal Relocation Arc written on it.' I hold it out to him.

He looks at it suspiciously, like he knows what's coming next. He doesn't want to take it, but he has little choice; everyone's eyes are on him now.

'Open it up.'

He unfolds it slowly.

'Choose one.'

He stares at me for a long moment and then turns his attention to the map. I watch as he studies each of the locations there, searching for the one to test me. At last he looks up and says *The Notch*.

The Notch is the codename for a bunker at a place called Bare Mountain, just outside a town called Hadley, Massachusetts. It's way north, certainly not anywhere I'd planned on us ever visiting. But that's okay. I've studied that map often enough over the winter that all I have to do is close my eyes and I can see the twelve numbers and letters written next to each of the locations marked on it. I call out the code he's asked for. When I'm done there's silence. I ask him if I've got it right.

He looks down at the map for a second, then starts to fold it up again.

'That doesn't prove anything.'

But now everyone's talking at once again.

'Peck still has the code.'

'He's bound to come back.'

'Or the soldiers.'

'They could already be on their way.'

'We need to leave, now.'

I glance over at Mags, but this time she doesn't meet my gaze. Lauren smiles triumphantly. I hold my hands up again for silence, only this time it's longer coming. At last things quiet down again.

'Has anybody got anything else to say?'

The Juvies look at each other but nobody speaks.

'Jake?'

He glares at me for a moment and then just shakes his head.

'I guess we should vote then. Everyone in favor of leaving raise your hand.'

Amy's arm's in the air almost before I've got the words out. Lauren raises hers too. Jake just shoves his hands into the pockets of his overalls. A couple of the Juvies who worked with him in the farms vote to stay too, but everyone else is in favor of quitting Mount Weather.

There's no need for a tally, but I do it anyway. Jake doesn't wait to hear the final result. He gets up while I'm still counting and marches off in the direction of the farms.

TWO DAYS LATER we gather by the lake again. This time there's little chatter. The Juvies wait, fiddling nervously with flashlights or adjusting the straps on their goggles, while Mags heads over to the plant room to power everything down. After a few minutes the faint background hum of the generator dies, leaving an eerie silence in its wake, and then one by one the arc lights blink out. There's a moment of darkness after the last of them shuts off and I hear a gasp that might be Amy, then the safeties kick in, bathing the cavern in their green glow.

We start making our way out. I wait at the blast door, standing to one side as they file by, leaning into the straps of their packs against the unfamiliar weight. I've loaded each till the seams were straining and the snaps would barely close. We have a long hike ahead of us, but if I've counted right we should be carrying enough for a return journey on short rations, should we need to make it.

The last of them leave and for a while I can still hear their footsteps, slowly receding as they shuffle off into the tunnel, and then it goes quiet again. I'm beginning to wonder where Mags has got to when she appears at the end of the corridor, pulling on a wool beanie. It's the first time I've seen her wearing one, but then her hair's yet to grow back and it'll be cold out there. The kid's got one too; he keeps reaching up to touch it, like it bothers him. She must have taken a detour to the stores, to pick them up. I would have fetched them for her, if she'd asked, but then I've hardly spoken to her since the vote. This last few days she's spent all her waking hours over at the plant. Seems like it's taken almost as long to shut

Mount Weather down as it did to get it up and running.

I hit the button to start the close sequence. There's the shrill whine of electric motors, then the familiar grumble of gears as the blast door commences its final inbound journey. Mags steps past me, out into the tunnel. Her pack's no less full than the others', but if the weight troubles her she doesn't show it. The pockets of her parka bulge suspiciously, too. I told her we'd have to leave her books behind - they were a luxury we couldn't afford - but I suspect a few of her favorites from the bookshelf have managed to stow themselves away, all the same. The kid hurries through after, like he's worried we might choose this moment to leave him behind. I stand there for a while after they've gone, just staring back into the cavern. Everything seems just like it did when I first arrived. Soon it'll be like we were never here.

I take a final look then follow them out. The Juvies' lights are already stretching off into the dark, quivering like fireflies as they make their way towards the portal. The soft glow spilling out from behind the blast door shrinks as the thirty tons of carbon steel slowly rumbles inward. Mags reaches into the side pocket of her parka and retrieves a flashlight. She cranks the handle to get the bulb burning then holds it out to the kid. He looks up at her, like he's unsure what to do, and I think I catch something passing between them. But then he nods, a quick bob of the head, as though he's remembered, and takes it from her. Another dynamo whirs as she winds one for herself, then she looks over at me.

'Ready?'

'You go on. I have to fetch it.'

'Alright. Be careful.'

They start out after the others, and for a moment I just watch them. The kid holds his flashlight low, aimless, like he's already forgotten he has it. Mags points hers ahead, slowly sweeping the tunnel floor. But there's something measured, mechanical, in the way she does it. It makes me wonder whether she needs it any more than he does.

The pitch of the motor drops, then dies. Behind me the sliver of light from inside winks out as the blast door clangs shut for the last time. I dig the windup from my pocket and crank the handle, then set off in the opposite direction.

From the blast door I count two hundred paces then I point the beam up onto the raised walkway and start scanning the concrete there. A little further along I find what I'm looking for: a shallow pile of rubble, stacked indifferently against the tunnel wall. I clamber over the railing and start lifting rocks from the top until my fingers settle on the olive-drab plastic of a rifle case. Not the most secure hiding place, but then the Juvies wouldn't have it inside. I can't say as I blame them.

I keep clearing debris until the entire container's exposed, then I play the flashlight over it. The plastic's a little scratched but otherwise it appears intact, and when I run the beam along the seal the rubber seems to have held. I brush the dust from the two heavy-duty catches and check they're still tight. I don't plan on popping them; I already know what's inside: Kane's stockpile of the virus, stolen from the armory on the day we fled Eden. I'd rather not have to bring it with us, but I don't reckon we have a choice. Its whereabouts was one of the things Peck was trying to get out of Jake when we interrupted him, so there was the proof, if we'd needed any, that Kane hadn't just forgotten about it. We can't risk leaving it behind for him to find.

I clear the last of the rubble then reach for the handle and lift it upright. Sweat prickles the skin between my shoulder blades as I imagine the delicate glass tubes shifting in their trays, clinking against the hard plastic that holds them in place. I'll need to get used to that. I have a long way to haul it.

I adjust my grip on the handle and set off after the others.

It's not long till I see the Juvies' flashlights ahead of me again. Those in front are already starting to wink out, as one by one the beams are lost to the curve of the tunnel. Soon I can hear the boots of the stragglers, scuffing the dusty concrete. And then I'm rounding the bend. Ahead lies the portal.

Outside the first reluctant grays of dawn are spreading slowly through the compound. Mags and the kid stand by the mangled remains of the guillotine gate. Tyler and Eric wait on the other side, next to the elevated walkway, their breath smoking in the cold. Something about that sets spidey off, but as usual there's no explanation why he's fussing. The only thing I can figure is the rifles they each carry, slung over their shoulders, but somehow that doesn't seem like it.

The rest of the Juvies are huddled further back, inside the arch of the tunnel, staring out. No one seems keen to venture farther. I make my way between them. They look up at me as I pass, their faces tight, anxious. I catch Lauren's eye. She smiles but it's fleeting, uncertain, like even she might not be sure of the course upon which we're about to embark. It's not been two days since we decided, but I suspect if I were to call another vote, right now, we might end up turning around and going back inside.

And maybe that wouldn't be the worst decision.

Our destination is farther than I've ever been, and a long way from certain. What if Fearrington's not what I've assumed? What if we make it there and Marv's codes don't work? What if I can't even get us there?

The dark windows of the control tower stare down through the twisted bars. Behind, clouds the color of coal dust squat low along the spiny mountain ridge.

Mags comes to stand next to me. She asks if I'm ready.

I'm not sure I have an answer for her, so instead I grasp the charred metal and squeeze myself through.

*

IT TAKES US ALL OF THAT FIRST MORNING just to clear the Blue Ridge Mountain Road. We stop for lunch in a barn just off the John S Mosby highway. The Juvies huddle at the back and eat quickly, their eyes darting over to where Mags and the kid are sitting by the door. Afterwards we cross the highway and continue south, into the mountains. I keep us to the valley floor, where the going's easiest, but our pace doesn't improve.

About an hour into the afternoon I stop at the crest of a shallow rise and set the container down in the snow, making sure it's settled before I release the handle. Mags pulls down the bandana she now favors in place of a respirator and asks if everything's okay. I tell her it's fine; I'm going to wait here a minute while the rest of them catch up. She should go on.

She looks at me for a moment, then pulls her mask back up and sets off again. I stand next to the kid, staring at the raggedy line of Juvies shuffling up the incline. They stumble through the drifts like a herd of indifferent turtles, lifting their snowshoes high, flapping them around like the good Lord Himself might not be sure where they mean to set them down. I have some sympathy for the chronically uncoordinated; long as I can remember it seems like my own limbs have been a measure too long for the body they came with, and rarely under any semblance of control. But this is unwarranted, even by those standards. Had it been this way when we set out from Eden? That trip had certainly taken an unconscionable length of time for the miles we had covered, but I don't remember it being this bad.

The kid pushes his goggles up on his nose. They're the ones I got him after we escaped The Greenbrier, when the light was troubling him. They were meant for an adult, so they're way too big on him, but they were the only ones that were dark, which at the time was important. He's removed the tape I bound the visor with, but I still can't see a thing through it, so I have no idea what he might be thinking. I'm about to ask when without warning he points his poles around and takes off after Mags.

I turn my attention back to the Juvies. One by one they drag themselves up the rise, snowshoes crunching clumsily through the ice-slicked snow. When they get to the top they shuffle on by, eyeing the drab olive container at my feet with suspicion. I wait till the last one has passed, then I reach down for it and set off after them.

I wonder what Marv would have made of it. I come to the conclusion he'd probably have shot one of the stragglers, for the example it might provide. I return to that idea more than once as the afternoon slips by, far faster than our progress.

The thought of it becomes sorely tempting.

We keep heading south, winding our way between peaks with names like Hardscrabble, Pignut, Watery, Lost. Our progress continues, painful slow. The Juvies stop often, and when they do it's always as one; it seems like we can't cover much more than a mile without a snowshoe that needs fixing or a bladder that needs to be emptied. Getting them to their feet again after is the devil's own work.

As evening draws in I take us off the road. I hiked this stretch, back when I visited Culpeper, so at least I know where to bring us for shelter. I choose a gas station just outside a place called Marshall. I head around back to find a place to stash the virus while the rest of them shuffle inside. When I join them Mags already has a fire going. The Juvies have arranged themselves on the far side of it, as though some line only they can see divides their territory from that assigned to her and the kid. They huddle close as they dare to the smoldering branches, picking at half-warmed rations, occasionally casting nervous glances over the reluctant flames. I pass around the first aid kit and then get to work on my own meal while they tend to whatever blisters or chafes have been earned that day. There's little in the way of chatter. Those that are done unfurl their sleeping bags and turn in, until soon there's only me, Mags and the kid left.

The kid finishes the HOOAH! I've given him, then he curls up on top of his sleeping bag and closes his eyes. Seconds later he's out. When we were leaving The Greenbrier Hicks warned me he wouldn't ever sleep, but the scanner seems to have cured him of that; since he came through he's developed a knack for it, almost like an animal. It's rarely for long, though - mostly little more than a catnap - but deep, complete. For the next while he'll be dead to the world; you could stand over him clashing cymbals and I doubt he'd stir.

I dig out the map and spread it on the floor, checking how far we've advanced by the light from the dying flames. It looks even less impressive measured that way. Mags sets her ration aside. She hesitates a moment, then reaches over and rests a hand on my shoulder. She says it'll be okay, I just need to be patient. It's only the first day; they'll soon settle to it, find themselves a pace. She says it was no better when we first quit Eden.

I don't recall it that way, but when I point this out she says I probably can't be relied on to remember on account of recently having being shot and not being that much use in a snowshoe myself. I'm not convinced, though. I mutter something about us being no better than those English rabbits.

'English what?'

I start to fold the map.

'Rabbits. They weren't built for long marches, either. It says so, right at the beginning, when Hazel and Fiver and the others first set out from the Sandleford warren.'

She looks at me like she has no idea what I'm talking about.

'"They spend all their lives in the one place, never traveling more than a hundred yards at a stretch. They prefer not to be out of distance of some sort of refuge that will serve for a hole."' I'm sure I have some of the words wrong, but I think it's pretty close. I think I can even hear Mom's voice in my head, reading them to me. 'It's from *Watership Down*, remember?'

She shakes her head.

'Was it among the books we had at Mount Weather?'

'No, but…'

I stop, mid-sentence. An uneasy feeling settles low in my stomach, that she would even ask. I could name every single volume we had on the bookshelf in our tiny apartment: the books I brought with me from under my bed in the farmhouse outside Eden; the ones that had been left behind by those who had fled when the bunker had been evacuated; the few paperbacks I managed to scare up on the scavenging trips I took whenever the storms would ease. She knows what was there as well as I do, better even. She'd read and re-read every single book on it, countless times over the long winter.

I look over at her. She smiles.

'Then I don't think you've told me that one. Sounds like a good story.'

She shifts a little closer, like she might be ready to hear it.

I'm not sure what to say. Every story I have, Mags already knows it. When I'd find a new book on the outside I could barely get back to Eden quick enough so we could go up on the roof of the mess and I could tell her about it.

But she's right, of course; I never did tell her that one. I didn't need to. It was the book she was reading when we first met, all those years ago, in the day room of the Sacred Heart Home for Children.

*

THE THREE DAYS THAT FOLLOW continue much as the
first.

The snow's settled deep in the valleys, and for the
most part we're forced to hike Indian file. Mags breaks
trail out front while I spend my time at the rear, with the
dawdlers and the lollygaggers. At first we switched up
every few hours, but that didn't work so well. The kid
insists on being at her side and the Juvies found it hard
to concentrate on the road ahead with him on their heels.
I asked if she got tired, breaking trail all day. She said
she didn't. Truth was she felt great, better than ever. The
morning after we quit Marshall she lifted Truck's dog
tags from inside her thermals and tossed them. There
was no need for them she said; it'd already been five
days since she came through the scanner, and that was
plenty of time for the virus to show. I pulled the cross I
took from Marv's grave from my pocket and handed it to
her. I explained how it'd been mine, when I used to go
outside scavenging. I said it had always brought me
luck, and I wanted her to have it. She studied it for a
while, then she smiled and slid it inside her thermals.
Afterwards she kissed me.

I felt bad about lying to her like that, but her not
remembering about the rabbits worries me almost as
much as what happened with Kurt in the cavern. I tell
myself I've forgotten things along the way too,
important things. At some point in the years after the
Last Day I stopped being able to call up Mom's face.
The voice points out that's not the same, however; I still
remember I *had* a Mom. I have no answer to that, so I
take to asking questions, probing for gaps in what she
should know. Herding the Juvies all day there's little

71

opportunity, but in the evenings, after we've found shelter and they've gone to sleep, there's plenty of time. The further back I go the sketchier she gets on the detail. After a while her answers grow short, like I'm being annoying, or maybe she suspects something is missing and it's the not-knowing that vexes her, so I stop. I wait till she's gone to sleep and then I check the cross. I do it every night, but the metal remains clear, or at least I find no marks other than the ones I put there with the *Patio Wizard* I used to fool Kane. I tell myself whatever work the virus has done, the scanner's put a stop to it.

It has to have.

The kid doesn't remember a thing from the time before he got sick.

Just shy of noon on the sixth day after we quit Mount Weather we hit a little no-stoplight place name of Warren. The Juvies have been dragging their snowshoes all morning; we've barely made a half-dozen miles since we broke camp, and I don't see us doing better with the afternoon. I catch her looking back at the long straggly line of them stretched out behind us, like even she may be beginning to doubt they have it in them to make this journey.

We wait out front of a *Gas 'n' Go* while they catch up. The kid stares off into the distance, fiddling with the strap on his goggles. Something's gotten into him today, too. We hit our first properly deep drifts earlier, not long after we broke camp. I bent down to pick him up, like I'd done countless times before, but he just stopped and shook his head, then set off again, without so much as an explanation. There were stretches where he was barely able to lift his snowshoes high enough to clear the snow, so I asked him again, but for some reason he wouldn't contemplate taking a ride. If it was just the three of us I might have made him, but the truth is it's not him that's holding us up now.

I turn around and look at the road ahead, watching as it winds its way through the valley floor. There's little of anything for what looks like miles, not even a barn or a stand of blackened trees to break the emptiness. This is as far as I've been; after Warren we'll be in new territory. I worry what that will mean for our progress. I can't risk keeping us out after dark, not in a place like this. From now on as soon as the sun starts dipping towards the horizon we'll need to turn over what remains of the day to finding shelter.

I guess Mags must have had the same thought, or maybe mine are just easy to read, because she announces she's going on ahead to find us somewhere to spend the night. I'm not sure I like that idea. I didn't particularly care for how he delivered the message, but Jake had one thing right: it's not safe out there; that much was true even before I learned the world's not as empty as I once thought it was. And there's another part to it, too; one I don't care to admit. The outside, scavenging, finding us places to stay - that's *my* job; it's maybe the only thing I know how to do. If anyone has to hike out to find us shelter, it should be me.

I don't say that last bit out loud, of course. Realizing how things might sound to others has always been what you'd call a development area for me, but even I can see that's not the kind of reasoning that's apt to appeal to Mags. So instead I remind her of the rule. You always scavenge in pairs. There are no exceptions.

She shakes her head.

'We can't both go. One of us needs to stay with them.'

'Then I'll do it.'

She hesitates for a moment, like she's trying to figure out a way to say what she has to.

'It makes more sense for it to be me. I can cover

more ground than you.'

She waits to see if I have anything to say to that, but I don't. After a few seconds she pulls up her hood, like it's decided.

I tell her to wait. I shuck off my pack and set it down in the snow, then dig in one of the side pockets, pull out a Ziploc bag. I have to take off my mittens to break the seal. For an instant there's the sweet smell of gun oil before the wind snatches it away again. I reach inside for the pistol Marv gave me and hold it out.

'It's already loaded. I took the bullets from the gun Peck left behind.'

She hesitates for a moment, then takes it from me. I show her how the safety works and how to chamber the first round. There's a soft *snick-snick* as she racks the slide. I cleaned and oiled it before we set off, so the mechanism should be good. She examines it for a moment, then closes her fingers around the grip. It looks too big for her hand.

'I don't know how to shoot it.'

'You just point and squeeze. There's not much more to it.' I say it with a shrug, like I might have spent my formative years terrorizing cattle towns alongside Billy the Kid and his Regulators, rather than counting tins for Quartermaster in Eden's stores. I see her eyeing the pistol, like she's not sure she really wants it, so I give her the talk Marv gave me, about how if she comes across people she thinks might be no good she should just point it up in the air and let off a round. That would be enough to get most folks to turn tail he said, although even as I hear myself repeat those words I wonder. I can't help but think it'd take more than a loud bang and a puff of gun smoke to get someone like Hicks to cut and run.

She checks the safety again then slides the pistol into the pocket of her parka, shifts her bandana back in place and sets off. I watch as she hikes out ahead. I wasn't sure at first, but I've been watching her these past few days and I know it now. Her strides are measured, deliberate, like she's checking herself, holding back; like she could go faster than she's showing me. Even so, she's breaking trail with a pace I doubt I could match. She's almost at the first bend when I hear the crunch of snow behind me. I turn to see Jake, hurrying up the slope. He draws level, unsnaps his respirator, but it's a few seconds before he has breath enough to ask his question.

'Where's she going?'

'To find us shelter.'

He looks up at me, incredulous.

'You...you just let her go? All by herself?'

I don't know what to say to that, so I don't answer, I just keep watching her. More of the Juvies are arriving now, huffing and puffing their way up the incline. They gather round, making sure to keep a respectable distance back from the kid. Jake pulls his goggles onto his forehead and stares at me, waiting for an answer.

'You want to stop her Jake, be my guest.'

He glares at me a moment longer, then points his snowshoes in the direction of the *Gas 'n' Go*. One by one the others follow until there's only me, Lauren and Johnny left.

For a while we watch Mags. As she nears the bend her stride seems to lengthen, and for the last few seconds before she disappears it's almost as though she's bounding through the snow. Then she's gone and there's nothing left but her tracks, the shallow indents already softening with the wind.

Lauren takes a step closer. For a while she says nothing, but then she turns and looks up at me.

'Is that normal?'

I don't answer. The truth is I'm not really sure what that means any more. She rests a mitten on the arm of my parka, squeezes once, then follows the others into the gas station.

WE LEAVE THE MOUNTAINS BEHIND, the serried peaks giving way to low, rolling hills that are much more to the Juvies' liking. They find themselves a pace, just like Mags said they would. It's barely faster than the one they set out with, however.

A week after we quit Mount Weather we pick up the interstate, a wide, furrowed scar winding its way through endless frozen wasteland. For mile after mile we cleave to it, trudging ever south. We pass exits for places called Thorn, Golan, Ruther, but take none of them. Our days take on a pattern. We start early, covering what miles we can while legs are fresh. When we stop for lunch Mags leaves us. I eat with the kid while the others huddle together in the far corner of whatever gas station or truck. stop we're favoring with our custom, although sometimes he waits outside, watching the road like he expects her to come back. Afterwards I lead us on again, but slower now. With little to do but coax the stragglers and watch for her return the afternoons drag. Each evening we trade the highway for whatever roadside diner or motel she's found for us, only to rejoin it the following morning.

I watch Mags for any sign of what I saw that first night back in Mount Weather, but there's nothing, or at least nothing I can detect. If anything she grows quieter; it's almost like with every day that passes now she draws a little further into herself. I ask her what it is, but she says nothing. I think I can guess, though. Sometimes with dusk settling I spot places from the highway that look like they might do for shelter, but she just shakes her head and says they're not for us. I don't ask her why, because I know. She's already been inside. It used to be

Marv's job to check the dark places, and for a short while after he died it became mine.

Now that job is hers.

On the morning of our thirteenth day on the road we see our first sign for Richmond, the almost-halfway point in our journey, but for the rest of that day and the next it remains always ahead of us, seeming to get no closer. At last we round a long curve in the interstate and an exit sign for the city hoves into view. I pick up the pace, ignoring the protests from behind me. Mags has been gone since early; I'm keen to catch up with her and get the Juvies to shelter while there's still a few hours left in the day. I know from the newspaper articles I used to collect that the city got hit in the strikes, but Marv's map shows it was a big place, once; there's bound to be something left I can scavenge, maybe stretch out our supplies a little. They could certainly use it; we've not been making near the time I had allowed when we quit Mount Weather. It'll probably be the last opportunity we get, too. South of Richmond we join interstate again, and that'll bring us all the way into North Carolina.

The kid senses the new urgency and sets off, his head bent to the snow. When he gets to the off-ramp he scurries straight up it without so much as a backward glance. I'm about to holler at him, but then he stops of his own accord and waits while I make my way up to join him.

From the interchange the land falls away before us and then lays flat, as far as the eye can see. I scan the horizon while I wait for the Juvies to catch up, searching for any hint of what lies ahead: a crumbling skyscraper, a listing apartment building, even the spindly jib of a tower crane; anything to break the featureless gray. But there's nothing, or at least as close to it as makes no difference.

As soon as everyone's gathered we set off again. The few buildings we pass now are little more than husks. I stare up at one as we trudge by. It's been stripped to its skeleton, its walls blown out, what little remains of its insides strewn with blackened debris. Spidey's been quiet since before we quit Mount Weather, but now he starts up again. It's low level, a not-so-urgent rumble I could probably drown out if I put my mind to it. But for once I understand what's got him on edge. I'm used to how the world is now; I've seen the work the virus has done. This is different, though; a manner of destruction I have not witnessed before. The Juvies sense it too. They grow quiet, like this place, the very air we're breathing, is thick with despair.

I spot a sign ahead. The gantry arm leans towards us, like something has pushed it over. The paint is blistered, making what's written there hard to read; it may say *Downtown*, but there's not enough of the letters left to be sure. As I pass underneath I look up. On the side facing the city the metal has been scorched black.

We start to hit traffic. At first just a vehicle here or there. A tractor-trailer on its side, the molten remains of its tires still clinging to the rims. The shell of a four-by-four, front wheels stuck in the low gully of the median, rump pointing skyward, like a steer down on its knees and waiting for the bolt gun. I drag my hand across its flank, dislodging an armful of ashen snow. Underneath the paintwork's bubbled, just like the sign.

More now, but all the same, until soon the road's choked with burnt-out wrecks, the glass blown from their windows, their insides melted. They rest on their sides or on their roofs; others protrude from the snow at improbable angles, like they were little more than *Hot Wheels*, held to the fire and then scattered, the work of a sulking child.

We keep going. Soon we have to pick our way

between them, our progress slowed by the weight of carnage. A stake-bed's impaled itself on the sheared iron of a guardrail; the kid ducks under but the rest of us have to squeeze past its slatted sides, one at a time. Up ahead he stops by the hood of a semi that's somehow managed to stay on its wheels and points forward with one mitten, like he's seen something there. When I catch up to him he turns to look up at me through his outsize goggles.

I set the container with the virus down in the snow. What I thought to be a low rise in the road is in fact the rim of a shallow crater; it stretches off on both sides, almost as far as the eye can see. Within its ragged circumference there's nothing left but the scorched char-pits of foundations exposed by the blast, mercifully filling with snow.

I let my gaze linger for a few moments, taking in the details of the cauterized bowl that was once a city. Nothing stands that might offer shelter. We have no choice but to cross, however; it's already too late to contemplate going around.

I wait for the last of the stragglers to join us then I start making my way down. The sides are steep; I hold my hand out to the kid but he just shakes his head, like he wants none of it. Without markers it's hard to tell where the road once was, so we just keep heading south. I keep my eyes on the opposite rim of the crater, expecting Mags to appear there at any moment. She would normally have returned to us by now, but I tell myself not to fret; she'll have had to travel farther than usual to find us somewhere to pass the night.

By the time we've hauled ourselves over the lip on the far side there's little left of the day. I can already feel the temperature starting to drop, so I pick up the pace, and for once there are no complaints from behind me. A couple of miles further on we reach a river Marv's map says is the Appomattox. A low concrete bridge, squat, ugly, but sturdy enough to have survived the blast, spans the sluggish gray waters. On the far side a lone figure, making her way towards us.

Nobody looks back as we cross.

*

WE PASS THAT NIGHT in a *Target* Mags has found for us just north of a place called Chester. I don't much care for the malls but she says it's the best there is, at least within any distance the Juvies might be capable of reaching this side of noon tomorrow. It makes me wonder how far ahead she's been.

I stand by the entrance as they unsnap their snowshoes and file inside. We've been on the road longer than usual and they look pretty beat. When I've counted the last of them in I head off to find a place to stash the virus. By the time I return there's already a fire going by the checkouts. I head down one of the aisles, making my way towards the back of the store, where Mags is waiting with the kid.

That was Lauren's idea. She took me to one side, not long after Warren, and suggested it'd be for the best. It wasn't her, she said; she felt bad even bringing it up. But the truth was the kid was making some of the others nervous. I can't say it was altogether a surprise. I remember how I'd felt, the first time I laid eyes on him, crouched at the back of his cage in that basement room in The Greenbrier's bunker. His appearance has improved a little since, but the truth of it is he's still pale as a sheet, coat hanger thin, and the shadows around his eyes are proving a lot more stubborn than Mags'. That habit he has of dropping to all fours persists, too. I know there's nothing in it; it's just from all the time he spent in the cage. It doesn't exactly set a mind at ease, however.

I wasn't sure how Mags was going to react, but she just said okay, almost like she'd been expecting it. I told her what Lauren had said to me: it wouldn't be for long. The Juvies'll get used to him, same as I did. It's the same as with the snowshoes. We just have to give them time.

I watch as he chooses a spot not far from us and rolls out his sleeping bag. Mags hands him an MRE carton and he lifts the flap and upends it, searching among the pouches and packets that spill out for the HOOAH! he favors. He tears the wrapper with his teeth and pushes the bar up; it's gone in a couple of quick bites. He spends a moment examining the foil for crumbs and then looks over at me hopefully. I wait until Mags is busy fixing herself a coffee and then dig mine from the carton. She'll be mad if she catches me; she says we have to wean him off them, get him on the food pouches, even though it's been a while since she finished one of her own. He's yet to show much interest in those, though, and he'll never get to a regular size if he doesn't eat.

When she's not looking I toss the candy bar over. He snatches it from the air and it disappears without a sound, I think up the sleeve of his jacket, but it happens too quick for me to be sure. Then he curls up on top of his sleeping bag and closes his eyes. Seconds later he's out.

I finish my meal and climb into the sleeping bag. The floor is hard, even through the quilted material, but I guess I must be more tired than I had figured; as soon as I lay my head down I feel my eyelids growing heavy. I hear the zip being drawn back and Mags slips in beside me. She takes off the beanie she wears and sets it on the ground.

I drape my arm around her, my fingers tracing a line across the taut curve of her stomach. She still has weight to gain back, but then I tell myself she was always thin. My fingertips come to rest on the angle of her hip. The skin there is chilled, like it's been left outside the sleeping bag. I shiver.

'You cold?'

She shakes her head but I pull her close anyway, hoping to warm her up. I'm already slipping down into that place where your thoughts unravel and you lose yourself to sleep. Without thinking I press my lips to the back of her head.

She lies there for a moment, not moving, then slowly lifts one hand and runs her fingertips across her scalp where I've just kissed it.

'It's not growing back, is it?'

I brush my lips over the skin there and tell her I hadn't noticed. The low, faithless voice inside my head pipes up before I have a chance to silence it.

Liar.

She just shakes her head.

'It's not, least not as quickly as it should. Back in Eden, when I had the mohawk, I'd have to shave it every couple of days.'

I slide my hand up from her waist. I checked the crucifix I gave her last night, while she slept, but now I reach for it again. I run my fingers over the crudely-cast metal, relieved to find the surface unchanged. For a long time she doesn't say anything, but I can tell she's still awake. The scanner gave the kid back some semblance of sleep but for Mags it's the opposite; I don't reckon she gets much more than an hour a night now.

She glances over at the small form curled up on the other side of the fire. He hasn't stirred, but she lowers her voice anyway.

'I don't think Johnny's hair's growing back at all. What do you think it means, Gabe?'

I kiss the back of her head again.

'I don't think it means anything.'

That answer doesn't seem to placate her any more than it does the voice inside my own head. It feels like it has something to say, but this time I hush it before it has a chance to get going. There's no way she's sick. No way. Whatever chance I might have had when we first set out, I couldn't hope to keep up with her now. I reckon it'd be the same with the kid, too, if it wasn't for those little legs of his.

She shifts around inside my arms.

'How old do you think he is, Gabe?'

The question takes me by surprise.

'I dunno. He doesn't look much older than we were, when Kane brought us to Eden.'

'But that would mean he would have to have been born after the Last Day.'

I say something about it being possible. It is of course, but somehow I'm not sure I believe it, any more than I reckon she does. Truck told us the survivors who found their way to The Greenbrier had shown up not long after everything had fallen apart. Before we arrived they hadn't seen anyone in years.

An image pops into my head, unbidden, of the girl I found in the closet in Shreve, all those years ago. I hadn't thought on her in a long while. I can still picture her, though; her face pressed to the backboard; the dark circles around her eyes; her ashen cheeks sunken and hollowed. Her hair had been white and brittle, like an old person's, but I remember thinking the same thing about her as I just did about Johnny: she couldn't have been much more than a first-grader. I wonder now if I got that right. I hadn't been scavenging more than a few months back then, but it had already been six winters since the Last Day. Kane scorched the skies not long after we first went inside the mountain, which meant she had to have been in that closet ever since. The dress she was wearing had hung in tatters from her tiny frame, but what remained of it had still fitted, like she hadn't grown in all that time.

There's a soft crack as a branch shifts in the fire. A

handful of red sparks rise in a swirl and then disappear. Mags looks over at the kid but he's still out of it.

'I asked him how long he was in that cage. He said he didn't know. He said it was hard to tell down there, in the darkness.' She pauses. 'A long time, I think. Months. Maybe even years.'

She doesn't say anything for a while. When she speaks again it's like it's mostly to herself.

'I don't know how he did it. I was only there for a few days and...'

She doesn't finish, just lets the sentence hang there in the darkness. I feel her shudder.

'I don't think I could do that again.'

I pull her close and tell her she won't ever have to. And right then I mean it, as much as I think I've meant anything in my whole life. Not that that matters. I should know better by now. The world doesn't bend itself to hopes and prayers, leastways not any I might have to offer.

I'll learn, though, soon enough.

Promises like that I simply have no business making.

*

HE WAKES FROM A DEEP AND DREAMLESS SLEEP, his eyes blinking wide. The transition is sudden, jarring, like someone has found the switch inside that works him and flicked it on. For long seconds he stares into the darkness, his pulse racing. Until his brain reboots he is empty, just breath and heartbeat and blood pumping, with no memory of who he is, what he might even be. Slowly it comes to him, in fragments at first and then all at once, a rush of sights, sounds, smells; what little he remembers. He presses his cheek to the sleeping bag, inhaling the warm, slightly musty odor. The quilted fabric does little to soften the hard floor, but it is a comfort nonetheless. He knows where he is now, and it is not the cage.

He blinks again, more slowly this time, his heart finally beginning to calm. He doesn't know how sleeping was, before, but somehow he doesn't think it was like this. He wonders if he will ever get used to it.

He lifts his head, taking in his surroundings. On either side rows of empty shelves, stretching off into gloom, the aisle between scattered with discarded packets, wrappers, here and there an abandoned shopping cart. Everything cast in grainy shades of gray, except around the fire, where a few motes of color still remain. He looks over to where the boy and the girl are sleeping. The boy's breath rolls from him in slow plumes, hangs for a moment in the still air, then vanishes. He cups one hand to his mouth and exhales slowly, watching. But there's nothing; his breath doesn't smoke like that. He wonders what it means.

Something shifts among the embers, then settles. The fire is dying. An idea comes to him, sudden, exciting: he could go outside and find more branches, build it back up. He knows how; he has watched the girl. He sits up. He won't sleep again tonight, and morning is hours away yet; it would certainly help pass the time. There is something about the idea that thrills him, too. For a very long time he wasn't allowed to go anywhere.

He looks along the aisle, towards the entrance. That is where the others are, though; he would need to walk right past them. He stares in that direction for a long while, watching for any sign of movement. It seems like they are all asleep now, but it is hard to be sure. He knows how to be quiet; he is very good at it. But what if the door is noisy and he wakes them?

It is better if he stays away, that was what the girl had said. Just until they got used to him. She had smiled then, but it wasn't her usual smile. There was something sad about it. And she had looked away right after, like she wasn't sure how much she believed it either.

It wasn't her idea, he knows that. It was the girl with the blond hair. He heard her, talking to the tall boy. It wasn't her she said; it was some of the others. She didn't mind him at all.

But she does, he can tell. The girl with the blond hair might be more afraid of him than any of them. She pretends not to be, and she is quite good at that. She smiles whenever she looks at him, so it never shows on her face, and she keeps it from her voice. He can smell it, though, every time she is near. Her fear has a bitter odor. She spreads it among the others with her questions, at night, when they huddle by the fire. She thinks he can't hear her if she whispers, but he can.

Earlier, did you see...?

Gabe says they're cured, but...

How can that be normal?

He looks back at the fire, already little more than a handful of embers, nestling in ash. It doesn't matter; he doesn't need it. The cold doesn't bother him, not really. If it did he could climb inside the sleeping bag, like the others do. He won't do that, though. The thick material is soft, but he does not like to be confined.

He remembers the candy bar the boy gave him. He reaches into his sleeve and takes it out, opening it slowly. He means to make it last, but it is too delicious and in a few bites it is gone. He pulls the wrapper apart, searching for crumbs. When he's certain the last of them have been had he puts it on the fire, watching as the foil shrivels with the heat. For a second the flames flicker bright around it as it is consumed, then they too disappear, as quickly as they came.

His gaze shifts to the trash-strewn aisle.

He doesn't have to go that way, of course; he could head towards the back of the store instead. There won't be firewood there, but maybe he'll find something else; something on the shelves that's been missed. The tall boy checked earlier and said there was nothing, but he might have more luck. He feels himself growing excited again. Maybe even another candy bar.

He gets up slowly, taking care not to make a sound. At the last minute he remembers the flashlight. He doesn't need it, of course, but it makes the others feel better, that's what the girl says. He picks it up and winds the handle slowly. The little motor inside hums; moments later the bulb glows orange, then yellow.

He sets off down the aisle, picking his way carefully among the debris. He is only tall enough to check the bottom shelves, but there's nothing there; everything has long since been stripped, plundered. After a while he gives up and just walks. The flashlight hangs at his side, already forgotten.

He wonders how long it will take the others to get used to him. The girl said not long, but he's not sure about that. He sees how they look at him. Mostly they pretend he's not there, but sometimes they can't hide it, like when the tall boy had bent down to carry him through the deep snow. They had stopped and stared, as though the idea of it was appalling to them. He won't let himself be carried anymore. It would just be another way for them to see he is different, and if they think he's different they won't ever get used to him. Besides, he's much better with the snowshoes now. He never falls down, and it's only when the drifts get really deep that he struggles. It's just because his legs are short, and there's nothing he can do about that.

He reaches the end of the aisle. The shelves give way to long racks of clothes. Some have been knocked over, the garments that once hung there lying in heaped disarray, but most still stand. He holds his hands out as he makes his way between them, letting his fingers brush the moldering fabrics.

A sudden flicker of light ahead, there and then gone again. He freezes and for a dozen hurried heartbeats peers into the grainy gloom. But it is only a mirror, for an instant catching the beam from the forgotten flashlight. He continues on, making his way towards it between the racks. As he gets closer he can see that the glass is broken. Only a few shards still remain, gripped by the frame; the rest have fallen to the floor. They crunch under his boots as he steps up to it.

He tilts his head to one side, studying his fractured reflection. He is still getting used to it. He does not remember what he looked like before, of course, and there were no mirrors in the cage; no surfaces that might have offered even the faintest clue as to his appearance. Sometimes when they are outside he catches himself in the darkened glass of an abandoned storefront, but it is never for very long and he is always masked, hooded, his eyes hidden behind the dark goggles he wears.

He leans a little closer, reaching up with the cuff of

his jacket to wipe the dust away. The beam from the flashlight wanders and for an instant the eyes that stare back at him flash silver.

His heart races; he glances over his shoulder, worried that somebody might have seen. But there's no one there; they're all still sleeping. He winds the flashlight and raises it, more slowly this time. When he finds the right angle he holds it up, forcing himself not to squint.

How long will it take them to get used to *that*?

A long time, he suspects. He remembers how frightened he had been when the doctor had come down and shone a light into 98's cage and he had seen her eyes for the first time. And he is much braver than they are.

He lowers the flashlight and closes his eyes for a moment, thinking. He reaches for the goggles that hang around his neck and pushes them up. They are a little big but the girl has adjusted the strap so they mostly fit, and the lens is dark; the tall boy got them for him when he was sick, to help with the brightness. He raises the flashlight again, but this time the goggles do their work; now there is nothing to see. He moves the beam closer, tilting his head this way and that until he is certain of it. Then he turns around and starts making his way back towards the fire.

It was lucky he found the mirror. He does not care to think about what might have happened if one of the others – especially the girl with the blond hair – had noticed first.

The thought that he might still be sick does not occur to him. He feels fine. And he has the metal tags he wears around his neck, the ones they took from the soldier. He checks them all the time and they never change. The tall boy says that proves it; the thing inside that made him dangerous has gone.

Well, not gone, exactly.

But not in control anymore.

Definitely not.

*

SOUTH OF WHAT WAS ONCE RICHMOND the interstate has little to say for itself, and for mile after mile we trudge on through empty, snow-shrouded flatlands. The days run one into the other. On the twenty-third morning after we set out from Mount Weather, when by my earlier reckoning we should already have arrived at our destination, we finally quit Virginia. The other side of the state line proves no more bountiful than what preceded it. Our packs grow light. I have the Juvies empty them, so I can check what we have left. I had counted on us arriving at Fearrington with enough food for a return journey on short rations, should we need to make one. I'm not sure exactly where it's happened, but somewhere along the way we've passed the point where that might have been possible.

We keep trudging on, ever south. Mags has to work hard to find us shelter now. Mornings she sets off before we've broken camp. I spend the days herding the Juvies along a stretch of interstate no different from those that have gone before. Afternoons I watch for her return, but often dusk's settling by the time I spot her hiking back towards us. Sometimes she says there's nothing we can reach with what remains of the day and we have to backtrack. I asked her once how far she goes when she leaves us but she just said *a ways* and wouldn't be drawn on it.

That's how she is most of the time now: quiet, withdrawn. Evenings she eats what little she cares for from her MRE and turns in without saying more than a dozen words. At first I tell myself she's just tired, on account of all the extra miles she's putting in, finding us shelter. I'm not sure that's it, though. I wait up each night until she passes into whatever it is she calls sleep, and then I check her crucifix. That crudely cast cross has become my talisman. I remember how Marv's had been, before he died. The virus had only had a couple of days to work on it, but already it had been pitted and pocked, like something had been eating away at it. Hers is always the same: the metal no different than how it was when I lifted it from his grave.

We pass our fifth night in North Carolina in a *Red Roof* she finds for us just outside of a place called Heavenly that has no business trading on that name. As day breaks we rejoin the interstate and point our snowshoes south once again. For once Mags won't be leaving us. Our next milestone is Durham, and barring calamity we should reach it before nightfall. Place that size there should be no shortage of places to sleep.

The drifts aren't bad along the first stretch so we can walk side by side. I settle in next to her, the kid between us. I make a few attempts at conversation, but she seems more comfortable with silence so I let it be. The kid looks up at her through those outsize goggles, then back at me. He wears them day and night, now; I can't recall the last time I saw him without them. I wondered about that when he first started doing it; I was worried it might be his eyes bothering him again. But when I mentioned it to Mags she got mad. She said I should stop trying to find problems where there were none. If it was the light that was troubling him why would he have taken to wearing them at night? I couldn't find a flaw with that, so I quit asking. I watched him close for a few days, all the same.

The morning slips by, our progress no better or worse than the days that have gone before. With each crest in the road I find myself scanning the horizon, eager for my first glimpse of the city. We're embarked on the last leg of our journey now. We'll be in Durham by evening and Fearrington's no more than a day's hike beyond; even accounting for our laggard pace we should be there by nightfall tomorrow. I should be relieved, but now that we're almost at our destination I'm nervous. I glance over at the pack Mags is carrying. It bears little resemblance to the one she set out with. Whatever rations we have left, they won't see us back to Mount Weather. Not even close.

I look behind me at the long, raggedy line of Juvies stretched out behind me on the interstate. We all voted, but I know the truth of it. They're here because of me, a bunker marked on a map a dead man gave me, and the things I told them about it: that I'll be able to find it; that Marv's codes will work to get us in; that there'll be food there to sustain us.

If any of those things prove false we're in a whole heap of trouble.

Sometime just shy of noon we pass an exit sign and not long after an overpass appears around a bend in the road. Ahead the interstate stretches off into the distance, with no apparent end to it. If we stayed on it would bring us all the way to 501, which in turn runs right by Fearrington. But the way I mean to take us – south through the city – is more direct; I reckon it could shave as much as a day off our journey. Our supplies could certainly use that, but mostly I just want to see what waits for us here. There was no mention in the newspaper clippings of Durham being hit in the strikes, but then there was no confirmation it had been spared either, and what we saw in Richmond has been on my mind since we came through it. Our new home's going to be a lot smaller than Mount Weather was. Even if it's stocked like I've assumed we're going to need things, and Durham's where I'll be coming to get them.

I lead us off the highway. At the top of the exit ramp a lone semi blocks the intersection; it looks like it was in the middle of executing one final turn when something called a halt to its advance. As I get closer I see what: the traffic light's given out just as it was passing under, staving in the roof of the cab. A single cluster hangs from the end of the collapsed gantry arm, creaking and groaning as it shifts in the wind.

From the junction the road slopes down. Drive-thrus line up one after the other on either side, their once-garish signs competing for our attention. A decade of weather has left them faded and tattered, but it's still a riot of color compared with what we've been seeing on the highway. My heart sinks in spite of it; the Juvies may not have much reading between them, but they remember enough to know what those signs mean. Behind me I hear the first of them asking whether it's time yet for lunch.

I turn my snowshoes around, but the rebellion's already caught hold. I look up to the sky. It's not yet noon but somewhere behind the clouds the sun will soon be contemplating its downward course. We're close to Durham now, though, so I guess I shouldn't sweat it. I call after them twenty minutes, knowing it'll be an hour if I'm lucky. They set off in the direction of a flat-roofed building the sign out front identifies as *Bojangles' Famous Chicken 'n' Biscuits*, a spring in their stride that's been sorely lacking all morning.

I shake my head and start to follow their tracks. As I enter the parking lot I get that familiar scratchy feeling, like stepping through cobwebs, only inside my head. Spidey's been quiet for days, but now something's woken him up. He hasn't yet reached for the alarm button, but he's telling me he's not happy about something, all the same. I stop, for the first time paying attention to the sorry-looking diner the Juvies have chosen. The roof's a little heavy with snow, but no worse than the Speedway or the Taco Bell on either side of it. It gives no indication it's likely to quit on us, least not until we're done with lunch.

Mags asks if everything's okay. I hesitate a moment then nod and we continue making our way towards the entrance. The door hangs back on its hinges and when I look closer I can see scratches around the lock where somebody's had at it with a pry bar. Spidey pings again at those, but the marks are old and he's giving no other clue as to what's suddenly getting him antsy. I set the container with the virus down and bend to my bindings. Mags is already out of hers and making her way in. I hear the snow crunch behind me and when I turn around the kid's standing there. He stares at me for a moment then follows her.

I step out of my snowshoes and join them inside. It takes a second for my eyes to adjust to the gloom, but when they do I see the Juvies have spread themselves across the available booths. There's still space left if they would bunch up and let us in, but no-one's showing any sign of that. They keep their eyes down, making busy work of unwrapping their rations. A few even shuffle closer to the end. I've been taking my lunches with the kid since she started hiking out to find us shelter, so I've kinda gotten used to it. It's been a while since she ate with us during the day, however, and now it seems like it's bothering her. I look for Jake - he can generally be relied on to find a spot for Mags - but he's got his back to the door and hasn't spotted us yet. I tap her on the shoulder, point to a couple of stools at the counter.

'Those'll do.'

She makes no move towards them. She stares at the Juvies a moment longer then she says she's not hungry; she's going to go on, find us somewhere to pass the night. Her voice is low, barely a whisper, but there's an edge to it that wasn't there a moment ago. I start to tell her there's no need. We're close now; as long as Durham isn't like Richmond there'll be no shortage of places there. But then I stop. Her hands remain by her sides, but her fists are clenched, and when my eyes return to her face her expression has hardened. And there's something else there too, something that makes me take a step back.

I tell her we'll catch up with her soon as we can. She pushes past me without saying a word and hurries outside. The kid runs after her like he means to follow, but then stops. We both watch as she crosses the parking lot, bounds up the embankment and rejoins the highway. Whatever efforts she had been making to conceal her pace, those are forgotten now; it's not long till she's little more than a speck in the distance.

I stand in the doorway after she's gone, uncertain what to make of what's just happened. I head back into the diner, choose a stool at the counter and shuck off my pack, but before I can sit Lauren sees me and waves me over. A space has miraculously opened up next to her; as I watch she shuffles in to make more room. I'm not sure what else to do, so I head over and sit. She hands me her canteen. I use a splash from it to get the heater in my ration working then hold the bottle to my lips and take a sip. The water's sharp with the cold; I can taste the ice crystals. I close my eyes and for a second, for no reason I can fathom, I'm sitting next to Mags outside a *7-Eleven*, the sun warm on my face. There's a white van in the parking lot, *The Sacred Heart Home for Children* printed in blue cursive along its side. I can feel the Big Gulp clutched to my chest, the first spike of brain-freeze from the soda I've just drunk too fast already on its way. Next to me Mags giggles, holds her hands out for it. I try to hold the memory, but then my head gives an involuntary shake and it's gone. I pass the canteen back, feeling the water I've just swallowed settle cold in my stomach.

Lauren smiles at me as she takes it.

'Not much longer now.'

*

AS SOON AS THE LAST food pouch has been emptied I get the Juvies to their feet and hustle them towards the door. The kid's waiting for us out in the parking lot. He looks up when he sees me, happy that we're on the move again. He scurries back to the interchange and disappears around the stricken semi without so much as a backward glance. I set off after him, but the Juvies show little interest in keeping up; it's not long till they're stretched out in their usual vagabond line behind me.

I ease back, resigning myself to their pace. My pack is light, barely worth the mention. With each step the container with the virus swings on its handle, but after weeks on the road I've grown accustomed to it. It hardly troubles me anymore; fact is there are days I even find it soothing. Marv said you always had to pay attention, but often, pounding the snow like this, with nothing to do but herd the Juvies along mile after mile of interstate my mind will slip out of gear and settle to an idle.

I'd be happy for it to do that now, but it won't.

I look at Mags' tracks, stretching out in front of me. I wonder how far ahead of us she is already. Probably in the city by now, the speed she took off. I tell myself it doesn't have to mean anything. Her crucifix is still clear; I checked it only last night. She's just pissed the Juvies are still being that way with her and the kid. She'll calm down soon enough; by the time she comes back to us she'll be fine.

The voice isn't going to let me have that, though. As my snowshoes crunch into the shallow indentations she's left it takes to whispering.

There was something else, though. You saw it.

My head dips inside the hood of my parka, before I

can stop myself. Because the truth is I did.

Something behind her eyes.

Yes.

Like with Kurt. Almost as though…

Almost as though whatever she was battling with then was back.

We make our way into Durham.

I keep following the tracks she's left, not really heeding much around me other than the occasional street sign. Little by little gas stations and strip malls give way to row houses with small yards, and then low-slung modern buildings. Spidey takes to grumbling again, but there's no sign here of the fire-blackened concrete, the blown out walls, we saw in Richmond, so I hush him. We crest a shallow rise and I catch my first proper view of Durham's skyline. Off in the distance small clusters of lonely high-rises huddle together, dotting the horizon. They seem in poor shape, listing this way or that or lying collapsed in rubble, the metal that once braced them virus-weakened, no longer able to bear the weight of concrete. They are a relief, nonetheless; proof that the devastation we witnessed earlier has not been visited here too.

Our pace slows the closer we get to the center. The Juvies stop at each cross street, craning their necks at the slowly disintegrating buildings, like each one we pass is a wonder. I stop often to let the stragglers catch up, making sure my charges don't get too strung out behind me. The streets get busy. Vehicles rest where they've been abandoned, their trunks popped, their doors agape. Others have mounted sidewalks, or folded themselves around light poles. Around Eden the virus did a pretty good job of quieting the roads, but then Providence, Shiloah, Ely, those were all small towns. It doesn't look like that was the way of it in the cities. Beyond the blast crater Richmond's streets were clogged, and it's no different here; Durham's final traffic jam appears to have been a doozy.

The wind's picked up a little while we've been making our way in and Mags' tracks are already fading. The kid runs farther ahead, following her prints as though fearful they'll be wiped clean before he's able to find her again. For once I'm less anxious about her return. She'll be back with us when she's ready; there's no shortage of places here we might hole up for the night. Best she takes the time she needs to sort out whatever's going on inside her head.

Every now and then spidey pings at something he refuses to share but I keep going, navigating the wrecks largely on autopilot, committing the occasional landmark to memory, until eventually the burned-out hulk of a tractor-trailer blocks our path. I lose Mags' tracks in a drift just this side of it, then I find them again, veering off through the parking lot of a VA medical center. The lot's full, a sea of humped gray shapes sitting silent under a thick blanket of snow. The building on the far side of it's in bad shape, even by the standards of what surrounds it. Its roofline sags pitifully and one entire wing has collapsed to rubble, twisted rebar poking out through the concrete like the ribs of a decaying carcass. Marv always kept us away from places like this. After what I saw in Blacksburg I can't say as I'd fault him for it.

I set the container with the virus in the snow while I wait for the Juvies to catch up. It's a relief Durham's not how Richmond was, but I can't say I'm much looking forward to working it, all the same. It might have been an okay place, once, but a straight shot of ferro, followed by a few hectic weeks of looting and then a decade of neglect has put paid to that. There's no shortage of hospitals here either; we're not halfway through yet and

I've already counted a worrying number of them. They're easy to spot, even from a distance; that was where the virus did its best work. I stare up at the crumbling remains of the VA. Rows of dark, broken windows march off towards its edges, and for a second I think I see movement behind one of them. But when I look there it's just the wind, tugging at the curtains. They flap uselessly, snagging on the edges of glass that still cling to the frames.

I wonder if it's all the hospitals that have been making spidey so antsy. I mull it over for a little while, but somehow it doesn't seem quite right. I look around, trying to work out what else it might be. It feels like it's right there, all around me; if I could just focus for a moment it'd come to me.

Lauren's snowshoes crunch the snow beside me.

'Something wrong?'

I let my gaze linger a moment longer then shake my head.

We make our way down into the parking lot, picking a path between the abandoned cars. I call back to the Juvies not to touch anything. What Kane did to the skies should have struck the virus from the metal, but this close to a hospital I certainly don't plan on taking chances. I breathe a sigh of relief when the last straggler clambers back up the embankment on the far side and we're through. I do a quick head count and then we set off again.

The kid's already picked up Mags' tracks, so I let him lead the way. Spidey's bleating grows louder, but I'm having no better luck working out what has him riled than earlier, so I just do my best to drown him out. A half-dozen blocks south of the VA I stop outside a Walgreen's while I wait for the Juvies to catch up again. I'm staring at my reflection in the darkened storefront, when for no good reason my gaze shifts from the glass to the wall nearby, settling on a section of concrete there.

I stare at it while my brain slowly joins the dots. And then a spike of adrenalin sends my heart racing.

*

I SWING BACK TO THE DOORWAY, silently cursing myself for not paying more attention. I check again, to be sure I haven't imagined it. But there's no mistake. My eyes jump to the next building along. Another. Across the street, more, all around us, everywhere I turn, obvious now that I know what to look for.

How long have I been missing them?

I look ahead at the prints Mags has left in the snow, and for a second I consider just taking off after her. I take a deep breath, tell myself to calm down; I need to think for a moment, try not to do something stupid. Lauren's been following in my tracks. She comes to a halt behind me.

'What's wrong?'

I tell her to get everyone off the road. Her eyes go wide and her mouth opens, like she might have a question, but something in the tone of my voice must convince her this isn't the time to have it answered. She turns around and starts ushering the Juvies into the Walgreen's.

I set the container with the virus down in the snow and turn my attention back to the street. Up ahead the kid's stopped. He looks at me, wondering why we're no longer following. I hold up a hand and beckon him to join us, quick. He hesitates for a second, eyeing what little's left of Mags' tracks like he doesn't care to give them up, but then he swings his poles around and starts making his way towards us.

Lauren's already herded most of the Juvies into the store as I begin retracing our steps. Jake calls out to me as I pass and asks what's wrong. I tell him I'll explain when I return; for now he needs to follow the others

105

inside.

I make my way back the way we've come, ignoring his protests. I remember I have Hicks' pistol, and for a moment I consider getting it out. But that would require digging around for it in my backpack, and in any event, it's not loaded. I don't plan to go far. A block or two, no more. Just enough to be certain.

The kid must have missed the memo about the Walgreen's; before I've gone more than a hundred yards I hear his snowshoes behind me. I turn around to find him looking up at me. I point back to where Lauren and Jake are herding the last of the Juvies out of sight, but he doesn't budge, just stares at me through the darkened lens of his goggles. I hold my mittens to my lips and he nods, once, like he understands. I set off again. He follows carefully in my tracks, watching as I search each doorway. When I reach the corner I cross over and check the next block, then the one after, just to be sure.

Tyler and Eric are the only ones still on the street when I return. They stand one on either side of the entrance to the Walgreen's. They've both slung the rifles off their shoulders. Behind them the Juvies huddle together back in the shadows. They press forward when they see me, anxious to know what's going on. Lauren squeezes her way to the front.

'What is it, Gabe?'

I point a finger at the wall.

'We've been passing them for a while.' That must have been what spidey was pinging at, in the parking lot of the Bojangles. 'Probably since we left the highway.'

She stares at the wall for a second and then her mouth draws taut. Behind her the Juvies crane their necks, anxious to see. There's more than one puzzled expression; not all of them have figured out as quickly as she has what the red 'X' sprayed across the concrete means.

'It's a scavenging mark, just like Marv and I used to leave on the places we'd visit, so you don't waste time working the same spot twice.'

From somewhere back in the shadows Amy pipes up.

'Maybe they're from a long time ago?' She says it hopefully, like all she wants right now is for me to tell her it's so. She's not the only one looking for that comfort; I hear others behind her, murmuring in agreement.

I reach up. Like everything else the wall's coated with a decade of grime. When I rub it the red comes off easy under my fingers.

'Paint's sitting on top.' I dust it from my mitten. 'I've been back a few blocks. The marks are older that way.'

Lauren continues to look at the wall.

'They live somewhere to the north.'

I nod.

'That'd be my guess. They come into the city to find what they need; probably been doing it a while. Each time they have to venture a little bit farther.'

'We could have walked right past them.'

I look over at Amy again. Her eyes are wide now, panicky as cattle. She sounds close to tears. The rest of the Juvies are exchanging worried glances. None of them need to be reminded what happened when Mags and I ran into the soldiers.

'I don't think so.' I say it with as much confidence as I can muster. I'll need to leave them now, to go find Mags, but before I do that I have to calm them down. Nothing spreads faster than panic, that's what Hicks had said, and right now the Juvies look no more than a couple of quick heartbeats from a stampede. 'I haven't seen any other tracks.' I'm sure I wouldn't have missed those.

I shuck off my backpack and set it on the ground. I undo the snaps and reach inside. My fingers find what they're looking for – a heft of cold hard steel, wrapped in old leather. I pull the pistol out and start to unravel the gun belt.

Lauren's gaze drops to the holster, and for a second it's as if her eyes brighten. She takes a step closer and looks out onto the street, following what remains of the prints Mags has left. She rests one hand on my shoulder and bends closer, lowering her voice. Behind her the Juvies shuffle forward, anxious not to miss whatever's being discussed.

'Should we be going on, Gabe? I mean, wouldn't it be safer to head back? It's like you said: we didn't pass anyone on the way in.'

Jake narrows his eyes at that suggestion, but most of the others are nodding in agreement. I look up into their anxious faces, uncertain what to say. The truth of it is I don't know. I have no idea who's working this place, or how many of them there are, or what their intentions might be towards strangers. All I know is whoever they are they most likely come from somewhere behind us, and we haven't yet reached the limits of their territory. Lauren could be right; they might be a few blocks ahead of us, even now. And if that's the case Mags will already have run into them.

I loop the belt around my waist and buckle it, feeling the weight of the pistol settle against my hip.

'You might well be right, Lauren. That's why everyone's going to wait here while I go find Mags. I don't expect I'll be long; she should have been coming back to us anyway.'

Unless she's already run into whoever's out there.

Jake pushes himself to the front.

'I'll come with you.'

I shake my head.

'I'll be quicker on my own.'

It comes out harsher than I intend, but I don't have to

explain it in a way that might save his feelings. I make for the door before he has a chance to argue.

Tyler and Eric are still standing guard by the entrance. Eric looks twitchier than I would have cared for. His eyes won't settle in one place and his finger darts in and out of the trigger guard like it expects to have business there soon; I daresay Hicks would have a thing or two to say about his gun manners. Tyler seems calmer. He clutches his rifle to his chest, the barrel held low, his eyes slowly sweeping the street. For a second he reminds me of Benjamin, waiting for us by the portal on the day we arrived at Eden. I pull him to one side on my way out.

'Can you keep watch out here, at least till it gets dark.'

He nods.

'They'll want a fire, but make them wait as long as they can, and then light it all the way in back, away from the windows. If I'm not back you stay here tonight, and then first thing tomorrow you head back to the highway. We'll find you on the road.'

'Don't worry Gabe, I got this.'

'Alright. See you soon.'

*

I SET OFF, following what's left of Mags' prints. Before I've got to the end of the block I hear the crunch of snowshoes behind me and I turn around to find the kid on my tail. I point in the direction of the Walgreen's, but he says no. I tell him he has to, I have no time for this now, but he just shakes his head and stares up at me through his goggles, like it's me who's holding things up. I can't think of anything to do other than shoot him, and tempting as that seems right now there's a good chance someone'd hear it.

'Alright then, but this time you have to stay behind me. And don't fall back. I'm not joking now; I'm not waiting on you.'

He bobs his head like he understands.

I check the streets are empty and then dart across, quick as I can. I meant what I said; I'm not making any allowances for his size. He's as good as his word, though. He follows hard on my heels; my snowshoes have barely cleared their tracks before I hear him stepping into them.

I keep us to the sidewalk, pressed to the buildings for what little cover they provide. The paint marks continue, growing fresher with each one we pass. A half-dozen blocks south of where I left the Juvies I stop. I realize I haven't heard the kid's snowshoes in a while. When I look behind me he's come to a halt under the faded yellow star of a Hardee's. I raise my hand to hurry him on, already cursing under my breath, but something in the way he's crouched gives me pause. I turn my snowshoes around and make my way back. I find him bent over a familiar shape in the snow. A discarded rattle can sits on top of a shallow drift, only a light dusting of windblown powder covering it. He lowers his head to it again, wrinkling his nose at the smell, but when I pick it up I don't get anything. The paint's still bright on the nozzle, however, like it's not been long since it was used. I drop the can and we continue on.

The marks are everywhere now. I slow us down, checking doorways, entrances, even the silted windows above, trying not to start each time I catch my reflection in the darkened glass of an abandoned storefront. Up ahead a delivery truck's mounted the curb, barring our progress. Mags' prints go up it then disappear. As I get closer I can see two words, scratched into its ice-crusted flank in letters each a foot high.

GO BACK.

I scurry forward and peer over the crumpled hood. A hundred yards beyond the block ends at another street. There's a *KwikPrint* on the corner, its weather-faded awning snapping and fluttering in the wind. Beyond I can just make out what looks like another set of tracks, coming out of the east. The wind's already flattening their edges, but they can't be any older than hers; whoever made them must have passed through right about the time she did. I look back down at the prints I've been following, trying to stay calm.

She had time to leave a message, which means she saw them before they saw her. Probably. I look down at the snow. Other than the prints she's left, and the set running up the middle of the cross street, it's smooth, unmarked. There's no way she would have let someone take her without a struggle, and there's no sign of that.

So where is she?

I feel the kid tugging at the sleeve of my parka. He points a mitten in the direction of the *KwikPrint*, and then without warning he takes off towards it. I hiss at

111

him to come back, but he's showing no greater inclination to heed what I say now than he did earlier. He crosses the street and disappears into the store. I hesitate a second longer then break from the cover of the truck and hurry after him.

The tattered awning flaps above my head as I step under it, into the shadow of the entrance. It takes a moment for my eyes to adjust to the gloom, but when they do I see a familiar figure, standing by the window. The kid's already out of his snowshoes, crouching next to her. I unsnap my bindings and hurry over to join them. She presses a finger to her lips.

'Didn't you see…'

I don't wait for her to finish, just throw my arms around her, hold her tight to me for a long while. Eventually she taps my arm.

'Hey.'

I wait a moment longer then let her go. She turns back to the window, but not before I catch what might be a smile. It occurs to me it's not an expression I've seen much of recently.

She looks over my shoulder, back towards the entrance.

'Where are the others?'

'As soon as I spotted the paint I got them off the street and came looking for you.' I hadn't intended it, but I realize that does sound pretty heroic, in a *Last of the Mohicans* sort of way. That was one of Mags' favorite films, back in Mount Weather, so I decide not to go into detail on how many blocks I had to pass before I finally noticed the big red X's sprayed on pretty much every building since we left the highway. I can't see how Hawkeye would have missed something like that.

She leans a little closer to the pane and goes back to looking out. Large cracks zig-zag their way across the glass, and what's not broken is coated with grime, all of which makes it pretty hard to see. I find a section that's a little cleaner than the rest and press my face to it.

'So what are you looking at?'

She points at a *Save-A-Lot* kitty corner opposite.

'The two men I almost ran into, coming up the street, they went in there. That was over an hour ago now. They haven't come out yet.'

For the next twenty minutes we keep watch in silence. Outside the day starts to darken, and I wonder if, whoever it is we're waiting for, they've settled in for the night. But then Mags and the kid both stir. I cup one mitten to the glass and peer out, holding my breath. At first I don't see anything, but a few seconds later there's movement by the doorway and a tall man steps into view. He's bundled up in so many clothes it's hard to tell much about him other than his height. He looks up to the sky, then gestures to someone else to hurry up. There's a pause and a second, shorter, man steps into view. He adjusts the straps on the pack he's carrying and then both set off up the street, Indian file.

I follow them until they're out of sight and then I step back from the window. An idea's starting to form, but I'll need to be quick. I glance at my pack, propped against the wall. I shouldn't need it; I don't mean to be gone that long. I start making my way towards the door.

Mags turns to look at me.

'What are you doing?'

'Going after them.'

She stares at me like I've taken leave of my senses.

'You're *what*?'

'Okay, I know how it sounds, but just think about it a second. Fearrington's going to be small; we know that, right? If we're lucky there'll be basic supplies, food, water, but probably not much else. Which means pretty soon I'm going to have to find us stuff. Marv's map says this is the only place of any size within a day's hike. The fact that someone else is working this place doesn't have to be a problem; I can stay out of their way, *as long as I know where they're going to be.* Now the marks I spotted earlier made me think whoever they are, they're coming out of the north.' I point out towards the *Save-A-Lot.* 'But the tracks those men made came out of the east and now they're headed west. I just need to follow them a little ways to figure out which it is. Otherwise sooner or later I'm going to end up running into them again, just like you almost did. Only next time I may not be so lucky as you were.'

She looks at me a while, like she's considering this. I guess she must see some sense in it, because she reaches for her backpack.

'Alright, I'll come with you.'

I shake my head.

'You need to get back to the others. I left them in a Walgreen's a dozen blocks back the way we came. The kid knows where it is.'

I see her weighing what I've just said. She doesn't look convinced.

'Some of them might be starting to fret by now.' *Might?* If Amy isn't already the proud mother of kittens I'll be amazed. I figure it's best not to overdo this last bit, however; Mags knows the Juvies every bit as well as I do. She thinks on it some more. In the end she nods reluctantly.

'Alright, but not far, okay? Seriously, Gabe - don't make me come looking for you.'

114

*

THE TWO MEN from the *Save-A-Lot* are already half a dozen blocks distant by the time I step outside. I watch from the shelter of the *KwikPrint*'s doorway to make sure they're not in the habit of checking behind them, then I wave Mags and the kid onto the street.

She steps into her snowshoes, pulls up her hood. She's about to set off but then she turns and grabs my arm.

'I mean it, Gabe: be careful, okay?'

'Don't worry; I'll be back here long before you. If I'm not bring the others as far south as you can while there's light, then find somewhere to hole up. I'll come find you.'

I watch until she and the kid have disappeared around the delivery truck, and then I turn my attention back to the two men. They're already little more than a couple of charcoal smudges, mostly lost to the swirling snow.

I pull off my mittens, unzip my parka and reach for the pistol on my hip. I saw no sign of a rifle slung over either man's shoulder, but I don't plan on taking any chances, all the same. I pry the hammer back and lever the loading gate open, then jiggle a round from the cartridge loops on my belt, drop it into the chamber and move the cylinder on a turn. The cold finds its way through my liners fast; by the time I'm pushing the last one home the tips of my fingers are starting to lose feeling.

I drop the gun back in its holster, pull on my mittens and poke my head out, just as my quarries disappear up a side street. I set off after them. My heart's beating a little faster, but as I cross the street I realize most of it's excitement. I meant what I said to Mags: I'm not going to do anything stupid. I don't plan on following them far, just enough to see which way they're headed. It'll make a welcome change from herding the Juvies down mile after mile of interstate. For the first time in weeks I feel useful.

I hurry along the sidewalk, keeping my eyes on the single set of prints they've left in the snow. When I get to the spot where their tracks veer off I stop and peer around the corner. I still haven't seen any sign they're checking behind them, but I hold back anyway, watching as they trudge steadily away from me. Maybe this is going to be even easier than I had counted on. They're headed north now. If they show no sign of deviating from their current course by the time I lose them again I'll take it as their destination and call an end to the pursuit.

I wait five minutes, then ten. I catch only occasional glimpses of them now, through gaps that open in the drift. I lift my goggles onto my forehead, squinting into the windblown snow, but it doesn't help. The sightings grow less frequent, and for a long while I don't see them at all. And then, just as I'm about to turn around and head back to the *KwikPrint* the wind drops, and for a second before it picks up again I see them cutting across the street, like they mean to leave it. I look up to the gunmetal sky. There's not much left of the day, but this might be my only opportunity to figure out where it is they're coming from. I hesitate a second longer, then pull the goggles back down and set off after them again.

For the next half hour I follow the men as they wind their way through the city. After the first few turns I think I have a sense of the general direction in which they're headed, but then suddenly their route seems to lose all reason. They switch this way then that, at times doubling back, until I start to wonder whether they know themselves where they're going. The wind strengthens. It drives the drifts in long, shifting ridges that snake across the road, clearing their prints; I have to keep shortening the gap between us to keep them in sight. They seem oblivious to my presence, however, and in any case the flurries of snow that obscure them will keep me hidden too.

They disappear down yet another cross street and I hurry to catch up, but when I get to the corner and peer around there's no sign and for a moment I think I've finally lost them. I look up. The sky's darkening and I can feel the temperature beginning to drop; I think it might be time to cut my losses and turn back. But then through a gap in the snow I see a flashlight wink on, followed moments later by another.

I set off after them again. Tracking their beams is easier so I allow myself to drop back a little, more comfortable now that I can keep a block between us. They finally seem to have found a heading they're happy with, too. The road begins to incline, and from the signs we pass it looks like we're almost back at the interstate. Ahead of me the flashlights stop and then perform a complicated little dance. I wait, peering into the gloom, trying to work out what's going on. After a few seconds the beams resume their onward march. I creep forward again, more slowly now, until I reach the interchange. Ahead the gantry arm from a stoplight lies collapsed in the snow, blocking my path; the light show I've just witnessed must have been them clambering over it.

The wind's strengthening; already there's little left of their tracks. I stand at the foot of the overpass, my arms hugged to my sides, watching the intermittent pinpricks of light until they finally lose themselves to the swirling snow. I've seen as much as I need to, though. I look around. I'm farther north than I expected and dusk's already settling; it's too late to go looking for Mags and the others now. I'll find somewhere to shelter for the night, catch them on the road tomorrow.

I make my way down off the interchange. There's a *U-Haul* lot right across the street. A single-story cinder block with a faded sign above squats in one corner, and as a bonus the door's already ajar, saving me the bother of busting it open, which is just as well given that the pry bar's sitting in my pack, back in the *KwikPrint*. I point myself toward it, already looking forward to the fire I'll soon have going.

I unsnap my snowshoes at the entrance and push the door back. The floor's dusty, scattered with debris. A long counter stretches the length of the far wall. There's a metal box mounted behind, its lock pried open, keys still hanging from hooks inside. Next to it a whiteboard, marked with the comings and goings of vehicles. To one side a stack of packing boxes that look like they'll hold a flame. I'm in luck; I won't even need to go outside again for firewood.

I step inside, pulling what remains of the door closed behind me. The sound of the wind recedes. But as I bend to undo my bindings I hear a soft *snick-snick* and I freeze. It's a sound I have recently come to know; the sound of the slide being pulled back on a handgun, as its owner chambers the first round.

A COLD KNOT OF FEAR tightens my stomach. I raise my hands and turn around to face a thin black man, bundled up in an assortment of rags. A pair of dark eyes, the whites tobacco yellow, stare back at me from deep in a wide, angular face. He holds the pistol he's just cocked sideways in front of him, at a flat angle, his finger already curled around the trigger. The muzzle's close enough that even in this light I can read the words *Smith & Wesson* stamped along the barrel.

Hick's pistol rests useless against my hip, under my zipped-up parka. The idea that I might draw it and fire a round in the air, and that that might frighten him off, suddenly seems laughable.

'Why you been following us?'

My mind races, searching for something to say. I can't tell him anything that'd make him think there's more than just me. I also really – and I can't stress this enough – *really* don't want to get shot.

'I…I thought you might have some food.'

His lip curls in a derisive grin, revealing a mouth full of gold teeth. If it was his intention to put me at ease, it doesn't work. There's something cruel, feral about it; a malice that infects the whole of his face. He inclines his head to one side, but the pistol doesn't move.

'Does it look to you like I might have any to spare?'

That sounds like a rhetorical question, but I shake my head anyway.

'You strapped?'

I stare at him blankly. I have no idea what he means.

'Are you packing?'

I'm still not sure what he wants me to say. My eyes flick over my shoulder. He must see I'm not carrying a backpack.

'Do-you-have-a-wea-pon?'

He says it one word at a time, punctuating each syllable with a short, agitated jab of the pistol into my chest. I nod quickly, desperate for him to stop doing that.

'Yes. Yes. Under my coat.'

'Take it out. Nice and easy, now.'

I unzip the parka and reach down to the holster, pulling Hicks' pistol out with my fingertips. When he sees it he whistles through his gilded teeth and snatches it from me. He stares at it for a moment and then it disappears inside one of the many folds in his clothing.

'Belt too.'

I unbuckle the gun belt and hand it over.

'Anything else?'

I start to tell him about Weasel's knife, but he's already rummaging through my pockets. He finds the blade, examines it for a second and then that goes the way of the pistol. My heart sinks when he takes out Marv's map, but all he does is study the cover for a moment and then toss it. It occurs to me now, too late, that I never thought to make a copy. Kane's master list of codes for each facility in the Federal Relocation Arc is sitting in the outside pocket of my pack, back in the *KwikPrint*, but without the map showing the bunker's location Mags might never find it. I glance down to where it lies, discarded, on the dusty floor. The snow outside will be wiped clean of my prints long before she'll think to come after me. How will she know to look for it here?

'That it?'

I nod.

'Travellin' a bit light aintcha?'

I don't know what to say to that so I just nod again.

'Alright, hold out your hands.'

An already looped length of cord appears from one of

his pockets. He pulls off my mittens and slips it over my wrists, drawing it tight. He runs the cord around a few more times, passing it between my hands in a neat figure of eight, and then ties it off with practiced efficiency, like he's done this before. He tests the knot. The work's good; I can already feel pins and needles pricking my fingertips. Satisfied, he picks up one of my mittens, removing a tattered, fraying glove so he can try it on. The fit must be close enough because he pulls off the other, smiling at me like he's happy with the trade.

I bend down to recover the gloves he's discarded, but he just pushes me in the direction of the door before I have a chance to retrieve them.

His accomplice waits for us up on the overpass. He's thin, like the first one, and no better groomed, but taller, a raggedy scarecrow of a man. He grips a flashlight in each hand, the yellow beams describing stretched out circles in the gray snow. The one with the teeth pushes me forward towards him. The scarecrow shifts a flashlight and holds me in its beam while he looks me up and down. The first man smiles, his eyes wet with excitement. The light from the beam glitters off the gold caps that crowd his mouth.

'Look what I found, Mac. Just wait till Finch sees him. Just you wait.'

The man called Mac pulls down something that might once have been a scarf. His skin is even darker than his companion's, the eyes that stare back at me black as coals. A patchy beard, straggled and unruly, salted with gray, covers the lower half of his face.

'Quit your yappin', Goldie. It's getting late, and we have a ways to go yet.'

*

WE LEAVE THE INTERSTATE behind and continue north. Crumbling strip malls slowly give way to houses with yards, then snow-covered fields. After a couple of miles the road branches at a water tower and we take the westerly fork. We keep to it for what seems like a long time. I close my eyes and try to recall what was on the map for this stretch, but as far as I can remember there wasn't much of anything. I really hope we don't have much farther to go. The last of the light's already draining from the sky and the temperature's dropping fast now; I can feel the ice-crust forming on the powder beneath my snowshoes. I flex the muscles in my wrists to keep the blood flowing, but the cord's too tight; my fingers are already numb. All I can do is I hold them to my face and blow into them to try and keep them warm.

We continue on, following the beams from the flashlights. The tall man stays quiet, but the other one, the one with the impressive dentistry, likes to talk. He keeps it up without pause. Mostly it's variations of the same thing, repeated over and over. Somebody called Finch is going to be very happy to see me. That seems to bode well for him, although it's unclear yet what it might mean for me. I find myself wishing for our destination in spite of it. Anything to get out of the bone-splitting cold.

We trudge up a long, straight section and then, just as I think we're about to start down into the shallow beyond, Mac takes a turn I hadn't even spotted was there. I search for a sign, any clue as to where we might be headed, but there's nothing. The road narrows to little more than a track. We follow it for an hour, maybe more, our snowshoes crunching through the ice-slicked

122

snow as it winds ever upward. At last we reach the ridgeline and now I see what must be our destination. In what little remains of the light I can make out little more than its size: a huge, walled fortress, sitting alone in the valley beneath us.

We make our way down towards it. Goldie grows more excited. He pushes me forward, jabbering continuously, barely stopping to draw breath. As we get closer I can see that the fortress's high stone walls are topped with tangled coils of barbed wire. A guard tower stares down from each corner. The nearest one on the western side looks like it's been set ablaze; there's little left of its structure other than a few charred beams, poking up into the darkening sky.

My heart sinks as I realize a building like this could only have one purpose.

Mac sets course for a tall iron gate that dominates the closest side. A rusting sign above confirms my fears: it announces we have arrived at *Starkly Correctional Institution*. Kane used to say if we were to happen upon others while out scavenging we were to give them a wide berth; that if there was anyone still left after all this time they'd most likely be desperate, dangerous men, lawless and Godless. Our President had his reasons for keeping us fearful, I know that now. But it gives me little comfort that my captors may not have had much of the law about them, even before the world fell apart.

We stop in front of the entrance. The gate towers above us; it must be three times as high as I am tall. Mac steps up to a smaller door set into the thick, riveted metal and pounds on it with his fist. After a long pause a latch slides back. A second later from somewhere behind there's the sound of bolts being drawn and the door creaks open.

I bend to undo my snowshoes. Goldie's eager to get inside now; he snaps at me to hurry, but my frozen fingers aren't up to the task of working the bindings. I finally manage one, but the second proves more stubborn. In the end he loses patience and shoves me. I trip over the foot that's still tethered and stumble forward. I try to get my hands out in front of me, but they're bound together and slow with the cold. My head bounces off the edge of something hard and then I'm falling through the door. I land awkwardly on the other side and just lay there for a moment, stunned, staring up at a wire-mesh sky. I feel something wet trickling down one side of my face, already growing sluggish in the frigid air. I raise my hands tentatively, trying to direct them to the spot. It takes longer than it ought. When I hold them out in front of me they're smeared with blood.

Something tugs at my boot and then rough hands grab me under my arms and haul me to my feet. I look around. I'm in some sort of holding pen. In front there's a step-through metal detector, like the one we had in the tunnel in Eden; beyond it a barred gate. Somewhere off in the darkness an indifferently muffled generator chugs away, marking out uneven time.

A small man sits in a glass-fronted booth, off to one side. At his elbow a low flame gutters in something that might once have been a candle, but is now little more than a pool of wax. The glass is pocked with frosted impact points, thin cracks spider-webbing out from the center of each. The pane seems to have been designed with such an assault in mind, however, because it's held.

Mac shucks off his backpack and approaches the booth. A metal tray slides out. He pulls a handgun from his coat, ejects the magazine and drops both in. Goldie does the same with his weapon, then digs in his pocket for Hicks' pistol. He pushes it up against the glass.

'I got to show this to Mr. Finch.'

The man behind the glass appears to consider the request for a moment, then simply says *Bullets*.

Goldie studies the pistol, turning it over in his hands, like he doesn't know how to work it. After a moment he holds it out to me, an irritated expression souring his dark features. My fingers are too numb to do it for him, so I explain through chattering teeth how he has to pull the hammer back to open the loading gate and then use the plunger to eject each round from its chamber. He struggles with it for a while before Mac steps over and takes it off him with a grunt. His fingers work the mechanism smoothly, rotating the cylinder so that one by one the bullets rattle into the bottom of the tray. When it's empty the man behind the glass draws the tray back. Goldie holds his hand out sullenly, and after a brief pause Mac gives the pistol back. It disappears into the folds of his clothing and then I'm being shoved forward again, in the direction of the metal detector. I tell him the dog tags I wear will set it off. He cusses me a few more times while he stops to yank them from my neck, and then I get pushed through.

Mac takes his turn after me. There's a loud beep as Goldie steps up to it. He turns to the man in the booth and pulls back his lips, pointing to his teeth.

'C'mon, man. Every time?'

There's a pause and then the gate buzzes and I'm hustled through into a large open area, a hundred yards or more on a side, like the keep of an old castle. A long gray building, three stories tall, its slab sides dotted with tiny slit windows, holds the center. A path's been cleared through the snow from the holding pen towards it. A handful of smaller structures huddle together at the base of the prison's high stone walls. By what little remains of the day's light it looks a hard place, devoid of either warmth or color, and I can't see how its appearance will have improved much by morning. Assuming I'm around to see it, that is.

Goldie pushes me towards a stout wooden door that

looks to be the entrance to the main building. Mac holds it open and I step inside. A metal stair zig-zags up into darkness. He turns to his companion.

'Bring him through. I'll go tell Finch.'

His boots clang up the stair. Goldie grabs me by the elbow, drags me along a short corridor that opens into a huge, dimly lit hall. As my eyes adjust to the gloom I can see it's open, all the way to its high, vaulted roof. Around the sides iron landings protrude from the gray stone and beyond I can just make out rows of cell doors. Most sit in darkness, but here and there the soft glow of candlelight seeps out from within. Shadowy figures lean against the railings in ones or twos, talking in low murmurs, here and there the glowing red tip of a cigarette passing between them. I feel the weight of their stare as I enter.

A long wooden table stretches off into shadow, candles in various stages of decomposition punctuating its length. Flames gutter in the shells of a few, but most are unlit. Goldie pulls out a chair near the end and manhandles me into it, then places Hicks' pistol on the table nearby.

He stands to one side, grinning down at me.

'Mr. Finch'll be down soon, don't you worry.' A giggle escapes his lips, like he can barely contain his excitement.

I stare down at the table. My head's starting to hurt from where I banged it, but I suspect whatever injury I've picked up there is soon going to be the least of my worries. I don't know who Finch is, but I can't say I share Goldie's excitement at the prospect of meeting him. There's not much I can do about that, however, so instead I tuck my frozen hands into my lap and sit there, awaiting my fate.

*

I DON'T HAVE LONG TO WAIT.

From somewhere behind and above there's the creak of a door being opened and then the slow, uneven clang of hard shoes on metal. The sound echoes through the hall, reverberating off the cold stone. The footsteps reach the end of the landing and take to the stair. They become more deliberate as they descend, until at last they reach the bottom. There's a pause and then they start up again, growing louder as they make their way toward me. And now the hollow click of heels is punctuated by another sound, an intermittent *clack* as something other than shoe leather strikes the concrete.

The footsteps come to a halt, right behind my chair. There's a long pause and then a short, neat man, dressed in a dark suit and tie, appears before me, leaning on a wooden cane. His graying hair is parted carefully to one side, and a pair of horn-rimmed spectacles perch precariously on his thin nose. He's flanked on either side by two much bigger men. The one on the left is burly, barrel-chested. An impressive gut hangs over his belt; a beard, wide like a shovel, adds to his scope. The other man is equally large, but whereas his companion looks like he might be running to fat, this one is muscular, powerful. His shaved head sits directly on a pair of broad shoulders without a discernible neck to separate the two.

The one with the beard steps forward, pulls out the chair at the head of the table. The smaller man I assume to be Finch lowers himself into it, then holds the cane up for the bearded one to take. He settles back in the chair, carefully placing one knee over the other. The cuff of one pant leg hitches up as he does it, revealing a

127

polished wingtip. He rests his elbows on the arms of the chair, steeples his fingers, and for a long moment just studies me over them. Then without warning he leans forward and reaches out a hand. The fingers are narrow, delicate, the nails clean, recently clipped. He smiles, revealing a perfect picket fence row of teeth.

'Garland Finch.'

The voice is low, soft like velvet, and yet somehow intense. For a few seconds I just stare at the hand, unsure what to say. There is something about him that is different, other. It's like he's wrong for this place; like he doesn't belong here. At last I stammer out my name. He repeats it, rolling the word from his tongue, almost like he's tasting it. I lift my hands from my lap to take the one he's offering, but it's a little difficult with my wrists tied together. He looks down at my bonds and his face wrinkles with displeasure. He tilts his head to one side.

'Mr. Goldie?'

The man with the teeth scurries forward out of the darkness.

'Yes, boss?'

Finch nods at my wrists.

'Why is Gabriel bound, Mr. Goldie?'

Goldie looks at me, and then at Finch, then back at me again, like he might not understand the question. The man who, for all his diminutive size, is clearly in charge of this place sighs. When he speaks it is patiently, as if to a slow-witted child.

'What do I detest more than anything Mr. Goldie?'

Goldie bobs his head, like he knows this one.

'Bad manners, boss.'

Finch looks at my bonds again, as if his point has been made.

Goldie leans closer, bows his head, so it's next to Finch's ear. He points at the pistol that sits in front of me on the table. His voice drops to a whisper.

'But boss, we found that on him.'

'Well no doubt he was carrying it for his own protection, Mr. Goldie. And I can't say I blame him, with hooligans like you running around untethered.' He smiles at me, apologetically. 'I'm sure he doesn't mean to use it on us, do you Gabriel?'

I shake my head.

'No, certainly not.'

At least not without the bullets it came with.

Goldie's mouth opens, like he might be about to protest some more. Finch closes his eyes and raises one hand to his brow. His narrow fingers press between his eyebrows, as if stanching a headache.

'Mr. Goldie.'

He doesn't raise his voice, but for those few syllables the tone changes. It loses all its softness and takes on a hard, flinty quality. From the dark balconies above there's a sound like I remember the rustling of leaves, as though the men there have suddenly all decided to draw breath at precisely the same moment.

Goldie's jaw snaps shut with an audible click. He hurries forward, fumbling in his pocket; Weasel's knife appears between his fingers. I hold my hands up. He slips the end of the blade between my wrists and starts sawing at the cord like his life depends on it. A few moments later the severed ends drop to the table. I rub my wrists, wincing as the blood returns to my fingers.

Finch looks at me as if embarrassed. He waits while I flex my fingers and then holds out his hand again. When he speaks his tone is once more pleasant.

'A pleasure to meet you, Gabriel.'

I shake his hand. The fingers that slip into mine feel slight, fragile, like there may be nothing more substantial than the bones of birds beneath the skin there.

'You will have to forgive Mr. Goldie. It may not

surprise you to learn that he has a long and troubled history with firearms.'

Goldie's already retreating, clearly anxious to be out of our presence, but the man with the beard steps forward, blocking his way. He folds a pair of meaty forearms across his chest and stares down at the shorter man.

Finch tilts his head to one side, the thinnest of smiles playing across his lips.

'Mr. Goldie, I do believe you've forgotten something.'

Goldie pauses then turns around and scurries back to the table. He deposits Weasel's knife next to Hicks' pistol, then hurries away again.

Finch turns back to me and shakes his head ruefully.

'You will need to be more careful with your possessions while you are with us, Gabriel.' He shifts a little closer, speaking into the back of his hand, as though the comment is intended for me alone. 'There is a regrettable criminal element.'

His fingers brush the knot in his tie. I'm struck again by how neat he appears. There's not a thing out of place. Even his shoelaces look like they might have been pressed.

'Now tell me: how have they been treating you?'

'Uh, fine, I guess.' At the last moment I remember his comment about manners. 'Thank you for asking.'

He smiles, but then something catches his attention. He leans forward, studying my face.

'I do hope that cut on your forehead wasn't caused by one of these ruffians.'

From somewhere off in the darkness I hear Goldie's voice again. He speaks quickly, tripping over the words, like he's anxious to get them out. Seems like the pitch might be a shade higher than it was just moments before, too.

130

'Wasn't me, boss. He fell of his own accord, coming in through the gate. Clumsy! Clumsy! I tried to help him, yes I did. Swear to God.'

Finch's eyes narrow at the lie; he lifts one finger and starts tapping the arm of the chair, like it vexes him. Nothing in our brief history should make me care for Goldie's wellbeing, but for some reason I can't fathom I nod, confirming his story. Finch stares at me for a long moment, his fingernail still marking out time. Then without warning he stops, spreads his hands, and the smile returns.

'Well I'm glad to hear it. Now, Gabriel, we were just about to eat. Will you join us for dinner?'

The inquiry sounds genuine, like I'd be free to get up and walk out if I chose. It's too late to go anywhere till morning, of course, but the fact that he makes it seem that way lifts my spirits a fraction, all the same.

'Um, sure.' I remember his comment about manners, and what Goldie said about them not having any food to spare. 'I'm afraid I don't have anything to contribute, though.'

Finch waves the idea away, like he wouldn't hear of it.

'Nonsense, you are our guest.' He tilts his head in Goldie's direction.

'Mr. Goldie, please run and tell Mr. Blatch we shall have one more for dinner.'

'One more for dinner, right boss.'

'And let him know he may serve whenever he's ready.'

GOLDIE'S FOOTSTEPS RETREAT as he scurries off on his errand. Those on the landings take it as their cue to join us. They shuffle down the stairs and across the hall, approaching the table cautiously. The positions they assume seem well rehearsed, though, as if this is a ritual they have performed countless times before. Finch introduces each as they step into the faltering candlelight. The names continue as more men emerge from the shadows; soon I've given up any hope of keeping them straight in my head and all I have is the count. The last two to arrive – thirty-six and thirty-seven – are the small man I saw in the booth as we came in, who Finch says is Mr. Culver, and Goldie's tall raggedy companion who he calls Mr. MacIntyre. None of these men look like they're carrying any extra weight. Their lips are parched, cracked, their faces chiseled gaunt by hunger. They keep their eyes down, focusing on the bowl and spoon each has brought with him. The two large men who entered with Finch are the last to sit, taking places on either side of him at the end of the table. Their size marks them out in contrast. The muscular man Finch introduces as Mr. Knox. The heavy one with the beard he calls Mr. Tully. If Finch had been the warden of this place I'm guessing Knox and Tully must have been two of his guards.

There's the dull groan of a door being opened somewhere behind me, followed by the quick, shuffling footsteps of someone hefting a load. I look over my shoulder, just as a long streak of a man with a narrow bloodhound face enters, struggling under the weight of a large metal pot. The table creaks as he sets it down at Finch's elbow. His mouth puckers into a frown as he sees me.

'I didn't know we was having guests.'

Finch offers me an apologetic smile. *You can't get the help*. He leans forward, as if sharing a secret.

'You will have to forgive Mr. Blatch, Gabriel. He is quite the genius in the kitchen, but he harbors an intense dislike for surprises. He will cluck like an old hen if I propose the slightest change to our dinner plans.' He turns to the cook. 'Now, Mr. Blatch, we must remember our manners.'

Blatch mutters something and then lifts the lid off the pot. Steam rises up, quickly disappearing into the darkness above. It smells of something that might once have been meat, but is now so diluted as to defy the identifying.

Finch leans forward and inhales theatrically.

'Why, it smells simply divine. Mr. Blatch, you may serve.'

Empty bowls make their way up the table. Blatch slops a ladle of piping hot liquid into each and then passes it back down. It's pretty cold in here; whatever it is he's serving won't hold its heat long. But nevertheless everybody waits patiently. When the last bowl has been placed in front of Finch Goldie steps from the shadows, fusses with a napkin for his lap, then scurries off again. The warden raises his spoon.

'*Bon appetit*, gentlemen.'

I'm not sure what that means, but the men seem to take it as a sign they can finally chow down. They bow their heads, each concentrating on his bowl with uncommon intensity. From somewhere behind me there's the chug of a starter; a motor sputters complainingly, then settles to a lump idle. And for a second I think of The Greenbrier, and how the lights had come on in the chandeliers at a similar sound. I look around at the stone walls, the iron landings, the barred cells behind. This place could hardly be more different.

A scratching sound brings me back. It's followed by the popcorn-crackle of an old record and from off in the darkness the thin, reedy strains of music drift out from a rattling speaker. It's a woman singing, in a language I don't understand. To hear music is a strange thing, and for a few seconds I just sit there and listen.

Goldie returns from the last of his errands and takes a seat a little further down the table. He leans forward, lowering his head to the soup, and starts slurping at it with a determination that's impressive to behold. Drops spill from his lips, running down his chin. He runs a grubby sleeve across his mouth, returns it to the table. The warden looks down the table at him and sighs.

'Mr. Goldie.'

Goldie looks up.

'Yes boss?'

'No uncooked joints on the table, if you please.'

Goldie withdraws his arms from the table. His chin drops to his chest and he tucks his offending elbows into his lap.

'Sorry, boss.'

He returns his attention to the broth, his fervor only slightly diminished by the reprimand.

Finch picks up his own spoon, but then he just holds it over the bowl and turns to me, as if waiting for me to go first. Tell the truth the broth doesn't look that appetizing, but I remember what he said about manners, so I try some. If Blatch was aiming for equal parts watery and greasy he's nailed it. There's little chunks of something gray that might once have been meat floating in it, too, but without the can they came out of it's hard to tell what it might be. It does have a certain flavor, though. I look up from the bowl and Finch is still staring at me. I hadn't really noticed it before, but his eyes are the palest of blue, and for the briefest instant it's almost

134

as if they burn a little brighter. He holds my gaze a moment then leans forward to sip his soup. When he's done he dabs at his lips with the napkin.

'Another triumph, Mr. Blatch, I do declare.'

I point my spoon in the general direction of the music.

'You have power?'

'Well, after a fashion.' He smiles down the table at the small man who was sat behind the booth in the holding pen. 'Mr. Culver was able to work his magic on a couple of old diesel generators we found in one of the sheds; he has an aptitude for that sort of thing. Fuel is hard to come by, of course, so we must be frugal. But music is so good for the digestion, don't you think?'

I have a better vocabulary than any of the Juvies, except maybe Mags, but sometimes the warden uses words and I don't know what they mean, except maybe from how he uses them. I think I can guess *frugal* from the context but I make a mental note to look it up, next time I'm in the vicinity of a dictionary.

'Can't say that I know.'

Finch looks at me for a moment, like he's considering this, then goes back to his bowl. I take another mouthful of the broth. Maybe it's just because I'm hungry, but the taste's kinda growing on me.

'So, Gabriel, what is it that brings you our way?'

I keep my eyes down for a moment. I knew sooner or later this question was coming, but my heart quickens a little nevertheless. I dip the spoon in the bowl and swirl the greasy liquid around, trying to sound as unconcerned about my answer as possible.

'Oh, I was just passing through. I noticed Mr. Goldie and Mr. Macintyre's prints and thought I'd follow them, see where they were headed.' I look up from my bowl, adlibbing a little to make it seem natural. 'I wouldn't normally have done that; I mostly make it my business to stay out of the way of others. But I haven't had a square meal in weeks and I was getting a little desperate.'

The warden's spoon is on its way back into his broth, but now it stops, and when he looks up at me his expression has darkened unpleasantly. I wonder if I've taken it too far. There's not much left of the rations we set out from Mount Weather with, but I haven't had to skip a meal yet, and compared to most of the wraiths sitting around the table I must look like I've been living high on the hog. Finch fixes me with those piercing blue eyes and for a moment it's as if I can't quite catch my breath. I want to look away, but somehow I think that would be a bad idea. Off in the shadows the woman's still singing, but otherwise it seems like the room's suddenly gone very quiet. The warden starts tapping his spoon against the rim of the bowl, slow, methodical, but in a way that's completely out of kilter with the music. The sound it makes seems as loud and deliberate as a hammer pounding an anvil.

'You were lucky you ran into us. City's not a place to be, least not after dark.'

Finch stops his tapping. His gaze stays on me a moment longer, then shifts down the table to Mac. At first I'm just relieved for the interruption, but as his words sink in I realize that's where Mags and the others are right now; she won't have got them clear of it before nightfall. I keep my eyes on my broth, trying not to let the concern show in my voice.

'What…what do you mean by that?'

Mac's spoon hovers over his bowl, but he doesn't look up. In the end it's the warden who answers for him.

'Oh, don't mind Mr. MacIntyre, Gabriel. He has the constitution of an old woman.'

Across the table Goldie giggles and then goes back to slurping his soup. I want to dismiss the tall convict's warning, but there's something about it that sticks with me. I remember the feeling I'd had, as we had made our way through the parking lot of the hospital, that we were being watched. I stare at Mac, but now he won't meet my gaze.

'Have you seen something, Mr. MacIntyre?'

For a long while he doesn't respond, then eventually he just shakes his head.

'No.'

Finch leans forward in his seat. The smile has returned.

'You really shouldn't worry, Gabriel. You're perfectly safe with us, all the way out here in the willy-wags.'

*

THE THIN CLINK AND SCRAPE OF CUTLERY continues as
all around me the prisoners concentrate on extracting the
last of the broth from their bowls. Then one by one my
dinner companions get up from their chairs, gather their
utensils and shuffle off into the shadows, returning to
their cells. Further down the table Goldie cuts a glance
in the warden's direction then lifts his to his lips, tilting
his head back for the dregs. I look down at my own
bowl, surprised to see it's almost empty. I guess dinner
was just the soup, then. I scoop out the last of it and set
the spoon down. I could definitely eat more, but there's
been no mention of seconds and seeing as I'm
freeloading anyway I say it was the best I've tasted and I
couldn't fit another mouthful. Finch seems happy with
that. He dabs at his lips with his napkin and smiles.

'It is kind of you to say, Gabriel. Now, I would love
to stay and chat but unfortunately I have an errand to
run.' He smiles, as if a pleasant thought has just occurred
to him. 'But if you'd care to join me I can offer you a
tour of our humble facility.'

I have nothing else planned for the evening so I say
that would be nice. Tully gets to his feet and pulls the
chair back for his boss while Knox fetches his cane.
Hicks' pistol is still sitting on the table in front of me,
next to Weasel's blade. I glance at them uncertainly.
Finch follows my gaze then flutters a hand in their
direction.

'Oh, by all means bring those with you.'

He accepts the cane Knox proffers, leaning his
weight on it to stand. When he's got his balance he limps
off. Tully lifts a candle from the table and lumbers after
him. Knox glares at me as I reach for the gun and knife,

but the warden was clear, so I shove both into my pocket and hurry after him.

We leave the main hall and enter a long, dark corridor. Iron-braced doors punctuate the stone at seemingly random intervals. Most are shut, but some hang ajar. I look inside as we pass. Behind one, rows of industrial-sized washing machines and tumble dryers, sitting gape-mouthed in the darkness. Another opens to what might once have been a pantry, but the shelves that line the walls now are dusty, bare.

Finch's heels and cane click-clack ahead of us, the sounds echoing along the passageway. The air grows thick with the smells of grease and smoke. We arrive at the kitchens, where I guess Blatch must cook up his masterpieces. The warden stops outside and sends Tully in to retrieve something while we wait. The candle he carries casts unreliable shadows, but I can make out things as he passes. Rows of steel countertops, stretching back into darkness. An assortment of pots and pans, their surfaces blackened from years of use, stacked precariously underneath. A collection of knives, saws, cleavers, the candlelight briefly playing over the honed steel. And for an instant in the far corner something long and gray, hanging from an old hook. I peer into the darkness, but Tully has already moved on with the candle and whatever it might be is lost again to shadow.

Finch shifts his weight on the cane.

'So tell me Gabriel, what is it you like to do with your free time?'

He says it like taking in a show, or visiting a museum or learning to play the piano might all be perfectly acceptable responses, so at first I'm not sure what to say. There hasn't been much in the way of free time since we quit Mount Weather, but there was enough of it over the winter for me to remember what having a spare hour feels like. I take a moment to sift through the possibilities. It doesn't take me long to settle on the answer I reckon is least likely to get me into trouble.

'Mostly I like to read.'

Finch looks up and once again I find myself caught in that piercing gaze. He continues to stare at me, as though measuring my age against the truth in that statement. One finger hovers over the head of his cane, as though he means to start that tapping thing again. But then the smile broadens.

'Well said, well said. There is nothing like a good book, is there?' He holds a hand up. 'Why, the library is right on our way. You must let me show it to you.' He raps the cane once on the stone floor, as though it's decided, then inclines his head in the direction of the kitchens, raising his voice a fraction. 'If Mr. Tully ever sees fit to return to us, that is.'

Moments later Tully emerges from the shadows carrying a battered looking metal flask, a length of fraying cord looped around the handle, and we set off down the corridor again. At the end there's a turn and a half-flight of stairs. I wait while Finch hobbles up them and then I follow his click-clacking footfalls down an even narrower passageway that ends in a small wooden door. He stops in front of it and reaches into his suit pocket, pulling out a key chain on which there must be a dozen keys. He selects one and inserts it deftly into the lock; the cylinders turn with a soft *snick* that suggests they have been oiled recently. He returns the keys to his pocket and opens the door, ushering me in with exaggerated courtliness.

I step through. It takes a moment for my eyes to adjust, but when they do I find myself in a square, high-ceilinged room. Two slender windows punctuate one wall, their grimed glass recessed behind thick iron bars. In daylight I'm guessing they would give views out onto the prison yard, but my gaze doesn't linger there;

something else has caught my attention. The walls that remain are lined with shelves that stretch from floor to ceiling. Each is crammed, two and sometimes three deep, with books. Hundreds of them, maybe even thousands, more than I've seen in one place since the Last Day.

From out in the hall I hear the warden telling Tully and Knox to wait, and then the sound of the door being closed, but I just continue to stare. At some point I become aware that Finch is watching me. I turn to face him, my mouth still open.

'How…how did you get so many?'

The warden leans on the cane, his other hand holding a candle he's taken from one of the guards. He smiles at the question, but not like earlier. Now it's as if his whole face shines with it, as though he's inordinately pleased with himself.

'Well, it wasn't all my doing, of course. The prison had a library before I was assigned here, although that was such a shabby collection as to be hardly worth the mention. Autoshop manuals; back copies of *The Reader's Digest*.' He waves the memory away, as though it causes him displeasure. 'I set to work immediately, of course. You wouldn't believe the letters I wrote, Gabriel. Senators, Congressmen, none were spared. But my pleas fell on deaf ears. Society is rarely at its most enlightened when it comes to the treatment of the incarcerated, and more books just wasn't where our representatives felt the public's hard-earned tax dollars needed to be spent. I cultivated a circle of more forward-thinking correspondents, and from time to time there would be a bequest from a private collection. There was the occasional donation from a public library. But this,' he raises the cane, an expansive gesture encompassing the room and everything in it, 'only really started to take shape later, ironically when things started to go wrong

141

on the outside.'

I look at him for an explanation.

'It's the men you see.' He smiles again, as though embarrassed by this revelation. 'They were grateful when I took it upon myself to release them, and they know how much I enjoy something new to read. So when they go outside, searching for supplies, they keep their eyes open.'

My eyes continue to roam the shelves, now and then lighting on a familiar volume. When at last I'm done my gaze shifts to one of the corners. There's a chair there, sitting back in the shadows. I had ignored it in favor of the books at first, but now I see it's no ordinary piece of furniture. Heavy, wooden, almost like a throne. The legs, arms, back are all made of stout timber, worn smooth with time. A large metal cap hangs from a hinged bracket above, a rubber cable wide as a hosepipe feeding into the top. Thick leather cuffs with heavy buckles circle the arms; more straps extend from round the back.

The warden follows my gaze.

'Ah, I see you've found Old Sparky.'

He hobbles up to it, setting the candle down on one of the arms. The guttering flame illuminates a spring-loaded clamp, bolted to one of the legs. The gate's open; inside I can see thick nubs of metal, bound together with rubber. Another cable runs from the base of it, snaking away across the dusty floor.

'It is a rather disagreeable piece of furniture, isn't it? It occurred to me to have it moved, but it turns out it is rather comfortable.' He turns and looks at me and for a second the smile twists, becoming slightly predatory. 'Would you like to try the hot seat?'

I stare at him for a moment. The chair doesn't look like it works, but all the same I can't think of anything I'd like less.

Finch shakes his head.

'No, of course not. Forgive me. How macabre.'

The part of my brain responsible for these things adds *macabre* to the list of words I need to look up. The warden lifts his cane, pointing it around the room.

'You said you liked to read, Gabriel. Tell me, do you have a favorite? You never know; I might just have it.'

I examine the shelves again, considering his question. There are so many to choose from. But then a spine I recognize catches my eye. It's the book about the English rabbits; the one Mags had, that first day we met, in Sacred Heart. Finch follows my gaze.

'Ah, *Watership Down*.' He hobbles over and slips it from its place. 'An intriguing choice.' He holds it up for a moment, turning it over in his hands. It's the very same edition, the one with the rabbit Mom thought was Hazel but I know to be General Woundwort, hunched in silhouette on the cover. Its ears are folded back, its teeth bared.

The warden leans forward.

'How the world looks at the bottom of the food chain. From the ass-end of the totem pole, so to speak. It really is quite a frightening read, isn't it?

It's been a long time since I read it, but I know the story well: Fiver's visions, of fields covered with blood; Bigwig caught in the snare, the wire slicing into his neck as he had struggled against it; the Owsla, the warren's secret police, and how they had ripped Blackavar's ears to shreds as punishment for trying to escape.

I nod.

'I hadn't thought about it that way, but I guess you're right.'

He shakes his head.

'I'm surprised anyone ever considered it a suitable book for children.'

He runs his fingers over the cover and then takes a measured step closer, holding it out to me.

'Why don't you hold on to it tonight? The hours can be long after dark. It will help you pass the time till morning.'

*

WE LEAVE THE LIBRARY.

The warden hands Knox the candle and then swings the door closed behind him, making sure to lock it. He returns the keys to the pocket of his suit and sets off down the passageway, back the way we came, heels and cane *click-clacking* off the dark stone. Tully picks the flask from the floor, gathers up its tether and sets off after him. We rejoin the hallway that led up from the kitchens. As we get to the end a door separates itself from the gloom. Knox hurries ahead to hold it open and I follow Finch through into another long corridor. This part of the prison is no more uplifting than the rest, but it does seem like it might have been more recently constructed: the walls and floor are concrete, not stone, and smooth; fluorescent tubes nestle in dusty ice cube tray fixtures set back in the low ceiling. At the end a guard booth waits, its thick glass reinforced with criss-crossed safety wire. Beyond, a large, barred gate. A sign above reads *High Security*; another *Maximum Control Unit*. A third warns against unauthorized entry.

We step through into yet another corridor. Cells with narrowly-spaced bars line one side, the doors hanging inward on their hinges. The metal is smooth; the locks sleek; I see no hole that might fit a key. Behind there's a small, windowless space, hardly big enough to be called a room. A narrow metal cot takes up most of the floor, a stainless steel toilet the only other furniture. It's been a while since I had Claus inside my head, but now a memory of him stirs, shudders. This would not have been a good place to spend time.

Finch turns to me, as if he's read my mind.

'Yes, it is rather unpleasant, isn't it? What you have

145

to realize Gabriel is that Starkly was where society sent its most undesirable undesirables, its most obdurate felons.' I add *obdurate* to my dictionary list. 'Most were housed upstairs, in the main cellblock, where we ate dinner earlier. But for some, the worst of the worst, the most irredeemable class of criminal, there was this place.'

I stare through the bars. I wonder if any of the men I've just had dinner with were confined here. I guess some must have been. Goldie must have been a shoe-in for the *Most Obdurate Asshole* award; Blatch had a mean look about him, too.

'And you just released them? Weren't you worried what they might do?'

Finch's mouth stretches out in a curious way, that might perhaps have been meant for a smile.

'Well, it was a risk, I'll grant you, but a calculated one. I didn't know each of the inmates personally of course, at least not at the time. But in my position I did have the advantage of access to their prison files, which in most cases were quite detailed. So I felt like I understood them, their strengths and weaknesses, their distastes and peccadilloes, how they had each come to be in a place like this.'

Peccadilloes? If I get out of here and can lay my hands on a Scrabble board I reckon I might be unbeatable.

The warden hobbles a little closer, leans over his cane.

'Some were deeply unpleasant men, there is no denying it. Most, however, were merely unsuited for the world, at least as it was then. And there was a truth to be faced. The very nature of their incarceration had changed. The society to whom they had once owed a debt no longer even existed. There no longer anywhere for them to escape to, either; no better place

146

they were forbidden to be.'

He holds one hand up.

'Besides, what else was I to do? Leave them in their cells and simply allow them to starve?' He shakes his head, as if answering his own question. 'How inconceivably barbaric.'

I nod. I remember how I had worried about leaving Weasel tied up in the KFC when Johnny and I were fleeing for Eden. As nasty a piece of work as he had been, I hadn't wished that end on him either.

Finch looks at me then, and for a second it's like he's just peered into my thoughts and read what's there.

'Good. So you understand.'

He turns and continues down the corridor, the candle throwing long flickering shadows ahead. I take one last look into the cell and follow him.

'Of course that's not to say we haven't had our difficult times. There have been misunderstandings. But I feel we've put those behind us now.'

We approach the end of the row. The last cell door's shut, secured by a length of chain and a heavy padlock. And now I understand the reason for the flask Tully's carrying. It makes sense there might have been one or two of Starkly's inmates who were beyond redemption; felons so dangerous not even a man like the warden could get comfortable releasing them. As we get closer I can see a strip of tape running down the center of the floor in front of the bars. Spidey doesn't care much for that, but I tell him to hush; whoever's still locked up back there, they seem secure. Ahead of me Finch stops. A chair has been placed in front of the cell, on the safe side of the taped line, but he chooses not to sit. Instead he turns to Tully, pointing to a spot on the ground with his cane.

Tully passes the candle back to Knox and slowly starts to unscrew the lid of the flask. He places it on the ground, taking a surprising amount of care for a man of his size, then pushes it forward with the toe of his boot.

For a moment nothing happens, then I think I see something shift in the shadows, but Knox is holding the candle too far back for me to see all the way into the cell. I lean forward for a better look, just as long, spider-thin fingers shoot through the bars towards me.

I STAGGER BACKWARDS, but something large, unyielding, blocks my retreat. I hear a grunted protest as I step on Knox's foot, and then a rough hand plants itself between my shoulder blades and shoves me forward. My boots scrabble for purchase as I try and get out of the way, but the fingers that shot through the bars have already closed greedily around the flask. The battered metal container clangs loudly as it's yanked back and then it's gone, swallowed whole by the shadows, the only evidence there was anything there a small amount of whatever was inside that's slopped over the rim, darkening the concrete. I take a breath, waiting for my heart to steady. It all happened so fast that if I'd have blinked there's a good chance I'd have missed it. Except I didn't; in that split second I saw what was there, lurking in the darkness behind. I look over at Finch.

'You…you captured one?'

'Well, it would be more accurate to say he fell into our lives.' He turns around, gesturing with one hand. 'Bring the candle over, Mr. Knox, so Gabriel can see.'

Knox hesitates. He eyes the bars warily, as though for all his size he's reluctant to come any closer. But after a moment's pause he does as he's bid and steps forward with the flame. The swaying light creeps into the cell. Spidey's still sounding a klaxon inside my head, but this time I'm ready for it. My breath catches in my chest as the candle reveals the cell's sole inhabitant, all the same.

The men I met at dinner were all painfully thin, but this final specimen appears inhumanly so. Rags that were once clothing hang from its emaciated frame. Here and there gray skin pokes through, stretched tight over bones like sticks; the contours of its skull showing

149

clearly through what little remains of its hair. Its eyes narrow to slits at the candle; it clutches the flask to its chest and tries to shuffle away. But there's only so far it can go, so instead it turns and bares its teeth. The pupils that glare back through the bars are unmistakably dilated; they glow silver as they catch the light.

'Yes, our friend was an infected.' Finch turns to me. 'In one sense we were fortunate, during those difficult times, in being so far out of the way here; we were generally untroubled by visitors of his kind. But somehow this one found us. Or rather we found him, just lying out there in the yard.' He looks over at me and says *No, really*, as if I had somehow challenged his account of it. 'He had managed to scale the walls and I suspect was up to no good in one of the guard towers when something must have caused him to fall.'

The creature in the cage raises the flask to its lips, which for some reason I can't fathom sets off a fresh chorus of alarms from spidey. It tilts its head back slowly, continuing to regard us with animal mistrust. Drops of something dark spill from its lips and run down its chin.

'It was Kane, scorching the skies. That's what did it.'

I say it mostly to myself, but after a moment I realize Finch is leaning forward on his cane, looking at me expectantly.

'The missiles, the ones the President launched. The explosions caused some sort of pulse that was intended to defeat its kind.'

The warden raises a finger to his chin, strokes it thoughtfully.

'Why, yes, the timing would certainly fit. I didn't witness that event myself of course; I was otherwise occupied at the time. But I've heard stories, from the men. And it was the very next morning I found him, just lying out there, in the yard, so still that at first I was sure he was dead.'

I think of the little girl, in the closet in Shreve, and how peaceful she had looked, too. At least until Marv had held the knife with his blood on it under her nose.

The fury drains the last of whatever's in the flask and lets it fall to the ground. It clanks hollowly as it hits the concrete, then comes to rest. It's hard to think straight, what with the sirens going off in my head, but there's something very wrong about this; something that doesn't sit with what I know of the virus.

Tully steps forward and picks up the end of the cord. I watch as he reels the battered container in, pulling it back through the bars. He waits till it's safely over the line then bends to retrieve it. Spidey kicks it up a notch as he replaces the lid, and now the sound inside my head's like a fire truck, trying to force its way through a clogged intersection. A dark thought pushes itself forward. The flask's ribbed metal sides are dented, scarred, but that's the extent of the damage there. I look over at the bars. They're smooth, untarnished.

The room tilts on some axis I did not know it possessed. I feel the blood drain from my face. I hear a voice that might be mine, asking a question I'm not yet sure I'm ready to have answered.

'It's…it's not infectious?'

Finch turns to look at me.

'Why, how very observant of you, Gabriel. Yes, our friend here can no longer transmit the virus.'

'You…you're certain?'

'Quite. We had to be, before we could risk letting him into a place like this, which is why the poor fellow spent so long in the hotbox. Besides, he's been down here for almost a decade.' He taps the bars with the tip of his cane. 'If he was still capable of passing on the virus I'm sure we would know about it by now.'

I'm aware he's still talking, but the warden's voice

seems to be coming to me from somewhere distant. My mind's running around in herky-jerky little circles, trying to fit this new piece of information into what I thought I knew of the virus.

The metal was how you could tell. Every time you go outside it was the same: you strip as much of it from you as you can, the rest you wrap in plastic. But there was always a single piece – a cross, dog tags – left exposed, worn next to the skin, so you would know if you'd been infected. That was how it always was, from my very first scavenging trip with Marv to the last time I saw him, on his knees in the snow, slinging the rifle off his shoulder.

I look into the cell. The fury glares back at me through the bars.

But this creature, it gives the lie to all that. And that can mean only one thing: the crucifix Mags wears, the one she took from Marv's grave, it doesn't prove a thing.

Beside me Finch is still speaking. I force myself to pay attention; there may be something I can learn, something that might help make sense of it. I replay his words in my head.

'What's a hotbox?'

He stops and looks at me, and I think his eyes narrow a fraction, like whatever he was just saying he might not care for my interruption. But after a brief pause he answers.

'A throwback to an even less enlightened time in the history of our nation's penal system, Gabriel. It's a wooden box, little bigger than an outhouse, dug into the earth. Most institutions of Starkly's vintage would have had one. Their position was chosen quite carefully; somewhere in the middle of the yard, a spot that would never catch the shade. A man shackled out there for a day in the Carolina sun would literally bake to death. The sun had abandoned us by then of course, so there was little danger of that fate befalling our friend here. I

152

regretted it nonetheless; the hotbox is an unpleasant spot to spend any amount of time.'

'When…when did he come around? Was it recent?'

Finch looks at me quizzically, and this time there's a longer pause before his answer.

'A week before you arrived.'

'Tell me about it.'

I remind myself I need to be careful; he's watching me closely now. I remember his comment about manners from earlier and add a *Please*.

'Why as chance would have it I was right here when it happened.'

He says it nonchalantly, like it was the funniest of coincidences, but I find myself glancing behind him to the chair pushed up against the wall, the seat shiny from use. I wonder how many hours the warden has spent down here over the years, just staring into that cell. He stares at the fury for a moment before continuing.

'Not that there's much to tell. One minute he was lying on the cot, the very same as he had been the past ten years. The next he's crouched on the floor, wide awake, like someone had just flicked a switch inside him.'

He tilts his head, leans forward on the cane.

'I must say, you seem remarkably well informed on this subject, Gabriel.'

I start to say something about it being a guess, but if that's the story I'm selling I'm not sure the warden's buying it. He starts doing that thing with his fingernail on the head of the cane again. It was Gilbey who warned me that we may not have long, but I don't plan to get into that with Finch. I turn my attention back to the cell, keeping my gaze on the thing crouched against the far wall while I rack my brains, searching for some answer that'll get me back on safer ground. The light catches its silvered eyes and it shifts its jaw, like it's grinding its

153

teeth. And for a second I think of Marv, as he was right at the end. I turn back to the warden.

'I had a friend, once. He reckoned his kind weren't altogether done for; that one day they'd rise up again. If it was the same thing put them all under, it'd make sense they'd come back at about the same time too. This is the first sign of it I've seen, and I've been watching. Makes me think it had to be have been recent.'

Finch continues to stare at me, as if weighing the truth in that statement, and what else it might be I'm not telling him. There's something in that piercing gaze that makes me want to keep talking. It's like I can't help it.

'What Mac…Mr. MacIntyre said earlier, at dinner, about there being something in the city…'

Finch's hand shoots up before I have a chance to finish.

'Mr. Knox, Mr. Tully, would you be so good as to give us a moment?'

Knox and Tully exchange a look, then they turn around and lumber back in the direction of the guard booth.

The warden leans forward on his cane.

'You must forgive me, Gabriel; interrupting you like that was rude. But it is a little early to jump to such conclusions. If the men were to get wind of this – as yet unproven – theory of yours I suspect it would be difficult to convince any of them to return to Durham.' He spreads his hands. 'And we are rather reliant on the city for the few meager supplies it provides.'

'I understand, Mr. Finch.' I glance down the corridor. Knox and Tully are out of earshot, but I drop my voice anyway. 'If the furies really are waking up, though, we're in for a whole heap of trouble.'

He studies me a moment longer, then at last he switches his gaze back to the cell.

'Yes, they are rather formidable creatures, aren't

they?'

'That'd be one way of putting it.'

The warden gives his head a little shake and smiles.

'Oh you must look past that ferocity, Gabriel; those inhuman sanguinary appetites.' He hobbles forward, shuffling across the line that's taped to the ground, and points the cane through the bars. The creature crouched by the back wall glances up at this new intrusion and raises its lip in a snarl. But if Finch is afraid of it he gives no sign. When he turns to look at me it's as if his eyes have brightened again.

'Regard our friend here. Hardly much of a physical specimen, wouldn't you say? And yet he was able to scale Starkly's walls without difficulty, and even to survive a fall from one of its towers.'

He holds the cane up a moment longer, then lowers it.

'Physically we are such a sad case in comparison. Look at us. Frail, fragile things, with our small, blunt, teeth, our delicate claws. In a fair fight we have never been a match for any animal approaching our size. It was only our intellect that placed us at the top of the food chain. And see how precarious that position has proven.'

He leans forward, his face only inches from the hardened steel. The fury curls its lip one more time, then turns its head to the wall. The warden smiles indulgently at it, as though it were a favorite pet.

'Remarkable.'

He shakes his head, then shuffles back over the line. He looks up at me and the smile broadens, revealing that perfect picket fence row of teeth. Later I tell myself it's just the shadows the candle was throwing. But for a second it seems like there might have been a few too many of them.

WE MAKE OUR WAY BACK to the main cellblock, where earlier we sat for dinner. I follow the warden as he hobbles up the metal stair to the second floor, then makes his way slowly along the landing. Here and there back in the shadows a candle still flickers, but most of the cells are dark. He finally stops outside a barred door that hangs open. I look inside. There's not much in the way of comforts, just a metal bunk with a threadbare mattress, a steel bowl for a toilet. I guess I should be thankful for small mercies. At least he's not putting me down in the basement with the fury.

He points with the cane. I hesitate for a moment, then step inside. The door creaks on its hinges, then clangs loudly as Knox pulls it closed. Finch gestures to the guard to hand me the candle then he reaches into the pocket of his jacket for the bunch of keys he carries. I tell him there's really no need, but he insists; he says he'll sleep better knowing I'm safe. I can't see how I have much of a choice in the matter so I say that'll be fine. He selects a key, inserts it into the lock and turns it. The bolt closes with a heavy clunk.

He returns the keys to his pocket, wishes me a pleasant evening, then points his cane along the landing. I stand at the bars for a while, listening to the slow shuffle and clack of his retreating footsteps. When at last they've faded to silence I set the candle on the ground by the leg of the bunk and sit.

The copy of *Watership Down* shifts in the pocket of my parka and I take it out, run my fingers over the familiar cover. I glance through the bars to check there's no one watching, then I hold it under my nose and riffle the pages, like I used to do when I'd find something new. I close my eyes and inhale the book smell, and for a second I'm not sitting on a metal cot in the main cellblock of Starkly Correctional Institution. I'm in the day room of the Sacred Heart Home for Children. A single shaft of dusty sunlight filters through a high window above, and the air smells of furniture polish and old newspapers. There's a girl sitting opposite me. Her head's down, buried in a book, the same one I'm holding. Her dark brown bangs obscure her face, but I know in a moment she'll look up, and I'll see her for the first time. I try to hold that image but I can't, and just as quickly as it came it vanishes again. I open my eyes and Starkly returns.

I lay back on the thin mattress. The cot's not long enough and I have to raise my knees to get my feet on it. I stare up at the bunk above, watching as the candle makes the shadows cast by the rusting springs shift and merge. There are things I need to consider now, but I'm not ready for that, not yet, so instead I open the cover. Another world waits for me in there, one where everything is still as it was when I first met her, and right now that's what I need. I turn to the first page, forcing myself to concentrate on the words.

Without anything to mark it the time draws out. Starkly grows quiet, save for the sound of the wind outside, moaning against the walls. A draft finds its way into my cell, disturbs the flame. For a moment it flickers, threatens to go out, then steadies again. I look down, surprised to see that the candle's almost done; all that remains is a charred wick in a shallow puddle of wax. But when I look back to the page I realize I've got no further than the paragraph I began on.

I set the book down. It's no use. The thing I saw, down in the basement, it will not be ignored. The truth of what it means drags at my brain, like a fishhook.

I've been checking Mags' crucifix every night since

we left Mount Weather. All the other stuff - how quick she is now; how she can see in the dark; how her skin is always cold - I'd convinced myself none of it mattered. The metal was how I'd know; as long as it stayed clear she wasn't going to end up like Marv.

The low, faithless voice has been quiet for some time, but now it whispers.

That's not true, though, is it?

It reminds me of something Gilbey told us; something I knew all along, but chose not to dwell on. The virus was a truly remarkable piece of engineering, she said, incredibly tenacious; so much more resilient than Kane ever gave it credit for. He fired all the missiles he had, but all that did was render those carrying it unconscious. For years it's been waiting, slowly building itself back up inside them, just like Marv thought. And now it's ready to return, and those that had it once are no different from how they had been before.

I lay my head down on the cot, letting that truth wash over me.

Kane scorched the sky; tore a hole in it; made the night burn bright with the force of a thousand explosions. And still he couldn't defeat it. What did Mags get? A few minutes in a glorified magnet; a machine designed to look inside you. Not even the time it had been set for.

How could I have ever hoped that would be enough?

*

HE PICKS HIS WAY through the darkened mall. On either side vacant stores, their trash-strewn aisles stretching back into gloom. He tries a few, searching the dusty shelves for anything that might have been missed. But there's nothing. Each has been ransacked, stripped of anything that might provide warmth, sustenance. In one he finds a box of plastic lighters, sitting by the cash register. He lifts one out, tries it. For a while it just sparks and he's about to toss it, but then finally it catches, holds. He stares at the blue-tinged flame until the metal grows hot, then he lets it die.

He steps back outside to resume walking the concourse. This is what he does now, while the others are sleeping. The girl does not like him wandering off by himself, so he has to wait until she has fallen asleep, too. She doesn't sleep for long now, hardly more than he does, so he can't go very far. But that's okay. He uses the time he has to explore. He likes it.

He makes his way through the food court. Packets and wrappers litter the floor, but there's nothing among them worth having. Occasionally he holds the lighter up, thumbs the wheel. He does not need it, any more than the flashlight in his pocket. But he likes the soft glow of the flame, the way the plastic feels warm in his hand after.

He finds an escalator, climbs it to the level above. He follows the walkway, examining each storefront he passes. A soft drinks machine lies toppled over, its front pried open. He checks the insides in case a can has been forgotten, like he's seen the tall boy do. The chute is narrow, but his arm is small and he can reach almost all the way up inside. There's nothing there, though, so he continues on.

He wonders where the tall boy is right now. He was supposed to have caught up with them already, but he hasn't. When they returned to the print store his pack was still there, right where he had left it. The girl stared at it a while then knelt to rummage in one of the side pockets. She took out a folded piece of paper, opened it to check something, then slipped it inside her parka. She stepped over to the counter, returning with a sheaf of paper. She pulled the stub of a pencil from her pocket and bent to scribble a note. When she was done she tucked it under one of the straps then headed back out to where the others were waiting. She led them on, picking her way between the cars and trucks that clogged the streets. Every few paces she would turn to check behind, but for the rest of that evening the road had stayed clear.

They had arrived at this place just as night was falling. The boy with the curly hair had brought them inside while she waited out on the road. When at last it had turned dark and there was no chance the tall boy might still be coming she had come in. The others already had a fire going, a way back from the entrance, where the flames would not be seen, but the girl showed no interest in joining them. She stayed by the doors, keeping watch over the parking lot. He could hear the others, whispering.

What's she doing out there?

Can she see in the dark, too?

How can she stand to be so far from the fire?

But if she heard she paid little attention. Some time later the boy with the curly hair had come out to join them. He had hugged his parka tight to him and his breath had smoked in the cold. He said she should come inside, that the tall boy would be alright. The girl nodded, but when he returned to the fire she made no move to follow.

He completes his circuit, returns to the escalator. Trash is strewn everywhere here; he has to pick his way among it as he makes his way up the ribbed steel stairs. At the top a single large room, stretching back into darkness. On one side a long counter; a sign above that would once have lit up. Large posters hang from the walls or lie curled on the floor beneath.

He heads for the counter, treading decade-old popcorn into the mulchy carpet as he goes. The glass is dusty; he has to wipe it with the sleeve of his jacket to see inside. He presses his face to it, hoping to spot a candy bar that's been missed. But the cabinet's empty. This place has been plundered, like everywhere else.

He holds the lighter up, cranks the wheel; his reflection appears in the glass. He turns his head to one side, studying it. He thinks it is a little better. The shadows around his eyes are finally fading, but enough of them remain to lend his face a hollow, sunken-in look. He is used to it now, but somehow it still feels unfamiliar, like this is not how he is supposed to look.

'Hello there.'

His fingers scrabble for the goggles hanging around his neck. In his haste to pull them up he drops the lighter and it blinks out, returning the room to grainy shades of gray.

He turns around slowly, still fiddling with the strap. A boy stands there, staring down at him, his hands stuffed into the pockets of a tattered leather jacket. The hood on the sweatshirt he wears underneath is pulled up, but there's enough of his face showing to suggest it's amusement that shapes his pale features. He turns his head, as though addressing someone behind him.

'Hey, check out the shades on this little dude.'

A girl appears at his side. Her hair is cut in a ragged bob; without the lighter it's hard to tell what color it might be. She wears a denim jacket with buttons pinned to the front. Underneath a dark t-shirt with a snaggle-tooth skull. Where the neckline dips he can see her collarbones. Her skirt is short and her legs are bare; they end in a pair of dirty high-tops. She tilts her head, her jaw working continuously. She flashes him a smile, says *Hey, cutie*, and goes back to chewing her gum.

One by one others step out of the shadows, until there are maybe twenty of them, arranged in a loose semicircle around him. Some are not much bigger than he is. None seem older than the girl, or the tall boy.

His brow furrows. He had not heard them, any of them. He can always hear the others, even when they are trying to be quiet.

The boy with the hood takes a step closer, squats down in front of him. His jeans are faded, his boots scuffed. He takes his hands from the pocket of the leather jacket and waves them in front of him, quick, almost too fast to see. A candy bar appears where before there was nothing. He holds it out.

'Y'all looking for this?'

He stares at the candy bar for a moment, then reaches down for the lighter instead. He holds it up, thumbs the wheel. The boy's pupils glow in the flame. He leans in, his eyes locked on the lighter, then pulls back the hood on his sweatshirt, revealing a shock of white hair.

'That's right, little dude. Just like you.' The boy holds his arms out, gesturing to the others gathered around him. 'We all are.'

He keeps his thumb on the lighter, holds it up. The girl cocks her head, pulls a face, goes back to chewing her gum. In the flame he can see her hair is bright pink, the same shade as the lipstick she's wearing.

The lighter grows too hot to hold and he snaps it off, returns it to his pocket where it glows like a coal against his leg. The boy's eyes turn dark again. His hand still holds the candy bar.

'It's alright.'

He hesitates a moment then takes it, peels the wrapper. The chocolate inside is gray with age. It tastes gritty, stale, but not altogether bad. He finishes it quickly. The boy smiles, like he's pleased.

'Want a drink?' He turns to his companions, not waiting for an answer. 'Hey, somebody gimme a soda.'

From somewhere back in the shadows there's the rasp of a zipper being pulled and a second later a can gets passed forward. There's the faintest of hisses as the boy pops the tab, hands it to him.

He takes a sip. What little gas is left stings his nose, makes his eyes water. It's so sweet it makes the roof of his mouth tingle. He takes a large gulp, then another, and another, until it's gone. He stands there for a moment, then belches loudly.

The boy laughs.

'Little dude likes it. Y'all got a name, little dude?'

He's about to tell them what he told the girl with the long blond hair, back in the mountain place: he doesn't know. But then he remembers how that went.

'They call me Johnny.'

The girl with the pink hair tilts her head again. She frowns, as though something about that answer doesn't sit right with her.

'And is that your name?'

He shrugs. The boy and the girl exchange a look he can't figure, then they both turn back to him.

'Well, Johnny, I'm Vince. And this is Cassie.'

The girl curtsies, flashes him another smile.

'Please-ta-meetcha.'

He holds up the can and the candy bar wrapper.

'Where did you find these?'

'Oh, around. You just need to know where to look.' He winks. 'Hey, Johnny, come with me.'

The boy with the leather jacket leads him back

towards the escalator. When they reach the guardrail he leans over, points down. Far below, towards the entrance, the cherry wink of a campfire; a collection of gray shapes, huddled around it.

'Those friends of yours?'

He hesitates. He's not sure what he should say. The girl is, for certain. And the tall boy, although he's not down there right now. He's less certain about the others.

'Some of them are.'

'Got it. Probably haven't known them long, am I right?'

He nods. That bit is true.

'And where are y'all headed?'

He pauses again. When he was in the cage the doctor said it was important to answer questions truthfully. He's not sure what he should say now, however. The place where they're going, the place that'll be their new home, he thinks it's supposed to be a secret. He doesn't know exactly where it is, anyway, except that it's close, but he's not even sure he's allowed to say that much. He considers it a few seconds more and then settles on an answer he thinks should be okay.

'South.'

'Y'all don't plan to stay here, then?'

He shakes his head.

The girl with the pink hair folds her arms across her chest.

'Told ya, Vince, no need to get your panties all up in a bunch. Just passin' through.'

The boy holds his hand up, like he wants her to be quiet.

'And what about the other one, the tall one, the one who took off after those men. Will they wait for him?'

He shakes his head again.

'He's going to follow us.'

'Wouldn't count on it, kid.'

164

The boy's features twist in irritation.

'Shut up, Cass.'

The girl rolls her eyes, goes back to chewing her gum. The boy turns to face him again. The smile returns.

'Sure about that, Johnny? The bit about heading south, I mean. Y'all definitely don't plan to stay here?'

He shakes his head and the boy's smile widens.

'Do you live here?'

The boy with the leather jacket goes back to staring at the campfire.

'Oh, here and there. Wherever we want.' He pauses a while and his face grows serious. 'You could stay with us, if you like.' He nods at the empty soda can. 'There's more of those. Loads more. We could show you how to find them.'

He shakes his head. The girl will be done sleeping soon. If she wakes and finds him gone she'll worry.

'I have to get back.'

The boy spreads his hands, like he understands.

'Alright. Well, Johnny, it was sure nice to meet y'all.'

He's not sure how he feels about having met them, so he just says thanks for the soda and the candy bar and hurries out onto the escalator.

He's barely made it back to the level where the others are sleeping when he hears a sound from somewhere off in the shadows. He turns towards it and the girl with the pink hair is there, waiting inside the entrance of a *Tastee Freez*. He looks back at the escalator. He came straight down; he's not sure how she made it here ahead of him. He opens his mouth to ask, but she presses a finger to her lips, beckons him over. He glances towards the fire then hurries over to join her. The gum she was chewing earlier has gone. She looks around nervously.

'What you said up there, about moving on, did you

mean it?'

He nods.

She looks relieved.

'That's good. Vince, he doesn't care much for warmbloods.' She glances out towards the entrance. 'Although all things considered Vince might not be the worst of your problems.'

He's not sure what she means by anything she's just said.

'What are warmbloods?'

The girl nods in the direction of the campfire.

'Your friends.'

'Why doesn't he like them?'

She tilts her head, like she's not sure what to make of his question.

'You kiddin' me, right? You don't remember what it was like?'

He shakes his head. He doesn't remember anything from before.

'Their kind, they hated us.' She keeps her voice low, but it grows hard. 'They wanted us dead, every last one, even those that had stopped being sick. They sent their soldiers, to hunt us down.'

He does know about soldiers. He remembers the mean one, with the zap stick; how he had looked at him, when he had come down with his food, like he was a dangerous animal, in a poorly built cage.

'It was Vince who saved us. Found us places to hide. Then the first winter came and that was it for their kind. Not enough of them left to be a threat to us anymore; for a long time now it's just been the men from the prison. They come into town every once in a while, looking for food. Makes Vince mad as hell. Me and a few of the others, we try and discourage them. The warmbloods, they're kinda dumb; they have to mark the places they've been, otherwise they forget. Makes it real easy to

166

figure where they'll go next.' She shakes her head. 'We strip whatever might be left before they get there; don't leave them hardly anything. But still they keep coming back.'

She inclines her head towards the campfire.

'So where'd you meet these ones?'

'They were living inside a mountain.'

She raises an eyebrow at that, but if she has more questions she doesn't ask them.

'Known them long?'

He shakes his head.

'But they're treating you okay?'

He hesitates a second then nods.

'Even the ones with the guns?'

He nods again.

'That's good.' She goes quiet for a moment, like she's thinking about something. 'Hey, Johnny, do you plan to say anything? About meeting us, I mean. Only I don't think it'd be a good idea if one of them was to take it into their heads to try and find us. You know, like the tall one did, going after those prisoners.'

He thinks about that a moment, then shakes his head. When the tall boy comes back he doesn't want him going off again.

'Alright.'

He looks back towards the entrance. The girl will be up soon. He's already been gone too long.

'I'd best get back.'

'Sure thing.'

She reaches in her pocket, holds out a candy bar. He hesitates a moment then takes it from her. As he turns to make his way back towards the entrance, she reaches for his shoulder.

'Hey Johnny, they're not your kind anymore. You know that, right?'

*

I DON'T SLEEP MUCH the rest of that night. I pick up the book again, but I make no more progress with it. The candle burns down, spends a little while working out whether it means to keep going, then simply winks out. After that it's just a matter of counting out the hours until at last somewhere far behind the clouds the sun rises and another gray dawn breaks over Starkly's walls.

Sounds drift into my cell - the creak of mattress springs, the scuff of boots on stone, the clang of metal - as around me the prison slowly wakes. I sit on the edge of the cot, waiting, but it's a long time before anyone comes to release me. At last I hear Finch's shoes and cane on the landing outside. I'm standing by the bars when he appears.

'Good morning, Gabriel. And how was your night?'

Truth is I've had better, but I remember how he feels about manners so I tell him I slept just fine. He smiles, like he's pleased to hear it. He reaches into the pocket of his jacket for the keys and takes them out, selecting one for the lock. He's about to insert it, but then he hesitates.

'I must say, it has been pleasant having you here with us. I feel like we have got along terribly well. It is nice to have someone who shares the same interests. Much as I have come to care for them, my charges are not the sort for whom a literary discussion is the preferred mode of entertainment.' He pauses, and for a second his pale eyes grow a little brighter. He presses his lips together, in what might be a smile. 'Tell me, would you give some thought to staying with us a little longer?'

The key hovers by the lock. I glance down at it, wondering how much of a bearing my answer might have on whether I'll be leaving this cell today.

'It's a kind offer, Mr. Finch, it really is. But I reckon I should be heading on.' I feel the need to say something more, to offer him a reason why. 'I heard there were survivors, down south. Won't be long now till winter's on us again and I have a ways to go yet if I'm to find them before it gets here.'

The smile flickers. One finger hovers over the head of the cane, taps it twice, then comes to rest.

'I want to thank you for everything, though. For the meal, and for lending me this.'

I hold up the copy of Watership Down.

'Of course, of course.'

He inserts the key in the lock, turns it, then stands back to let me out. I step past him onto the landing. Knox and Tully are waiting a little further along, by the stair.

I hand him his book.

'How far did you get?'

'Not very.' I glance back into the cell at the puddle of wax that used to be a candle.

He looks down at the paperback. His fingers fiddle restlessly along the edges, as though he is deciding something. In the end he pushes it back towards me.

'Why, you must have it, to take with you. To remember us by.'

I start to tell him I couldn't, but my hands betray me; they're already reaching for it of their own accord. Any book is a treasure, but this one means so much more.

'I insist. And who knows, maybe someday you will be in a position to do me a similar favor.'

He says it like he expects our paths to cross again, but the truth is I have no plans to return to Starkly. I figure there's little mileage to be had in pointing that out, however.

'Well, if you're certain.'

He nods, once. But when I go to take the book from

him his fingers suddenly tighten around it. I look up and something has changed, a hardening of whatever is behind his eyes.

'Maybe I shouldn't take this from you, Mr. Finch. Books are hard to come by, and it's obviously one of your favorites.'

And just like that it's as though whatever spell he was under has been broken. He pushes the book into my hands.

'Nonsense. I won't hear of it, Gabriel. Never let it be said that Garland Finch was an Indian giver.'

We make our way down the stair. The mittens Goldie took from me are waiting on the table where the night before we sat for dinner. There's no mention of breakfast, and I don't enquire after it. I wasn't certain when I checked in last night I'd ever be checking out again, so all things considered I reckon I'm up on the deal.

I exchange goodbyes with the warden in the hall. He says his leg's no good in the snow, but Mr. Goldie will show me to the gate. Goldie bobs his head and smiles broadly, as if nothing could conceivably bring him greater pleasure.

I follow him outside. I can't say daylight's improved Starkly any, but then my expectations weren't high to begin with. Goldie jabbers at me all the way to the holding pen. Mostly it's how sorry he is about our misunderstanding; how he hopes I don't hold it against him. I tell him not to give it another thought, but he keeps up his jawboning regardless. His apologies don't put me much at ease. I haven't known him long, but I'm pretty sure remorse isn't among this particular inmate's limited catalog of feelings.

He holds the gate open and I step through. Culver's sitting behind the pockmarked screen, just like he was when I came in last night. Goldie bangs on the glass with the side of his fist and the tray slides out. He hands me the gun belt and then busies himself gathering up the bullets that were emptied from Hicks' pistol while I loop the leather around my waist and cinch the buckle. When I'm done he hands me the cartridges with a smile. I slip them into my pocket while he runs on ahead to work the bolts on the door set into the main gate.

I take one last look back into the yard. Finch is still standing by the entrance to the cellblock, leaning on his cane. He holds one hand up to wave me goodbye. I hesitate for a moment then return the gesture. Behind me the last of the bolts slide back and I hear the door swing inward.

My snowshoes are waiting, right where I left them. The snow's been wiped clean of the tracks we made coming down, but that's okay; I'll be able to find my way just fine without them. I tighten the bindings and set off. I think I hear Goldie's voice calling after me, but whatever he says is lost to the wind. I don't turn around; if he has parting words for me I don't need to hear them.

I don't stop until I've crested the ridge. I pull off my mittens and dig in my pocket for one of the bullets Goldie handed me as I was leaving. I angle the tail to the light, searching for what I thought I saw there earlier. I hold it under my nose, to be certain. I check each of the others, to make sure there's no mistake.

There isn't. They're all the same. Dollars to donuts the ones nestling in the gun belt's cartridge loops won't be any different.

I weigh the bullets in my hand one last time, then throw them as far off into the snow as I can.

IT'S ALREADY EDGING into the afternoon by the time I find my way back to the interstate. I glance behind me then hurry up onto the overpass. The pistol shifts on my hip underneath the parka as I make my way across. There's not many things I can say I'm grateful to Hicks for, but he did show me how to check a weapon, and that included the ammunition that went with it. The primers on the cartridges that were returned to me had been soaked in something, from the smell my guess'd be oil, to make sure they wouldn't fire.

It's possible Goldie did that on his own initiative, of course, but somehow I doubt it. I've seen nothing to change the impression I had on our first meeting: there's little more to him than a fast mouth run by a slow brain. Which means it was the warden told him to do it, and that's a lot more worrisome. I could offer you three guesses as to why he'd go to that trouble when it'd be just as easy to have Culver hold back the bullets in the first place. But unless your name's Angus or Hamish I doubt you'll need more than one.

Nope, he wanted me to walk out of those gates feeling good and relaxed, like my dealings with Starkly Correctional Institution and all its inmates were firmly in the rearview. And there's only one reason I can think of for that: he means to send someone after me, to see where I'll go. Could just be idle curiosity, of course. I guess even with all those books time must sit heavy on your hands in a place like Starkly. I wouldn't bet on it, though. Well, I've been fooled by that trick before. I certainly won't be falling for it again.

I make my way down off the overpass and head straight for the U-Haul. I cross the lot and hike up to the low cinder block where Goldie jumped me. The door hangs back on its hinges, just how I left it. I snap off my snowshoes and step inside. Marv's map's lying on the floor. I return it to its rightful place in my pocket and make my way back to the interchange.

I need to get back to Mags and the kid now, quick as I can. Someone will be coming down that road after me, however, and I can't lead them right to the Juvies. I lift my goggles onto my forehead. On either side the highway stretches off into the distance, far as the eye can see.

One way looks as good as the other so I choose left, then set off down the on-ramp. The wind picks up, but not enough to clear my tracks. For now that suits me. I want whoever's following to pick up my trail. At first I swing around every few paces, expecting to find the dark shapes of whoever Finch has sent on the road behind. But each time it's empty, and after a mile or so I allow myself to relax a little. My thoughts return to what I saw at Starkly.

I have a theory now about the virus, of sorts. I reckon the furies that found themselves somewhere that was shielded the night Kane scorched the skies, those ones can probably still pass it on. Hicks certainly seemed to think so, and if he was wrong about that he put Ortiz to his end unnecessarily, after he got attacked by that one in the basement of the hospital in Blacksburg.

For those furies that were out in the open when the missiles detonated it might have been different, however. The pulse that was released didn't strike the virus from them, and it's been building its way back up inside them all this time, just like Marv suspected. Whatever ability they had to transmit it was lost, though. The crucifix Mags wears, I can't rely on that anymore.

I tell myself none of it means she's going to get sick again. The voice has been quiet since I quit the prison, but now it pipes up. It wants to know about all the other things: how quick she is now; how she can see in the dark; how her skin is always cold.

How she was with Kurt.

It seems like it has a lot more to say on the subject, but I hush it. None of that has to mean anything either. It's already been weeks since Mags and the kid came through the scanner, and they're both still fine.

If something was going to happen to them it would have done so by now.

I stick to I-85 as it winds its way west. I pass the exit for 501, the road that would take me south to Fearrington, but I don't take it. About a mile further on the interstate elbows north at a place called Eno and shortly after runs through what must once have been forest. I slow down. This is far enough. If I'm going to find my way back to the Juvies I'll need to cut south again, and here looks as good a spot as any. I have no backpack to drag in my wake, so I take out Weasel's blade and cut a branch from the withered remains of a tree that's still clinging to the embankment. I return to the center of the highway and keep going until the gnarled trunks on either side are as densely packed as I think they're apt to get, then I quit the road, using the branch to sweep the snow behind me. When I reach the tree line I look back. I doubt what I've done would've fooled Marv, or Truck, but with a little help from the wind it might do. It'll have to. Right now it's as much as I can manage.

I head cross-country for a while until I hit a little place name of Blackwood. I stop on the far side of town, lift my goggles onto my forehead and look west. From here I could go directly south to Fearrington, but I have one final detour to make. My backpack's sitting in a print store, south side of Durham. I don't care much to go back to the city, not after what I learned in Starkly,

174

but there are items in it, chief among them the box of bullets for Hicks' pistol and the list of codes for each facility in the Federal Location Arc I took with me from Eden. There's a good chance Mags will have taken the list with her when she returned with the Juvies, but I can't be certain of that. There's no information on it that isn't already in my head, but Mac and Goldie were scavenging right across the street when Mags ran into them.

I can't take the risk that they'd find it.

Traffic clogs the streets as I approach the city. I pick my way among the wrecks. The buildings grow taller the closer I get to the center. I keep looking up, thinking I catch movement behind the darkened windows, but each time I check there's nothing.

I arrive back at the *KwikPrint* just as the last of the light's slipping from the sky. My pack's right where I left it, propped against the wall in the corner. There's a note from Mags sitting on top, saying she's taken the Juvies on ahead. I'm sorely tempted to head right back out after them, but it's too late for that. There's no way I'd catch up, not with the head start they have; I doubt I'd even make it out of the city. Better to rest up, get back on the road early.

I head back to the entrance to check the street again, then wedge the door shut. I return to my pack and break out one of the last of my MREs. While it's heating I search the aisles. I find a few cardboard boxes and a ream of paper in the storeroom that's been overlooked, enough for a fire. I set it in back, as far from the windows as I can. When I've got the paper lighting I break down the boxes and feed the pieces to the flames while I wait for my ration to heat.

Soon as my food's passable warm I tear it open. I haven't had anything but watery soup since the night

175

before and I'm ravenous. I don't lift my nose from the pouch until there's nothing but a half-dozen sorry-looking beef ravioli left in the bottom. I lean back against the wall, wipe my mouth with the back of my hand, then reach for the canteen to wash down what I've just eaten.

As I unscrew the cap I glance up, just in time to see a flash of something through the silted glass of the storefront as the first of them come for me.

*

THE CANTEEN SLIPS from my fingers. It hits the ground, teeters drunkenly as the contents slosh around inside, then topples. Water spills from the neck, darkening the dusty floor, but that's not my concern now; I'm already on my feet, running to the window. I press my face to the cracked pane. A single flashlight beam, jitterbugging its way down the street as whoever's behind it picks their way between the abandoned cars.

How did they find me so soon?

I waste precious seconds staring at it in disbelief, watching the beam grow steadily closer. It looks like just the one, but I've been fooled by that trick before. I snap myself out of my stupor. How they found me matters little now. I turn back to the fire. It's too late to worry about extinguishing it, so instead I reach down for Hicks' pistol. The grip is still unfamiliar, but the heft gives me courage, at least until I remember it's not loaded. I rush over to where my backpack rests against the wall and upend it, scrabbling through the items that spill out for the box of ammunition. I pry the hammer back and fumble the loading gate open. I shake the bullets onto my palm, not caring that most of them end up on the floor. I've been inside long enough for my fingers to have thawed, but haste makes them clumsy; it takes an inordinate length of time to jiggle each cartridge into its slot, rotate the cylinder and push the next one home. The last bullet slides into place just as I hear a sound from outside. I look up. The beam's come to a halt right in front of the store.

I snap the gate closed and cock the hammer, just as a lone figure steps up to the entrance. The flashlight makes it hard to tell who it might be, but from his height I'm

177

pretty sure it's Goldie's companion, Mac. He raises both arms above his head. The wind's gusting and he has to shout to make himself heard.

'I don't mean you no harm. I only want to talk.'

'Is it just you?'

'It is.'

He turns his head, like he's checking for something further up the street, then looks back to the door.

'I'd appreciate if you'd hurry up and let me in. You can shoot me inside just as easy as out.'

I hesitate a moment, weighing my options, then I call back that he can enter. The door opens and he stumbles in, a flurry of snow swirling around him. He pushes past me and makes straight for the fire, paying little mind to the pistol I have on him. He drops to his knees, shuffling as close to it as he can, his hands held out like he would grasp the flames to him if he could.

When he's warmed himself enough he pulls the scarf he's wearing down and turns to me. If he has a weapon I don't see it, but I certainly don't plan on taking any chances. I make a show of leveling the gun at him, trying to keep my hand steady.

'It's loaded, so you know. And not with the bullets I left Starkly with.'

I nod in the direction of my backpack where the ammo box lies on its side, a dozen cartridges scattered in the dust around it. His eyes dip to it and then return to stare at me.

'Fair enough. Just remember I walked in with my arms raised. Don't know why I'd have done that, if I planned to hurt you.'

I don't have a good explanation for that, but I see no upside in dropping my guard just yet, either.

'How'd you track me here?'

He shakes his head.

'Didn't have to. You weren't carrying a pack when

we picked you up. A person wouldn't get very far without supplies, not out here. I reckoned you must have stashed it somewhere after you picked up our trail. Seemed like a good bet you'd come back for it. I figured I'd just retrace the route Goldie and me took earlier, see if I got lucky.'

He looks around the room. His gaze settles on the remains of my MRE, sitting by the fire.

'Don't suppose you'd be done with that?'

I wasn't, actually, but the dark eyes that flick back to me are filled with so much hunger I tell him he can have it. He holds my gaze a moment longer, then grabs the pouch as though he expects me to change my mind at any moment. I watch as he pulls off his mittens and sets to, using his fingers to scoop what was left there into his mouth. It doesn't take long. When he's got the last of it he runs one finger round the inside and licks it clean. Then he reaches for the carton it came in and upends it. The various packets inside tip out. He seizes on the HOOAH! and looks at me for approval. I nod, watching as he tears the wrapper open. The candy bar disappears in a couple of bites. He talks as he sifts through the remainder of the carton's contents.

'I'm here to give you a warning. You and whoever else you're traveling with.'

I start to deny it, but he just shakes his head.

'You might have done enough to fool that bonehead Goldie, but not me, and certainly not Finch.' He finds a ketchup and tears the corner, squirting it straight into his mouth. His eyes close for a moment, and then his tongue darts out to lick the corner of his chapped lips.

'Alright; have it your own way. Probably best I don't know anyway.' He nods at the fire. 'You can sit if you want. Ain't nobody else coming, leastways not tonight.'

I think on that for a while. It sounds like he's telling the truth, but I shake my head at the invitation anyway.

179

'Suit yourself.'

'How many of you did Finch send after me?'

'Six. We split up when we hit the interstate. Goldie took the rest of them off after the tracks you laid down. He'll follow them till they run out, just like I expect you intended.'

He checks the last of the packets, grunts at nothing in particular, then breaks out the little plastic toothpick that comes with each meal. He sets to work with it on a row of chipped yellow teeth.

'Why does the warden care where I go?'

He stops what he's doing and looks up at me slowly, like he doesn't understand. Then his eyes crease with humor. I watch as a slow smile spreads across his face.

'Garland Finch? The warden?' He gives a snort, like what I've said amuses him. 'What gave you that fool idea?'

'He said he was.'

'You sure about that?'

I open my mouth to tell him I am, but now that I think back I can't recall him ever saying as much, at least not specifically. I guess I just assumed from the way he talked, his suit, the shoes, the bunch of keys he carried.

He gives a shake of his head, goes back to work with the toothpick.

'I doubt it. Hard to know what rules a man like that lives by, but I ain't ever heard him tell no lie. He considers it the height of bad manners.'

I run back through our conversations in my head, trying to find any other evidence for my assumption.

'He said he released you all.'

He worries at something with the pick a moment longer, then runs his tongue over the front of his teeth.

'Well, that he did.' When he looks up at me again his mouth is doing something that might be a smile, but this time it doesn't stretch to his eyes; those have darkened considerably. 'Eventually.'

'So who was he, then?'

He picks up the empty MRE box and turns it over in his hands like he means to check inside it one more time. His eyes stay there a moment longer, then he looks up at me.

'Only the most dangerous man ever to set foot through the gates of Starkly prison.'

*

HE SHAKES THE CARTON one last time to be sure, then shoves it onto the fire. The flames grow brighter for a second as they consume the card, then die down again.

'How old are you, anyway?'

I tell him seventeen. Truth is I'm not quite there yet, but I figure an extra year goes a lot better with the pistol.

'So you was what, when it all ended? Six? Seven? I guess you would hardly have been outta diapers when they caught him.'

'Caught him? You mean he's just a prisoner?'

I don't mean no offense by it, words just have a habit of coming out of me that way. Mac's mouth hardens at the comparison. He rakes the embers with the side of his boot; sparks rise in a shudder and die in the blackness overhead. He leans toward me, and when he speaks again there's an edge to his voice that wasn't there before.

'Don't let the cane and that gimp leg fool you, kid. Garland Finch, he ain't like nobody else.'

'What...what was he in for?'

'Murder.' He pauses while he goes to work with the pick again. 'Not that that'd distinguish a man in a place like Starkly; ain't nobody ever been sent there on wino time.' He shakes his head. 'No, what set Garland Finch apart was the manner of his crimes. They reckon he was responsible for more than a hunnerd deaths, all told. Nobody's exactly sure how many, of course. They never did find a single body.' He smacks his lips like he's finally dislodged whatever he was hunting for. 'Probably because he ate 'em.'

At first I'm not sure I've heard him right, and for a few seconds my brain does that thing where it replays the words, trying to work out an alternative meaning that more closely fits with what I know of reality. Mac mustn't notice, or maybe he doesn't care, because he keeps talking.

'Starkly was a mean place to do time, maybe the meanest, so I guess it made sense they'd send him to us. The *warden*,' he looks over at me as he says it, 'was a prime asshole by the name of Stokes. Prided himself on being a real hardcase. But even Stokes was smart enough to know what he was dealing with, with a man like Garland Finch. He didn't take no chances. Soon as he arrived he emptied out HCON. All those who'd been down there – the snitches, the punks, the chesters, anyone who'd earned himself a stretch in solitary, even those on death row – he transferred back into the general population, so Finch would have the place to himself. Said it was for his own protection.' He gives a short, humorless laugh at that. 'First five years he was with us no one even laid eyes on him.'

'So how did he come to be in charge?'

Outside the wind moans, rattling the door in its frame, then settles down again. For a long moment Mac just stares into the fire, like he's considering whether he wants to tell me the next part. When he speaks again his voice has lowered.

'Whole world got turned on its head, is how.' He goes quiet, for longer this time. I begin to wonder if that's as much explanation as I'll get when without warning he hitches in a breath and starts talking again.

'You wind up in a place like Starkly, you try not to think too much about the world outside. How it's going on without you. Ain't much comfort to be had in that. There was the TV, of course, least for the hour each day Stokes allowed it. We knew from the news reports that things had taken a turn for the bad, but we figured it'd pass. The President had been on. The scientists were working on a cure, she said; wouldn't be long till they had it sorted.'

'The warden, he's a cautious man, though. He sticks the entire prison on lockdown. No one in or out; no visits, no furlough; hell, we weren't even allowed into the exercise yard. Can't say anyone cared much for that; more time in your cell's not something a con wishes for. Stokes, he says it's temporary; just till it all blows over.'

He prods the embers with the toe of one boot, sending another rush of sparks swirling up into the darkness.

''Cept things didn't seem to be getting no better, on the outside. Wasn't long before we're beginning to feel it, too. Starts with a few of the COs not showing up for their shifts. The screws were a mean bunch, so that didn't seem no bad thing, least not at first. It gets worse, though. Soon the warden's saying he doesn't have enough men to watch us at mealtimes, so we'll be taking our food in our cells, for the foreseeable.'

He leans forward, holding his hands a little closer to the dying fire.

'The future's something a con in a place like Starkly dwells on even less than what's going on outside. Mostly you teach yourself *not* to think on it. But by now the wise blood's starting to wonder how much longer our room service is going to hold out.'

He looks up at me.

'Well, the answer to that question was: not much. Starts with just a meal here and there being skipped, but before long getting fed's proving to be the exception rather than the rule. Never thought I'd miss a single one of those assholes, but that first morning no guard shows up to walk the block I knew it: we were screwed. The TVs in the main block are on, day and night now - I guess whoever was last out the door didn't bother to turn them off - but the coverage is getting pretty sketchy.

Most of the channels have shut down and the ones that are still broadcasting are showing the same bulletins, over and over. It was pretty clear: the world outside had fallen apart. Wasn't nobody goin' to care much about a bunch of prisoners, stuck in some Godforsaken place out in the middle of nowhere.'

He takes a breath, lets it out slow.

'Once that realization sinks in all hell breaks loose. Cons start banging on the bars, hollerin' for the warden, the guards, Jesus; anyone they thought might listen. It stays like that for a couple of days, then all of a sudden it turns eerily quiet, 'cept for the few TVs that were still on, just pumping out static now.' He points a finger at nothing in particular, as though remembering. 'That was strange. Starkly hadn't ever been a peaceful place, even at night.'

He pauses, and for a while he just stares into the flames. Outside the wind gusts, rattling the door on its hinges, and he returns from wherever he's been.

'I'd been stashing food for a while; anyone with any sense had. What little I'd managed to squirrel away didn't last long, though. After that it was just a matter of taking to your cot, to wait for the end. Days passed like that; I can't say how many, so don't ask; by then they were just blending into each other. Then one night all sorts of weird shit starts happening. Outside the skies go white, like it's the middle of the day, only brighter. I was pretty sure I was trippin', you know, on account of not having eaten for so long. It stays like that for a while, the light comin' and going' in waves, like fireworks. Some of those that had found religion start hollering like it's Rapture. Then just as sudden as it lit up everything dies: lights, TV, the works. Starkly gets its final curfew.'

He goes quiet again, for longer this time. I realize I've let the pistol drop to my lap. I look down at it, then over at him. I don't reckon he means me any harm, so I

185

ease the hammer back down.

'So how did you get out?'

'It was like Finch said. He let us out.'

'But how did he escape?'

'He was being held separate, remember, over in HCON.' He looks up. 'You must have seen it, when he was givin' you the tour? I bet he showed you that thing he keeps down there, too, didn't he?'

He grunts, like he doesn't much care for Finch's pet fury.

'It was the only modern part of the whole compound. They built it when the state designated Starkly a supermax. The cells had those fancy electronic locks, magnetic.' He wiggles his fingers in the air as he says it, as though as far as he was concerned they might have worked on magic rather than electricity. 'So when that weird shit happens in the sky and everything with a circuit gets fried, those locks, they just give up. The doors down in HCON spring open and Garland Finch he walks right out, free as a bird.'

'And he released you.'

Mac nods, only this time he doesn't say anything, just takes to staring into fire again. When at last he speaks his voice is little more than a whisper.

'That he did, eventually. First he walked the block, though, up and down with that leg of his, setting it out in terms he thought we'd understand. The world was a changed place, he said. Lean times were upon us. There were truths to be faced, hard ones. There wasn't going to be enough to feed everyone, and something had to be done about that, starting right then. So he'd come to a decision. He'd only let one man out of each cell, and only when there was nothing left of the other.'

I HEAR THE WORDS but my brain chooses not to accept them. I look over at Mac, hoping he's going to offer some alternative explanation for what I've just learned. Any other explanation.

'Yeah, at first we didn't think he was serious, either. But once you've known Garland Finch a while you realize that's not his style. You learn to take him very seriously.' He shakes his head slowly. 'He was every bit as good as his word, too. There were upwards of four hundred cons in the main block of Starkly, most of us two to a cell. When the last of those doors were opened what was left counted for not much more than a hunnerd-fifty. Weren't no cell where more than one man crawled out.'

The truth of what's he's told me finally sinks in. I stagger to my feet and take a step backwards.

'You *ate* your cell mates?'

I can hear the revulsion in my voice even as I say it. Mac looks at me over the fire, fixing me with a stare that makes me wonder if I should have kept the pistol cocked after all. He keeps his voice low, but there's a hardness to it now that reminds me why a man like him might have ended up in Starkly in the first place.

'You'd do well to keep that tone from your voice, boy. You prob'ly think you understand hunger 'cuz you had to skip a meal every now and then. You ever tried to eat the ticking out of your mattress? You ever spend your days praying for a roach to wander by your cell so you can slap your boot on it, maybe wash it down with a handful of water from the toilet bowl? You try that for a week or two, we'll see just what you would and would not do.'

He glares at me for a long moment, the embers from the fire burning red in his eyes. I tighten my grip on the pistol, reaching my thumb down to cover the hammer.

'Whatever shit I done, you think I deserved that? You think any of us did? Hell, I didn't even have that long. My time was short.'

'You were about to be released?'

He shakes his head.

'I wasn't ever going to see the outside of Starkly's walls. I had my ticket for the Big Bitch. The Stainless Steel Ride.'

I stare at him blankly; I have no idea what he's talking about.

'I was due to be executed. It was okay, though; I'd made my peace with it. When the time came the state was going to pay up for some expensive pharmaceuticals to take me over the line.'

He prods the fire with the toe of his boot again.

'I didn't sign up for any of it.'

His voice trails off and for a long while neither of us speak. My mind's still baulking at what I've just heard. I gaze into the fire, trying to make sense of it.

'But why would he do something like that? If he was worried about food he could just have released a bunch of you, forced you to leave, let you take your chances outside.'

Mac shakes his head.

'I thought about that a lot, after. What Finch done, it wasn't just about thinning our numbers, see. I think he figured he could give us a taste for it.'

He shakes his head, quick, like he's denying it.

'He sends us out, looking for supplies, but we never bring back enough. I guess the city had been picked over long before we got to it.

I'm not sure why he's telling me this, but all of a sudden I get a feeling, deep in the pit of my stomach. He keeps talking, but now it's like whatever he's about to tell me I'm not sure I want to hear it. It's too late for that, though. There's a part of my brain that's already racing ahead, working it out.

He said Finch released a hundred and fifty of them from their cells. There was only thirty-seven when we sat for dinner.

'And then there's the winters, when we can't hardly go out at all.'

As I had passed the kitchens, something gray, back in the shadows, dangling from an old hook.

'So when it gets tight we have ourselves a lottery. Supposed to be the same odds for everyone, but I doubt you'll ever see Tully or Knox's name get drawn. Nobody thinks it's going to be them. Until it is.'

I feel the blood draining from my face as I realize what he's telling me.

'The soup...'

He nods.

'Best not to think too hard 'bout what ends up in Blatch's cookpot.'

I stagger backwards but I don't make it as far as the door. Next thing I know I'm on my knees, still clutching the pistol, as what's left of the beef ravioli I had earlier comes flying out of my mouth. I continue to retch long after my stomach's expelled the last trace of it. When I think I'm finally done I wipe my mouth with the back of my hand and return to the fire.

Mac's still sitting, staring into the flames. He looks over at me as I take a seat. Whatever anger was there earlier has gone.

'I'm sorry, kid. I shouldn't have laid that on you. No reason for you to have to carry that around.'

I set the pistol down beside me. If I don't learn one more thing about Starkly for as long as I live I reckon it'll still be too soon. We sit in silence for a while, then

Mac picks up the toothpick again. He digs around for a while till he finds something, holds it out to examine it, then goes back to work. One by one the embers wink out, until there's only a handful left, nestling among the ashes.

'So what do you mean to do?

He stretches his hands out to the fire.

'I done what I came to, which is give you a warning. I don't know how many of you there are, or where you're hidin' out, and I don't care to. Garland Finch has taken an interest in you, and believe me that ain't no good thing. If you've any sense you'll clear out of here, quick as you can, and you won't ever show yourself again, least not anywhere within a couple of days' hike of Starkly, or Durham, or anywhere else he might send us looking for you.'

'And you'll just head back?'

He nods.

'First light. I'll say I followed your tracks south into the city, but then I lost you. Goldie and the others'll tell the same story. You let me have that book he gave you it might go a little easier on me.'

I reach into my pocket for the copy of *Watership Down*, but as I pull it out I find myself hesitating, reluctant to hand it over.

'Won't he wonder how you came across it, if you couldn't find me?'

He shakes his head, like he's already thought about this.

'I'll tell him you tossed it, before your trail went cold.'

I stare at the cover a moment longer, then hand it over.

'I appreciate it. Man sure loves his books. You find him one, your name don't go in the lottery for a while. I'm surprised he let you leave with it.'

He looks over at the backpack lying against the wall. Most of its contents lie scattered on the floor from when I upended it looking for the bullets.

'Maybe you could spare one of those food cartons, too? You know, for the journey back.'

I open my mouth to tell him I don't have any extra to spare, but then I see how he's staring at me. He has the look of a man who's been on the wrong end of every deal going for longer than he can remember. I nod. He reaches for the closest one and it disappears inside his coat.

'Much obliged.'

Outside the wind gusts against the front of the *KwikPrint*, harder this time. There's a loud crack as it flexes the fractured pane. Mac spins around and takes to staring at the window. I remember how he had hurried in off the street when he first arrived, like he was more concerned about what might be out there than he was with the gun I had on him.

'What you said over dinner last night, about the city not being safe after dark. What did you mean? Have you seen something?'

He stares at the window a little longer then turns back to the fire.

'No, not exactly. It's just sometimes, when I'm out...I dunno...I get this feeling. Like I'm being watched.'

I remember thinking the same thing, when we cut through the parking lot of the VA medical center, on our way down through Durham. I tell him what Marv told me; how he reckoned the furies weren't gone for good; that one day they'd rise up again.

He studies me for a long moment without saying anything.

'Your friend one of them scientists?'

I shake my head.

'Then how could he know?'

But there's no conviction in his words; it's like he's only saying them because he needs it to be so. I consider telling him about Gilbey. She *is* a scientist, probably the only one left whose opinion counts for a damn, and she thought the same as Marv. I don't, though. Doesn't seem like he's trying to trick me into talking about stuff I'd do better to keep to myself, but if I'd been a little more suspicious of Hicks from the get-go things might have been different. Besides, I don't need to mention what happened at The Greenbrier to convince him.

'The fury Finch keeps, down in the basement.'

'What of it?'

'It's awake.'

He looks up at me like he's not sure what he's supposed to do with that information.

'When did that happen?'

'Just last week, according to Finch. He doesn't want anyone to find out about it. Says it might discourage those he sends out scavenging.'

'Son of a bitch.'

His eyes shift back to the street. He looks like he might be about to say something, but then he just takes to staring at the ground between his boots.

'Why are you going back to Starkly, Mac? I mean, why don't you just stay away yourself?'

He shakes his head.

'First thing Finch'd do is send Goldie and a few of the others out for me, then I'd wind up on the sharp end of Blatch's knife, for sure. Besides, where would I go? That place is all I got; it's all any of us got. Nuthin' else left on the outside, not anymore.'

His voice drops and he glances around furtively, as though someone might be listening.

'Besides, I reckon Garland Finch's time's getting short. There's not many of us left now, so that lottery of his ain't lookin' like the deal it used to. I reckon it won't be long before some of the brothers take it on themselves to bump titties with Knox and Tully. I figure I just gotta keep my head down, bide my time, pray my number don't come up in the meantime.'

WHEN I WAKE THE FOLLOWING MORNING the fire's died
and the room's bitter cold. I draw the sleeping bag tight
around me and watch as my breath rolls out in fat, white
plumes. It hangs above my head for a few seconds
before vanishing into the frigid air. I wipe the sleep from
my eyes and look around. There's no sign of Mac. My
gaze flits to the backpack, resting against the wall on the
far side of the blackened remains of the fire. I climb out
of the sleeping bag and hurry over to check the contents,
but nothing's missing beyond what I offered him.

I get dressed quick as I can, then pack up my things. I
don't bother with breakfast. I'm anxious to be on the
road now, and besides, my appetite hasn't yet recovered
from what I learned about Starkly. I hoist the backpack
over my shoulder and head outside. A single set of
tracks leads away from the *KwikPrint*, the wind already
softening their edges. I stare at them for a moment and
then point my snowshoes around and set off in the
opposite direction, picking my way between the
abandoned wrecks that clutter the street, swinging
around every few paces to check behind me. A few
blocks south a sign points to the turn for 501, but I don't
take it. I plan to stay off the main roads, least till I'm
well clear of Durham. It's a fair bet Goldie and the other
men Finch sent are already out there somewhere,
looking for me. I have no intention of making it easy for
them.

Listing high-rises give way to crumbling warehouses
and then finally to darkened strip malls as I make my
way out of the city. Little by little the roads start to clear.
I pass a *Kmart*, squatting long and low on the far side of
a vast parking lot. Mac said there was little left here; that

the city had been picked clean. I don't think he was lying to me about that, not with how thin he and most of the other inmates were, but I'd like to go in and check what's on the shelves, all the same, to see for myself. Seems strange there wouldn't be something worth scavenging, not in a place this size. There'll be time for that later, though. Right now I need to get back to Mags and the others.

One by one the last of the malls drop away and the road snakes out into open country. I follow it as it curves this way then that, trudging up each incline, hurrying down into the shallows between. When at last I reckon I'm far enough from the city, I cut west and start heading back towards 501. An hour later I pick up the highway and turn south again. I keep checking behind me, but less often now. The road stays clear.

Morning stretches into afternoon, then evening. As dusk's getting ready to settle I come to a large wooden yardarm, poking up through the snow just off the hard shoulder. The sign that hangs there shifts back and forth, creaking in the wind. Its paint is flaked, peeling, the timber underneath split, rotten black, but there's just enough of the faded cursive left to tell me I'm entering Fearrington Village.

I hurry on by, following the highway into town. It doesn't take me long to get the measure of the place. It's little more than a wide spot in the road; not even a diner or a gas station, just a couple of stores clustered around a stoplight, most of their windows broken, those that remain thickened with grime. I make my way quickly through. There'll be time later to explore, but I can't say as I hold high hopes for what I'll find for us here.

I pass another sign on my way out, this one buried in a drift. I bend down and scrub snow from the metal until I can read what's there.

Mount Gilead Church Road.

I recognize the name; according to Marv's map the bunker waits somewhere down that way. I'm about to point my snowshoes around when I stop. Mags has the list of codes she took from my backpack, but without the map I'm carrying there'd be little hope of her finding the bunker. It's more likely she'd have chosen a spot close, got the Juvies off the road, then settled in to wait for me.

I take another look along Mount Gilead. I can't see anything that way that'd do for shelter, so I turn back to the road I've been following. A little further along, right on the edge of town, a single low brick building, set a little ways back from the highway, its roof heavy with snow. I stare at it a moment longer then start making my way towards it.

As I get closer I see a weather-faded sign: *The Suntrust Bank.* Out front a small parking lot, empty save for a lone sedan, sunk on its tires under a blanket of gray powder. The snow is smooth, undisturbed, but that doesn't mean anything; if the Juvies got here more than a few hours ahead of me the wind would have taken care of their tracks. I scan the building again, more slowly this time. A narrow ATM lobby stretches the length of the front. To one side of the entrance the corner of something pokes from a drift. I don't have to stare at it long to work out what it is: the container with the virus.

I start to make my way down off the highway then I stop, remembering how twitchy Eric had been with his weapon when I'd left them in Durham. I pull my mask down and call out, like I used to do with the Guardians when I was about to crawl back into Eden's tunnel. There's a pause, then movement from back in the shadows and a second later the kid scampers into the lobby. He drops to a crouch in front of one of the ATM machines and raises a hand like he means to wave but then he stops, the gesture interrupted. He tilts his head.

It's hard to tell on account of the goggles he wears, but it looks like he's checking the road behind me.

Tyler shows next, cradling his weapon to his chest, followed by Eric. The rest of the Juvies crowd into the lobby after them, staring out as I make my way through the parking lot. I wait for Mags to appear, but there's no sign of her. As I bend to snap off my snowshoes Lauren pushes her way to the front.

'Gabe; thank God. I was...' She stops herself. 'I mean, we were all worried about you, of course. What happened? Did you find out where those men were coming from?'

I open my mouth to tell them about what happened at Starkly, but just then Jake appears at her shoulder. From the look on his face it's clear not everyone's as happy to see me as she was.

'Where's Mags?'

'She's not with you?'

He shakes his head.

'She brought us down here last night. First thing this morning she went back out looking for you.'

'Which way was she headed?'

It's a stupid question; I know it before I'm done asking. Where else would she go? I'm already re-fastening the bindings on my snowshoes even as he points behind me, north, back towards the city.

Lauren hugs her arms to her sides.

'What are you doing?'

'There are men there, looking for me.'

The Juvies' eyes shift as one, out to the parking lot, like I've just pointed to a horde of them, gathering behind the sedan. Jake mutters something under his breath I don't catch.

Lauren takes a step closer.

'Wait, Gabe; are you sure it makes sense to go back out? I mean, it's already getting late. I'm sure Mags will be here soon.'

I stop for a second. What Lauren's saying makes sense. Mags knew there were others out there; she would have been careful. When she doesn't find me in the city she'll go looking for shelter, somewhere to hole up for the night.

I look up to the darkening skies. That might be more than I'll manage. I doubt I'll even make it back to where I joined 501 before I lose the light, and there was little in the way of shelter along that stretch; I know because I've just hiked it. Marv certainly wouldn't be taking us out again, not this close to nightfall.

But that doesn't change the fact that she's up there right now, while Goldie and whoever else Finch may have sent are looking for me. I finish tightening the straps on my snowshoes and point them in the direction of the highway, before I can think of any more reasons not to go. The kid's still crouched in front of the ATM. He looks up at me through those outsize goggles he wears.

You should warn them.

I'm not sure how to do that, though, and right now I don't have time to figure it out. I turn to the Juvies crammed into the narrow lobby.

'Go back inside, all of you, and stay out of sight.'

They don't need to be told twice. The ones closest the door are already tripping over themselves to get out of the lobby.

I wait till Eric's gone back inside then I call Tyler over.

'Can you stand watch while I'm gone?'

His brow furrows.

'You really think they'll find us, all the way out here?'

I let my gaze linger on the highway a moment longer than it needs to before I answer, like I'm giving serious consideration to his question.

'I hope not. But there *are* men out there looking for me. I've left a trail, and if Mags is on her way back here she'll be doing the same. That's how the soldiers found us last time.'

He looks to the road, like he's considering what I've just told him.

'Alright.'

'One more thing.'

I turn to the kid.

'Johnny, will you stay out here and keep watch with Tyler?'

He hesitates for a moment, then turns his head in Tyler's direction. It's hard to tell behind those dark goggles, but it looks like he's taking in the rifle held across his chest. Tyler glances down at him then looks back at me.

'It's okay, Gabe, really. I got it.'

I shake my head.

'I need him out here as much as I need you, Tyler.' I lower my voice, not wanting the others to hear. 'The truth is he can see in the dark like you can't.'

Tyler cuts another glance in the Johnny's direction and I see his grip on the rifle tighten, like I've just disclosed the kid's favorite food is Juvie-brain and he hasn't been fed in an age. But then he nods, once, like he's getting himself straight with it.

'Alright.'

I pull my goggles down and set off across the parking lot. I can't see how anyone's coming down this road for us, not so late in the day, and if they are I'll run into them first. But at least out here the kid'll be away from the others. And Tyler will watch him close, without me having to tell them why.

As I pass the buried sedan I glance back towards the lobby. The kid's settled himself underneath one of the

199

ATMs. Tyler stands by the entrance, the rifle still clutched to his chest.

It'll be fine. Tyler's calm. He won't freak easy, not like Eric, or one of the others. I tell myself that's why I chose him, and there's truth to that. The voice pipes up as I make my way up the embankment and rejoin the highway. It thinks there might be another part to it, too, whether or not I care to admit it.

It wonders whether I picked Tyler because he has a gun.

I CAN'T RIGHTLY SAY what my expectations might have been for the rest of that evening, only that they weren't met.

Not even close.

I've barely gone a mile when a lone figure appears around a bend in the road, not twenty yards ahead of me. She stops when she sees me, shifts her goggles onto her forehead and pulls down her mask. For some reason spidey pings at that, but as usual there's little explanation for it, so I put it down to the same surprise I'm feeling at finding her so soon. By the time I've shifted my brain back into gear she's already closed the gap between us. She stands there for a moment, then throws her arms around me. I grunt as the air's squeezed from my lungs.

'Easy.'

She doesn't let up.

'Asshole. You had me worried.'

Eventually she releases her grip.

'It's getting late. We should head back.'

I shuffle my snowshoes around and we set off back towards *The Suntrust Bank*.

'So what happened? Where were you?'

I tell her about getting surprised by Goldie and how he and Mac brought me to Starkly to meet Garland Finch. I describe how I took dinner with the inmates, but I don't go into detail on what might have been in Blatch's cookpot. I'm not sure I mean to tell anyone about that, ever, not even Mags. I describe the tour of the prison I got from Finch afterwards, including the library and the copy of *Watership Down* he gave me, but when the time comes I don't mention what I saw in the basement there either. It'd not take her long to work out the significance of a fury being held behind metal bars, and I haven't yet made up my mind how to tell her about that, or even if I mean to. I finish up with the warning Mac gave me about staying clear of Durham.

'I didn't see anyone there.'

'How far'd you go?'

'Just to the print store. When I saw your backpack was gone I figured you were on your way back down to us and somehow I'd missed you on the road.'

We walk for a while in silence. The *KwikPrint* was on the south side of Durham, but that's still more miles than anyone should have been able to cover in a day.

A normal person, you mean.

I tell the voice to be quiet. Up ahead the sign for Fearrington shifts on its yardarm; beyond it the stoplight and the turn off for the Mount Gilead Church Road.

'I guess the city's off limits then?'

I nod, still a little distracted.

'Unless we want to risk running into more of Finch's men.'

I tuck my thumbs into the straps of my pack, suddenly aware of how little heft there is to it; it weighs hardly more than the canvas it's made of.

This place I'm bringing us to, it'd better be stocked.

Mags stops, turns to look at me. It takes me a moment to realize I've said the words out loud.

'You want to see if we can find it?'

'Now?'

She nods.

I take a look down the Mount Gilead Church Road. Dusk has already settled over the snow-shrouded fields; it won't be long till darkness draws down behind it. I know what Marv would say; we've already pushed our luck enough for one day. But according to the map in my pocket the bunker's only a mile or so east of here.

I turn back to face her.

'I   do.'

WE SET OFF INTO THE FAILING LIGHT. I scan the road ahead for signs. It curves east for a while, then straightens again. The bunker should be somewhere around here, at the end of a lane neither Marv nor the map had bothered to name. Up ahead I spot a turnoff that seems in about the right place. I push my goggles onto my forehead. A narrow track runs through open fields for a couple of hundred yards and then ends at what was once dense woodland. I look across the empty snow, my breath smoking in the cold as I try and decide what to do. The temperature's falling fast now; there's not much of the day left to us.

Beside me Mags pulls down her mask. Spidey pings again, like he did when I first saw her earlier, and it seems like he has something more specific he wants to say, but I'm too busy trying to stop my teeth from chattering to focus on whatever it might be. I ask her what she can see. She doesn't say anything for a while, but then eventually I just get *Trees*. She goes quiet again.

'How far down there was it supposed to be?'

I don't need to get the map out to give her an answer.

'Not far. Half a mile maybe.'

I stamp my snowshoes, trying to keep warm. She looks at me for a moment, like she might be measuring my ability to go on. In the end she must come to a decision because she pulls her mask up again.

'Let's give it another ten minutes. If we haven't found anything by then we'll turn back. Okay?'

'Alright.'

I open my mouth to ask her if she's cold but she's already off, a new purpose to her stride. I try to keep up, but by the time we're halfway across the field she's

204

already more than a dozen paces ahead of me. She doesn't slow for the tree line, just disappears among the gnarled trunks. I hesitate for a second and then follow her in. Long-dead trees push up through the snow on either side; their blackened limbs swiping at my parka as I make my way deeper into the wood. Darkness quickly fills the space between, until there's little to see but the moldering remains of those closest to whatever trail she's following. I'd get out the flashlight, except I don't want to fall any further behind, so instead I try and focus on the sound of her snowshoes crunching the ice-crusted powder. They're getting harder to hear above the sounds of my own breathing. The air is sharp with the cold now; it burns my lungs. This is crazy. I'm about to call out to her to suggest we go back when I realize that she's stopped.

As I catch up I see something ahead, jutting from the ground to waist height, blocking the way. She brushes snow off it, then turns to look at me. I dig in my parka for the flashlight, fumbling with the stubby handle while I get my breath back. Spidey pings again as the beam spreads, but I'm too distracted by what she's found to pay attention. I play the light over the obstacle, trying to keep my hand steady against the cold.

A barrier, the kind that rises right out of the road, the rusting metal painted in wide yellow and black stripes. On either side a high fence stretches off as far as the shuddering beam will allow. A single weather-faded sign hangs forlorn from the chain-link. It says we're on government property and right now we're trespassing. Beyond it the trees stop, as abruptly as they began.

We clamber over the barrier and make our way into the compound. A small guard shack squats on the far side, the snow drifted high against its aluminum sides. It's almost full dark now and inside my parka I'm shivering so hard my teeth are rattling together. I crank the flashlight again, the fingers inside my mittens already stiffening with the cold. The dynamo whirs and the bulb grows momentarily brighter, but the beam soon reaches its limit and won't be pushed further; all I can see are the tracks Mags is making in the snow. She seems to know where she's going, though, so I give up on winding the handle and follow her. A rusting pole appears out of the darkness; a tattered windsock shifting back and forth on its fraying tether. This must be where Gilbey and the soldiers landed in their helicopter, all those years ago. I look around for other landmarks that might confirm it, but find none.

Ahead the ground starts to incline and soon I can make out a raised embankment. As we get closer a pair of giant concrete cubes slowly emerge from the darkness. I play the flashlight over their sides. The beam won't stretch all the way to the top, but from what I can see it seems like the concrete sweeps inward to a point in the center, almost like a huge dish has been molded there.

Mags makes for the space between, where a narrow funneled entrance cuts into the ground. I can just make out the top of a metal door, right at the end. A camera stares down from a rusting bracket above, its single lens cataracted with ice.

She steps forward and starts scooping snow from in front of the door. I hang back a moment then join in, but my hands are numb with cold and I end up spilling as much as I clear. When we've managed to clear an area big enough for the door to open I stand back and crank the flashlight again, trying to hold the beam steady. It's little more than a Hobbit hole, hardly bigger than the vault door in the Exhibition Hall back at The Greenbrier. A large wheel handle sits at its center. The only other feature is a small window at eye level above. It's about the same size and shape as a letterbox, its metal surround held in place by heavy bolts. The thick glass is rimed with ice; I scrub it clear with the edge of my mitten and shine the flashlight inside, but I can't see a thing.

I search the wall to one side, relieved to find a keypad just like the one in Eden. I clear the snow from around the cowling and hit the reset button. For a moment nothing happens, but then there's the faintest of flickers from the light at the bottom, like it's deciding whether it cares to rouse itself from its decade-long slumber. The light gradually grows brighter, and then for a heart-stopping moment it goes out, before finally returning to blink at me in long, steady pulses. The rest of the keypad slowly illuminates.

I close my eyes and the section of Marv's map that showed Fearrington, complete with the code he had written next to it, appears before me. I start to punch in the sequence but my fingers are shaking so badly I keep having to start over. After the third attempt Mags taps me on the shoulder. I step away and call them out so she can do it.

She enters the twelve letters and numbers and stands back. The light underneath switches from red to green, and then there's a pause. A faint whine rises from somewhere behind the door, builds to complaining pitch, and then from deep within there's the grinding of gears. The handle in the center of the door begins a hesitant, anti-clockwise rotation. For a few seconds there's the muted screech of metal being dragged against metal as bolts slide back into their recesses, then it reaches the end of its travel with a loud clunk. Silence returns once again to the darkness.

I grab the wheel with both hands and pull but the door allows me only a fraction and then immediately retreats, like there's something else holding it in place, preventing it from opening. I kick the last of the snow from the base and try again, this time bracing one boot against the concrete to the side. Behind me I hear Mags asking if she can help, but I just keep yanking desperately at the handle. At last I think I feel something give. I renew my efforts. It takes a few more frantic tugs, but at last there's a soft sucking sound and the door finally surrenders, swinging back out towards me with a dull metallic groan.

I WIND THE FLASHLIGHT and shine it inside. A thick rubber seal runs around the edge of the recessed frame, explaining its unwillingness to yield. Beyond there's a small chamber, no taller or wider than the entrance. At the end another heavy steel door, identical to the first.

I step in. The air smells fusty, stale, like it hasn't been disturbed in years. I play the beam over the walls. The metal looks old, its surface covered with tiny whorls, scratches, the dull patina of age. The floor is steel grating, and when I point the flashlight upwards it finds more of the same. In the hatched shadows behind I can just make out the curving blades of what look like ventilation fans.

I step up to the inner door and try the handle, but it won't turn. I search the frame for a keypad; there's none. Instead a large green button protrudes from the wall, the plastic cracked, faded, the word CYCLE stenciled above. I push it, but nothing happens. I wait for a few seconds, listening, then try again. This time I press my ear to the cold steel, straining for any sign of activity within. But there's only the sound of my breathing.

I point the flashlight at the edges. Another strip of rubber compressed between door and frame, just like the one behind me. I grab the wheel and lean into it. The soles of my boots squeak as they compress against the grating but it won't budge, not even a fraction.

I step back and hit the button, harder this time, feeling the panic begin to rise. We can't have come all this way to be denied entry now. Mags rests a hand on my shoulder.

'Gabe.'

I turn around. She looks back at the door we've just

come through.

'Let's try closing that one. Maybe the inner door isn't designed to open unless the outer one's shut.'

'Okay. Yeah. Good idea.'

She reaches for the handle to pull it shut.

'Wait.'

I dig in my pocket for Marv's map, but my fingers are numb with the cold and I have to fumble with it to pull it out. I look up. My breath hangs heavy in the air between us, and suddenly I understand what spidey's been trying to tell me since we left the Juvies. Because it's only my breath I see, roiling yellow in the flashlight's faltering beam. I stare at her, studying her slightly parted lips, the almost imperceptible flare of her nostrils as she exhales. There's no mistake; her breath is clear.

I wonder what that means.

'Gabe?'

It doesn't have to mean anything. She's not freaking out like you are, that's all. Besides, right now I have other things to worry about. If I don't get this door open we could freeze out here.

You might. She won't.

I squeeze my eyes shut and to my surprise it works; when I open them again the voice has gone.

'Gabe, you okay?'

I nod, hold the map out to her. The faded blue-red cover with the Standard Oil logo trembles in my hand. I tell her through chattering teeth to go back outside.

She looks at me like she means to argue, but I shake my head.

'W-who knows how much juice is left in the b-batteries? If they die before the cycle's c-complete I need you out there to f-figure a way to get me out.'

She hesitates for a moment like she doesn't care much for this plan. I guess she can't think of a better one, though, because in the end she takes the map and steps back outside.

I pull the door closed behind her, turning the wheel to lock it. This time when I hit the button there's a series of muted clicks, followed by more silence. I hold my breath, waiting for something else to happen. After what seems like an eternity there's a buzzing sound from above my head and I point the flashlight up just in time to see the fans in the ceiling start to rotate. They stutter at first, but then the pitch builds until they're nothing more than a blur. I feel a pressure in my ears as the air's sucked out of the tiny chamber. The motors run for a while then die, and for a long time after there's more silence. I'm starting to think there might not have been enough left in the batteries to complete the cycle after all, when at last I hear a click from the door in front of me and then the whine of another motor, followed by the low grinding of cogs as the mechanism grumbles through its internal processes. In front of me the handle slowly starts to turn, and from inside the door there's the familiar sound of bolts working their way home. When the wheel reaches the end of its travel it stops and silence once again returns to the small chamber.

I press my shoulder to the steel and push. It takes another couple of tries to break the seal on the inner door, but in the end it gives just like the outer one did. I shout over my shoulder that I'm in. I've no idea whether she can hear me through the steel, but I tell her to wait while I find a way to open the door manually.

I step out of the airlock into a tiled area, no wider than the chamber I've just left. A fat metal drain in the center of the floor; a showerhead, round like a sunflower; a metal chain you'd pull to make the water flow. A sign on the wall with instructions. Beyond the decontamination area, a concrete passageway stretches off into darkness. I find a metal hatch, low on the wall. It opens with a creak, revealing a handle with the word OVERRIDE stenciled in red above, an arrow telling me the direction it needs to go. The mechanism's stiff, but after a little coaxing I get it to move. I step back into the airlock, and this time when I grasp the outer door's wheel it turns. I keep winding it until the bolts have been drawn back. I push the door open and Mags joins me.

We make our way along the passageway, following a run of rust-spackled pipes that hang from the low ceiling. No more than a dozen yards from the entrance it ends abruptly at a narrow concrete-lined shaft. A short walkway with guardrails on either side leads out to a metal staircase that spirals down into darkness. I shine the flashlight over the edge, but the drop is deeper than the beam will show me. I stand there for a second, inhaling the spent air. It feels dank, clammy. There's something else, too: a smell, heavy, unpleasant, drifting up from the depths.

'Everything okay?

I nod, make my way out onto the gangway. The metal looks old, worn, just like in the airlock. It groans worryingly as it accepts my weight, but it doesn't feel like it's about to give, so I keep going, out to the stairs. When I reach them I rest a hand on the rail. Paint still clings to the underside, but on top the steel's burnished smooth from years of use. When I point the flashlight down at the tread plate it's the same there: in the corners the raised diamonds still show; in the center where my boots fall there's little left but their outlines.

I start down. Inside my head I begin the count, measuring our progress in steps descended. The shaft is tight, the walls close enough to touch. Small vents punctuate the concrete at intervals I take to be equal to a floor, the area beneath each streaked brown with rust. I shine the flashlight on one. My breath still smokes in the beam, but less than above; already it feels a little warmer. I pull off a mitten and stretch my hand out to the grille. A gentle breeze slips between my fingers.

We continue on, round and round, each spiral taking us deeper into the bunker, our footfalls echoing and rebounding off the concrete as we descend. The walls get no closer, but somehow the shaft seems to press in, becoming more confined the lower I go. I push that thought from my mind and focus on the count. By the time I've reached two hundred I'm beginning to worry. I lean over the railing and point the flashlight down into the blackness below, desperate for evidence of anything other than this never-ending spiral. But the beam finds only more steps.

I pick up the pace. My hand skims the rail and my boots ring out on the tread plate, sending little clouds of dust shivering through the flashlight's herky-jerky beam that disappear off into darkness. I can feel my heart beating faster, but not from the effort of our descent. Hicks said the silo was only thirteen stories deep. I had assumed each of those would have living space, like the floors of a tall building, only buried underground.

But what if for most of it there's just this stair?

*

AT LAST I THINK I SEE something below me and I force myself to slow down. After a few more turns the stair drops through a grated ceiling and the shaft opens out. A narrow gangway juts into emptiness. I lean over the handrail. Beneath me the stair continues its spiraling descent, but the flashlight's no match for the inky blackness; I have no idea how much farther it goes.

A bead of sweat breaks free inside my thermals and trickles down my side. It's definitely warmer down here. I unzip my parka and step onto the catwalk, pointing the beam ahead. The gangway joins the stair to what looks like a doughnut-shaped floor that surrounds the shaft on all sides.

I make my way across. On the far side metal desks, lined up in neat rows that stretch back into darkness, their surfaces crammed with gauges, switches, readouts. Swivel chairs sit neatly under each. There's something not right about that, but I can't work out what it might be, so instead I lean closer and wipe dust from a few of the dials. The markings look old, antiquated. I continue along the row until I reach the end. The wall curves around gently, punctuated here and there by more grilles like the ones I saw in the shaft. But when I hold the flashlight up the surface isn't concrete; it has a dull luster, like it's sheathed in something metallic. In the yellowing beam it looks green, but in a different light it might also be blue.

'Copper.'

I turn around, surprised to see Mags standing right there. I hadn't heard her come up behind me. Her hood's pulled back and she's taken her mittens off. She reaches a hand out to the metal.

'It was on the walls of the plant room in Eden, too. Scudder said it was put there to shield the machinery from the effects of a pulse, like what Kane did, when he scorched the skies.'

I study her face. I can't see her breath, but then when I look in the flashlight's beam I can't find mine either. I take off my mittens, reach for her cheek. Her skin feels cold, but then we have just come from the outside.

She pushes the hand away.

'Hey, we're supposed to be checking this place out, remember?'

But as she turns her head away she flashes me a smile.

We head back to the stair and keep going down. The next level's similar to the first, only in place of the workstations there's stacks of what looks like computer servers, mounted on thick rubber shocks. A rat's nest of wires trails from the back of each; more snake along the floor; others hang in thick bunches from the low ceiling. The machines look clunky, old, like they belong in a museum.

We return to the shaft and continue our descent. The level below was clearly the mess. I count four long tables, each bolted to the floor. Chairs are tucked neatly underneath, just like upstairs. Something seems wrong with that, too. I stare at them for a while, but I have no more success figuring out what than I did earlier, so in the end I move the flashlight along. The beam finds a row of industrial-looking ovens, mounted on heavy springs. Large stainless steel hoods hang down, their elbowed vent pipes disappearing into the ceiling above. To one side, counters where food would have been prepared. Further along, rows of metal shelves, stacked with pots, pans, bowls.

I return my attention to the nearest table and play the flashlight over the scuffed metal. Mags takes a step closer, runs a finger across it, dislodging thick motes of dust that swirl through the beam before starting their lazy descent to the floor.

'It all looks so tidy. Do you remember how long it took us to clean up in Mount Weather?'

And then I see. Mount Weather's mess had been, well, a mess. The tables had been covered in plates of half-eaten food; the chairs had been pushed back, knocked over. We knew why, of course. On the morning of the Last Day Kane had contacted the base commanders of each of the facilities in the Federal Relocation Arc and ordered an emergency evacuation; anyone inside would have left in a big hurry. Afterwards he'd changed the codes on the blast doors remotely, preventing anyone from getting back in. Thankfully Benjamin had been listening, and had thought to write the new codes down, so that years later Marv could hand them to me.

There's no evidence anything like that happened here. The tables are bare, the chairs lined up neatly underneath. I point the flashlight over at the shelves. Plates, bowls, cups, all in perfect stacks; everything squared away, just so. I look back at Mags, but she's already worked it out.

'Whoever was here had plenty of time to tidy up before they left.'

I nod. It'll be good not to have to clean up like we did in Mount Weather. But there's something about it makes me feel uneasy, all the same.

We make our way back to the stairs and keep going down. The next level is stores. Metal shelves stretch back into darkness, all the way from the central shaft back to the silo's copper walls, like the spokes of a giant wheel. I'm relieved to see most are packed tight with boxes. I play the beam over the nearest one. The cardboard's old, speckled with mildew, but the faded letters printed on the sides are still mostly legible.

U.S. Army Field Rations ~ Type C.

I point the flashlight along the row. They're all the same. I drag one down. I don't need Weasel's blade; the adhesive's long dried; the tape lifts easily when I get a finger to it. Inside, small cans, each large enough for maybe a single meal. I lift one out and examine it. The contents are stamped, military-fashion, on the lid: the tin I've chosen says *Meat Stew with Vegetables.* I examine the sides but there's no further clue as to what animal it might have been taken from. If it's like Eden it won't resemble anything in God's creation; the army seemed to have only the vaguest grasp of what food actually tasted like. But cans are good; as long as the seals have held what's inside shouldn't have spoiled. I drop the one I've been inspecting back into its slot and return the box to its place on the shelf.

We head back to the main shaft. The floor below looks like it's been given over to provisions as well. From the stair my flashlight won't reach between the shelves, but when I set foot on the gangway to cross Mags says there's no need; it all looks the same as above. We continue on. The air grows heavy around us. I catch the smell I picked up when I first came through the airlock again, stronger now.

We wind our way down, deeper into the silo. The levels beneath the stores house the dorms. I count the cells as we cross the gangway: twelve to a floor. I push the door back on the nearest one, lifting my boot over the raised threshold. Inside is shaped like a slice of pie, narrow near the front, wider towards the back. Two metal-framed cots hinge down from the wall, just like in Eden. There's no more in the way of comforts than there was in our first home either, just a single bulkhead lamp mounted high on the riveted steel opposite.

I step back out, return to the shaft. Mags says the

217

floor below looks identical to the one above so we stick to the stair. The next level down is ablutions. We find rows of narrow stalls, shower cubicles barely big enough to accommodate a body. The plumbing is rust-streaked, crusted with grime; by flashlight it all looks pretty grim. Here and there a rubber joint has given out, but most of it seems to have held. Beyond the final stall a row of washbasins, bolted to the silo's curving wall. Above each a square of steel that would once have served as a mirror.

I try one of the faucets, but it won't budge, so I move along to the next. It's seized solid, too. Mags steps up to the basin beside me and grasps the handle. For a second it looks like it won't yield either, but then she adjusts her grip and it turns with a low metallic groan.

She looks at me and smiles.

'Weakling.'

'You just got an easy one.'

We wait. At first there's nothing and then from somewhere above the sound of pipes clunking and shuddering. Finally something brown that might be water spits and sputters from the pipe in chaotic bursts. It doesn't look very appealing, but Mags says it's probably okay; at least whatever passes for a reservoir here hasn't run dry or frozen. She lets the water run until the stream steadies and starts to flow clear, then she shuts the faucet off and starts making her way back to the main shaft. I check she's not looking then I try the next one along, but I can't get it to turn any more than I could the first two. I wipe my hand on the outside of my parka and follow after her.

Beneath the showers the stair spirals down through another couple of turns then ends at a floor made of sections of thick, riveted steel. A large metal hatch, a wheel handle in its center, like the kind of thing you'd find on a submarine, waits for us at the bottom. I grasp the handle with both hands and heave it open, then point the flashlight through the opening. A narrow ladder drops to a grated landing; beyond, more steps.

I climb through the hatch and we rejoin the stair. There are no more floors now, just a single cavernous space. The sound of our footsteps changes, taking on a hollow, watery reverberation. The air is thick, the smell pungent.

I wind the flashlight until the dynamo hums and the bulb's burning bright as it can. I hold it out over the handrail, sweeping the darkness as we descend. Large-bore pressure pipes, their surfaces spackled with rust, circle the walls; others crisscross the open space between. Here and there gangways leave the stair, extending out to machines in an assortment of shapes and sizes. In the yellowing beam they all look old, decrepit.

Behind me Mags steps off onto one of the narrow catwalks. I turn around to see where she's going, but she's already lost to the darkness. I'm about to point the beam after her to light the way, but then I remember she doesn't need it. I lose her footsteps and for a few seconds there's nothing, but then I hear a tapping from somewhere above me that sounds like she's checking the level in one of the tanks. I stand there for a moment, uncertain what to do. I've had several weeks now to get used to how she and the kid can manage without the light, but the truth is I still find it a little unnerving.

I wind the flashlight and continue my descent. Less than a turn of the stair later the tread plate suddenly becomes slick and I feel my boot slide from under me. A jolt of adrenalin rushes my system and I grab for the handrail. The flashlight slips from my fingers, clatters off down the stair.

I take a deep breath and pull myself upright. From somewhere above I hear Mags, asking if I'm okay.

I call back that I'm fine.

I look down. The flashlight's come to rest on a narrow landing a few steps beneath me. I make my way down to retrieve it, gripping the handrail tighter now. I pick it up. The lens is cracked and when I shake it there's a rattle that wasn't there before, but at least it still seems to be working. I wind the handle. There's an unhappy grinding from somewhere within and for a moment the bulb flickers, but then it brightens. I point it over the edge. The beam reflects back off something dark, oily, and I see why the steps have suddenly become so treacherous, and where the smell's been coming from. Beneath me the staircase disappears into water. The bottom of the silo's flooded. I hold the beam close to the slowly undulating surface, but there's no way to tell how deep it is.

I shout up at Mags. A moment later her voice echoes back to me from somewhere in the blackness above. I point the flashlight to where I thought I heard her, and for a split second the beam picks out two pinpricks of silver, there and then immediately gone again.

The blood in my veins turns to ice water. An image flashes before me: a dark shape, spider-thin, slipping from behind an operator booth, and for a moment I just stand there, paralyzed with fear, just like when that thing attacked Ortiz in the basement of the hospital in Blacksburg. And then I'm bounding back up the stair. My mouth opens to shout a warning, but what comes out is wordless, incoherent. I feel Hicks' pistol bouncing on my hip, but the narrow steps are treacherous and I need my reaching hand for the rail.

Mags must sense the alarm in my voice because I hear her boots above me now, hurrying across the gangway. She meets me where it joins the stair.

'What's wrong?'

I push past her and point the flashlight along the

catwalk, searching for the thing I saw only seconds ago. But the gangway's empty, at least as far the beam will show me. I inch forward, holding it out in front of me. My other hand drops to the haft of the gun. Ahead the fuel tank Mags was checking slowly separates itself from the darkness, its rusting flanks disappearing up into the gloom. I keep going, all the way out to the silo's curving walls.

'What is it, Gabe?'

I sweep the beam over the guardrails, the grating, the blue-green copper. This is where it was, right here, I'm sure of it. But there's nothing; nowhere for anything to hide. I lift my hand from the pistol's grip, letting it slide back into the holster.

I feel her hand on my shoulder and I start. Another possibility occurs to me then, settling cold in my stomach. I swing the flashlight around, but she's too fast. Her hand closes around my wrist, so quick it surprises me. She pushes the beam away before I have a chance to see.

'Hey! Careful with that.'

She stares up at me, a quizzical expression on her face.

'You look like you've seen a ghost. What's wrong?'

I manage to stammer out something about the silo being flooded. She holds my hand for a second longer then lets it go.

'*That's* what freaked you out? I could have told you there was water down here as soon as we came through the airlock.'

She turns around and steps out of the beam, disappearing into the darkness beyond. I think I hear her boots on the stair, but it's hard to tell above the sound of my own breathing. When I point the flashlight over the guardrail it finds her crouched by the water's edge. She studies the oily surface for a moment, then comes back up to join me.

'It's okay. This far underground they'll have had to pump the water out, just like we did in the deeper parts of Eden. With the power off all this time it's seeped back in, that's all. Once we get the generator running the pumps should kick in and clear it out.'

I nod, like this is good news. She looks at me strangely, like she's wondering what it is I'm not telling her.

'Well, I guess we've seen as much as there is'. She dusts her hands off. 'Ready to head back up?'

I nod again, still distracted by what I think I've just seen. She studies me a moment longer, like she's still trying to work it out, then heads for the stair.

*

WE MAKE OUR WAY BACK up to the hatch, clamber through, then rejoin the spiraling stair. When we reach the mess I set the flashlight down on one of the tables and start digging in my pack for the last of my MREs while Mags wipes the dust from the old steel. I open the cartons, add a little water from my canteen to the chemical heaters to start the reaction and then leave the pouches to warm. When they're ready she tears the foil off one and starts poking at the contents with the plastic fork that came in the packet. She skewers something the carton says is a Chicken Chunk and holds it up.

'Hey, I've been meaning to ask. Do these taste funny to you?'

'Like what?'

'I dunno. Stale?' She shakes her head, like that's not it. 'Dull. Boring. Like it's missing something?

I shrug. My meal tastes like every other one I've had. She goes back to digging half-heartedly in the pouch for a few moments then abandons the Chicken Chunks in favor of the HOOAH! that came with them. I steal a glance across the table as she removes the wrapper. The flashlight with its freshly cracked lens sits further along the table. The sorry puddle of light it casts is slowly receding, but it's enough to see by. She looks okay; still a little thin perhaps, but the shadows have all but gone from her eyes. She finishes the candy bar and looks over at mine.

I slide it across the table towards her. She flashes me a smile and then unwraps it. When she's done she busies herself fixing a coffee. We haven't bothered with a fire, so all that's left to warm the water is the heater from the MRE carton. She takes a sip, grimaces, then looks

223

around the room.

'So what do you think?'

My mind's elsewhere, still fretting over what I think I saw in the plant room, so at first I miss what she says. She glances around, the gesture clearly meant to encompass more than just the mess. She looks at me expectantly.

'Well, it's thirteen stories, just like Hicks said. He just forgot to mention most of them don't start until you're almost that far underground.'

She raises the mug to her lips, letting her gaze rove one more time. I find myself stealing glances at her eyes, searching for anything unusual there. But there's nothing. The memory of what I thought I saw in the plant room is already growing less certain. Did I imagine it? Was it just my own eyes playing tricks on me?

I'm waiting for the voice to chime in; it seems like just the sort of thing it would have an opinion on. But for once it stays quiet.

'It seems old, doesn't it? Maybe even older than Eden was. What do you think they built it for?'

I force myself to pay attention.

'I dunno. This far underground, the shielding on the walls, the way everything's mounted, it was definitely built to survive a blast. It must have something to do with that equipment up there.'

She takes another sip from the coffee, sets it on the table.

'There's bound to be a set of manuals. I bet they'll tell us.'

She looks right at me. Her pupils are definitely wide, but then the only light we have is from the flashlight's tiny bulb. And they're dark, normal, with no trace of what I thought I saw, earlier.

I must have imagined it. It was pitch black down there, after all. And I had been staring into the floodwaters. Maybe what I saw was the afterglow of the flashlight, reflected off the oily surface.

That would explain it.

I wait for the voice to contradict me, but it remains silent.

A trick of the light, that's all it was.

I nod to myself, as if to confirm it. I'm being foolish, letting my imagination run away with me. And right now there are plenty of other things I need to concern myself with. I look at the handful of tables arranged around us. I certainly wasn't expecting anything on the scale of Mount Weather, but this place is smaller than I had imagined. *Way* smaller. The dorms only sleep forty-eight, and that's assuming two people bunking together, which would be pretty cramped. *Seriously* cramped. I'm not sure the cells are even as big as the ones we had in Eden.

'It certainly doesn't look like it was designed to hold many people.'

I say it mostly to myself. Mags reaches for the mug again, raises it to her lips.

'Good thing there aren't many of us, then. At least it's warm, and there's food, and water. As long as we have those things we can make it work.'

Two levels devoted to stores *is* good. Not a lifetime's worth of food, but several winters at least, as long as we're careful. I realize I should feel better about that than I do.

'Yeah, but only cans. Isn't that strange?'

She shrugs.

'I guess. I'm just glad we won't have to clear out stuff that's spoiled. Do you remember how long that took us in Mount Weather, and we didn't have that stair to contend with.'

I nod, still a little distracted.

'I'll need to check the stores, properly.' There's

bound to be other things we'll need. And now that Durham's off limits I have to figure out where else I can go to get them.

She reaches across the table for my hand.

'You can do that tomorrow. Come on, let's go pick out our room.'

She drains what's left of her coffee while I bag our trash, and then we head back out on to the stair. I stop to charge the flashlight. The handle sticks and grinds for a few turns, like there's still something amiss with its innards, but then the bulb brightens. I point it along the gangway, but Mags has already disappeared into the darkness. I hesitate a moment then set off after her. When I reach the dorms she's waiting for me by the guardrail.

'Okay, which one?'

I sweep the light over the bulkhead doors that circle the landing. The cells all look identical, so I settle on the closest one.

'Excellent choice.'

She pushes it open and steps through, but instead of following her in I wait. It's been weeks since we've been alone together, without either the kid or the Juvies nearby. I should be looking forward to this. But somehow I can't help my thoughts returning to what I thought I saw in the plant room earlier.

I shake my head.

I'm being stupid.

I take a deep breath and step over the threshold.

The cots bolted to the walls are too narrow to share so she takes the thin mattresses off, lays both side-by-side on the floor, then latches the frames out of the way. I unpack our sleeping bag while she wriggles out of her thermals and slips under the quilted material. I set the flashlight down so I can get undressed, not paying attention to where I point it. Her eyes narrow at the

226

beam, and in the second before she reaches to turn it away I glimpse again what I had almost convinced myself I had imagined down in the plant room.

I freeze, one foot still caught in the leg of my pants, but she's busy pointing the flashlight at the wall and doesn't notice. The pale cone of light reflects dully off the tired steel. Even as I watch it shrinks, the weakening bulb shifting from yellow to orange as it dies.

'Hurry up, slow poke.'

I finish getting undressed, making much more of a deal than I need to of folding my clothes. She props herself up on one elbow, watching my progress from inside the sleeping bag.

'Really? *That's* your priority right now? Should I be worried, Gabe?'

She says it like it's a joke, but when I look down the smile that goes with it is less certain. She holds back the flap. I don't know what else to do so I climb in beside her.

The flashlight flickers for a few seconds, steadies, then finally blinks out. For a moment afterimages of the dying bulb swirl across my vision, then they too fade, leaving only blackness. I close my eyes then open them again, like I do when I'm trying to get them to adjust. It makes no difference, though; I can't see a thing. We lie there for a while, barely touching, then she takes my wrist, guides my hand to her side. After a moment she moves it down to her hip. Where there should be cotton my fingers feel only skin.

I think of the nights I have spent since we quit Eden, trying to find a way past that narrow stretch of material; the daylight hours spent in contemplation of how it might be achieved. My efforts never came to anything. Whatever subtlety, distraction or boldness I attempted, the result was always the same: my hand would gently be relocated elsewhere.

I let my fingers rest where she has placed them.

All I can think is how cold she feels.

She murmurs something I can't make out, shifts closer. I feel her arms slip up behind my neck. Her face is only inches from mine but the darkness is complete, impenetrable; I can't make out anything there.

But she can see you.

She stretches up, pressing into me, and now I feel her breath on my neck. An image appears, unbidden, the flashes of silver I saw earlier. I feel myself tense.

She pauses. I screw my eyes shut, trying to push it away, but the image reappears, and this time the voice returns with it. It effects a drawl, the last thing Hicks said to me as we stepped out of The Greenbrier's tunnel.

When the time comes there'll be no warning. It'll be like a switch has been flipped.

I know it's Mags, but I can't help it. As she leans in to kiss me again I flinch.

She stops.

'What's wrong, Gabe?'

My heart's pounding and there's a tightness in my chest, a weight, just beneath my ribcage, like I'd get when I'd go out in the tunnel in Eden.

'Nothing. I…I guess I'm just a little tired.'

I feel her pull back. I can't see a thing, but in my mind's eye I picture her, examining my face, searching it for proof of the lie I've just told. It won't be hard to find. I'm sixteen years old; most of the time it feels like I was standing *way* too close to the front of the line when hormones were being handed out. Nobody knows that better than Mags. This isn't an invitation she'd ever have expected to be declined.

She exhales slowly, and then for what seems like an eternity there's just the darkness and the weight of her stare. Finally she turns around. I slip my arm hesitantly around her waist, but this time she doesn't press back into me.

HE SITS ON HIS SLEEPING BAG, his back to the wall. The lobby is small, narrow. A row of bank machines at one end, their long-dead screens gray, filmed with dust. At the other a small trashcan, lying on its side. Scraps of crumpled paper spill out onto the moldering carpet.

The remains of his meal lay spread out around him. He picks at the pouch's contents with the plastic fork. The girl says he has to eat as much of it as he can, so he takes another bite. He tells himself it's not so bad. It doesn't taste of much at all, really, but if you stir it like she showed him at least it's not gritty, and that helps.

He looks out into the parking lot. The girl was supposed to be back by now. The tall boy's gone to get her. He wonders if he should have told him about the others he met, in the shopping mall. But then the boy might have tried to find them, and the girl with the pink hair said that wouldn't have been a good idea.

He takes another forkful of the food, chews it slowly. Even mixed up properly it's not as nice as the candy bar. He eyes the HOOAH!, still in its wrapper, sitting on the sleeping bag next to his goggles.

The boy with the dark skin is gone now, so he doesn't have to wear them anymore. The boy stayed as long as he could, but eventually it got too cold and he had to go back inside. He offered to make him a fire. The girl lets him build them so he's gotten quite good at it. He knows how to stack the firewood and where to place the kindling, and to blow on the flame when it catches to so it will spread up through the branches and not die. But the boy said they couldn't have one, not out here. Somebody might see.

He looks out to the parking lot. The wind has picked

up; it sends snow swirling around the abandoned car.

A fire would have been fine. No one could be out in that.

At least not one of them.

He likes the boy with the dark skin, though. He seems okay. He was nervous at first, even though he tried not to show it. But after a while he rested his gun against the wall and sat down. Not close, but not as far as he could have sat either. He even spoke to him a few times. Mostly just to ask what he could see, so not a conversation exactly, but better than silence. Much better. Back in the cage he wasn't allowed to talk at all.

The other boy came out to them a few times, but he never stayed long. He kept to the far corner, clutching his rifle, and pretended to stare out into the darkness. He was pretty scared. He could smell it, even from all the way at the other end of the lobby.

After the boy with the dark skin went back inside he could hear them, whispering their questions.

What was it like?

Did it say anything?

Weren't you frightened?

The boy who stayed in the corner said he wasn't; he had a gun. The boy with the dark skin told him to shut up. After that it had gone quiet again.

They'd get used to him, that's what the girl said.

But it's been a long time now.

Outside the wind gusts against the glass, flexing the pane. He catches his reflection as it shifts. Maybe if he looked more like them. He tilts his head, studying the still-unfamiliar face that stares back at him. The grimy glass makes for a poor mirror, but it shows him enough. The shadows that darken his eyes seem to be fading at last, but slowly. He reaches up, takes off the cap the girl makes him wear, runs the fingers of one hand over his scalp. He feels something there, like the beginnings of stubble. It is hard to tell just by looking. The hair that grows there is white, just like his skin. He can't be sure, but he doesn't think that was the color it was, before.

He looks down at the food pouch, eyeing it guiltily. He will definitely finish it later. He hesitates for a moment and then reaches for the candy bar. He's busy tearing at the wrapper with his teeth, so at first he doesn't hear the footsteps. Then the door creaks open behind him. He drops the HOOAH! and scrabbles for his goggles just as the beam from a flashlight dances into the lobby.

The boy with the curly hair steps through, zipping up his parka.

'What're you still doing out here?'

He turns away from the light while he sorts out his goggles. Once he's got them situated he looks back at the boy and says he's keeping watch.

The boy hugs his arms to his sides and glances back over his shoulder, to where the others are huddled around the fire.

'Aren't you cold?'

He shakes his head. The truth is he's not. It is colder out here, but it doesn't bother him. Not really.

The boy stands there for a moment, as though he's considering that. He steps back into the other room but then he returns, carrying an armful of branches from the firewood they collected earlier. He dumps them on the ground and then heads over to the corner and bends to the trashcan.

'We're not supposed to have a fire.'

The boy doesn't look up from his task.

'Nobody's coming now.'

He returns with a handful of crumpled ATM receipts. The flames are reluctant at first, but slowly they creep up through the kindling and then start to lick at the wicker of blackened limbs above. When he's certain they've caught he sits back on his haunches and dusts off his hands, but he makes no move to leave. He watches the fire for a while, as though measuring his work.

'So what's with your eyes? Are they troubling you?'

He shakes his head. The tall boy asked him that too, when he first started wearing the goggles. But the truth is they're not, or at least nothing like they used to. The light outside sometimes hurts, but only in the very middle of the day, and even then not much. When he's wearing his goggles he hardly even notices it.

'Why do you wear those all the time then?'

He shrugs. The boy looks at him for a while like he might press him on it, but he doesn't.

'Is it true you can see out there?'

He hesitates. Being able to see in the dark is another way he's different. But the tall boy already told the boy with the dark skin about that, so they probably all know by now. He nods.

The boy stares into the fire for a while as though he's considering this. He looks like he has another question he wants to ask, but it takes a long time for him to get to it.

'Mags too?'

He's not sure what to say. He's pretty certain the girl doesn't want the others to think she's different, any more than he does. That's why she wears the cap and pretends with the flashlight. But he doesn't think this boy means her any harm. He sees how he looks at her, when he thinks no one's watching. Sometimes he feels a little sad for him.

He nods again.

The boy with the curly hair keeps looking at the fire. Eventually he says *Okay, then*, as if to himself, and then he gets up and goes back inside.

I OPEN MY EYES SLOWLY, still fuggy with sleep. The cold darkness, the thin mattress, the unyielding steel, all are familiar, and in those first uncertain moments between sleeping and waking I think I'm back in my cell in Eden, waiting for the buzzer to sound, and everything that has happened since we left, all just fragments of a dream that, however vivid, will soon begin to fade.

I pull the sleeping bag around me. Not so much a dream as a nightmare. I close my eyes and wait for it to recede. The dream is stubborn, however; I find myself wishing for the bulkhead lamp to blink on and banish it. But for long seconds nothing happens. I open my eyes again as it slowly begins to dawn on me where I am.

I stretch out one hand, sweeping the cold metal for the flashlight. I pick it up and crank the stubby handle. It graunches a complaint but after a few turns the bulb starts to glow, slowly illuminating my cramped sleeping quarters. I play the beam over the worn steel. Even with the bunks latched out of the way it feels tight in here, confined. The reluctant cone of light continues its journey, coming to rest on a pile of clothes by the door. I stare at them for a moment, vaguely aware that something's not right. Far too neatly folded for my hand. And Mags certainly isn't in the habit of picking up after me.

Mags.

The thought of her brings everything else back. I swing the flashlight around, but I'm alone. I struggle out of the sleeping bag, pulling my clothes on as I stagger out to the landing.

I waited until she'd lapsed into whatever passes for sleep for her now, then I checked her crucifix again. I had no reason for doing it other than habit; I already knew what I'd find. After that I just lay there, waiting, trying to keep images of things I have seen in dark places from popping into my head. She woke with a start some time later. I listened while her breathing calmed, pretending I was asleep. I don't think she was fooled, but she mustn't have had anything to say to me either, because she didn't call me on it. For a long while we just stayed like that, not speaking. I hadn't meant to, but I guess at some point I must have drifted off.

And now she's gone.

I lean over the guardrail and call out to her, but the only answer I get is my voice echoing back up through the silo. I tell myself there's no reason to be concerned. She'll have got bored just lying there and gone off to do something, maybe see if she can find those manuals she was talking about, that's all. But my heart's beating a little faster than it should as I cross the short gangway and start down the stair.

The steps spiral down, past the dorms below, then the showers. I call out as I go, but still there's no answer. The voice pipes up; it has something it wants me to see. It shows me a long tunnel, a flashbulb image of something pale, impossibly thin, bounding towards me. I screw my eyes shut, trying to banish it, but the voice grows bold with the darkness. It shows me another. The basement of a hospital this time; a dark shape slipping from behind an operator booth.

I grip the handrail.

I'm being stupid. It's Mags. She wouldn't hurt me.

Marv this time, on his knees in the snow, silver eyes staring back at me from inside the shadow of his hood as he slips the hunting rifle from his shoulder. My hand drops to my hip. I realize I've left Hicks' pistol back in the cell.

The voice wonders whether it might be a good idea to

go fetch it.

I put that shameful thought from my mind and climb through the hatch into the plant room. At the bottom of the ladder I pause, listening. I think I hear a sound now, drifting up from below. A tapping: hollow, metallic. It stops for a second and then resumes.

I rejoin the stair. Every few steps I call out; still there's no answer. I keep following the flashlight around, forcing my boots to continue their downward journey. The air grows thick, dank. I feel like I should be close to the bottom, but I've forgotten to count, so I can't be certain. I listen for the sound of lapping water. It's hard to hear over my own breathing, though.

The tapping grows louder. It seems to be coming from the end of one of the gangways. I point the flashlight there, but whatever might be causing it is beyond the beam's reach. I crank the handle. Something inside grinds in protest and then the dynamo whirs; for a few seconds the bulb grows brighter.

I step off the stair and make my way along the catwalk. An access panel lies propped against the guardrail, the old steel dented, scarred. I find her just beyond it, lying on her back on the metal grating, peering up into the belly of one of the ancient machines, an assortment of tools spread out around her. There's a windup flashlight among them, but she must not have need of it because she's allowed it to go out.

I call her name again. There's a pause and then she puts down whatever it is she's working on and starts to wriggle herself out. My heart races again as she sits up, but she gets a hand up to ward off the beam before I have a chance to see whatever might be there.

'Point that somewhere else, will you?'

I hesitate for a second, then let the beam fall to the grating.

'What is it, Gabriel?'

The long form of my name; never a good sign.

'I...I was calling for you.'

'I heard.'

I want to say something about what happened last night, about what I saw in Starkly, about what might be about to happen to her. But how do you begin with that? *Hey Mags, guess what? The scanner I thought would cure you? Yeah, it didn't do that after all. Turns out you and the kid both still have one-way tickets to Furytown.*

In the end I just point the flashlight at the generator and ask if she needs help.

She tilts her head and stares at me for a moment, like she wants to know if that's really the question I want answered. When I don't come up with another she just shakes her head and slides back under the old machine.

I tell her I'll go back and fetch the others, then. But the only answer I get is the sound of the tapping resuming.

*

I CLIMB BACK UP THROUGH THE HATCH, trading the
plant room's depths for the compressed levels above. At
the dorms I step off, grab my parka and backpack from
the cell, then continue my spiraling journey up through
the silo. When I reach the concrete shaft I pause to crank
the flashlight. The handle sticks but then the bulb burns
brighter, throwing confused shadows over the rust-
streaked walls that shift and merge as I climb. Tight
spaces don't bother me anything like they used to, but
there's a weight that has lodged itself behind my
breastbone, an ache that is at the same time hollow and
heavy, just like I'd get when I'd step into Eden's tunnel.
I quicken my stride, anxious to be outside again now.

At last the shaft ends and I hurry along the
passageway and into the airlock. I push back the outer
door, step outside, and for a moment I just stand there,
waiting for that feeling I'd get when I'd crawl out
through the portal, like an invisible burden had been
lifted. But the weight in my chest remains.

I look up to the sky. Somewhere off to the east
dawn's already breaking. The light that filters through is
gray, flat, but sufficient to grant me my first view of our
new home. There's not much to look at. Blackened trees
circle the compound, pressing themselves up against the
rusting chain-link, like they might still hold a grudge for
the clearing they were once forced to concede. The part
of Mount Weather that was above ground was busy with
buildings: storage sheds, a barracks, a motor pool, the
control tower; even a hangar for a helicopter, but here
there's nothing other than the two huge concrete cubes
that guard the entrance and a single tattered windsock,
clanking listlessly against its pole. I guess I shouldn't be

surprised. Mount Weather was an underground city; the silo's only a fraction of its size. I can't escape the feeling something's missing, all the same; something that should be here, but isn't.

I pull my hood up and set off, heading for the gap in the fence that marks the entrance. When I reach the guard hut I stop and turn to scan the compound again, but whatever it is won't come to me, and right now I have other things on my mind. I clamber over the security barrier and make my way in among the trees, following the tracks Mags and I made last night. Without them I'm not sure I'd be able to find my way, even in what passes for daylight. I don't know how she managed it, in the dark.

Yes you do.

An image, sudden, unwanted: a pair of silvered pupils, caught for an instant in the flashlight's beam.

I squeeze my eyes shut against it. It doesn't mean she's sick. She can't be. I've seen firsthand what that looks like: by the end Marv wasn't able to lift a boot from the snow. She hiked all the way to Durham and back in a day, a distance he couldn't have covered at his best, and it took nothing from her; I couldn't keep up with her last night.

I hold tight to that thought as I pick my way between the withered trunks. But whatever comfort it might bring, the faithless voice won't allow it. It starts to whisper.

Hicks was pretty quick, too, remember?

Hicks knew he had the virus, though. He told me he could feel it, working its way through him. Mags says she feels fine.

The voice shows me another image. This time it's Finch's fury, crouched at the back of its cell. I shake my head, desperate to dislodge it. If that were going to happen it would've happened already. It's been weeks

239

since she and the kid came through the scanner.

I have little more than hope to back that theory up, however, and the voice knows it. I try and hush it, but it won't be quieted. It has things to say now, and it means to be heard.

You thought it would be that easy?

I know what's coming next. I shout at it to shut up, but it makes no difference; it carries on regardless.

Kane launched every missile he had, enough to turn the night sky bright as day.

I quicken my pace until my snowshoes are pounding the snow. But the voice is in my head; it can't be outrun any more than I might hope to silence it.

Hicks had it burned from his flesh, but that didn't work either.

I reach the end of the woods, strike out into open fields.

Gilbey's a scientist. *She knows more about the virus than anyone. She* invented *it. She's been searching years for a cure and she hasn't found one yet.*

You really thought you *could do better?*

I force my legs to work faster, anything to escape it. My lungs burn with the effort. Sweat soaks my back, my legs, more than my thermals can hope to wick away. It runs down my face inside my goggles, stinging my eyes. I yank down the thin cotton mask I wear, desperate for more air. And still the voice continues, over and over, a never-ending loop inside my head.

You think the few minutes you got Mags in the scanner could do what Gilbey couldn't?

How could you?

You don't understand how it works, any of it.

You're just a kid.

I have no answer for any of it. I only know what happened to Marv, and Hicks and Finch's fury can't happen to her.

There's no reason.
It just *can't*.

I keep it up for as long as I can. My legs are accustomed to the snow, but not the pace I've set them. I feel the muscles there come to the end of their endurance, become unreliable. I catch an edge with a snowshoe, stagger into a drift. I throw my hands out against the fall, but I land awkwardly, my arms sinking deep into powder. I stay like that for a while, just sucking in air. The voice has finally fallen silent, but its work is done. A cold darkness wraps itself around my heart.

At last I struggle to my feet. Snow has found its way inside my mittens; it sticks to my cheeks, my mask, my goggles. I don't bother to dust it off. I point my snowshoes toward the road, but my knees have turned to rubber. It takes longer than it ought to make it the final few hundred yards back to the SunTrust Bank.

As I stagger into the parking lot I see the kid, sitting by himself in the ATM lobby. He stares at me through those goggles. I should have paid more attention to that, I see it now. When did he first take to wearing them at night? I try to remember, but the days since we left Mount Weather have blended into each other and I can't be sure. I unsnap my snowshoes, meaning to go in and ask him about it, but as I step out of them Jake appears at the door, blocking my way. He looks past me, over my shoulder.

'Where's Mags?'

I tell him we went to check out the bunker; that she's back there right now, working on getting the power back on. He stares at me like I might have sprouted another head overnight.

'Seriously, you just left her, by herself? What if something's hiding in there, like when you went to Mount Weather?'

Something hiding.

If only he knew how absurd that sounds. I feel something inside my chest start to convulse, and I realize I might actually laugh. I can feel it, bubbling up inside me. I have to grit my teeth to suppress it.

Mags *is* that thing, you muscle-bound moron.

Or soon will be.

Jake's still glaring at me, waiting for an answer. In the room behind the Juvies have stopped whatever they're doing to tune in to this latest drama. I take a breath, start to explain that it's okay. Fearrington wasn't that big; we checked everywhere. It's clear he doesn't care much for that explanation, however. He turns on his heels and heads back inside before I've got more than a couple of words out. I stand there for a moment, aware that the Juvies are all watching me.

I feel the heat rising in my cheeks. I follow him inside, meaning to make him listen to what I have to say, whether or not he cares to hear it. But before I've made it half way across the room Lauren steps into my path. She slips one hand through my arm and the next thing I know I'm being led over to where the rest of them are huddled around the fire.

'So, Gabe, what's it like?'

I look at her, distracted, for a moment unsure what she means.

She tilts her head, smiles.

'The bunker?'

I glance over at Jake. He's stuffing his sleeping bag into his pack.

She squeezes my arm and I feel the anger beginning to subside. I study the faces gathered around me. They stare up, anxious for details of our new home.

'Well it's a little smaller than Mount Weather.' *Way* smaller. 'But there's food, and water.'

I'm not sure what else to say. I find myself repeating

the words Mags told me, the night before, in Fearrington's mess.

'I...I think we can make it work.'

WHILE THE JUVIES ARE PACKING UP I head back out to the lobby. The kid's sitting under one of the ATMs, smoothing out a candy bar wrapper he's picked up from somewhere. I check no one's within earshot then I squat down next to him, ask how he's feeling. He nods and says fine, but when I reach for his goggles he pulls back.

'You have to let me.'

He looks at me uncertainly.

'It'll be alright, I promise.'

I lift the goggles onto his forehead. He squints a little against the light but keeps his eyes open. I dig in the pocket of my parka for the flashlight and crank the handle. It grinds for a turn, then the bulb starts to glow. When it's as bright as I can get it I hold it close. The beam barely competes with the light filtering through the clouds, but when I shift it back and forth I catch a glimpse of what I knew I'd find there. I was ready for it, but my heart picks up a little all the same.

'You're feeling okay, though? No different?'

He shakes his head.

'Are you going to tell the others?'

I think about that for a moment. There's no prizes for guessing how the Juvies will react if they find out about Mags and the kid; there's a good chance they'll make them leave. I'm not prepared for that, not yet. I shake my head, tell him to put the goggles back on. He pulls them down, settles them in place.

I flick the flashlight off.

'You'd let me know, wouldn't you? I mean if you felt even a little bit strange?'

He nods, then reaches inside his jacket for the dog tags he wears. He holds them up. The thin slivers of pressed steel rotate slowly on the end of their chain. The metal's still smooth, but I hadn't expected it to be otherwise. I examine them, mostly because he seems to want me to, then I tell him to put them away.

The Juvies have no tricks up their sleeve; there's no sudden burst of speed they've been holding back to carry us over the finish line. For once I'm grateful for it. I have some thinking to do before I bring them to our new home.

I settle to their pace, letting my snowshoes follow the trail I left on my way back to the Suntrust Bank. The kid runs on ahead. Every now and then he stops and turns to look at me, like he's wondering what's holding us up. The Target, outside Warren, not long after we set out; that's when he took to wearing them night and day. How many weeks ago now? Four? More? I really should have paid more attention.

He says he feels fine, but I'm not sure how much comfort I can take from that. The voice has an answer. It replays Hicks' words, the same ones I heard last night, in the cell with Mags.

There'll be no warning. It'll be like a switch has been flipped.

It shows me the thing that got Ortiz again, in the basement of the hospital in Blacksburg. How fast it had moved; not even Hicks had been quick enough to save him. I imagine what something like that would be like, loose inside the silo. I set the container with the virus down in the snow, pull the mask I wear down, take a breath, then another. I can't let my thoughts get dragged that way; no good will come of it.

I pick up the container and set off again. There has to be a solution; something I can do to fix this. I call up everything I know about the virus, anything Marv ever told me, anything I read in the newspaper clippings I used to collect, anything I might have heard Hicks say. It doesn't take long; there's not that much. I lay it all out in my head anyway, examining each piece of information, like I'm trying to find a place for it in a puzzle. It does no good, other than to remind me how little I understand of any of it. I keep returning to the same conclusion. There's only one person who might be able to help: the person who knows more about the virus than anyone; the person who invented it.

The one who infected Mags in the first place.

That can't be the answer, though, and even if it is, there's no way I'd ever convince Mags to come with me back to The Greenbrier. Not after what happened to her there.

I pull the mask back up and set off after the kid.

There has to be another way.

I just need to figure it out.

It's already late morning by the time we make it to the Mount Gilead Church Road. I lead the Juvies single file across the open fields and in among the trees, picking my way carefully between the withered trunks, until at last I spot the raised security barrier ahead. I wait with the kid while one by one they clamber over. When the last of them has made it in I look down at him. The barrier's too high for him to clear; it's almost as tall as he is. But when I hold out my arms to hoist him up he just shakes his head.

I tell him he can make his own way over then. I throw my leg over and slide down the other side. I send the rest of them off in the direction of the two concrete cubes, then I pick up the container with the virus and bring it behind the guard shack. I set it down in the snow, lay it carefully on its side and scoop armfuls of powder over it until there's no trace of the olive drab plastic. I'll need to come up with a better hiding place,

246

maybe somewhere deep in the woods, where it'd never be found. That's for later, though, once I've got the Juvies inside.

I head back, planning to haul the kid over the barrier if I have to. But when I make my way around front of the guard shack he's standing on top of it, holding his snowshoes. He looks at me for a moment then slides down the other side, steps back into them and starts making his way across the clearing. I stare at the barrier a moment longer, unsure how he did it, then set off after him.

Up ahead the Juvies have gathered by the entrance. I follow the tracks they've left in their wake, a swathe of churned up snow cutting through the smooth, unmarked powder. Sometimes when your mind's focused elsewhere solutions to other problems you didn't even think you were still working on float to the surface. It suddenly occurs to me what's missing from the compound.

Vent shaft covers.

I look around, searching for the telltale bumps in the snow, but there's nothing. Those grilles in the shaft were definitely for ventilation; I could feel the breeze when I placed my hands over them. The pipes must lead to the surface somewhere; if not inside the perimeter then maybe beyond the fence, among the trees. I look at the blackened trunks pressing up against the chain link, wondering whether that's something I should be worrying about too. But the vents were way too small for someone to crawl down. No one's getting into Fearrington the way I snuck back into Eden.

I unsnap my snowshoes and make my way into the narrow opening. The keypad accepts the code and I haul the blast door open. As I step into the airlock I realize I'm holding my breath. I'm hoping for the lights in the passageway beyond to be on, but when the inner door swings back it's to darkness. Mags hasn't got the power back on yet.

Assuming that's what she's still working on.

I tell the voice to hush. The kid's still fine. He got the virus way before she did; carried it far longer. It makes no sense she'd turn before he did.

You're sure about that? He was taking Gilbey's medicine a long time too, remember?

I close my eyes, pushing that thought from my mind.

'Everything okay, Gabe?'

When I open my eyes Lauren's standing next to me, a concerned look on her face.

I nod quickly.

'Yeah. Absolutely. Just letting my eyes adjust.'

The kid squeezes past, hurries along the corridor. When he gets to the stair he pushes the goggles up onto his forehead and looks over. He stays like that for a moment and then starts down the shaft without so much as a backward glance; by the time I reach the gangway I've already lost him to the turn of the stair. The pitter-patter of footsteps drifts up, echoing off the concrete. He hasn't bothered with his flashlight, but if the darkness impedes him he shows no sign of it.

Lauren leans over the guardrail.

'How does he...?'

She says it softly, under her breath, so I doubt the question's directed at me. Which is just as well, seeing as the answer I have isn't one she'd much care to hear. Behind her the Juvies are already crowding into the corridor. I dig in my pocket for the flashlight and hold it up.

'The power's still out. You'll need these.'

There's the inevitable shuffling while they fumble in pockets or backpacks for the windups they each carry, but finally I hear the whir of the first dynamo being cranked, followed seconds later by others. It rises to a soft drone then one by one the flashlights blink on, casting overlapping shadows that shimmy and bounce along the passageway's concrete walls.

We make our way out onto the stair. The old metal complains at the weight of so many boots, but it holds steady. Behind me flashlights curl up into the darkness, a raggedy helix of fireflies. I lead them down. For a long while there's just the long drop of the concrete shaft, but finally we reach the upper levels and the silo opens out.

Mags must hear us coming, or maybe the kid fetches her, because when we reach the mess she's waiting. She sits on one of the tables, her boots dripping water onto the worn tread plate. Her fingernails are dark with something that might be grease or maybe engine oil. A smudge of it marks her cheek, another her temple. A single flashlight rests on the table next to her, the yellowing bulb casting weary shadows over the scuffed steel. The kid stands to one side, watching our approach.

She looks up as she sees me, but her expression's hard to read. Behind me the Juvies continue to file down out of the darkness. As they see her they come to a shuffling halt and a dozen flashlights swing in her direction. I hurry across the gangway and stand in front of her. I turn to face them, holding a hand up against the beams.

'Hey, point those somewhere else, would you?'

There's a moment's hesitation, then one by one the beams drop. The Juvies hang back, gathered on the gangway or bunched up on the stair; no one seems keen to follow me into the mess. I step to one side, her cue to go on. But for a moment she just stares at me, like she's wondering what the point of all that was.

'Well, there's plenty of diesel.' She pauses, then continues. 'The problem is the generator; the flooding's done more damage than I thought.' Uneasy murmurs greet that news; fuel or not, if we can't get the power on this is going to be a shorter stay than any of us had bargained for. She raises her voice. 'I think I can fix it; it might just take a while.'

'Like when we got to Mount Weather,' I add, like anyone needs reminding of the bright, underground city I traded us for this place. 'It took a few days to get everything working there too, remember?'

I study the faces crowded onto the gangway, assembled on the stair. They've already seen as much as they need to of our new home and I can tell they don't care for it. It's right there in their furrowed brows, the turn of their mouths, expressions even I can read. I can't say as I blame them. I don't care much for it either, and it was me who brought us here.

Mags lifts the flashlight from the table and stands, then makes her way past me to the stair. The kid hurries after her, like he's worried he might get left behind. When she reaches the gangway she stops. It takes a second for Lauren to realize she means to get by and then there's confusion as she tries to get out of the way. Those behind shuffle back, pressing themselves against the guardrail or retreating up the stair. Mags takes a step back, allowing Lauren and a few of the others forward into the mess. When the gangway's clear she squeezes the kid's shoulder and they cross. For long seconds their boots echo up out of the darkness and then it goes quiet again.

'Okay, well, I guess we'd best get settled in. Dorms are three levels down. Everyone gets their own...' - I'm about to say *cell* but catch myself just in time - '...room.' I don't have it in me to sound cheery, and even if I did, I'm not sure it'd do much good.

There's a pause and then those nearest the front turn towards the stair. As they start to make their way down I remember I'm not done; I have one more piece of bad news for them. I'd prefer not to have to deliver it so quick on the heels of their arrival, but there's really no helping it. I take a step forward, hold a hand up.

'But before you go I need you to empty your packs.'

Jake looks at me suspiciously.

'Why?'

'I still need to do a proper count, but I reckon there's food here to last us a few winters, as long as we're careful.' I pause, letting that one piece of good news sink in. 'But it's in cans.'

A groan travels up the stair. After a decade in Eden they know all about C-rations. What comes in the MRE pouches may not be great, but it's way tastier than anything you'll find in a tin, at least one that has *U.S Army* stamped on it.

Lauren looks around, and I get the sense that's she's taking a measure of things, like she did by the lake in Mount Weather, right before we voted to leave.

'Why can't we just finish off what we brought, Gabe? I mean we're here now, right? We've made it. We'll be eating out of cans soon enough.'

I see heads nodding, murmurs of agreement. I close my eyes. Maybe she's right. There can't be much of our travelling rations left, now; does it really matter if we eat the last of them? I have a much more immediate problem to worry about.

It's Jake who answers for me.

'Because at some point we'll be leaving again, Lauren. And when that time comes every ounce of food we can carry will matter. So all of you, just do as he says: hand them over.'

The Juvies shuffle to the tables and start unloading their packs. When the last of them have been emptied there's even less than I had hoped for, just a few pitiful stacks of cartons. Jake looks at each for a few seconds, like he might be counting what's there. He turns to me.

'Just to be clear though, these are for when we leave.'

A few of the Juvies look puzzled, but I have no trouble working out what he means. In Eden MREs were in short supply. Marv and I used to get them from Quartermaster, for when we'd go out scavenging. I also had my own deal going on with Amy and some of the other Juvies who worked the kitchens; they'd get them for me in exchange for stuff I'd fetch from the outside. But for everyone else they were rationed pretty tight; before Mount Weather I doubt Jake or any of the other Juvies who worked the farms had seen one in years.

I shake my head.

'I'll be eating the same food as you while we're here, Jake. We all will. Nobody's getting any special treatment.'

He holds my gaze a while longer, like he's not sure how satisfied he is with that answer, but in the end he just points his flashlight toward the stair and starts making his way down. One by one the others follow, until there's no one left in the mess but me and Lauren. Eventually she swings her pack onto her shoulder and goes to follow them. As she's about to step off the gangway she stops and turns around, offering me an apologetic smile.

'I'm sorry, Gabe. I didn't mean to cause trouble, about the food, I mean. I just thought...'

'It's alright, Lauren.'

She stands there for a second, then she bobs her head, smiles again.

'It'll be okay, you'll see.'

I nod, like of course she's right. She looks at me for a second longer, then turns and sets off down the stair after the others.

I WALK OVER to one of the tables, drag out a chair. I
slump into it and sit there for a while, just staring at the
scuffed steel.

What just happened, with Mags and the flashlights,
that was close. Until I've figured out what to do I need
to find a way to keep her and the kid apart from the
others, as much as possible. The flooding in the plant
room, maybe it'll turn out to be a blessing. She'll be
working on the generator till she gets it running; after
that there'll be other machinery needs fixing too. Who
knows how long that might take? The kid, he won't
leave her side, and the Juvies won't venture down there;
they'll want to stay out of her way, much as they can. I
think of them just now, shoving themselves back up the
stair to let her pass.

It's hardly a plan, but it'll have to do while I come up
with one. I push the chair back, head for the gangway. I
make my way down, not really sure where I'm going,
just letting my boots find their own way. When I look up
again I'm at the stores. I stop. Row after row of metal
shelves, each laden with boxes, stretching back into
darkness. I had planned to inventory what's there
anyway, and counting things has always helped. Maybe
it'll be like with the vent shaft covers earlier, outside in
the compound. If I can just take my mind off Mags and
the kid, even for a little while, perhaps the answer will
come to me.

I cross the gangway and step in among the shelves. I
tear a strip of card from the lid of the nearest box and
make my way along the aisle, a nub of pencil from my
pocket in one hand, the flashlight in the other. I shine the
beam over the stacked rations, wiping dust from their

flanks so I can read what's printed there. Occasionally I drag one down, to confirm the contents match, but mostly I keep counting, not wanting to give my thoughts a chance to catch up. When I reach the end of the first aisle I hurry on to the next without stopping. It doesn't take me long to finish the upper level. As soon as I'm done I move down to the one below.

A half-hour later I come to the end of the last shelf. I look back along the stacks of boxes. It took me the best part of a week to go through everything that was in Mount Weather's stores, and when I was done my lists had filled a notebook. I glance down at the card. My scribbles don't even cover one side of it. Aside from a single ammo can of *Sterno*, a box of candles and a couple of crates of bottled water it's canned food, and more of it. There's only three meals to choose from: *Ham and Eggs*, *Meat Stew with Vegetables* and *Beans with Frankfurter Chunks in Tomato Sauce*. We're going to be mighty sick of those by the time we're done, but as long as I haven't messed up the counting there should be enough to last us a couple of winters, maybe three if we're careful.

I drag a final box off the shelf and set it on the floor. Motes of dust tumble through the flashlight's beam, see-sawing down to settle on the worn tread plate. The flap says meat stew and when I look inside the contents are a match. I lift one of the cans out and hold it up to the flashlight. The metal looks dull, tarnished. Mags said she thought this place was at least as old as Eden, and I've seen nothing that'd make me doubt that view. I reckon Fearrington must have been abandoned long before the Last Day, mothballed, just like Eden had been, before Kane decided he had a use for it after all. It would explain how we found it: nothing on the shelves that might spoil and everything else just so, with no trace of a hurried evacuation. I point the flashlight down the aisle, playing the beam over the stacks. If that's right then what's on these shelves has been sitting here for half a century, maybe even longer.

I hear noise on the stair and when I look up Jake's silhouette's standing on the gangway. One by one the other Juvies appear behind him. From their faces it's pretty clear they haven't found anything in the lower levels to make them feel any better about their new home.

I return the tin to its slot and close the flap, then pick up the box and slide it back into place. Jake looks past me to the shelves.

'So how does it look?'

'Three winters.'

He repeats it, like he's testing what I've just told him, or maybe he's simply contemplating spending that much time in a place like this.

'You're sure?'

I am, but I find myself looking down to the strip of card anyway.

'Long as we're careful.'

'We should start work on some growing benches, then.'

I catch Lauren rolling her eyes at that, but I tell him I think it's a great idea. Setting the farms up again will be a lot of work, and if the Juvies are busy up here there's even less chance they'll go wandering down to the plant room to check on Mags.

I say he can take this level. There's as much space as he'll find anywhere in the silo and the shelves should provide him with the materials he'll need; all we have to do is move what's on them. He looks at me for a moment, then steps past to examine the closest one. He runs his fingers over the steel, testing the bolts that hold the shelves to the uprights, like he's trying to find a problem with what I've offered. I guess he mustn't see one, because he starts organizing the Juvies into groups, then dispatches them into the aisles.

I stand back and watch as they go to work. I have to hand it to him; it's all pretty efficient. The Juvies at the end are already lifting boxes down, passing them along and out to the landing, where others are waiting to stack them by the guardrail.

I glance back at the stair. Forming a line up to the level above would have been better, but I'm not about to suggest it. Now that he's got a project Jake almost looks happy again; he's dragging boxes off the shelves and tossing them along the line like there's little he'd rather be doing. I pick up the closest one and start making my way towards the gangway with it.

Neither of the Guardians got assigned a place on one of Jake's chain gangs and now Tyler steps forward, like he means to help. As he reaches for a box another thought occurs to me. I tell him to hold up.

'Listen, I'm sorry to have to ask, but can you and Eric take the rifles and stand watch outside?'

Eric's face falls. The silo may not have a lot going for it, but being inside where it's passable warm beats being out in the cold.

'I'm sorry; I know we just got here, but the journey took us way longer than I expected. Peck will have reached The Greenbrier not long after we set out; whatever went down between him and Hicks, that'll have played out long ago. One or other of them's probably on the road already. We can't let them surprise us.'

'Alright, Gabe, you got it. C'mon Eric.'

'And when you come back in, leave the rifles up in the airlock, yeah? It's the only way in. Makes no sense having them down here.'

He nods.

'Sure thing.'

I watch as they both set off back up the shaft. It's not long till I've lost them to the turn of the stair and all that's left is the echoing clang of their boots on metal. Soon that too fades.

I hoist the box back onto my shoulder.

What I said about Peck and Hicks is true, and it's reason enough for wanting to post a guard. But there's another part to it, one I scarcely dare admit to myself.

I don't know how long I have before Mags and the kid go the way of Finch's fury. That moment lies an unknowable amount of time ahead, but it's on its way; I'm as certain of that now as I once was that the dog tags and crucifix proved otherwise.

And if that time comes before I've figured out how to stop it I need the two Juvies with the rifles to be as far from her as possible.

*

I SET TO WITH THE BOXES, hauling the rations Jake and
the others are clearing from the shelves up to the level
above.

It's harder work than I had anticipated. The print on
the side says fifty pounds, but it soon starts to feel like a
lot more. I learn quick to check bottoms and seams. The
damp air's got to the old card, and some of the boxes are
no longer up to the task of holding their contents
together.

After a few trips Lauren decides her time's better
spent helping me than among the shelves, on one of
Jake's details. I tell her I'm fine, but she just shakes her
head and says Jake has enough helpers already, and I
look like I could use the assistance. Problem is two
people's not sufficient for a chain. and the stair is too
narrow for more than one person. We try it for a while,
but each time we meet and I have to squeeze past her it's
awkward. I suggest maybe it'd be better if she worked
on clearing space from the shelves above instead. For a
split second her face rearranges itself into an expression
I can't quite read, but then just as quick the smile
returns. She says *Sure* then turns and disappears up the
steps, the hank of her ponytail swinging after her.

Without Lauren to distract me I settle into a rhythm,
of sorts. My thoughts return to Mags and the kid. I run
through everything I know about the virus again, but at
the end of it the conclusion's no different than it was on
our way here: Gilbey's the only one who might be able
to help. There's no way I'll get Mags to go back to her,
but maybe I don't need to. Gilbey has medicine,
medicine that can hold back the virus. Not forever,
certainly, but a long time. Hicks must have been taking it

since he got infected, back in Atlanta, and that was ten years ago now. The kid almost as long, if Mags is right about the time he spent in that cage. It's a long way from a cure, I know it, but right now I'd take it, in a heartbeat.

I return to the level below, pick another box from the nearest stack, heft it onto my shoulder.

Problem is Gilbey's not just going to give it up, though, not without wanting something in return.

Something big.

I make my way back up the stair. As I'm crossing the gangway Lauren appears from between the shelves. She collects another box from the end of one of the rows, flashes me a smile. I hear Hicks' drawl in my head even before she's disappeared back into the darkness.

Warm bodies, and lots of them.

Eden was the prize; that's what he told me, that night in the main cavern, right before Mags burst out of the tunnel. It's the only reason Gilbey had been willing to let her and the kid go: Hicks had promised he'd get her the rest of the Juvies if she did.

I stand there considering it, for perhaps longer than I ought. I can't give up the Juvies for Mags, though.

But maybe I don't have to.

I slide the box I'm carrying off my shoulder and set it on top of a stack next to the guardrail.

How many inmates had I counted at Starkly?

Thirty-seven; half again our number. Would that many warm bodies be enough for Gilbey? Would she trade me as much as I could carry of her medicine for their location?

I start off down the stair again.

She might.

I spend the rest of the afternoon trying to think of anything else I have to offer, anything she might want instead. But there's nothing. Starkly's my best shot.

My only shot.

I tell myself it's not like they were innocent men, any of them. Murderers for the most part. *Ain't nobody ever been sent to Starkly on wino time,* those were Mac's exact words. If Finch were in my shoes he'd do it, in a heartbeat, I have no doubt of that. He'd do it and sleep sound that night, and all those that followed. Only one reason I walked out of that place alive, and that's the same reason I escaped The Greenbrier. Finch knew I was travelling with others; he wanted me to lead him to them so there'd be more for Blatch's cookpot.

I set the box I'm carrying on top of the nearest stack and start making my way back down.

We may not be done with him yet, either. He'll keep sending Goldie and those other men out looking for me, hoping they'll pick up my trail. Looked at that way it'd be no more than self-defense. I'd simply be making sure they were dealt with before they got around to finding us.

Little more than a question of timing, really.

Even as I think it I realize that was exactly how Hicks managed to get himself straight with what Gilbey had done to Mags, and Johnny, and all the other survivors that had found their way to The Greenbrier.

I tell myself this is different. It's only information I'd be offering; just the fact of their existence, a location, nothing more. Given enough time Hicks might even have stumbled on to them by himself. He was out looking for subjects for Gilbey to experiment on when he ran into Mags and me, after all. And Starkly's not that far from The Greenbrier.

Even if I give him the location, it's not like I'd be sealing their fate. That place is as much fortress as prison now; there's no certainty Hicks would even be able to find a way in, let alone overcome those inside. And Finch would be a more than capable adversary. *The most dangerous man ever to set foot through Starkly's gates*, that's what Mac had said.

These and a dozen other excuses run through my head as I heft one box after another up the stair. I try each on for size, hoping to find the one that'll make the decision sit that bit easier. None of them do, no matter how many I come up with; no matter how I dress them up.

I can't even pretend I'd be doing it to fix the world, like Gilbey, or Hicks. It might not even save Mags, while we're at the business of truth-telling. Most likely it'll just postpone the inevitable. I'll do it, all the same; I've known that since the idea first came to me. I'll trade the thirty-seven souls living inside Starkly's walls if it means there's even a chance to save her, maybe the kid too if I'm lucky and can make it back in time. And there's only one reason when it comes right down to it: those other people don't mean anything to me, and she does.

I think of Gilbey; the necklace around her neck, the one that belonged to her daughter, Amanda; the box in the storeroom with her things inside. Hicks told me he'd blown up the scanner just in case it could have been used to cure her, to make sure Gilbey wouldn't lose focus. It occurs to me then that all the terrible things she did, it would have begun just like this: weighing the value of a life, one she cared about more than anything, against others, less important to her. I can't know the exact circumstances of it, but in the end those matter little.

That first step she took would have been no different to mine.

This is how she would have gotten started.

*

I KEEP GOING, hefting one box after another onto my shoulder, planning my return to The Greenbrier as I haul each up the spiral stair.

If I cut cross-country, hike sun-up to sundown, I reckon I can reach Sulphur Springs in six days, maybe five. I don't know how long it'll take Gilbey to prepare all the medicine I'll need, but I'll have to assume a few more. Coming back will take longer. I'll have to return via Starkly, to prove my side of the deal. I could show them on a map, but I can't see Hicks taking me at my word. He'll want to see it for himself. That's when he'll try and double-cross me, like he did in Eden, but this time I'll know it's coming. Assuming I can figure a way to get away from him, it'll take me another couple of days to get back here. All that means I'll be gone two weeks, maybe a shade longer. Mags must have that time. The kid's already had that eyeshine thing the best part of a month and he hasn't turned yet. Hers has just started.

I step off the gangway and look around. Boxes are still stacked four- and five- deep waiting to be taken up, but the shelves behind are mostly bare; Jake's already started dismantling the first of them. Upstairs the last of the empty spots have been filled and now Lauren's placing boxes anywhere she can find space – in the aisles, at the end of the rows, against the railing that circles the shaft. Another day at most and I reckon the stores will be all squared away. It'll take Jake a little longer to get the farms up and running, but I won't hang around for that. I'll leave at first light, whether or not Mags has the power back on. I'll tell the Juvies I'm heading out scavenging; Jake will need things to complete his growing benches, so they'll buy that. I'll leave a note for Mags; something she won't find until after I'm gone. I'll need to warn her to start tethering the kid again, too. I have no way of knowing how long he might have left.

I set the box I'm carrying on top of a nearby stack. I can't say I'm excited about the prospect of returning to The Greenbrier, but I've had long enough to think of an alternative now to realize there isn't one coming.

I hear the sound of boots on metal, echoing through the silo, and I look up. Tyler and Eric, returning from outside. Their footsteps grow steadily louder, until at last a pair of flashlights materialize on the railing above and begin circling their way down through the darkness. Moments later Tyler appears around the curve of the stair, still bundled up in his parka. His eyebrows are white with ice; more of it thickens his lashes. The crystals stand stark against his ebony skin.

'We stayed out as long as we could, Gabe. I can't see anyone coming tonight.'

Behind him Eric nods quickly, like he's worried I might yet send them back to the guard hut. He asks through chattering teeth whether we've eaten yet.

I shake my head.

'You're just in time.'

I reach for a box sitting atop a nearby stack. The writing on the side's faded, obscured by mildew, but enough remains to make out *Beans with Frankfurter Chunks in Tomato Sauce*. That was as close as we got to a favorite in Eden; it'll do for our first meal here. I pick it up, hold it out to him.

'Bring this up to the mess while I fetch something to heat them up.'

He takes the box, cradles it to his chest, sets off up the stair.

Lauren emerges from the shelves, dusting her hands on the front of her pants. She flashes me a smile.

'Somebody mention food?'

I nod.

'Yep. Can you go and tell the others?'

She hesitates, one foot on the gangway. The smile remains, but now it looks hesitant, uncertain. She looks at me, like she's waiting for confirmation. I suddenly remember.

'Just Jake and the others. Mags will be busy with the generator; she won't want to be disturbed. I'll bring her something later myself.'

Her expression relaxes and she disappears off down the stair.

I make my way back in among the shelves. The mess has a couple of large industrial-looking ovens, but like everything else here they're useless without power. I spotted something while I was going through our supplies that should help, though. I return to the aisle where I thought I saw it and there it is, peaking out from between two mildewed cardboard boxes: an ammo can with the word *Sterno* stenciled across the top. I drag the old metal container out, spring the catch and lift the lid, reaching inside for one of the little blue fuel blocks. There were a couple of crates of them in Eden, back when we first arrived; Marv would bring a handful with us each time we'd go scavenging. They were useful to get a fire going, or if we managed to scare up a tin of something on the outside. They smell pretty bad when you light them, but what's here should keep us in warm meals until Mags can get the power back on. I fasten the catch, sling the container over my shoulder and head back to the stair.

Word about dinner spreads fast; the Juvies are already making their way up as I step out from between the shelves. I cross the gangway and join the last of them. When we reach the mess I deposit the *Sterno* on the table next to the box of cans. They gather round, anxious to find out what's on offer now that MREs are off the menu. A few like Jake might have enough reading to be able to make out what's printed there, but for most I suspect the letters stenciled on the mold-spackled cardboard might as well be hieroglyphics.

I pull back the flaps, reach inside and lift out one of the tins, setting it on the table. The Juvies press forward, looking on expectantly. Lauren hands me a can opener. I figure I'll get the first of the tins heating and then bring something down to Mags and the kid while she sees to the rest. I press the opener into the lid, but the cutting wheel's dull with age and for a second the metal resists. I squeeze the handle tighter and finally it gives with a high-pitched squeal, like a whistle being blown. It keeps that up for a couple of seconds then settles to a sharp hiss.

The Juvies lean closer, puzzled looks troubling their faces. I know what's wrong, though; I've heard that sound before. I grab the pierced can. The opener unclamps itself from the rim, clatters to the floor. No time to retrieve it. I toss the can into the box and scoop it off the counter, thinking if I'm quick I might just make it. But the Juvies are all around, blocking the way.

Beside me Amy reaches for the table, and out of the corner of my eye I see Fran, one hand already clapped to her mouth. I held my breath as soon as I heard, but now I catch the first whiff of it too: a vile smell, the rank odor of decay. A hot acid rush hits the back of my throat and my stomach feels like it's about to do something that could well be projectile. I grit my teeth and swallow hard, then shove my way through them.

The Juvies have finally figured out something's wrong. They clear a path for me, but it's too late. Behind me I hear the first of it: the strained sounds of retching, followed seconds later by something wet spattering on metal.

I push my way out onto the gangway and start up the stair. I have no thought other than to get the box as far away from the others as possible, but as I follow the steps up past servers and workstations into the concrete confines of the shaft, a simpler reality displaces that goal. I'm never going to make it all the way on a single lungful of air.

I set the box down, press my face to one of the rusted grilles and breathe deep. When I've had enough I take the pierced can, cover the hole with my thumb and carry on, stopping close to a vent whenever I need to take another breath. When I get to the airlock I spin the wheel, shoulder the outer door open. I've come up without my parka and the blast of icy air bites immediately, finding its way through my thermals with ridiculous ease. I toss the can out and heave the door closed, then set off back down the stair to retrieve the box of unopened cans I left behind.

I'm sweating as I make it back to the airlock for the second time. I drop the box in the corridor outside, open the access panel and yank the handle back, cancelling the override. I drag the box into the chamber, close the inner door behind me and hit the green button to start the cycle. It's only as the ceiling fans stutter to life that I realize I've left the can opener back in the mess. I dig in my pocket for Weasel's blade and unfold it, holding it over the first of the lids. Above me the fans are turning faster; I wait for them to get up to speed and then I start puncturing metal. The tins squeal like pigs as they're stuck, the high-pitched shriek quickly settling to an angry hiss that's mostly drowned out by the thrum of the fans. When they finally shut down I hold my breath and wait for the cycle to finish. As soon as it's done I open the outer door and toss out whatever's bad.

The third time I run the fans they start up as usual but never really get beyond half-speed, and when I cycle the airlock for the fourth time they manage no more than a dozen lazy rotations before grinding to a halt. Whatever juice was left in the batteries, I've had it; I can no longer rely on them to purge the chamber of the stench that escapes from each can I puncture.

I yank the recessed handle to the over-ride position then head back into the airlock and open the outer door. The wind blows snow around the thick steel, sending it dancing into the small chamber in furious flurries. I work quick as I can, but within minutes the fingers that grasp the blade are starting to go numb. I grip the knife in both hands and stab at the lids that remain, puncturing as many as I can while my breath holds, tossing those that hiss or squeal out into the snow before the smell has a chance to linger.

When there are no more tins left in the box I stagger to my feet and pull the outer door closed again. My fingers have already begun to claw and it takes me longer than it should to turn the wheel handle. As soon as it's done I slump to the floor and jam my hands into my armpits. I lean back against the frigid steel and stare at what remains of the cans I hauled up the stairs.

This isn't good.

I'd figured on some spoilage, maybe a few tins in each box where the seal had failed. But nothing like this. There were enough cans in that box to keep us in lunches or dinners for the best part of a week. I count up what's left: barely enough for a single meal.

I glance back towards the inner door. The Juvies are waiting for me to return. If they see how few cans I've been able to save they'll freak.

I take a deep breath, tell myself to calm down. I gather up the cans and begin placing them inside the cardboard. That was just one box; the others won't be like it. They can't be. I reach for a tin, examining the ragged hole Weasel's knife has made in the lid. Problem

267

is there's no way to be sure, not until each one's been opened.

I place the can with the others and look around, as if the answer might somehow be found among the scuffs and dents that scar the airlock's walls. But the old metal is unhelpful; if it has the answer it refuses to reveal it.

My breath starts to come quicker so I screw my eyes shut, try to bring it back under control. It's okay; there's no need to panic yet. I'll bring another box up, try some more cans. As long as those aren't spoiled then there's a good chance this was just a stupid, unlucky box.

I gather up the last of the tins, place them with the others sitting at the bottom of the box. I get to my feet. I feel a little better now that I have a plan, but mostly I just want to run down to the stores and grab another box, right away. That'll have to wait until after the Juvies have gone to bed, however. There's no sense letting them know about this, not yet.

Not until I'm sure.

THEY'RE ALL WAITING in the mess when I return. I step off the stairs, clutching the box with the cans I managed to salvage to my chest. I make my way over to the table. The surface has been wiped clean, but the tang of vomit remains. From the looks on some of the faces I'm guessing it was more than just Fran and Amy lost whatever they had last eaten. I set the box down, aware that everyone's staring at me.

'It was just a random can. What are the odds it'd be the first one we opened?'

I say it like it really was the funniest of coincidences. Lauren smiles back, but she might be the only one. I start unloading the punctured tins.

'I've brought down enough for our meal tonight.' I stack the cans neatly to one side, trying to sound casual. 'The rest I've left up in the airlock.'

I figure I'll be safe in that lie. The airlock's all the way at the top of the shaft; the Juvies have no reason to venture anywhere near it, at least not tonight. Lauren picks up the can opener and sets to work on the already punctured lids. I keep talking.

'Yeah, I reckon I'll open them up there and bring down what we need each day. Better safe than sorry, right?'

Another smile. It goes unreturned, just like the last one. Jake gives me a funny look, like he's already suspicious of my story.

Lauren removes the lid from the first of the cans and empties its contents into a metal bowl she picks from a stack on the counter behind her. The beans hold the shape of the can for a while, then slowly start to collapse.

269

I pop the catch on the ammo can of Sterno and free one of the little blue fuel tabs from its wrapper. I take the tin Lauren just emptied and start punching holes in the side with Weasel's knife, just like Marv showed me. When I figure there's enough to let the air flow through I take one of the tabs and drop it in. I dig in my pocket for a lighter and hold the flame to the fuel until I'm sure it's caught, then I set it on the table and place the bowl on top.

Tyler's been watching and now he gets to work on the cans Lauren's discarded. Before long there's a dozen of the makeshift stoves, each with a tin of congealed franks and beans resting on top. My eyes are watering from the fumes, but the little *Sterno* tabs are doing their job; I can already see the sauce in the first of the bowls starting to bubble. The beans that float in it look a little anemic, and I seem to remember there being more in the way of franks in our rations back in Eden, but at least our first meal here won't be cold.

One by one the Juvies shuffle forward to collect a bowl. They take them off to other tables, away from the still lingering smells of vomit and the stinging odor from the fuel blocks. They eat in silence, their heads bowed. I hear spoons scraping metal before I've handed out the last of them, then the dull screech of chairs being pushed back. Nobody seems inclined to linger.

Good; the sooner they leave the better.

My beans are already cooling, but I force myself to go slow. Cleaning up the mess outside the airlock, that can wait till morning; as long as I'm up there before Tyler and Eric, everything will be fine. The other part of it won't, though. I need to fetch another box of cans up from stores, to convince myself that first one was just a fluke, a random piece of bad luck.

One by one the Juvies finish eating and make for the stair, until soon there's only Lauren, me, Jake, Tyler and

Eric left. Across the table Jake gets to his feet. He brings his bowl to the counter, mutters a goodnight and then heads for the gangway. Tyler takes a final mouthful of beans, sets his spoon down, wipes his mouth with the back of his hand.

'Guess I'll be turning in too. See you both tomorrow.'

Eric leaves with him. I watch as the two Guardians make their way toward the stair. For a while the sound of their boots echoes up out of the darkness and then those too fade.

I go back to pushing the last of my frankfurter chunks around with the spoon, pretending to study the greasy patterns they make in the congealing sauce. Lauren's already done with her bowl, but she's showing no sign of getting up. I will her to go downstairs with the others, but she doesn't move.

In the end I drop my spoon into the bowl.

'Well, I reckon I'm done, too.'

But when I glance across the table she's still sitting there, just looking at me.

'It'll be okay, Gabe. Really. Things will seem a lot better after we've had a good night's sleep.'

I nod, like I believe it.

She hesitates for a second and then reaches across the table and places her hand over mine, like Mags did, when it was just the two of us here, last night.

I glance over at the counter, to where the last of the makeshift stoves are burning.

'Mags and Johnny; we forgot to bring something down for them.' I look back at her. 'Hey, would you...'

I was only meaning to ask if she'd mind if I tended to that, but I never get the chance to finish the sentence. She draws her hand back, and for an instant the smile becomes uncertain, like maybe she's worried I was going to ask her to do it for me. She gets to her feet, a

271

little faster than I guess she means to. Her chair teeters like it might fall; she holds a hand out to steady it.

'Well I guess I should let you get to that.'

She makes for the gangway without waiting for my reply.

HE SITS ON THE NARROW CATWALK, his elbows resting on the bottom guardrail, his feet swinging into empty space below. The flashlight the girl gave him lies on the grating, next to his goggles. It went out hours ago, but he hasn't bothered to wind it.

Far below he hears her, at work on one of the machines. It's the important one, she says, the one that will make this place run again. He asked her if she could fix it and she said she thought she could. He hopes she can. He's not so sure, though. The girl is smart, he knows that. But not everything can be fixed. And most things down here smell old, broken.

He rests his chin on the metal and stares out at the silo's curving walls. He hasn't been to many other places, at least not that he remembers, so he doesn't have much to compare this place to. There was the place inside the mountain, where the girl and the tall boy brought him first. He had been very sick when they arrived, though, and they had left right after, so his memories of that place are broken, incomplete, like when he first woke up in the cage.

They had gone to the other place next, where the rest of them had been living. It had been much nicer there. Inside a mountain too, just like the first, except it hadn't felt like it. It was *way* bigger, for a start. He liked that. He spent a long time in a box not large enough even for him; he does not care for tight spaces anymore. It wasn't safe there, though, that's what the tall boy had said. The man with the gray eyes and the gun had left, but he would probably be back.

And now they are here. He lifts his head and looks down, past the catwalks that crisscross beneath, all the

273

way to the bottom, to the rusting machines rising from the oily floodwaters. He wrinkles his nose at the smell.

This place isn't so nice.

He returns his gaze to the gangway. His new perch is okay, though. He chose it carefully. It is the highest of the walkways, passing through a space for the most part uncluttered by pipes or cables, yet still far enough beneath the ceiling above that he does not feel it pressing down on him.

The plant room falls quiet and he realizes the girl has stopped whatever she was doing. He wonders if she is finished. It has been a while since he ate and he thinks he might be hungry. He has decided he will finish all of the food in the pouch today, before he opens the candy bar. That will make her happy. He listens, waiting to hear her boots on the stair. But then the tapping resumes as she goes back to work.

He hears another sound and he looks up, following the steps that spiral towards the ceiling. All afternoon he has listened, straining for any sign that one of them might be about to come down. It was difficult at first. The sounds in this place are unreliable; they echo, bouncing off the curving walls, so it is hard to tell their source. But he thinks he is getting the hang of it.

There has been no one, though, not even the tall boy. A little while ago it seemed like they all stopped what they were doing and then there was the hollow clang of boots as they took to the stair. He scrabbled for his goggles, but when he listened closer the sounds were heading up, not down, and he had relaxed again. Soon after there had been a commotion, and just one of them – he thinks maybe the tall boy; he knows his footsteps well – had set off up the steps, only this time he had been running. Soon after there had been a smell; faint at first, but growing steadily stronger. It was horrible; he had to bury his face in his hands to try and block it out.

Things stayed quiet for some time after that. When at last the boy had returned other smells had started to drift down. Those had been all jumbled up, and it had taken him a while to untangle them. There had been smoke, that one had been easy. But not the thick, wet odor of the branches he is used to. This had been different: a sharp, peppery smell that had burned his nostrils and stung his eyes. And underneath the smoke, something cooking. Not like the food they normally eat, though, the kind that comes in the plastic pouches. This was different. Not a bad smell exactly, at least not bad in the way the first one had been. But there had been something about it, something familiar, that at the same time had made him feel uneasy.

The girl must have noticed the smells too, because she had stopped whatever she had been working on, and for a long while the whole silo had gone quiet except for the occasional noise from above, much more subdued now: the thin clink and scrape of cutlery; the dull screech of a chair being drawn back. Then the sound of boots on metal again as the first of them had started to make their way down through the silo. He had reached for his goggles again, but it soon became clear none of them planned to venture beyond the hatch. For a while that had continued until he had been sure the last of them had gone to bed.

Now somebody *is* coming down, however. Their footsteps are awkward, like they're carrying something, but it's the tall boy, he's sure of it. They continue, past where they should have stopped if he were going to bed, like all the others. He looks down, searching the plant room's depths. The girl continues to work on the machine. Maybe she hasn't heard yet.

The footsteps grow closer, stop. There's a long pause and then the hatch creaks open and he sees the wink of a flashlight above. Food smells, stronger now. It is the tall

275

boy, bringing them something to eat. He tilts his head, scenting the air. There's something about the smell that is unsettling, but that doesn't matter. He'll eat the food and then there'll be a candy bar for after, maybe two; the tall boy always gives him his. For a second the thought consumes him. He picks himself up and scurries along the catwalk. It's only when he nears the end that he realizes he's left his goggles behind. He looks up, just as the flashlight appears on the handrail where the ladder drops through the ceiling. A shape appears, but it is nothing more than a shifting of shadows behind the light, a movement in darkness not even his eyes can penetrate. It is definitely the tall boy, though; he is certain of it now. The flashlight starts circling its way down. He glances back towards the goggles. He still has time to fetch them. But then he remembers. He doesn't have to wear the goggles around the tall boy, not anymore.

He already knows.

The footsteps come to a halt just above his perch, on the far side of the column supporting the stair. The boy calls the girl's name. The sound echoes off the walls, but she doesn't answer. For a long moment the boy waits, and then he continues, more slowly now. He takes the last few steps around and then peers over the guardrail, canting his head to one side, as though listening. The boy is right at the end of the gangway, only a handful of yards away, but he hasn't seen him yet. It is too dark for his eyes.

The boy bends down. There's the soft clank of something metal being laid on the grating. He has to shift his grip on the flashlight to set the second bowl down. As he does he loses control of the beam; it darts along the catwalk.

The light is a surprise and for a second all he can think is that he must not look away. Because not looking at the flashlight is a sign, just like not eating your food.

The boy's eyes suddenly grow wide. He drops the bowl, takes a startled step backwards. The bowl clatters to the grating, for a second teeters on the edge like it might go over, then rights itself.

The tall boy bends down, pulls the bowl back.

'Jesus, Johnny. You scared me.'

He tilts his head, testing the air. He knows. He can smell it.

The boy glances over his shoulder, as if reassuring himself that that way is still clear. He reaches in his pocket for a couple of spoons, sets them next to the bowls, then takes another step back.

'Listen, I have to go. Can you make sure Mags gets one of those?'

The boy turns and hurries back up the stairs, not waiting for an answer. Seconds later there's the sound of his boots climbing the ladder and then the creak of the hatch closing behind him.

He picks himself up and crawls along the gangway.

The bowls sit side by side on the metal grating. He bends over the closest one.

His brow furrows as he sees what's there.

*

I MAKE MY WAY slowly down through the narrow shaft, the flashlight sweeping the gray walls. A vent grille appears in the beam, long fingers of rust staining the concrete beneath. I'm not sure how far I've come. For once I'm not counting, simply following the yellowing cone of light as it circles the spiral stair.

This is bad.

Really bad.

The first box I picked at random, from nowhere near where I got the franks and beans. I chose ham and eggs. I figured I'd open just what was needed for the Juvies' breakfast. That'd be enough. It's pretty cold up in the airlock, so whatever I tried would keep until morning, and that way there wouldn't be any waste.

The smell from the eggs was even worse than the franks and beans. I tossed the shrieking cans out as quick as I could, but without the fans to clear it the stench was overpowering; the first time I threw up I barely made it out to the snow. After that I dragged the box close to the airlock's outer door, trying to ignore the icy wind that howled around the edge of the thick steel. When I was done I heaved it closed again and counted up what remained. There wasn't enough for a single meal. Not even close. I had to make another two trips to the stores, just to give me the numbers I needed for breakfast.

That's four boxes I've opened now, each worse than the last. Assuming the rest are like that we won't make it through a single winter, let alone two or three. Our food will run out long before the storms break.

The thought makes me want to throw up again. I stop and reach for the handrail. My knees fold underneath me and I slump to the narrow step. I rest my forehead against the cold steel and wait for it to come. But there's nothing left. After a while I get to my feet again and continue on, letting my boots find their own way down the spiraling stair. The voice starts to whisper. It reminds me of what Mac said, about how things got in Starkly when the food ran out.

It won't get to that. I'll figure something out.

I keep going, following the flashlight around, fighting to stop the panic from rising.

One problem at a time. There's enough cans in the airlock for the morning. It's too cold outside to clear the ones I had to discard from in front of the blast door, but I'll head back up first thing and deal with those. All I need to do now is bring another box of franks and beans up to the airlock, to replace the one I opened first.

The concrete ends and the silo opens out to silent rows of workstations. When I drop to the level beneath I stop among the dusty server stacks and listen. But the mess is dark, quiet. I continue on, treading as lightly as I can. At the stores I step onto the gangway. The old metal groans under my boots as I cross, but I learned in Eden how to tread lightly; the sound won't carry to the dorms.

On the other side boxes circle the central shaft, piled high against the guardrail. The shelves start beyond, stretching back into darkness. They're crammed tight, the empty spots from earlier now filled; Lauren's already started stacking boxes against the walls at the end of each row. And this isn't all of it; there's more yet to come up.

I stop in the middle of the gangway, then reach for the strip of card in my pocket, the one with the inventory of our supplies. Back in Eden it was Quartermaster's responsibility to keep track of our provisions, and because I'd worked with him all those years, in Mount Weather it became mine. It'll be no different here. Most of the Juvies don't have enough reading to know what's printed on the side of the boxes.

I stare at the stacks, my mind already starting to sketch out the bones of the deception. Boxes waiting to be opened can go in the decontamination area next to the airlock, and in the passageway beyond. I can stash them in other places too: under the workstations and between the banks of servers on the levels above. The airlock's where I'll keep the cans I've already checked. It's hardly convenient, having them all the way up there, but after what happened in the mess earlier, when I opened that first tin, there won't be any objections.

I feel a glimmer of insane hope.

As long as I make sure the Juvies have sufficient food for the time I'll be gone nobody needs to know. Not yet. Not till I get back from The Greenbrier.

I return the strip of card to my pocket.

I'll make a start tonight.

The flashlight's about to die so I wind the stubby handle. It clicks and grinds but after a few turns the bulb brightens, then takes to flickering. I give it a shake, as though that might solve the problem, then I step in among the shelves and start probing the dusty boxes with the faltering beam.

It doesn't take me long to find the one I'm looking for. I drag it down, crouching over it to check the contents are match. But as I lift the flap I suddenly realize I'm not alone. I stagger to my feet, startled, take a quick half-step backwards. I hadn't heard anyone on the stair. I point the flashlight along the narrow aisle. There are two figures standing between the shelves.

Mags raises a hand to ward off the beam. The kid peeks out from behind her. He's put his goggles back on.

The flashlight continues to flicker. Mags waits until I've pointed it down, then she takes a step closer.

'What're you doing, Gabe?'

I can't help an incriminating glance at the box at my

feet.

'I…I was just bringing some cans up to the airlock. For tomorrow's breakfast.'

Her eyes drop to the lid. The cardboard's mildewed but the print's legible through it: *Beans with Frankfurter Chunks in Tomato Sauce.*

She looks at me, waiting for the rest of it.

'…and dinner. Thought I'd get a head start on tomorrow.'

So far I'm still within spitting distance of the truth; now would be a good time to let her know about our supplies. I can almost feel the relief that would come with it. But if I tell her about the cans she'll insist on getting the others involved, and who knows what will come of that? I certainly can't wait around to find out; I need to set out for The Greenbrier as soon as possible. Before I'm aware I've even made a decision I hear myself repeating the same thing I told the Juvies earlier.

'Yeah, one of the cans in the first box we opened had gone off. So I'm going to open all of them up there. Just to be safe.'

This time I notice the lie slips out a little easier than before. But then I guess lying's no different to most things: to get good at it just takes practice. I think I even manage a smile.

The flashlight falters, like it might die, then steadies, goes back to flickering. She looks at me like she's trying to work out what it is I'm not telling her. I don't want her dwelling on that too long, so instead I ask what her *she's* doing in the stores. I hadn't practiced that one, however, and it comes out weird, like I'm accusing her of something.

'I came up to get something for Johnny.'

I glance down to the kid, then back to her.

'I brought food down, for both of you.'

She cants her head to one side and looks at me, like

that's something else she wouldn't mind an explanation for, as long as we're on the subject. When I don't say anything she continues.

'Yeah, I saw.'

She doesn't raise her voice but there's an edge to the way she says it, like there's a whole litany of things wrong with what I've done. She stares at me for a long moment, like she's waiting for my thoughts on the subject. When it's clear I don't have any she continues.

'You didn't stop to think what it was you were giving him?'

The kid looks up at her, mumbles something about it being okay, he's really not that hungry. Mags pays him no mind.

'Cold beans, Gabe?'

The kid says the beans weren't actually cold, not really, but she ignores that too. I guess I'm a little distracted, or maybe I'm having a slow day, because I'm still not sure what she means.

'That's what Truck was feeding him, in the cage. You couldn't have found something else?'

I'm not sure what to say to that. I open my mouth to explain, but then realize I've got nothing, so I close it again.

'Well I guess it just didn't occur to you.' She glances at the shelf. There's a box that has *Meat Stew* stamped on the side right by her head. 'It's okay. One of those will do.'

She reaches for it and now I feel a spike of fear. I've no reason to believe the contents of that box will be any different to the four I've already opened tonight. I step forward, placing a hand across the box's flank. It happens to be the one holding the flashlight.

Her eyes narrow at the beam, like it troubles her, but not enough to make her step away. And for long seconds I just stand there, transfixed. Her pupils are wide, and what's behind them glows, incandescent. This close it's not silver, though, but palest gold.

I stammer out something about there not being enough. Her eyes flick to the boxes stacked all around us, then return to me.

'Then I'll trade him what I'm having for breakfast, Gabriel.' She says it slow, like she's trying to figure out how deep this new streak of asshole goes.

She stares back at me. I want to look away, but I can't. I shake my head.

'I already told the others: no one's getting special treatment. That goes for you and the kid too. I'm sorry. Franks and beans is what we have. He'll just need to get used to it.'

She takes a step closer, and for a second I think she might just take the box anyway.

And you might not be able to stop her.

The kid grabs hold of her arm and says it's okay, he's not hungry.

She keeps looking at me, her eyes shimmering with something that might now be rage. The kid says it's okay again, louder this time. She holds my gaze for a second longer then lets her hand fall from the box.

'C'mon Johnny, let's go.'

HE HURRIES AFTER THE GIRL, out of the shelves, past the stacks of old, tattered boxes that push up against the guardrail. As they cross the gangway he remembers his flashlight. The girl said they should use them whenever the others are around, but hers hangs forgotten from her wrist, bouncing on its tether as she takes to the stair. It died on the way up from the plant room, but she hasn't bothered to wind it.

He follows her as she makes her way around, quickly dropping through the level below. Boxes line the guardrail here too, just like above. Beyond, more shelves, stretching back into grainy shadow. Most are empty now, the closest ones already in various states of disassembly. The girl said they were going to grow things here. Food. He's not really sure what that means. The only food he's ever known comes in cans, packets, wrappers.

She keeps going down, passing silently through the floors where the rest of them are sleeping. Most of the doors are shut, but here and there one has been left ajar. The soft night sounds they make drift out from behind.

He feels bad. He should have just eaten what was in the bowl. Not eating your food is a sign; he knows that, better than anyone. How could he have forgotten? Does the tall boy think he's getting sick again? Is that why he was scared, just now?

But that doesn't make sense. The tall boy checked his dog tags; they prove it. And he had been frightened earlier, too, when he first brought the food down, before he could have known he wasn't going to eat it. He hadn't been wearing his goggles then, of course. But he didn't think he had to, not in front of the tall boy. He already knew.

They leave the dorms behind. He doesn't know what to make of any of it, and something behind his eyes feels scratchy, now. He raises one hand to his goggles, then stops. He knows what that feeling means, and rubbing them won't help. He just needs to rest. Only one more floor and the hatch and then he will be back on his perch, high above the machines, and he can sleep, just like they do.

But when the girl reaches the next gangway she suddenly stops. She stands on the stair for a moment, listening, and then she crosses, quickly disappearing among the narrow stalls. He hesitates, unsure what to do, then he follows, making his way between the dark cubicles. He finds her standing in front of the row of washbasins.

She steps up to the nearest one and places her flashlight on the lip of the shallow basin. She leans forward, examining her reflection in the square of steel above. Her fingers probe the skin under her eyes. He wonders what she's looking for. It may still be a shade darker there, but it's hard to tell now. Those shadows have all but disappeared.

When she's done examining her eyes she turns her attention to the rest of her face. A smudge of grease marks one cheek; another follows the line of her jaw. She reaches for the faucet. It sticks for a moment, but then turns with a dull groan. There's the sound of pipes clunking and then water spits from the tap, quickly steadying to a stream. She cups her hands under it, then brings them to her face and starts scrubbing at the marks there with the cuff of her overalls.

When she's finished she shuts off the faucet and checks her reflection again. She hesitates for a moment then pulls off the cap she wears and sets it on the washbasin next to the flashlight. She leans closer to the mirror. Her hair is growing back faster than his, but after all these weeks it's still little more than stubble. A wide swathe of it darkens the top of her head, continuing all the way back to the nape of her neck. She lifts one hand, runs her fingers over it. She tilts her head first this way, then that, examining the sides. He follows her gaze, trying to work out what she's doing. At first he thinks it hasn't grown back as quickly there. But then he sees it's not that; it's just that what's there is flecked with white.

And then at last he thinks he understands. He hesitates a moment then lifts the goggles from his face, settles them around his neck. He reaches for the flashlight and starts to wind the handle. The dynamo whirs and after a few seconds the bulb begins to glow. The tangle of rubber-jointed pipes throw complicated shadows against the wall behind.

The girl looks down to see what he's doing. He holds the flashlight up, pointing it back towards himself. The beam isn't that bright, but his eyes have grown accustomed to the darkness and he has to force himself not to squint. When he thinks he has the flashlight in the right place he looks up so she can see.

The girl's eyes widen; she starts to take a step backwards. He quickly reaches for the tags he wears and holds them up. The slivers of pressed metal hang in the beam, slowly twisting at the end of the beaded chain.

Her gaze flicks from his eyes to the tags, then back again.

When he thinks she's seen enough he holds the flashlight out to her. She stares at it for a long moment. At first he's not sure she understands, or maybe she doesn't care to. Then she takes it from him.

She turns back to the mirror and holds it up, searching for the right angle, just as he did. When she finds it she stops, and for a long time she stays like that. Then she closes her eyes. She leans forward, her hands

286

grasping the side of the shallow washbasin.

He tells her it's okay. They're not sick. The tags, the cross she wears; they prove it. He starts to tell her what she told him, back when they first set out. The others, they'll get used to it.

But then he stops. He's not sure that last bit's really true. It's been a long time since they left the mountain place. And now the tall boy is frightened of them, too.

Perhaps it's like the girl with the pink hair said, in the shopping mall.

Their kind, maybe they're just too different after all.

WHEN I RETURN TO THE DORMS they're dark, quiet. I push back the door to the cell, half expecting to find Mags in there, waiting for me. But it's empty. Tell the truth I'm a little relieved. I don't think I've ever seen her as mad at me as she was earlier, down in the stores, and I haven't got the words to make it better. I step inside, wind the flashlight and set it on the ground, then lower myself onto the thin mattress next to it.

My legs ache, my shoulders are numb from hefting boxes and I've lost track of the times I've been up and down the stair. But the first part of it's mostly done. Enough of the rations are now distributed between the upper floors of the silo and the corridor by the airlock that it'll be impossible for anyone to keep track of what we have, even if they wanted to.

I lean back against the cold steel. All I want to do is climb into the sleeping bag, curl up into a ball and pretend none of this is happening. But I can't. Up on the surface dawn can't be more than an hour away. I can't let Tyler or Eric find all the cans I've had to toss out of the blast door.

I'll go back up there soon, bring the Juvies down their breakfast, let the Guardians know I'll take their shift. They can stay in the silo, help Lauren with whatever of the boxes still need moving. I can't see either of them objecting to that. Soon as I've dealt with the discarded tins I'll set to work opening more. When I've got enough to last through the time I mean to be away I'll leave. It shouldn't set me back more than a few hours.

I'll just take a little rest first. I feel my eyes start to close so I sit up straight, blink them open. I can't afford to drift off. My backpack leans against the wall by the door; the cell's small enough that I can reach it just by leaning forward. The snaps are already undone and I reach inside. Hick's pistol sits on top, wrapped in the gun belt. I lift it out, set it down beside me. Cartridges nestle in their loops, the stamped brass ends glowing dully in the flashlight's waning beam.

I return to the backpack. In a Ziploc bag buried near the bottom there's the container of gun oil I took from Hicks' pack before we left Eden, the worn nub of a toothbrush and a half dozen cotton swabs. I part the seal, shake the contents onto the floor next to the gun belt. The smell of the oil wafts out. I reach down for the pistol, draw it from its holster. The carrion bird etched into the grip feels rough against my palm. I turn the pistol over in my hands, pointing the muzzle up so I can get to the base pin.

I still need to work out what to do with the Juvies, when I get back. I look over at the pack. The map Marv gave me is in the side pocket, but I don't need to take it out to know what it'll tell me. There are only two locations on the map I haven't yet been.

The first is a facility called The Notch, at a place called Bare Mountain. It's the one Jake tried to test me on, when we were deciding what to do about Peck.

Would they have voted to leave if you hadn't risen to the bait?

I push that thought from my mind. What's done is done; wishing things were different won't make it so, no matter how much I'd like it to. I just need to figure out a way to make it right.

I turn my thoughts back to the map. Bare Mountain's no good. It's all the way up in Massachusetts, even farther north from Mount Weather than we are south. The second facility is a place called North Bay, on the shores of a small body of water called Lake Nipissing, about a third of the way up Ontario's eastern border. It might as well be the far side of the moon; whatever chance we have of reaching Massachusetts, there's no prospect of us making it to Canada.

I jiggle the base pin free, set it aside and slide out the cylinder.

In the bottom corner of the map, in Marv's careful hand, there's a list of codes for other places. *Crown, Cartwheel, Corkscrew, Cannonball, Cowpuncher*; each name less likely than the one before. A few have lines drawn through them. Marv didn't get round to explaining why he'd done that, but I reckon those were places that got hit in the strikes. Whether I'm wrong or right on that score makes little difference. There's no corresponding mark on the map for any of them, which suggests either Marv didn't know where they were, or they weren't on it. Either way, I have no hope of finding them.

I pick up the container of gun oil and one of the cotton swabs and set to work on the back of the cylinder, where the ratchet touches the frame.

The last code given is for a facility called Cheyenne Mountain. It's not marked on the map either, but at least for Cheyenne I understand why: Marv's written *Colorado* after it. I'd need to find an atlas to check, but I think that's way out west somewhere.

The Juvies don't have it in them to make any of those places, even if we had the supplies for it. And why would they trust me to embark on such a journey, anyway? I know even less about those places than I thought I knew about here. There's every chance each one is just the same: ancient, mothballed, long-abandoned relics; their machines all broken, whatever supplies might still be there long since spoiled. Mount Weather might be the only place left where we ever stood any chance of surviving, and I led us away from it.

I need to get them back there.

It's less of a decision, more a lack of other options. A measure of relief comes with having arrived at it, all the same.

I set the swab down, reach for the toothbrush. I turn the cylinder over and start on the chambers, working the bristles up into each. The smell of the oil fills the tiny cell. I think of the wooden stool I found behind the door, in Eden's armory, the seat shiny from years of use, testament to the hours Peck must have sat down there by himself, tending to each weapon. I think I understand now. The ritual is somehow calming. I hold my hand to my mouth, stifling a yawn.

There's not much time. Winter's still a couple of months off, but I can't risk them getting caught out in it; I need them back inside before the first of the storms arrive. The journey down took over a month, which means I have four weeks, no more; by then they need to be back on the road. The good news is they should be able to follow the route we took coming down, for the most part. I can't risk sending them back through Durham, of course, not with Finch's men out looking for us, but finding another way around won't be difficult, and it shouldn't add much to the journey; once they're clear of the city they can rejoin the interstate and from there it'll be easy. They've hiked that road already; they know where the shelter is to be found. The interstate has another advantage, too, one I hadn't appreciated before Starkly. Whatever might be starting to wake up out there, the danger will be in the towns, not out in open country.

I finish with the cylinder, wipe it down, set it to one side.

Supplies will be a problem. There's precious few of the MREs we set out with left, maybe enough for the first couple of days, but not much more than that. I can't rely on there being anything worth scavenging along the way, either, even if they knew how to find it. Which means they'll have to survive on whatever they can take from here.

Pounding the snow's hard work; I figure even on short rations each of them will need three cans a day, which means a hundred apiece for the trip. Plus basics: canteen, sleeping bag, fixings for a fire. A heavy load; more than they set out from Mount Weather with.

You think they'll manage?

They'll have to.

I'll need to do something about the cans, to make sure they last, even with the lids punctured. I can't risk them eating food that'd make them sick; there's no place for that on the road. The holes I can reseal, like I used to do with the containers with Kane's medicine, when I was smuggling them back into Eden. Wax should do the trick; there's a box of candles in the stores. The cold will help. At night they can leave their packs outside. Maybe I can rig something up for during the day; line the insides with garbage sacks, pack it with snow.

How do you think they'll take the news that they're leaving again?

I pick up the pistol and set to work on the barrel.

I'm not going to tell them, not until I get back from The Greenbrier.

And you're certain, about the other thing? About not going with them?

I lean back against the steel, close my eyes.

I am.

I WAKE TO DARKNESS. At first I think it's still the middle of the night and all I want to do is drift back down to sleep. But then through the metal walls I hear the muted sounds of others stirring.

I lift my chin from my chest, wincing as an unexpected jolt of pain shoots down my neck. I reach up with one hand to rub it. Something I didn't realize was there slips from my fingers. It lands in my lap, the weight of it startling. I open my eyes to try and make sense of it, but the blackness is complete. I struggle with simple concepts like up and down for longer than a right-minded person has any business doing, but eventually I work out I'm sitting upright. I rub my eyes, trying to clear the sleep from them. The smell of gun oil is heavy on my fingers. Hicks' pistol. I must have fallen asleep cleaning it.

I reach out with one hand, find the flashlight, wind it slowly. The mechanism grinds out its now-familiar complaint but eventually the bulb glows, spreading its light slowly over the steel.

The pistol's reassembled and loaded; there's brass in each of the chambers bar the one under the hammer, just like Hicks showed me. The box of ammunition I stole from him sits nearby, but the mattress it was resting on last night is gone. I glance up at the door. I closed it behind me when I came in, but now it's ajar.

Mags.

She must have been here at some point while I slept. I think of her, staring down at me in the darkness. I wonder what it means that she took the mattress. It can't be good, but the sounds from the adjacent cells are growing louder, reminding me I have things to attend to.

I'll worry about that later. First I need to find Tyler and Eric, let them know I'll be standing guard this morning.

I slip the pistol into its holster, loop the gun belt around my waist, tighten the buckle and make for the stair.

I hurry up to the airlock, load one of the boxes with enough of the ham and eggs for the Juvies' breakfast and return to the mess. I get the Sterno stoves lighting and start transferring the yellow mulch the Army reckoned would stand for ham and eggs to the tin bowls. The first of the bowls is already starting to bubble by the time I see the Juvies' flashlights circling the stair. One by one they shuffle out of the darkness, take a bowl and make their way over to the tables.

Lauren comes over to stand next to me, an expression of concern troubling her features. She rests a hand on my arm.

'Gabe, you look exhausted.'

'Yeah, couldn't sleep.'

'I noticed the stores as I came up. Seems like you were busy last night.'

I shrug, hoping to get her off the topic.

'Figured I might as well be useful.' I notice the two Guardians on the gangway. 'Hey, Tyler, Eric, can you guys help Lauren with the boxes this morning? I'll keep watch outside.'

Lauren's face rearranges itself into a frown, but Eric seems relieved. Tyler asks if I'm sure.

'It's only fair. You guys were out yesterday.'

Jake takes one of the bowls off its stove.

'What about Mags? Is she coming up?'

A few of the Juvies raise their eyes from their bowls, like they're waiting for my answer. I shake my head.

'No, I...she said she was in the middle of something with the generator. I'll bring her and the kid their breakfast before I head outside.'

Jake looks at me for a moment like he's not sure what to make of this, but then he collects a spoon and heads over to one of the tables. Lauren lifts a bowl from its makeshift burner.

'Don't you want to eat first?'

I look down at the yellow mulch she's offering. Truth is I've never cared much for eggs. The powdered substitute we had in Eden bore more than a passing resemblance to the paste Miss Kimble used to give us when we were doing art, and what's in these cans looks like it's from no better stock.

I shake my head.

With what I have planned for the day I doubt I'd be able to keep it down anyway.

I bring a couple of bowls down to the plant room. The kid's sitting on the same catwalk where he'd startled me the night before. He looks up as I make my way around the stair. After what happened in the stores I'm not sure what to say to him so I just leave the bowls on the grating nearby and ask him to bring one down to Mags.

A few minutes later I'm back in the airlock. The wind's picked up overnight. I can feel it, pushing against the blast door as I heave it open. Gray flakes swirl around the edges and dance into the narrow chamber.

I smear UV block across my cheeks and then pull up my hood. Outside the snow is littered with the cans I tossed out of the airlock. I pick up one of the cardboard boxes and start gathering them into it. The contents have frozen overnight so there's hardly any smell, and what little remains the wind carries away, but I pull the cotton mask I wear up over my nose anyway. When the box is full I snap on my snowshoes and set off through the compound, cradling it to my chest. The tattered windsock snaps angrily on its tether as I pass.

At the guard shack I rest the box on the raised security barrier while I clamber over, then pick it up and carry on. I follow the trail for a while, until the gnarled, blackened trunks grow thick around me. I glance back over my shoulder to make sure no one's watching, then I turn off the track and start making my way deeper into the wood. Dead branches whip and claw at my parka as I squeeze myself between them. After a few minutes I arrive at a small gap in the trees, hardly big enough to count as a clearing. I glance back over my shoulder. Somewhere a little further from the trail would be better but I'm in a hurry now, so I upend the box and dump the cans into the snow.

A couple more trips and all the tins I threw out of the airlock have been relocated to the place I've found for them in the woods. When I've disposed of the last of them I collect the container with the virus from behind the guard shack and carry it out there too. I bury it in a drift a little way off to one side then I go back to the airlock and start over, opening cans from the boxes I brought up last night. I come up with a system: I puncture each tin on the bottom, in the crevice between rim and base, where it's harder to spot. For those handful of cans in each box that haven't spoiled a drop of candlewax seals the hole. I get pretty good at it. By the time I've done a dozen of them I doubt anyone would notice, unless they were told where to look.

When I get to the bottom of the first box I go outside, collect the spoiled cans from in front of the airlock and ferry them off into the woods. I'm about to turn around and head back but then I stop, pick one of the cans from the pile and set it in the crook of a tree. The clearing's mostly sheltered from the wind, so I don't need to spend much time digging it in. I turn around and measure out ten paces. That's not very far in snowshoes, but I reckon it makes sense to start with a realistic goal.

I slip off my mittens and unzip my parka. The gun belt sits low across my hips, the old pistol snug in its holster. I take a deep breath, let it out slow, watching it turn white before it's carried away. I picture how Hicks was, in the hospital in Blacksburg, when the fury attacked Ortiz. I was looking right at him, but it happened so fast all I have now are a series of disconnected images. One second his hand had been empty, the next there'd been a pistol there. A burst of shots in rapid succession, his off hand little more than a blur as it worked the hammer, his other pumping the trigger, just like one of those gunslingers from the movies.

I flex my fingers against the cold, then reach down and practice sliding it out. The pistol feels heavy, awkward in my hand. I bring it up slow, keeping the hammer down and my finger away from the trigger until I've got the barrel pointed roughly where I think I need it to be. I doubt I'll get the drop on anybody that way, but at least I'll stand a chance of walking away with all my toes accounted for afterwards.

I reach for the hammer with my thumb. The mechanism's stiff and it takes some effort to cock it. I settle the sight back on the can and squint down the barrel, lining the blade at the end with the groove at the back so that both rest on the target. A random gust of wind picks up the snow, swirling the flakes in little eddies around the tree, but I have no thoughts of correcting for it. I just hold the grip steady as I can and slowly squeeze the trigger. The hammer snaps forward before I'm ready for it. There's a loud bang and the pistol bucks, jumping skyward with the recoil.

When the smoke clears the can's where it was, undisturbed, just like the tree it was resting in, and as far as I can tell, all the others that surround it. I have no idea where the bullet went.

I return the pistol to its holster. I tell myself it'll be alright; I'll have more time to practice with it on the road.

Besides, my plan doesn't depend on me being a sharpshooter.

The stack of cans inside the airlock grows steadily. By mid-morning the passageway that leads to the shaft is once again clear of boxes, but I reckon I'm done. There's enough rations there now to last the Juvies while I'll be gone.

I gather up the last of the spoiled cans and set off across the compound. If there was any doubt before, there can be none now; most boxes had no more than a handful of cans that could be saved. I have no reason to think what's down in the stores will be any different. I don't need to check the card in my pocket to know that's nowhere near enough to see the twenty-four of us through the winter.

A gust of wind picks the windsock up, sets it clanking against its pole as I pass.

What's there should stretch for three, though.

When I return from The Greenbrier I'll send the Juvies back to Mount Weather. Mags, the kid and me will stay here for the winter. I doubt there'll be too many objections to that, not after they find out where I've been, and why I went there.

I reach the security barrier, rest the box on top of it.

When the storms clear I'll find Mags, the kid and me somewhere else to go.

That's months from now. You're certain Gilbey's medicine will see them through till then?

I have no answer for that, so instead I clamber over and set off into the woods on the other side.

I'M HALFWAY DOWN THE SHAFT from the airlock when I hear something like a cough from way down deep in the silo. I stop to listen. For a long moment there's silence and then I hear it again. On the third go it catches, sputters, almost dies, and then settles into a lumpy rattle. A few seconds later the bulkhead lamp closest to me flickers to life. I look over the railing, just in time to see others coming on beneath me.

I hurry down, taking the steps as quickly as I can. The noise grows louder as I drop out of the shaft into the silo's upper levels. I continue round the spiral stair. All around me bulkhead lamps are lit. Here and there a bulb has blown, and more than a few falter like they're on the verge of it. But enough are burning to bathe the ancient workstations, the dusty server stacks, in their soft yellow glow.

When I reach the farms the Juvies are gathered around the guardrail. They lean over, eyes fixed on the source of the sound, but none seem keen to investigate. I continue past them, round and round the spiral stair. Jake's waiting for me at the bottom. He stands by the open hatch, like he wants to go down, but something's giving him pause. I peer into the plant room's depths and now I see what's troubling him. Above me the silo's lit up like Christmas, but below there's only inky blackness.

'Why would the lights not be on down there?'

He says it without looking up, like maybe the question's not meant for me. Whether it is or not there's a voice inside my head that's ready with an answer.

I don't wait to hear it. I unzip my parka and lower myself through the hatch, searching for the rung of the ladder with the toe of my boot. When my feet touch the grating I step off and reach into my pocket for the flashlight. I hesitate. Now that I'm down here Jake's question's got me thinking too. Mags might not need the lights, but that's no reason to turn them off.

Unless they bother her.

I look up through the hatch, but Jake shows no sign of following me, so I rejoin the stair and start making my way down. I go more slowly now, probing the gangways I pass with the beam. I find the kid in his usual spot, sitting by the guardrail, his legs dangling over the edge. He looks up as the flashlight finds him, then goes back to staring down into the darkness.

I continue on, calling out to her as I go. The harsh clatter from the generator grows louder; soon I have to raise my voice above it. I can feel the reverberations in the handrail now, too. I keep sweeping the darkness with the flashlight until finally I spot her, halfway out along one of the gangways, right on the edge of the beam. The top of her overalls are tied around her waist and she's working a pipe wrench almost as long as her arm, tightening the mounting bolts at the base of one of the ancient machines. The muscles across her narrow shoulders cord with the effort as she leans into it.

I call her name one more time and she stops what she's doing, hoists the wrench onto one shoulder. The air is thick now, humid. Her skin gleams with sweat; the thin cotton of the vest she's wearing clings to it.

She waits till I've lowered the flashlight, then turns to look at me. The beanie she's been wearing ever since we quit Mount Weather is gone, but the mohawk's back. It looks like it's been done recently, too; there's a nick just above her ear where she's pressed too hard with the razor.

I wonder what that means.

'What do you want, Gabriel?'

300

The long form of my name again, but there's no trace of the anger I heard in her voice last night. Mostly she just sounds weary, like she might not care any more. I can't decide if that's worse.

'I dunno, I...' I glance around, searching for something to say. 'Why is it dark down here? The lights are on in the rest of the silo.'

It's her turn to look away.

'I stripped the bulbs from the bulkhead lamps. Jake'll need them for his growing benches.'

I want to tell her that no, he won't. The Juvies won't be here to see a single crop from the farms; they'll be gone long before he has a chance to plant the first chits. But she can't know those things, not yet, so instead I just shrug.

'Well, you did it.'

She inclines her head. Maybe.

'What's wrong?'

She hesitates a moment then sets the wrench down and walks toward me. I back up to let her by and then she sets off down the stair without saying another word. I assume she has something she wants to show me, so I follow her. When she reaches the bottom she makes her way out onto the last gangway. This close to the generator the racket is deafening, but I can just make out another sound, underneath it. I point the flashlight over the railing. Beneath me the steps disappear into water. Where it was still before the oily surface is agitated now, countless ripples splashing and lapping off the metal below.

Mags is waiting for me by the clattering machine, so I follow her out onto the catwalk. The thin mattress she took from our cell lies spread out on the grating. I have to step over it to join her.

This close to the machine it's hot. I unzip my parka. Her eyes drop to the pistol at my waist. They linger there for a second then she looks up at me again. She says something, but it's just moving lips. I bend down to hear what she's saying. She hesitates a moment and then leans in. This close to the machine she has to shout to make herself heard.

'This is the one I got working. The other's beyond fixing.'

I feel her breath on my neck. I have to force myself to concentrate. My eyes just want to follow the chain from the crucifix as it disappears inside the neck of her vest.

'Okay, but we can manage with just one generator, though, right? I mean without all that equipment up there to run?'

She nods.

'Yeah, but that's not the problem.'

She looks at me like I should understand, but I don't. She hesitates again, then takes my arm by the cuff of my parka and directs my hand to the casing. I can feel the heat, now, radiating from the metal. And something else: a thrumming, heavy in my fingertips. When I lay my hand flat it travels up through my palm until my whole arm is vibrating.

'Something in there's not right.'

'Can you fix it?'

She looks doubtfully at the shuddering machine.

'I might be able to, if I took it to pieces. I've watched Scudder break down all sorts of things. But there's no guarantee I could put it back together again, after. We'd need fresh seals, gaskets, lubricant. Is there anything like that in the stores?'

I shake my head, no. I'm not even sure where I'd start looking for some of that stuff on the outside.

'So how long will it last?'

She returns her gaze to the generator.

'I don't know. As long as it doesn't get any worse it might hold out for years. It could give up on us later

302

today.'

I close my eyes while I digest this latest piece of bad news. It may not matter for the Juvies; in a couple of weeks they'll be on their way back to Mount Weather. Mags, the kid and me, we won't be making that journey with them, however; this will be our home for the winter. I hadn't figured on spending those long months without heat, or light. I don't care much to think about what that would be like.

She steps away from the machine, back into the shadows. When she returns she's carrying a cardboard box.

'I'll need to run the generator for a while to clear the flooding. Those vibrations will work things loose pretty fast, so I'll be staying down here to keep an eye on it. Okay?'

I nod, still a little distracted by what she's just told me.

'Good.' She hands me the box. Inside are the bulbs she's removed from the bulkhead lamps. 'And Gabe, I'll be busy, so maybe it'd be best if I wasn't disturbed. Can you let the others know?'

I doubt they'll need telling, but I nod again anyway.

'Sure.'

Her eyes drop to the mattress for a second.

'That means you too.'

She turns away before I have a chance to say anything.

'You can leave rations for Johnny and me by the hatch. If you can see your way clear to swapping out his franks and beans for something else I'd appreciate it. Hard enough to get him to eat regular food in the first place.'

I MAKE MY WAY BACK up through the plant room.

I have to balance the box of light bulbs on my shoulder to climb the ladder. Jake's waiting for me at the hatch. I hand it to him.

'She thought you'd need these.'

I expect questions about that, but I don't get any. He just stares at the box.

I swing the hatch closed, but the noise from the ailing machine is only slightly reduced. It travels up through the silo with little to stop it, like the walls had been designed to hold it in, to amplify it.

'Is everything alright?'

'There's a problem with the generator. She doesn't want to be disturbed.'

'What does that mean?'

'It means she doesn't want anyone going down there, Jake.'

I don't have time to explain it further, even if I had a mind to. Things are worse than I thought. Mags knows something's wrong with her; that's why the lights are off, why she's shutting herself down there, making sure everyone stays away. I'm not sure how much time I have, but it's probably a lot less time than I counted on.

I set off up the stair, taking the steps two at a time. At the dorms I step off and run across the gangway to my cell. I never really got around to unpacking, so it takes only seconds to stuff what I'll need into my backpack. I return to the stair and continue on up.

When I reach the farms the Juvies are still gathered around the guardrail. Jake's with them, still carrying the box I gave him. He calls out to me from the gangway.

'Hey, where are you going?'

Their eyes settle on me, waiting for an explanation. I glance behind them. Growing benches in various stages of completion stretch back into shadow; it won't be long until the first of them are ready. Too bad they're wasting their time; those benches will never see a harvest. They give me the excuse I need, however.

'Outside.' I nod in the direction of the benches. 'Those look almost done, and now Mags has the power back on.' I point to the box of bulbs he's carrying. 'You're going to need more than what's there to get the farms up and running.'

He hesitates a moment, then sets the box down. He reaches into his pocket and pulls out a scrap of paper, holds it out to me.

'Here. I made this.'

I take it from him and unfold it, pretending to study his large, careful handwriting while he stares at me, waiting for questions. Some of his spellings are pretty out there, but there's nothing I can't make out or guess at; I know as well as he does what he needs. Most of the important stuff – garbage bags for the skirts; aluminum foil to wrap the lights; containers he can use as drip trays – I could probably pick up right there in Fearrington Village. But I have no more intention of telling him that than I do of actually looking for anything on his list. I stuff the scrap of paper into my pocket.

'I'll be gone a while.' Nobody seems interested in asking why, but I have an explanation ready so I deliver it anyway. 'Now that Durham's off limits I'll need to go further afield to find everything. Mags is having problems with the generator so she's going to stay down there till it's fixed. She said it'd be better if she wasn't disturbed.'

A few of the Juvies exchange glances at that, like they already suspect there's more to it than I'm telling them. It doesn't matter; all that matters is that they stay away. I search the faces for the one I'm looking for.

'Lauren, are you mostly done sorting out the stores?'

She nods.

'Good, because I'll need Tyler and Eric to stand watch outside again.' I find the two Guardians. 'Get your coats and follow me up. I'll see you in the airlock.'

I return to the stair before any of them have a chance to ask questions. I make my way past the mess and the upper levels, into the concrete shaft. When I reach the airlock I shuck off my backpack and count in two weeks' worth of supplies. Soon as that's done I grab an empty cardboard box and set it on the ground. I dig out the list Jake gave me, flip it over and start scribbling a note for Mags. It explains everything: what I saw at Starkly, what I think that means for her and the kid, what I intend to do about it. When I'm done I place it at the bottom of the box and then start stacking tins of *Meat Stew* and *Ham and Eggs* on top. As long as she doesn't think to empty the box it'll be a week before she finds it. By then it'll be too late to stop me, even with the pace I know she's capable of.

I'm transferring the last can when I hear Tyler and Eric on the stair. A few moments later they step into the airlock, rifles already slung over their shoulders.

I get to my feet.

'I'll be relying on you guys to bring food down for the Juvies while I'm gone. You need to check each tin up here before you bring any down. Make sure the fans are running first. Most seem to be good, but every now and then you'll hit a bad one.'

I've left a few tins I haven't checked among the stacks, to make sure that they will. Word will soon spread that it's not safe to test rations outside the airlock. I don't want the Juvies thinking they can just wander into the stores for a box whenever they feel like it.

'No worries Gabe, we got it.'

I bend down and pick up the box I've filled with cans for Mags and the kid.

'Can one of you bring this to the plant room? Don't worry - you don't need to go down there. Just leave it by the hatch and she'll come get it.'

I HURRY ACROSS THE COMPOUND, clamber over the security barrier, and make my way into the woods.

I have less time than I thought. I need to get Mags some of Gilbey's medicine, quick. The Greenbrier's due north from Fearrington, a distance just shy of two hundred miles. I reckon I can make it in five days if I go as the crow flies, which I intend to do. That means going through Durham, which I had hoped to avoid, but tacking west around the city would add the best part of a day to my journey, and that's time I don't have. I tell myself it'll be okay, long as I'm careful. I'll stay off the main roads, out of the way of whoever Finch might have out looking for me. I'll give the hospitals a wide berth, too. Most of those I spotted on the way down were close to the center anyway, and there's no reason for me to venture in there.

I make it to the outskirts with little of the day's light left to spare. Depots and warehouses line the road on either side, their windows silted or smashed, their corrugated roofs sagging under the weight of snow. I hurry between them, searching for somewhere that'll do for shelter.

As night falls I spot a junkyard, nestling between a railway siding and a cluster of squat gas tanks. I stop in front of it and peer through the fence. Vehicles lie in haphazard piles, their doors missing, their trunks agape. It looks like they were once stacked five or six high, but whatever attempt at order there was before has long succumbed - only here and there a few teetering columns remain. Dotted among the wrecks are other shapes, dark, hulking: huge, tracked machines with powerful hydraulic limbs, raking claws; elsewhere the square-toothed jaws of giant, slab-sided compactors. They all rest silent now, their operator compartments deserted, filling with snow. It's a sorry-looking spot and no mistake, but I couldn't hope for better. Nobody in their right mind would bother to scavenge a place like this; stands to reason they wouldn't come looking for me here either.

The gate's padlocked, but the fence has been breached before; it doesn't take me long to find a spot where the chain-link's parted company from the uprights. The wire scratches and claws at my parka as I squeeze myself through. I find what I'm looking for near the back, behind an old Airstream trailer: an unremarkable cinder-block with a low, sloping roof. The temperature's dropping so I hurry towards it, already contemplating the fire I'll soon have going. I reckon it'll be safe enough to light one; the building's set well back from the street, hidden from view by the piles of vehicle carcasses that clutter the lot.

I make my way up to the entrance and step out of my snowshoes. When I try the door it's locked, but the wood in the frame is old and doesn't stand long to the pry bar. I hurry inside, a little windblown snow following me in. I close the door behind me and wind the flashlight. The beam shows me an open space, laid out like a waiting room. Threadbare sofas push up against the walls, low tables slung between them, here and there an armchair. Beyond, almost at the end of the flashlight's reach, a long wooden counter that runs the width of the room. What looks like tall metal shelves behind, stretching back into darkness.

Spidey's antsy about something, but as usual he's not sharing the detail. It seems pretty low-level, though, and he's been on edge ever since we made it back to the city, so I shuck off my backpack and prop it against the busted door. I step over to one of the sofas and sit. The cushion sags and I can feel the springs beneath, but at least the fabric's dry. There's even a stack of magazines, neatly arranged on one of the tables. I won't even have to go searching for kindling.

I sit there for a moment, just listening, but there's nothing except the sound of the wind outside. I glance over at the counter, the shelves beyond. This wasn't a place folks would have chosen to live, before, so I can't see how anything'll be waiting for me back there. I guess I'd better go check it out, all the same. I hesitate, watching my breath hang in the flashlight's yellowing beam. It's been a while since I've had to do this. These past weeks it had become Mags' job, on account of it was she who was finding us shelter. I didn't like that it fell to her to do that, but I can't say I missed it much, either.

I look over at my backpack, resting against the door. I'll tend to it once I've got my dinner on. I undo the snaps, dig out one of the cans I've brought, hold it up to the flashlight. There's no sign of leakage; the wax I've used to seal the hole's still doing its job. I shouldn't get my hopes up, though; it hasn't yet been a day. We'll see what shape the tins are in in a couple of weeks, when I get back to Fearrington.

If *you get back to Fearrington.*

I return to the pack and pull out one of the Sternos and a makeshift stove. There's no point doubting myself now; it's the only plan I've got. Gilbey will go for it; there's no reason she wouldn't. All I'm asking is for some of her medicine. Hicks was ready to cut me a deal for the location of the Juvies; what I'm offering this time is even better.

I don't care to revisit what that might mean for the current inhabitants of Starkly prison, so instead I busy myself opening the can and setting up the jury-rigged burner. When it's done I fumble in my pocket for the lighter. Seconds later the little blue Sterno tab is aglow, filling the air with its acrid fumes.

I step back while it warms my meal. I'd like to get started on a fire, but spidey's still jangly about something or other so I wind the flashlight and make my way back to the counter. On the far side rows of wide-spaced metal shelves, stretching all the way up to the ceiling.

I hesitate a moment, then step in among them. On either side, high as the flashlight will show me, car parts: springs, shocks, mufflers, body panels, here and there what looks like an entire engine; the innards pulled from the vehicles outside. I head further back, letting the beam sweep the laden shelves. After a dozen or so paces cardboard boxes take the place of hubcaps and chromed fenders. I set the flashlight down and pull one out. A few motes spiral lazily through the faltering cone of light. Spidey takes it up a notch at that, and for once I'm way ahead of him. I run a finger along the shelf, then hold it up. Hardly any dust. When I check the floor it's the same, almost like it's been swept recently.

I lift the flap on one of the boxes, point the flashlight inside. I'm expecting more car stuff, so at first when I see what's there I think it's my eyes playing tricks on me.

Candy bars.

Scores of them, maybe hundreds. *Hershey's*; *Twizzlers*; *Oreos*; *Peanut Butter Cups*. A dozen other names, some I haven't seen in more than a decade.

I pull out a *Butterfinger* and hold it up to the light, then tear off the wrapper. The chocolate is gray and when I take a bite it tastes a little gritty, but otherwise it's fine. I check a couple of other boxes from higher up on the shelf. The contents are all the same. I pocket the *Butterfinger* and reach for a box from the other side of the aisle. It feels heavier, and when I drag it down I see why. Inside, instead of candy bars, soda cans, packed most of the way to the lid. I lift one out, pop the tab. The soda's flat, but it's good all the same; way nicer than the snowmelt from my canteen that tastes of plastic and ash and the cloth I've used to strain it.

I take another sip and return my gaze to the boxes stretching up into darkness. At last, a piece of good luck. Candy bars are way lighter than tins. If all the boxes are like the few I checked there should be more than enough here to see the Juvies back to Mount Weather, without me having to worry about whether some stupid wax seal will hold.

I finish the *Butterfinger*, pocket the wrapper. I wonder who stashed all this stuff here, though, and what happened to make them just abandon it? I return the box of sodas to its place on the shelf and start off again, the beam dancing ahead of me down the aisle. The cardboard boxes continue for a while and then stop, as abruptly as they had begun. At first I think the shelves beyond are empty, but when I shine the flashlight further along I see they're not. The beam catches a familiar shape, just beyond the next upright: a pair of stockinged feet. Spidey bleats a warning, begging me to run, but instead I stop, take a breath. It's been a while since I've come across a dead body, but it's hardly my first. Over the years I've seen my fair share of them, grown as used to the experience as I expect a person can. I can't say I'm thrilled at the prospect of finding another, but I'm certainly not about to abandon a find like this over it.

I take a breath, steady the flashlight. At least the mystery of who stocked this place has been solved. I have to hand it to them: they picked a good spot to hide their stash, a place no one would think to check; the fact that it's gone undiscovered all this time is testament to that. I guess they set up camp right next to it, presumably meaning to guard it against those who would have taken it from them. At some point along the way the cold's had another idea, however, and the cold, being a vicious bitch, has prevailed: they've frozen to death, long before they had a chance to consume what they'd gathered. I shift the beam forward, trying to ignore the fresh caterwauling inside my head as it shows me a pair of hands, folded neat across a shallow rise of chest. It's a girl, or at least once was. A girl no older than I am. The light slides up over collarbones thin as pencils, to a slender neck. Spidey's pinging like crazy now, and at last I start to realize my mistake. This is no corpse. Her skin is pale, smooth, unblemished by decay. She looks just like she's sleeping.

I cover the windup with my hand before the light can land on her face, afraid that it might wake her. Spidey's pleading with me to get out of there, but instead I glance over to the other side of the aisle. Another one, a boy this time, hands just the same, neat across his breastbone. I slowly angle the flashlight up, sweep it carefully over the shelves above.

On either side, more of them, as far as the beam will show me.

I TAKE A QUICK STEP backwards, then another, my heart racing. Looks like these furies are all still out of it, just like the ones in the basement of the hospital in Blacksburg, but after what I saw in Starkly I might not be willing to bet the farm on it. I turn around and hurry back towards the counter. Outside night's already fallen; under normal circumstances I wouldn't even be contemplating a fresh search for shelter. I'll have to take my chances, however; I don't plan on spending another minute under the same roof as whatever's back there.

But as I step from between the shelves I stop. The door I thought I had closed behind me when I came in hangs ajar, and when I look there's no sign of the backpack I had propped against it. That's not what has spidey dialed all the way up to DEFCON 1, however. I glance over at the sofa. The little Sterno's still burning away in its makeshift stove. The flame is low, the light it casts next to useless, but sufficient to show me a dark shape, hunched over it.

I freeze and for a dozen heartbeats just stand there, staring. The figure on the sofa doesn't move, least not as far as I can tell. I can't even be sure it's seen me. I realize I'm still holding the soda can I took from the shelves. I set it on the counter as quietly as I can and reach down for the pistol. As my fingers close around the grip whatever it is that's sitting there looks up from the flame.

'Hey! How're y'all doin?'

The hand on the pistol relaxes a fraction and I allow myself to exhale. I shine the flashlight in the direction of the voice. The hood of a sweatshirt covers his head, hiding his face, but whoever this latest interloper in the run of poor choices that has become my life might be, at least he's not like one of those things in back. I know this for one simple reason: furies can't talk.

That undeniable piece of logic does little to calm spidey, however. I try to quiet him as I make my way around the counter, but with little success. The figure on the sofa speaks again.

'My name's Vince, by the way.'

I hold a finger to my lips then use it to point behind me.

'Nice to meet you Vince, but you need to keep it down now. There's a bunch of furies back there.'

I half expect him to up and bolt for the door at this news, but instead he looks past me, into the shelves, like he's considering what I've just said. After a moment he just says *Good to know*, then gestures at the can of franks and beans bubbling away on the stove.

'This yours?' He leans forward. 'Sure don't smell very good.' He shakes his head, as if to confirm it. 'Hey, y'all wanna see something neat?'

He doesn't wait for my answer, just pushes up his sleeves and places his hands over the makeshift stove. His arms look thin, like he may not have eaten recently. He flips them over, so his palms are facing down, then starts moving them in slow interlocking circles, like he's a magician, performing a trick. His hands speed up, going faster and faster until they're a blur. After a few moments he pulls them away with a flourish. The stove's still there, the remnants of the Sterno burning away inside it. But the can that was sitting on top a moment before has disappeared.

'Pretty neat, huh?'

He keeps his head down, but I get the feeling he's waiting for a reaction, maybe even some applause. I just stand there with the flashlight, uncertain what to do. I begin to wonder if there's something not right with him, like maybe not all his dogs are barking. I know he heard what I said, because he responded to it.

'Alright, let's see what else y'all got in here.'

He bends forward and reaches down between his knees, his hand disappearing into something that looks like it might be my backpack. He pulls out a can, appears to study it for a moment, then discards it. It clatters noisily to the floor.

I glance over my shoulder, nervous that something back there might have heard.

'Hey, stop that now. We got to get out of this place.'

He keeps rummaging through my pack, like he doesn't hear me, or if he does he doesn't care. I take a step closer.

'Listen, friend, I don't know what your deal is, but I mean to be on my way, and if you have any sense you'll come with me. It's not safe here, you might want to trust me on that.'

He doesn't lift his head from the pack. Instead he pulls out another can, sends it sailing over his shoulder. It crashes to the floor somewhere behind him.

'Hey, quit that! I mean it now. That's my stuff.'

'It's only fair. That candy bar y'all ate was ours. The Coke you drank, too.' He pulls out another can, tosses it. 'And then there's the door you busted.'

Ours? Does he live here, among the furies? That'd make him crazier than a sprayed roach, and I don't care much to tangle with an insane person. Spidey's begging me to just cut my losses and get out of here. I glance over at the door, then back at the hooded figure hunched over my backpack, still pulling stuff out it. But I can't just leave; I need what's in that pack to get me to The Greenbrier.

I pull the pistol from the holster and hold it up so he can see.

'Hey, asshole! That's enough. I mean it now; I have a

gun.'

If he hears me he gives no sign of it. Another tin gets discarded, skitters across the floor, rolls noisily off into darkness. I level the pistol at him, like I mean business. He continues to ignore me, so I lever the hammer back with my thumb. There's a loud click as it locks into position.

That finally seems to get his attention. The hood lifts a fraction, like he might be considering what I've just said. He tilts his head to one side and raises his voice.

'Y'all hear that, Cass? Sundance here says he's got a gun.'

I'm wondering if whoever he's talking to is real or just a figment of his imagination, when all of a sudden out of the corner of my eye I catch movement, a shifting in the darkness, almost too fast to comprehend. My brain's still contemplating what instructions it might want to issue to the rest of my body when I feel the pistol wrenched from my hand.

I snap my head around, startled. Where a second ago there was nothing now a girl stands. She's wearing a denim jacket, a bunch of buttons pinned to the front: *This Is Not The Life I Ordered; Stare All You Want; Bite Me;* a bunch of others I can't read. Beneath it a short skirt, scruffy-looking high-tops. Her hair is cut in a ragged bob. In the flashlight's yellowing glow it seems orange, maybe even pink. Her bangs hang down, hiding most of her face, but where they end I can see her jaw working. She turns the pistol she's just taken from me over in her hands, points it at the ground, squints along the barrel.

'Hardly a gun, Vince. More of an antique.'

I point the flashlight at her. She looks at me sideways through the strands of hair – definitely pink – that fall across her face.

'What, you couldn't have found something older?'

She lowers the hammer, studies the pistol a moment longer, then with a flick of her wrist sends it spinning towards the sofa. My eyes twitch left, trying to follow the shallow arc it takes, but I'm *way* too slow. By the time I catch up Vince is already on his feet, and now he's standing atop the low table. He snatches it from the air with an almost alarming grace.

I take a step backwards, finally beginning to realize how wrong I've got this. I swing the flashlight in his direction. The beam shows me faded jeans, snugged down over a pair of scuffed work boots, a leather jacket. The sweatshirt he wears underneath has an eagle's head on it and the words *Lynyrd Skynyrd*. I don't know what that means; it doesn't even sound like English. I hesitate for a second and then angle the flashlight up. The beam slips into the cowl of his hood, suddenly setting his eyes ablaze. He narrows them a fraction, but doesn't look away.

He steps down off the table and pulls back the hood, revealing a shock of white hair. His face splits into a lopsided grin. If it was his intention to reassure me with that gesture, he's missed the mark, and by some margin. He regards me the way a fox might a chicken that's just wandered into its den, all of its own accord.

I stand there, rooted to the spot, just staring back at him.

He holds me in his gaze a moment longer, then he looks over my shoulder and whistles through his teeth.

*

THERE'S A SOUND FROM BACK IN THE DARKNESS, faint, like I think I remember the flutter of birds' wings, and when I swing the flashlight around others are appearing from among the shelves. They take up positions all around me, by sofas or armchairs or backed against the wall. Others hop up on the counter, like it's nothing to them. Some are small, little bigger than the kid. With the exception of maybe Vince none seem older than I am. They keep coming, one after another, until I count maybe twenty.

When the last of them has emerged I turn back around. Vince is standing right in front of me now. I take a half-step backwards, surprised by his sudden proximity. I hadn't heard him step closer.

'So y'all are the one the prisoners been out looking for.' The smile disappears and his face creases into a frown, like something's troubling him. He leans in, tilts his head, like he's testing the air, then looks over at the girl. 'Why ain't he more afraid of us, Cass?'

My brain's still trying to come to terms with what I'm seeing, but I realize he's right. My heart's doing a little giddy-up, for sure, but there's something else, another feeling, for the most part keeping the fear in check. It takes me a moment to recognize what it is.

Relief. I'm almost light-headed with it. The stuff with Mags and the kid, I've had it all wrong. They're not sick anymore, not like Marv was. They're on their way to becoming whatever Vince and Cass and all these others are.

The girl with the pink hair shrugs, like she could care less. She takes to studying a fingernail that's already been bitten back to the quick.

319

'I dunno, Vince. Could be he's too dumb to realize the fix he's in.'

The once called Vince looks me up and down, like he's considering this.

'Could be, Cass, could be. He sure don't look that bright, even for a warmblood.' He glances around, as though waiting for a reaction from the others. 'Tall enough though, ain't he?' He leans back on his heels, cups one hand to his mouth. 'Hey, up there! Y'all got a name?'

I shake myself from my stupor, manage to stammer out an answer.

'Gabriel. Gabe.'

He stares up at me for a moment, like he's considering that. I feel like I should say something. I have so many questions, but my mind's still running 'round in herky-jerky circles, which makes it hard to put them in any sort of order.

'What are…I mean, how did you come to be this way?'

The one called Vince holds my gaze a second longer then turns to the girl with the pink hair.

'Where's this guy been, Cass?'

She doesn't look up from her fingernails.

'Hidin' out inside a mountain, Vince.'

I open my mouth to ask how she knows that, then close it again. Vince has slipped his finger through the trigger guard on Hicks' pistol and has taken to spinning it, slow lazy rotations, first this way then that. It seems like I should pay attention to that.

'So waddya think, should we hand him over to them?'

Cass just shakes her head.

'You could, Vince, but it'd be a mistake. I keep telling you: the prisoners, they ain't a problem. Hell, they don't even know for sure we exist. That'd soon change if you give this one to them, though. You can be sure he'd tell them where we're at, too.'

Vince's face scrunches into a scowl and he glares at me, like I've already done the thing I've been accused of.

'What should we do with him, then? Give him to the crazies?'

Crazies? I look over at Cass, but she's already shaking her head.

'You don't want to get them any more riled up than they already are.'

Vince stops twirling the pistol for a second and looks at her.

'I ain't afraid of their kind.'

She flicks the hair from in front of her face

'I never said you was. All the same.' She hesitates a moment then looks up from her fingers, cuts a glance at the pistol. 'You let me have that back, I'll take care of him for you.'

Vince looks at her.

'Y'all would?'

She takes a step closer, nodding quickly.

'You were right about this one, Vince; I can see it now. He's different. Pokin' his nose in where it don't belong; stealin' our stuff; wavin' his gun around at us.'

A slow smile spreads across Vince's lips, like he likes the way that sounds. I start to explain I hadn't been looking for them; that me stumbling in here was just chance. He swings the pistol in my direction so fast it makes my head spin.

'Now y'all just need to stay quiet while us grown-ups discuss this.' He looks back at the girl. 'Sorry about that, Cass. Rude. Go on, now.'

'Like I said, Vince, you had it right, before. I should've just let you deal with him, with all of them, back when we had the chance.'

Vince waits a moment, like he's thinking on it, then he tosses her the gun. She catches it effortlessly then waves it in the direction of the door, like whatever she has planned for me, she's anxious to be getting on with it.

'Alright, let's go.'

I open my mouth, meaning to protest my innocence again. I get rewarded with a jab of the pistol to my ribs. Not hard enough to hurt, but the speed of it surprises me. I step towards the door. As I pass Vince he leans in. His nostrils flare and then his face creases into a smile.

'Hey, Cass - I think he's finally startin' to get it.'

*

OUTSIDE IT'S ALREADY FULL DARK; the cold bites before I've even stepped through the door. My snowshoes are where I left them, up against the wall. Cass pokes around in the snow a little further along, then picks up what looks like a tennis racket, the bindings improvised out of duct tape. Her fingers are bare, but if the temperature bothers her she shows no sign of it. She bends to retrieve another then drops both to the ground and steps into them.

Vince appears in the doorway behind me.

'Where y'all bringin' him?'

'The railway line.'

'Why don't y'all just do it right here?'

'Really? You wanna have to step over him every time we go outside?'

Vince scratches his head, like he's considering this. The thought of him stepping over my frozen corpse brings home to me the trouble I'm in, and I feel the first quickening tendrils of panic wrap themselves around my insides, urging me to bolt. I take a deep breath, push the fear back down. I wouldn't make it more than a half-dozen paces. I'll go along with the girl, for now. Wherever she means to take me, I have a better chance away from the rest of them.

I step into my snowshoes without waiting for an instruction. Vince watches me. He waits till I'm done tightening the straps, then points at my feet.

'Hold up now. Fancy snowshoes like that are hard to come by. It's not far to the fence. He can walk it.'

Cass gives a little shake of her head, sighs.

'Alright, you heard him.'

I bend down and unsnap the bindings, step out of

323

them. My boots sink into the snow, but not too deep; the trailer provides a measure of shelter and in front of the building the snow hasn't had the chance to drift. I stamp my feet, anxious now to get moving. It won't be long before the cold makes my limbs unreliable, and however I plan to escape, I need to do it before that happens. Cass waves the pistol into the darkness, motioning me on. I wind the flashlight and set off, following the direction she's indicated. Vince and the rest of them hang back by the door, watching.

Beyond the trailer the snow deepens. Within a few paces it's above the tops of my boots; I have to lift my knees high to clear the drifts. It's an effort, but at least it'll keep my muscles warm, least for a while. I risk a glance behind me. Cass isn't close enough that I might try reaching the gun.

And you think if she were you could take it from her?

I might not care to hear it, but a part of me knows the voice is right. I've seen how quick she is. I'll have to be smarter than that. I wait till I reckon we're far enough from the others then I stop, pretending like I need to get my breath back.

'So what are you, exactly?'

I say it mostly for something to say, to get a conversation going while I come up with a plan. But even as I hear the words I realize part of me desperately needs to know. Satisfying my curiosity doesn't seem to be high on Cass's list of priorities, however. She just tilts her head and shows me the gun, like *Really, this is what you want to talk about, now?*

I start forward again.

'But you're some kind of fury, though, right?'

I don't expect a response; my brain's already trying to come up with something else to say that might distract her. This time her answer comes back quick, however, and now there's an edge to it.

'Wrong.'

I stop again, like I need another rest. I try to turn around so I can face her, but the snow's up around my knees and it's too much effort. I look over my shoulder. She's a little closer, maybe, but still keeping her distance. I don't know how much farther the railway line is, but whatever I'm planning on doing, I'll have to get to it soon. The fingers that grip the flashlight are already starting to ache with the cold.

'You must have been once, though, to be the way you are.'

She brings the pistol up, in a single fluid motion. It happens too fast for me to see it, but I hear a click as the hammer cocks.

'You're just as dumb as all the rest of them.'

I'm not sure who *the rest of them* might be but I jerk my hands up, worried she means to shoot me right here.

'Sorry!' I pause, trying to choose my next words carefully, worried they might be my last. 'I didn't mean anything by it, really. I don't understand how it works, any of it. I want to, though. I have these friends...'

The gun drops a fraction.

'The one you call Johnny?'

I want to ask how she knows about the kid, but it seems like she might be about to tell me something else, something more important, and I don't want to interrupt her.

'He'll be fine. It's not him you should be worrying about right now.'

'How...how do you know?'

I wait for an answer, but I don't get one, so instead I search for something else to say, a line of questioning less likely to get me shot. Maybe it's the cold - I can feel its barbs sinking into me now, slowing me down - but I can't think of anything. I raise my hands a little higher.

'So I get that you weren't a fury. You must have been

infected, though, right? I mean, to be the way you are.'

She doesn't say anything for a moment.

'I was. I'm not any more.'

'But, how?'

'That thing with the sky.' She shrugs her shoulders. 'I don't remember much more than how bright it was. But when I came to I wasn't sick anymore. None of us were.'

She pokes me in the ribs with the gun again.

'Alright, Gabriel, question time's over. Start movin'.'

The snow's settled around my legs and it takes longer than it ought to work my boots free. When I finally manage it I set off again, lumbering through the drifts in the direction she indicates. I'm shivering inside my parka now, in spite of the effort it takes to keep moving. Cass isn't exactly dressed for the outdoors, but if the cold's bothering her she gives no sign of it.

'S-so, are there more…more of you, then?'

She shakes her head.

'We're all there is.'

The virus does its work quick, I know that; there's only a small window between being infected and turning. What Kane did to the skies would have had to coincide with that. Still, though; something about what she's said doesn't seem right.

'Isn't…isn't that s-strange?'

'What do you mean?'

I don't answer her right away. I sense we're getting close to wherever she means to take me, and I need to draw her in. This might be my last chance.

'It j-just doesn't seem enough. N-not for a city…the s-size of Durham.'

She goes quiet and for a while I'm not sure I'm going to get an answer. I shuffle around to face her. Her eyes narrow at the flashlight, but she doesn't look away. The gun's pointed square between my shoulder blades;

behind it her expression has hardened. I begin to suspect I've made a terrible mistake continuing with my questions.

'There used to be more of us, but then the soldiers came. They didn't care; they hunted us down, just the same as the crazies. First winter took care of them, though; took care of all of you. Your kind aren't a threat to us anymore. There's only a handful of you left now, hanging on to life outta little more than habit. Soon enough you'll be gone.'

She gestures for me to move on.

My teeth are chattering, and I don't seem able to stop them. I start to tell her what I was trying to explain to Vince, back inside: I wasn't looking for her, or any of them. I was on my way to The Greenbrier, to trade the prisoners for a medicine for Mags and the kid. A pointless errand, seeing as it turns out neither of them need it. I don't get very far into the story before she cuts me off.

'Save your breath. I'm not interested.'

I lift a boot from the snow, stumble forward. Somewhere in the darkness ahead I think I hear the creak of fence wire, and when I point the flashlight that way it finds a stretch of chain-link. There's a section right in front where it's been breached, the diamonds cut, pulled back to create a gap.

I feel the panic rising up inside me as I realize this must be where she means to do it. I freeze, trying to think of something to say, anything to make her change her mind. Something hard jabs into the space between my ribs.

'Quit stallin'.'

I shuffle forward until I can feel the snow crumbling under the toes of my boots.

'Okay, that's far enough.'

I point the flashlight down but there's nothing, just a

black chasm into which the snow twists and tumbles. This is it, then. The end of the road. I meant to do something, to fight, to run, but I've left it too late. There'll be no struggle. No last-minute attempt to overpower my executioner, to wrest the pistol from her grip. I can't even turn to face her; my boots are wedged too deep in the snow. I hold my arms out.

'Listen, Cass, y-you don't have to do this. Just…just let me go and I p-promise, you'll never…'

I don't even get to finish the sentence. There's a bang, shockingly loud, and something hits me hard, right between the shoulder blades, knocking the wind from me. My mouth opens in surprise, even as the force of it pitches me forward.

And then I'm falling, breathless, into darkness.

NOW, YOU COULD SAY I'M NOT OLD ENOUGH to know for sure, but I reckon there are moments in your life you don't ever forget, no matter how long you live. You take those snapshots because the thing that happened in that moment is significant, remarkable. It can be something good; something you desperately want to cling to. Or the opposite: something so terrible your mind just won't let go, much as you might wish for it. Memories like that don't fade, or dim, because every time you call them up the details get etched a little deeper, until each is a record cut so deep it will endure a lifetime. I have a few of them. Sprinting hand in hand with Mags across the White House lawn on the Last Day. The first time she kissed me, on the roof of the mess, back in Eden. My first glimpse of the fury in Mount Weather's tunnel, bounding towards me out of the darkness.

One of those moments is from the farmhouse outside Eden, the place Marv and I would visit, before we'd head out scavenging. I didn't know it then, but it was the last time I'd be there with him. He was sitting opposite me in the kitchen. There was a pistol on the table between us, wrapped in a Ziploc bag. I was afraid, certain he was about to shoot me with it. A question had popped into my head, nevertheless; in the circumstances a stupid, pointless curiosity. I'd read somewhere, in a book or maybe a magazine, I forget now, how you never hear the shot that kills you. Something to do with the bullet travelling faster than the sound it makes.

These shots I hear just fine.

The pistol booms a second time, even as I'm falling. A third shot follows, fast on its heels, and an instant later something hits me, hard, like a hammer, from a direction

I wasn't expecting. The impact is even more shocking than the first. I feel something inside me give, even as the force of it spins me around. I open my mouth, but there's no air left in my lungs to give voice to the cry. My shoulder bounces off something unyielding and I land heavily. Pain explodes up the side where the second bullet found me, sending starbursts swirling and exploding across my vision. The sheer magnitude of it threatens to overwhelm me.

Another shot rings out, but I don't even have it in me to flinch. I just lie there, like a stood-on bug, waiting for the bullet to find me. A pause, a final shot, and then a thud, directly above. Snow rains down on my head and then it grows quiet, save for the crunch of powder beneath me as I rock back and forwards, trying to force air into my lungs. Each attempt sends a fresh spike of pain down my side, but I can't stop; the need to breathe again overrides everything else.

After what seems like an eternity I manage a shallow, hiccupped breath, then another. My mind switches to the task of gathering reports of the damage I've suffered. The pain isn't so bad where I got hit first, between my shoulder blades, but rather worryingly I think I can feel something wet trickling down my spine there. The real action's coming from my side, however. The pain there is medieval; it feels like someone's jammed a pry bar between my ribs, spread them, then ripped my lungs out through the gap between.

For a while I just lie there, rocking back and forth, mouth agape, marveling that somehow I'm still alive. The cold seeps inside my parka, wraps itself around me. It's oddly soothing. Little by little the pain starts to recede, becoming almost distant.

I know what comes next, though. I can't stay here. I need to find shelter; I've already been outside too long.

I lift my head from the snow. I'm not even sure

where I am; it's too dark to make out anything. The flashlight's still tethered to my wrist, but I don't want to wind it. Cass might still be up there, considering whether she needs to come down and finish me off. Instead I reach out a hand, grope around in the snow. There's an excruciating reminder from my side that all is not well there; I have to push my face into the snow to stifle a cry.

When the pain subsides I try again, this time making my explorations gentler. I seem to be lying on a narrow metal ledge; if I brush away the snow I can feel the small, ridged diamonds of tread plate just beneath the surface. When I stretch a little farther my fingers close around metal. The upright of a guardrail? I wriggle towards it. The movement causes fresh agony from my side, making my head swim, but inch by inch I haul myself upright.

I take a couple of shallow breaths then shuffle along the ledge, one hand gripping the rail, the other clutched to my ribs. After a few steps the walkway ends at what feels like a narrow metal door. I grope around until my fingers brush something that might be a handle. It sticks a little as I press down then turns. I lean my shoulder into it and stumble inside, pull it closed behind me.

I reach into the pocket of my parka for the flashlight. I hesitate a moment then give the handle a couple of slow turns, just enough to get the bulb glowing. It shows me a small cabin, a cushioned seat mounted on a thick pedestal, a footrest at its base. Beyond a narrow windscreen, the glass dark with snow. I brave a few more turns of the windup. The bulb grows brighter, revealing a control panel, busy with levers, switches, dials. *Engine Start*, *Brake Power*, *Throttle*, *Dynamic Grade*. A plate riveted above says *GM Electro-Motive Division* and underneath *La Grange, Illinois*.

Cass said she was bringing me to the railway line. I

must be in the cab of a locomotive.

I lean against the seat and gently unzip my parka. Each movement sends fresh bursts of pain down my side, but all things considered I'm in way better shape than I should be, considering I've just been shot.

Twice.

I remove a mitten and feel along my ribs on the side I was hit. When I hold my fingers up to the flashlight I expect them to come away sticky with blood, but somehow they're dry. My spine feels cold, damp, but I'm beginning to think that might just be snowmelt.

She was right behind me. How could she have missed?

She couldn't have, not from that range.

She must have shoved me off the ledge, then fired Hicks' pistol up into the air to convince Vince she'd done as she promised. Just my luck I found a freight train to break my fall.

But why would she spare me?

I think on that for a while, but can't come up with a reason, other than the desire any human might have not to end the life of another.

Except she's not...

I hush the voice before it can get going. Whatever her reasons, I can't be here when the sun comes up. I look down at my boots. Without snowshoes I won't be going very far, though. My first thought is to try and make it back up to the junkyard, steal back the ones Vince stole from me. It doesn't take me long to realize that dog's not for hunting. I don't think I fell that far, but I doubt I have it in me to climb back up, not with my ribs the way they are. Vince and the others can see in the dark, too, and if they're anything like Mags and the kid are now they won't be much for sleeping. If one of them spots me I'll be done for.

I wind the flashlight and look around the tiny cab. A

newspaper, yellow with age, lies folded beneath the windshield, the headline proclaiming the end of days. An old thermos on its side next to it. I move the beam along. A drop-down seat, a sidewall heater bolted to the wall, what looks like a locker between them. I squat in front of it, wincing at the protest from my busted ribs, and slide the latch. Inside there's a pair of work gloves and a large metal flashlight, the end furred where the batteries have leaked. Next to it a single spiral-bound volume, thick with dog-eared pages. I reach in and lift it out. Across the front, printed in large letters under a GM logo: *Locomotive Engineers Manual*. I consider it for kindling, but it's way too small and poorly ventilated in here for a fire, and cracking the door would defeat the purpose. I'm sorely tempted nonetheless. I might be out of the wind, but there's little to the cab's walls. It's like an icebox in here.

I take the items out, one by one, set them aside. In the darkness behind the beam finds an old hinge-top toolbox, the metal dented and scarred. My side hollers again as I reach for the handle. I slide it towards me as gently as I can, unsnap the catches and shine the flashlight inside. A motley collection of tools: screwdrivers, wrenches, a claw hammer. A socket set on a rust-spackled rail, half of the sockets missing. Underneath, a large roll of silver duct tape, a rattle-can of WD-40.

I sit back on my heels, considering. I look over at the heater again. A length of hose runs from the underside, back towards the control panel. I reach over and work the end free. The rubber's old, but when I flex it it doesn't split.

I reach into the toolbox, pull out one of the wrenches, hold it up for size.

It might just work.

HE JERKS FROM SLEEP, eyes wide like saucers, blinking in his surroundings. In every direction unfamiliar metal, stretching and twisting and spiraling off into grainy shadow. He reaches for the mattress, clutching the musty fabric, waiting, heart pounding, for the memories to come back. One by one they return, slow at first, disjointed, then all in a rush.

He lies there for a while, letting his breathing slow, then he sits up, shuffles himself over to the edge. It is quiet now, only the occasional wheezing gasp from the air purifiers to punctuate the silence. It was louder earlier, with all the machines running. *Way* louder. The roar from the old diesel generator had been deafening. He had fled to his perch and covered his ears with his hands, but it had done little good; there was no escaping it. The noise was a physical thing, a vibration he could feel in his chest, his teeth. The girl said she was sorry but they needed to clear the flooding. He watched as inch by inch the waters dropped, until at last beneath the oil-slicked surface you could make out the huge springs on which the silo rests. Once the pumps had done their work the girl shut the machine down, but it had taken a while for his ears to stop ringing.

The hatch had creaked open shortly after. A voice had called down, asking if anything was wrong. It was the boy with the curly hair. He had sounded nervous. The girl had shouted back that she needed a few hours with the generator off, so she could tend to whatever had worked its way loose. He should go back up, use the time to get some sleep.

He hears her now, working on it. He rests his chin on the guardrail and for a few minutes just stares out into the darkness, listening.

He hears another sound, different, and he lifts his head. At first he thinks it is the girl, starting the machines up again. But he knows the noises they make – the shrill whine of the starter; the way the generator coughs before it catches; the labored whine from the bilge pumps. That wasn't one of them.

He tilts his head, trying to determine where it's coming from. His ears are no longer ringing, but the sounds in this place are difficult and he's not used to them yet. He's pretty sure it's not something the girl is doing; he doesn't think it even came from down there. He looks up towards the hatch. It's not one of the others either; they have yet to stir. It seemed almost like it came from within the walls. He picks himself up and scrabbles along the gangway. When he reaches the end he presses one ear to the metal and waits, holding his breath.

Again, louder this time. A muffled crump, like an explosion, from somewhere on the other side of the curving wall, followed immediately by another, then a third. He feels a tickle in his nose, like he might sneeze, and when he looks up he sees a fine rain of dust, filtering through the grille above his head.

He looks down. Beneath him the girl is still at work on one of the machines; she hasn't heard it yet. He scampers back across the gangway and climbs the stairs, padding lightly up the worn tread plate, until he reaches the ladder that leads to the hatch. He clambers up the rungs and pushes the hatch up, poking his head through. He doesn't like being up here, where the others are, but he's pretty sure they are sleeping now.

He stops, listening.

Another sound: faint, intermittent, the ringing chime of metal striking metal. But uneven, not mechanical. And coming from somewhere else, somewhere…

He scurries back down the ladder and rejoins the

stair, his hand skimming the railing as he descends. He continues, round and round, all the way to the bottom. He jumps off the last step, splashing through the last six inches of groundwater the pumps have yet to clear. On either side of him huge springs, each several feet in diameter. Even compressed by the weight of concrete and steel above the coiled steel is higher than he is tall.

The girl has her back to him. She stands ankle deep in floodwater, working on one of the dampers, leaning her weight into a wrench. She turns at his approach, swings the wrench on to her shoulder. She wipes her forehead with the back of her hand and looks down.

He points to his ear and then up, up. She looks at him for a moment, her brow furrowing. She cocks her head to one side and closes her eyes. She stays like that for a moment and then her expression changes. The wrench slips from her hands. She's already at the stair before it hits the water.

He catches up to her at the console. Her hands move over the switches, then she reaches underneath, transfers something to the pocket of her overalls. She takes off again, bounding up the steps, taking them two at a time. The machines that scrub the silo's air draw one final wheezing breath, exhale, then fall silent.

He follows on her heels, dropping to a crouch so he can keep up. At the dorms some of the others have emerged from their cells. They stand on the landing, looking up, their faces anxious. Others peek out from behind the narrow cell doors, blinking sleep from their eyes. They can hear it now too. The boy with the curly hair hurries across the gangway like he means to confront her, but she just shouts at him to get out of the way and he freezes, lets her pass.

By the time they reach the upper levels she's already several turns of the stair ahead of him. She continues up into the shaft without pausing. The sound is louder now;

it echoes down towards them, reverberating through the long drop of darkness above.

He reaches the gangway at the top of the stair, hurries along the narrow passageway, into the shower room beyond. At last he finds her, standing by the inner door. Sweat glistens her shoulders, but her breathing is calm, regular. She pauses a moment, listening, but there is only the same, persistent clanging. She takes hold of the handle. The wheel grumbles through a rotation, reaching the end of its travel with a heavy clunk. She pulls the door back and steps into the chamber.

The clanging grows louder.

He follows her into the airlock. At the outer door she pauses, as though steeling herself. She reaches up and slides the hatch back, leaning forward so she can see through the narrow slot.

The clanging stops.

Something in her face changes and she steps away from the door. She closes her eyes, one hand clenching into a fist at her side. After a long moment she takes a deep breath and returns to the slot, gesturing at whoever's on the other side of the door to back up.

He tugs at the leg of her overalls.

'What is it?'

She closes the hatch and squats down in front of him.

'The man who was at Mount Weather, he's found us. I have to go outside to talk to him.'

Her eyes flick over his shoulder.

'I need you to go back in there and stay out of sight. Whatever happens you don't come out. Okay?'

He is frightened now, but he nods anyway.

She reaches into the pocket of her overalls, pulls out the handgun she collected from the console. She pulls back the slide, checks something above the grip, then tucks it into the back of her waistband. She turns to the outer door, spins the handle until the locks click, then pushes it back. A flurry of wind-blown snow swirls through the opening and then she steps through, pulling it closed behind her.

*

I STOP ON A BLUFF overlooking a place the map says might be Calvander. My right boot has worked itself loose again; it'll need tending to before I can go any further.

I lower myself into the snow and set to. The mittens make for clumsy work. I have to pull them off to remove the tape that's frayed, but once that's done it's a quick job to rebind the boot at toe and heel. The other one still seems solid. I add a couple of strips anyway, then lean back to admire my handiwork.

Not the prettiest, but with a little luck these repairs will see me back to Fearrington. It was Cass gave me the idea, or rather those tennis rackets she had jury-rigged into snowshoes. They looked like nine parts hope, one part Hail Mary, but they seemed to do the trick all the same. I figured with what was available to me in the locomotive's cab I should be able to come up with something similar. Didn't need to be anything fancy; whatever I could throw together only needed to get me back to the bunker.

The rubber pipe I pulled from the sidewall heater, that would do for the base. I cut it into two lengths, both about as long as my leg, then bent each back on itself and taped the ends together until I had a pair of teardrop-shaped loops that looked about the right size. A couple of the smaller wrenches across the midsection of each, the ends bound in place, to give it some structure; a place for my boots to sit. Then a shedload more tape, wrapped tight around the frame I had constructed, and my makeshift snowshoes were starting to take shape. I considered working up bindings, just like the ones Cass had on hers, but in the end I figured there was no need for anything so fancy. They only needed to last me one trip; it'd be far easier just to stretch the tape over my boots before I set out.

When I was done I propped my newly constructed footwear against the door and reached for the newspaper. I might not be able to use it for a fire, but the paper would at least provide some extra insulation to get me through the night. I began tearing pages from it, crumpling them up and stuffing them inside my parka. When I couldn't fit anymore I pulled the zipper up as far as it would go, tightened the drawstrings on my hood, hugged my knees to my chest and sat there to wait for the dawn.

I return the remains of the tape to my pocket and get to my feet, wincing at the pain from my busted ribs. I set out before the first gray smear of dawn had begun to trouble the horizon, but with my side the way it is and the stops I've been making to fix my footwear I certainly haven't been setting any snowshoeing records. If I can hold to this pace, though, I reckon I can be back at Fearrington before the afternoon's out.

I lift a snowshoe high to clear a drift. Underneath my parka Hicks' pistol shifts in its holster. It was sitting on the roof of the locomotive when I stepped outside; Cass must have tossed it down after she was done emptying it. My backpack's gone, however, which means the only ammunition I have left for it is what's tucked into the gun belt's loops, less than a dozen shells all told.

My ribs ache with every breath. I have no food, not even a canteen. And when I get back to the bunker I'll have to come clean to the Juvies: admit to the lies I told about our food and break the news that we'll be leaving again, not even a week after we arrived.

But it doesn't matter, any of it.

Behind the mask I feel the corners of my mouth pull upwards into a smile.

I can scarcely believe my luck.

I don't have to go back to The Greenbrier. I don't have to convince Gilbey to give me any of her medicine, and I don't have to trade Starkly's inmates for it. Mags and the kid, they don't need it.

They never have.

I think back to the newspaper reports I used to collect, when I was out scavenging with Marv. Among them was an interview with a scientist, one of those tasked with studying the virus, in the hope of coming up with a cure. The world had come to know ferro as a weapon, she said, something that had been designed to kill. But what she'd seen didn't support that theory; the way it worked was just too complicated for that to be its purpose. She reckoned those that had become infected, it was like the virus meant to rebuild them, on the inside, to replace their internal wiring with its own.

Problem was the circuits the virus meant us to have were *way* faster, and our bodies had never been designed for that kind of speed. Most people who got infected simply didn't survive. Those few that did became something else, a transformation you'd be hard pressed to consider an improvement.

Except it didn't have to go that way - Vince and Cass and the others from the junkyard are the proof of it. If the virus got interrupted before it overwhelmed you, before you turned, there's a chance you could become something else.

Something better.

Faster.

Stronger.

Getting Mags and the kid back to Eden and into the scanner, it must have done that for them. I don't understand how exactly, but that doesn't matter now. Once the Juvies understand they'll stop being afraid. We can all return to Mount Weather together.

I pick up the pace, ignoring the protests from my side. There's already several weeks' worth of rations in the airlock; it won't take long to add enough to that for the journey back. We can be on the road within a couple of days, and safely back inside the mountain long before the storms arrive.

*

THE HANDLE COMPLETES ITS ROTATION and comes to a jerky halt. He stares at the metal door, undecided. The man with the gray eyes is dangerous, he knows that; the girl shouldn't be out there alone with him. He hesitates a moment longer and then steps into the airlock, crossing quickly to the outer door. The slot is too high, so he drags a box of cans over from the stacks that line the wall and steps onto it. He has to go up on tiptoe, but now he can see.

The girl is standing in front of the door, her back to him. A little way beyond the dangerous man waits, his arms held out from his sides. He's holding something in one hand. The glass is thick, rimed with ice, so it's hard to tell, but it doesn't look like a gun. At his side is a boy he also recognizes, from that night inside the mountain. He stares at the girl through strands of lank brown hair. His nose looks funny, like what the girl did to it, it didn't set straight. A lazy grin plays across his lips. Three others kneel in the snow in front of him, their heads down, their hands behind their backs. The two on either side he knows immediately; it's the boy with the dark skin and the other one, the one who goes outside with him to guard the silo. There's a third figure between them, a bag over his head. The plastic blurs his features, but he thinks he recognizes him. It's one of the two large boys from the first place inside the mountain they visited, the place that had the machine, the one that fixed him. He can't tell which of them it might be, however, because those boys were difficult to tell apart.

Behind him he hears noises as others reach the top of the stair and start making their way along the passageway. The girl with the blond hair is the first into

343

the airlock. When she sees him she comes to a sudden halt and shouts at those behind who are still trying to push forward. The boy with the curly hair squeezes past her and steps up to the door. He shuffles over to make room for him. The boy cups one hand to his brow and presses his face to the slot.

'What's she doing out there, without a parka? She'll freeze. And what's…'

He stops midsentence and takes a sudden step backward. His hands drop to the handle.

'She said we were to wait.'

'That's Peck. I'm not leaving her out there with him.'

He grips the wheel, but the girl has set the lock; when he tries to turn it it just clanks against its stop. The sound is loud inside the small chamber. Outside the girl must hear it too. She doesn't turn her head, but one hand slides behind her back and she splays her fingers.

Stay.

The boy with the curly hair doesn't say anything, but after a moment he lets go of the handle and presses his face back to the glass.

Outside the dangerous man is saying something to the girl. The man's voice is muffled by the thick steel, but he can still make out most of his words.

'…need to watch carefully now…not do anything stupid.'

The man turns and nods at the boy with the grin. He steps behind the large boy in the middle. The large boy looks frightened, but the boy with the grin lays one hand on his shoulder, like he means to reassure him, and that seems to calm him down. With his other hand he reaches for a corner of the plastic, pinches something there, then takes a quick step backward.

For a moment nothing happens, and then the large boy's eyes suddenly go wide and his whole body convulses. Something white that looks like foam spews from his mouth, spraying the inside of the bag. He tries to stand but fails in the attempt, and instead falls forward, landing face first in the snow. He twitches once, twice, and then goes still.

The girl reaches behind her back, draws the gun. For a second the man's expression changes, like the speed of it might have taken him by surprise, but then he recovers. He raises his hand and now he can see the thing he's holding is a radio.

'Those explosions you may have heard, they were grenades, dropped into each of the vent shafts to open them up. Jason, Seth, Zack, Sergeant Scudder, they each have a canister of the same stuff that just did for Angus there. Some sort of nerve agent Gilbey had us pick up from Fort Detrick. It's nasty business, make no mistake.' His eyes drop to the body lying in the snow. 'Only took the tiniest little capsule of it to do that.' He holds up the radio. 'They're waiting for me to tell them whether or not to drop those canisters down the shafts.'

The girl takes aim at the man's head.

''Course if they don't back hear from me, or if they hear a gunshot, their orders are to drop them anyway.'

The girl pauses for a moment, like she's considering this.

'What do you want?'

'Why, you. And the other one Gilbey had been working on, the little one.' He turns to the boy beside him, the one with the grin. 'What'd she say his name was, Kurt? 99?'

The one called Kurt smiles, nods.

'That's it.'

The man raises his voice, as if he's addressing not just the girl now.

'Gilbey doesn't care about the rest of you anymore. She's only interested in the two who were infected and found themselves a cure.'

He hears murmurs from behind him as this news makes its way back along the passageway. The boy with the curly hair tells them to be quiet. Outside the girl still has the gun trained on the dangerous man.

'You working for Gilbey now, Randall?'

'I serve at the pleasure of the President, little girl, same as I ever did. I guess you thought you were being smart, sending him back to her like that? You think a man like Kane wouldn't be able to cut himself a deal?' He looks at her for a moment, as though he's expecting a response. When he doesn't get one he continues. 'So here it is: I fetch you and the kid back, she lets him go.'

The girl shakes her head.

'You won't drop those canisters. If you do you'll kill us all. And if I'm dead you have nothing to bring back to Gilbey.'

The man just stares back at her.

'You might want to think that through a second. Without you and the kid Kane's dead anyway. Or worse. So you decide. What's it to be?' He raises his voice again. 'You and the kid, or everyone in there dies.'

'You can't have Johnny.'

'I'm not sure you're in any position to be making demands.'

The man nods at the boy he called Kurt. He pulls a plastic bag from his pocket and takes a step towards the boy with the dark skin who's still kneeling in the snow. The girl shifts her aim and he freezes. The smile disappears from his face.

'You can't have him because he's already dead, Randall. He turned the same day we left Eden. Gabe had to put a bullet in him. His body's lying in a ditch, not more than hundred yards from the railroad crossing, right there on the other side of the state line. Go look for yourself if you don't believe me. Should be easy enough to find.'

The dangerous man studies her for a long moment, as if considering. In the end he nods.

'Well, Gilbey said that might happen. I guess you'll just have to do then.'

The girl nods, like she understands. She lowers the gun.

'I need to gather my things.'

She turns back towards the entrance.

The dangerous man calls after her.

'Don't be long.' He holds up the radio, as if to make his point. 'I'm not in a patient mood.'

THERE'S A SERIES OF CLICKS as the girl enters the code, then the grumble of gears and the handle starts to turn. He steps off the box. There are too many of them in the room beyond the airlock and he doubts they will let him hide among them, so he scurries over and crouches behind the stacked rations. A second later the door swings back and the girl steps inside. She grabs the wheel and pulls it closed behind her.

The boy with the curly hair steps forward.

'That was just to buy some time, right? I mean, you have a plan, don't you?'

He says it like he needs it to be so. The girl looks past him, into the faces pressed into the passageway beyond the airlock. Her eyes settle on one near the back.

'Amy, can you run down to the dorms and fetch my backpack? My parka too; it's behind the door.'

There's a pause and then the sound of footsteps, growing softer as they descend the shaft.

The boy shakes his head, like he doesn't want to believe it. His mouth opens, but he looks like he's struggling to arrange words into sentences. He finally manages to get one out.

'You can't go with them.'

The girl with the blond hair had pushed herself back among the others, but now she steps forward again.

'She has to, Jake. You heard what Peck said. It's her or all of us.'

She looks around. A few murmurs of agreement, but most of them just stare down at their boots. She points a finger in his direction.

'The little fury; he should go too.'

He does not want to go back in the cage, and for a

moment the thing inside him takes control. He snaps his head around, bares his teeth. The blond girl yanks her hand back like it's just been burned. The smell of her fear flares in his nostrils.

He feels the girl's hand on his shoulder.

'Johnny's not coming with me, Lauren. I hear that suggestion again, though, and someone else will be.'

The girl with the blond hair glares back, but after that she stays quiet.

The girl digs in the pocket of her overalls, retrieves the nub of a pencil. She glances around, searching for something to write on. Her eyes settle on the boxes. She tears the lid from one, presses it against the wall.

The boy with the curly hair looks around, desperate for something to say that will change her mind.

'What about the airlock? We can move the cans; hide in here.'

The girl doesn't look up from what she's doing.

'We'd never all fit. And even if we did, then what? If Peck dumps whatever that stuff is into the vent shafts the whole silo will be contaminated. We couldn't go back inside.'

Footsteps echo up the shaft as the girl she sent to get her clothes returns. There's only one thing left that might convince her. He doesn't want to say it out loud, but he also doesn't want her to leave with the dangerous man, and he's running out of time.

He takes a step closer, tugs at her overalls. His voice drops to a whisper.

'The doctor will take you into the other room.'

As soon as it's out he's sorry. Of course the girl knows this. The pencil stops scratching its way across the card and she closes her eyes as the fear rises up in her. He can smell it now. She takes a deep breath, stepping down hard on it so she can concentrate. The nib of the pencil returns to the paper, resumes its path. When she's done she reaches inside her vest and lifts out the crucifix. She presses it into his hand with the note.

'Give that to Gabe when he gets back.'

The girl she sent to get her things appears among the others, her face flushed. They part quickly, letting her through. The girl takes the backpack she offers, undoes the snaps and starts pulling out what's inside. When she finds her thermals she stops, lets the pack fall to the floor. She takes the gun from the waistband of her overalls and hands it to the boy with the curly hair, then starts to undress.

There's a loud clang as something strikes the blast door and her eyes flick that way. She shouts that she's coming, then goes back to putting on her clothes. When she's done dressing she pulls on her boots, laces them up, stands. She reaches for her parka and steps over to the door.

'Coming out.'

She closes her eyes, bracing herself, and then turns the handle.

The seal breaks with a soft sigh and she pushes the door back, slipping through without a backward glance. It closes behind her. There's a series of clicks as she enters the code and then the grinding of gears as the handle turns to lock it.

He drags the box of cans back over, steps up on it, peers through the slot.

She stands in front of the entrance, her arms held out at her side, while the boy named Kurt checks her for weapons. When he's done he pulls her hands behind her back, loops something around her wrists, ratchets it tight. Then he bends down and does the same to her ankles.

'You planning to carry me all the way back, Randall?'

The dangerous man doesn't answer. He says

something into his radio. There's a long pause and then he sees the girl tense. Moments later the huge soldier with the beard and the empty eyes appears, lumbering through the compound. The dangerous man points at the girl. She tries to back up, but her legs are bound. He lifts her as if she weighed nothing, throws her over his shoulder.

The dangerous man unzips his parka and reaches inside. The girl sees what's coming and starts to struggle, but the huge soldier holds her easily. There's a single gunshot and the boy with the dark skin slumps forward into the snow. The other boy stares at his body for a second, then tries to get to his feet. The man adjusts his aim and fires again. He joins the other two in the snow.

'What are you doing? We had a deal.'

The dangerous man returns the pistol to his jacket.

'I said Gilbey wasn't interested in the rest of them. I never said anything about Kane. He doesn't much care for being betrayed.'

I FOLLOW A TWO-LANE FEEDER Marv's map says is the old North Carolina highway south from Calvander. My snowshoes start to unravel in a serious way just outside a place name of Dogwood and I lose more time than I would like fixing them. Somewhere far behind the bruised clouds the sun reaches its peak and starts tracking for the horizon, but I'm close now. In a few miles I'll pick up 501, and from there it's not much more than an hour's hike to Fearrington.

I spot the tracks not long after I join the Mount Gilead Church Road: a wide swathe of churned up snow, cutting across the field from the woods that surround the bunker, then turning south. That many prints, at first I think it must be the Juvies. They wouldn't have left Fearrington without me, though, not unless something very bad had happened. And why would they have taken off in that direction if they had? The only places they know are north of here. I stare at the tracks a while, trying to make sense of it. Then I spot a set of prints, off to one side, indentations so deep they could only belong to one person. I feel something in my chest tighten.

I take off for the trees, the pain in my side forgotten. Branches swipe at my parka, but I pay them little mind. I clamber over the security barrier and stagger into the clearing.

It's Tyler I see first, his frozen corpse face down in the snow. Eric's lying on his side a little further on. His head is turned away, the gray powder beneath stained dark with his blood.

I find Angus last. His hands have been cable-tied behind his back, just like the others, but his method of execution was different. I bend closer to examine the bag that's been taped around his neck. He stares back at me through the clear plastic. His eye are wide, the whites bloodshot, the pupils little more than pinpricks. There's something around his mouth that looks like foam. More of it sprays the inside of the bag.

I head for the blast door, fumbling my mittens off to punch in the code. I heave it open, step inside, close it behind me. Someone must have canceled the override because I have to wait for the airlock to cycle. At last the fans die and the wheel on the inner door rotates. I push it open. The corridor beyond is lit, but the bulkhead lamps are dimmed and I don't hear the generator, which means they're running off the batteries. A backpack I recognize as Mags' lies on its side. The snaps are undone; items of her clothing lie strewn across the floor.

I hurry through the showers and out onto the stair. I make my way down the concrete shaft, taking the steps two at a time.

The Juvies are gathered in the mess. They sit around the tables, but no one's talking. Some have their heads in their hands, others stare down at their boots. A few glance up as I step off the gangway, but most keep their eyes down, unwilling to look at me. I seek out Lauren, ask her where Mags is. For a moment she meets my gaze, then she looks away again without saying anything.

I return to the stair. I find Jake by himself in the farms, tightening the bolts on one of his growing benches. I call across to him from the gangway.

'Where is she?'

He shakes his head, but doesn't look up from what he's doing.

'I couldn't stop them.'

I hurry past him, down to the plant room, still not wanting to believe it. I climb through the hatch, calling out to Mags as I clamber down the ladder. The kid's waiting for me on the landing below.

'Is she down there?'

But all he says is he's sorry.

He hands me something, wrapped in a scrap of card. It's the crucifix she wore. I study it for a moment then turn the card over, read the message she's left.

I PUSH THE BLAST DOOR OPEN and stagger out, pulling my goggles down as I go. I grab a pair of snowshoes from the pile by the entrance. I stare at Angus's corpse as I adjust the bindings to my boots. The wind's drifting gray flakes over his body, already starting to cover him up.

I had a hand in it, what happened to him. It was me who sent him off after Peck, him and Hamish. And now he's been returned; a reminder from Kane to the rest of us: the price of betrayal. Tyler and Eric lie slumped forward in the snow next to him, bearers of the same message.

I sling Mags' pack onto my back. There's little heft to it, but it has everything I'll need. Behind me I hear Jake shout something, but whatever he says is lost to the wind. I set off across the compound, heading for the gate. He catches up to me at the security barrier, grabs my shoulder.

'Are you going after them?'

I shake my head. That would be pointless.

'Then what?'

I can't bring myself to say it out loud. Instead I tell him to follow me.

I turn and throw my leg over the barrier, dropping into the churned up powder on the other side. I hear him scrambling over behind me. I follow the trail for a dozen paces and then push my way in among the gnarled, blackened trunks. The branches claw at my parka but I stagger on, snowshoes crunching through the drifts until at last I reach it. Jake steps into the small clearing seconds after me. He stops and stares at the tins that litter the ground.

'What's this?'

I cross to the far side of the clearing, drop to my knees. I tell him about the cans while I dig. If he has thoughts about why I chose to hide the truth of it from them he keeps them to himself.

My fingers hit something hard. I scoop the snow away in handfuls, revealing a familiar olive drab container. I work my way quickly around the edges. When the lid is clear I sit back on my heels. Behind me Jake leans a little closer.

Sweat prickles the skin between my shoulder blades as I pop the catches. The case hasn't been opened since we fled Eden and the lid is snug; I hear the contents shift inside as I try and lever it open. I hesitate. What if something inside has broken? But that concern seems trivial now, absurd.

There's a soft sigh as the seal gives. I lift the lid. The inside's lined with a layer of charcoal foam, molded in an egg-crate pattern. Beneath, sheets of the same dark material, square cutaway sections accommodating the trays I took from the cabinets in Eden's armory. I examine the neat rows, each vial standing to attention in its individual slot. None of them seem damaged.

I pull off my mittens. The cold bites but I hardly notice. I reach inside for one of the tubes. Behind me I hear Jake take a step backwards.

'Gabe! What are you doing?'

My hand shakes as I lift out the delicate vial, clinking the glass against the hard plastic of the tray. I hold it up, examining it in the ashen light. The liquid inside shifts sluggishly against the glass.

I tell him what I mean to do. Just hearing the words out loud is enough to make my blood run cold. I realize how scared I am; how much I don't want to do this.

I stare down at the vials, lined up neat in their trays. I reach down, lift another one out, hold it up to him. An unspoken plea.

If there were two of us.

He stares at it for a moment and then takes a step backwards. His eyes drop to the ground and he shakes his head.

'I…I can't.'

I slip the vials into my pocket.

'Alright.'

I close the lid, snap the catches.

'You were right, Jake; coming here was a mistake. I thought I could put it right, but it's on you now.'

I reach inside my parka, pull out Marv's map, hand it to him.

'You need to get the Juvies back to Mount Weather.'

He takes it from me, studies the cover for a moment, then slips it into his pocket. As we make our way back I explain what he needs to do with the rations, how to seal the cans that can be saved, the route he needs to take to avoid Durham. I talk quickly because there's not much time. When we reach the trail I turn to leave but he calls after me.

'Gabe, I'm sorry, for giving you a hard time, about everything. About Mags. It's just…she's…I mean, I always thought…'

'I know.'

'But when they came for her I couldn't do anything either.'

'It's alright, Jake, really. I have to go.'

I set off through the woods, the only sound my breathing and the crunch of my snowshoes. The trees end and I strike out across open fields, following the tracks Peck and the others have cut through the snow. When I reach the junction where the Mount Gilead Church Road runs into 501 I stop. Their tracks swing south, and for a long moment I just stare after them.

I wasn't to come after her; that's what her note had

357

said. It would do no good.

I can't argue with that. Peck, Kurt, Scudder, the Guardians, Jax; there's just too many of them. All I have is an old pistol I can't shoot worth a damn and a handful of bullets.

I have no hope of beating them.

Not like this.

I reach into my pocket for one of the vials. But as I unscrew the cap I feel my resolve start to slip away.

The voice inside my head is pleading with me now. It shows me image after image, of things I have seen in the dark places, of creatures once-human, now pale and bent and spider-thin, their minds lost to whatever bloodlust or rage now consumes them.

Before I can lose my nerve I lift the vial to my lips, tilt my head back and drink what's inside. The taste is a shock: like nothing I have ever experienced before. Bitter, metallic, like how it might taste if you melted down aluminum foil, only a thousand, thousand times worse. I drop to my knees, my stomach already heaving. I cover my mouth with my hand and swallow hard to stop myself throwing it right back up.

I wait until the urge has passed, then look up to the skies. I reckon I have at best three hours of daylight left. There's a Walmart just this side of Dogwood; I passed it on my way down. If I hustle I reckon I can make it by nightfall. I don't have a second to waste; the clock's ticking now.

When I told Jake my plan he looked at me like I'd lost my mind.

But I'm not crazy.

Not yet.

I reckon I have three days before that happens.

I MAKE IT TO THE WALMART not long after dark. The door's already busted open. I hurry inside and dump the firewood I gathered behind the checkouts.

My side still aches from where I belly-flopped onto the freight train, but it's not the only place now. The muscles in my back and legs are getting in on the act, too; they feel all sprung out of joint, strained and achy. I tell myself it's from the hike, but there's a headache brewing just behind my eyes that says otherwise, and it seems like it means business. I resist the urge to pull the dog tags from around my neck to check them. There'll be nothing to see yet; this is only the first day.

I don't much feel like eating, but I'll need my strength for what's to come, so I get a fire going and break out one of the MREs I took from the stores before I left Fearrington. While the chemical heater's doing its work I walk the aisles looking for something to dull the pain. But there's nothing; the shelves have been stripped bare. I wish I'd thought to bring some Tylenol with me, but then I remember my first aid kit's still with my pack, in a junkyard south side of Durham.

I head back to the fire and wait for my dinner. When the carton stops hissing I tear open the pouch and poke around at the contents, but I don't manage to finish more than a few mouthfuls. I set it to one side, thinking maybe I'll feel like it in the morning, then I climb inside my sleeping bag. The branches I managed to gather on the way up were black and moldering, and once the Sternos I use to get them lighting are spent they do little more than smoke up the place. I shuffle as close as I can regardless, but they provide little comfort.

It's only been a few hours, but already I feel it

coming. I thought I'd have longer. I wonder if I should have waited another day to take the virus. There was never time for that, though. Even if he takes the long way around to avoid the mountains Peck'll be back at The Greenbrier in a week, no more.

I can't let him get there before me.

The fever sets in not long after I take to my sleeping bag. It rises in ominous waves that break and crash against my body, growing larger with each set. I know this is just the beginning, but already I feel worse that I ever thought possible. One minute I'm shivering, long shuddering spasms running up and down my spine, rattling my teeth together. The next I'm burning up, my back and legs drenched with sweat; heavy, salty beads of it roll from my scalp, into my eyes and mouth. And through it all, a jack-hammer of a headache that no amount of Tylenol could hope to tame.

Sometime in the early hours the fever breaks, and the chills settle in for the long haul. I drag my parka over the top of the sleeping bags and throw more Sternos on the fire, but it does little good. My bones ache with the cold, like someone's hollowed them out and packed the space there with ice. My hands are the worst. I try rubbing them together, but with the latex gloves I've taken to wearing it's hard to get the friction.

Exhaustion finally overcomes me and I drift off, but it's thin, sketchy dreams that haunt my sleep. Some are familiar: of dark, endless tunnels and faceless things, long and bent and spider-thin, that stalk me through them, a shrill voice I haven't heard in a long time, urging me to run faster.

Others are new.

In one a girl with pink hair shakes me awake, but when she sees what I've done her eyes go wide and she staggers backwards, disappearing into the night. That dream seems more real than the rest, but later when I check I can find no evidence she was ever there.

When I wake the following morning the fire's died and it's bitter cold. My thermals are drenched and for a while I just lie there, shivering, barely able to contemplate getting out of my sleeping bag. I feel hammered hollow. My head aches like someone's trying to drive a spike into the space behind my eyes; my muscles feel like they've been strung with razor wire. Not even a day has passed since I drank what was in the vial. How could Marv have lasted the hike to Mount Weather? It suddenly occurs to me I may have miscalculated. I assumed Marv got the same dose I took, but the truth of it is I have no idea how much of the virus Peck gave him. And it was put in his respirator, not swallowed straight like I took mine.

The realization jars me into action. I might not have three days, or anything like it. I clamber out of the sleeping bag and start gathering up my things. Last night's food pouch lies next to the blackened remains of the fire, but I don't even look at it. As soon as I'm packed up I head outside and rejoin the road.

I make my way north through the city, my head down, my arms held tight to my sides, shivering inside my parka. I stumble into the drifts; struggling to lift my snowshoes high enough to clear even the shallowest of them. After what seems like hours I finally come to the *U-Haul*, where Goldie surprised me with the gun. The low cinder block that once served as the office sits on the far side of the lot. The door's still open; it swings back and forth on its hinges in the wind. I stagger up onto the overpass and continue on, leaving Durham behind me.

By the time I reach the stretch of highway I think I remember the day's already dying. I trudge along it, searching for the turnoff. There's no sign, and I have to backtrack a couple of times before I find it. The road narrows to little more than a track, then starts to incline. Each step now is a Herculean effort.

When I finally reach the ridgeline I rest for a dozen breaths, my hands on my knees. My lungs burn, my sides pumps like a bellows. Inside my parka my thermals are soaked with sweat; it runs freely between my shoulders, down my back and thighs. I shuck off Mags' backpack, fumbling for the snaps. My fingers sing out in protest, like someone's packed the space between my joints with ground glass. I take out what I need and cover the canvas over with snow. Then I pick myself up and stumble down into the valley. The gray fortress grows steadily closer, until finally its stone walls are looming over me. I stagger up to the gate and pound my fist on the rusting iron. For a long time there's nothing, and then the sound of movement behind and the hatch slides back.

A pair of eyes appear at the slot. It takes a moment for Goldie to recognize me, and then his mouth drops open and for a moment he's at a loss for words. I don't care to let him get started. I hold up the Ziploc bag with the handful of books Mags brought with her from Mount Weather.

'I have something...for Mr. Finch. Tell him...it's important...tell him he needs to come out and see me.'

I push the bag through the slot before he has a chance to object. There's a pause and then the hatch snaps shut. A wave of exhaustion hits me, threatening to drag me under. I put my hand out to the wall for support, but it's not where I expect it to be and I end up slumping into the snow. My head falls between my knees and for a long time I just sit there, sucking in air in long, rasping gasps.

At last from somewhere above my head there's the

clang of bolts being drawn back. I stagger to my feet just as the smaller door set into the gate creaks inward. Goldie beckons me forward and I stumble over the threshold into the holding pen. I glance over at the guard booth. The small man Finch had called Culpeper (*no, that's not right; Culver*) watches me closely from his seat behind the pock-marked glass.

Goldie tells me to wait, then he hurries off into the yard. I stand there for what seems like an eternity, shivering in the cold. I'm not sure how long I can trust my legs to hold me upright. It feels like they could give out again at any moment.

At last the gate buzzes and I look up, just as Tully steps through. He stands to one side, holding it open. Moments later Finch appears in a heavy overcoat, the collar trimmed with fur, a thick scarf wrapped around his neck. The hands that grasp the cane are clad in soft leather. I have the same thought I had when I first saw him: that he is other, exotic, not of this place.

Knox steps into the pen after him, holding the Ziploc bag with Mags' books. Behind him I can see other figures making their way across from the main building. They gather around the holding pen and take to staring at me through the wire.

Finch leans forward.

'Gabriel. What a pleasant surprise. I really hadn't expected to see you back here so soon.' He looks me up and down, slowly. 'But I must say you do not look the better for our time apart. You have something of a desperate air to you.'

'I brought you a present, Mr. Finch.'

'Yes. I received your books. Very thoughtful, very thoughtful indeed. It was quite unwise for you to deliver them in person, however. But I like you, Gabriel, I really do. And so I will accept your gift, and give you something in return, as good manners dictate. A piece of advice. One you have no doubt already received, but for reasons I cannot quite fathom, have chosen to ignore. Best you leave here, right now, this very instant. And never return. Lest you wish to find yourself in Mr. Blatch's cook pot, like our friend the recently departed Mr. MacIntyre.'

I shake my head.

'The present's not the books, Mr. Finch. That was just to get you to come out here. The present's me.'

I reach in my pocket. A pistol appears in Knox's hand and he steps forward, but Finch waves him back. My fingers close around the second vial of the virus I brought with me from Fearrington. It's sealed up in a zippy, just like the books. I pull it out slowly, hold it out in front of me.

Tully steps forward and takes it from me. He hands it up to Finch, who examines it for a long moment.

'Now where did you come by this?'

'I've infected myself with one just like it.'

There's a rustle of uneasy murmurs and the inmates who have been gathering on the other side of the wire shift back, like they may not trust the protection the holding pen offers. Finch just stares at me, his expression implacable. I can see I have his attention now, though, and that's good. My plan depends on it. It sends a chill through me, all the same, one that has little to do with the approaching night, or whatever is coursing through my veins. The curiosity of a man like Finch is not something to be wished for lightly. It's the kind of thing that makes a snake slip its head into a bird's nest; that will lure the fox into the henhouse.

'And tell me, Gabriel, why would you have done something as foolhardy as that?'

For starters, in case you had thoughts of adding me to the cook pot, like you did Mac. I don't say that out loud, however; Finch might take it as rude. Besides, there's no need. He'll already have worked that bit out for himself.

'Somebody has taken something from me, Mr. Finch. Something important; more important than all the rest of it. And I mean to have her back. But to do that I need your help.'

He looks at me a moment longer then snaps his fingers. There's a commotion behind him and I see a chair being passed forward. Goldie hurries to the gate to collect it. He makes sure it's settled in the snow, then he wipes the seat with the cuff of his jacket. Finch orders another for me and he fetches that too. My chair doesn't get a wipe-down and I notice he steps back smartly as soon as it's been delivered. I slump into it, grateful that I no longer have to stand. Two of the other prisoners roll an old oil drum into the pen. They busy themselves building a fire inside it while Finch goes back to studying the vial. The prison's walls offer some shelter against the wind, but the air's turning frigid nonetheless. I get up to drag my chair closer, but Knox steps forward and waves me back with the pistol. I sit back down and clutch my arms to my sides against the cold.

When the flames are licking up over the rim Finch turns his gaze back to me.

'Well then, you must tell me what you need, Gabriel. But I warn you, this time you will have to be more honest than on our last encounter. You must tell me absolutely everything.' He holds a finger up. 'If you lie to me, if you leave out so much as the smallest detail, I'll know, and it won't go well for you. Do you believe that?'

I nod, because I do.

'Good.'

He leans back, crosses one leg primly over the other.

'You may begin.'

*

DUSK SETTLES OVER THE YARD. On the other side of the wire more fires are lit.

I tell them everything. The Last Day, the White House, how Kane brought us to Eden. The ten years we spent there, our escape to Mount Weather. How Mags and I went looking for another home for the Juvies and instead found Dr. Gilbey and the soldiers. I describe our escape from The Greenbrier, first to Eden and then to Mount Weather, our journey south to Fearrington. How Peck found us there.

One by one the fires burn down. More wood is brought out, dumped into the drums, sending showers of sparks swirling up into the darkness. I talk till there's little strength left in my voice, and it feels like I'm croaking out whispers. The prisoners shuffle closer to the mesh, anxious not to miss the details of my story.

I leave out nothing, just as Finch warned me. A low murmur rumbles around the outside of the pen as I tell of my plan to trade them for the medicine I thought I needed for Mags, but Finch holds up a hand and it dies just as quick.

When I've divulged the last detail I lay out what I mean to do and the things I need from him to get it done. I tell him what I'm offering in return. When I'm finished he remains quiet for a long moment, the light from the fire playing across his glasses.

'That is indeed an interesting proposition, Gabriel. You have certainly given me a lot to consider. You must let me sleep on it.'

I want to remind him not to take too long, but to a man like Finch that might appear impolite, so I hold my tongue. I've already told him what happened to Marv,

366

and I was very specific about how little time that took.

'But what to do with you in the meantime?' He looks around the holding pen. 'I can't just leave you here. And I'm afraid I can't offer you one of the cells either. There is simply far too much metal for someone in your condition.'

I glance behind me.

'It's alright, Mr. Finch. There's a farmhouse, up on the ridge. I can spend the night there, come back at first light.'

He shakes his head, offering me an apologetic smile.

'I'm afraid I can't have you just roaming around outside, either, Gabriel. You seem lucid right now, but from what you've told me the progress of the virus can be somewhat…unpredictable. Our friend in the basement seemed to have little difficulty scaling our walls, and he is a rather fragile specimen next to you.'

He presses one gloved finger to his lips, as though considering the dilemma, then his eyes brighten.

'Ah, I think I have it.' He turns his head. 'Mr. Goldie.'

Goldie appears at his shoulder.

'Yes boss.'

'Do you think you and a couple of the men could open up the hotbox for me?'

Torches are lit from the fire pits; the inmates set to work with shovels. Finch watches their progress for a while and then gestures for the Ziploc bag with the books I've brought him. He opens one and starts flicking through it. I hunch forward in the chair, desperate for whatever I can get of the fire's warmth. Tully and Knox keep their pistols trained on me the whole time. I can't see how it's necessary; I'm not sure I have it in me to stand, let alone do them harm.

When enough snow has been cleared Goldie hurries

over to fetch us. Finch hands the book back to Knox and retrieves his cane while Goldie holds the gate open for him. Tully waves me up with the gun.

As I get to my feet the pain in my head flares; it feels like my skull might explode with it. My vision narrows and for a moment I'm unsure if my legs will bear my weight. I get no offer of assistance from either of Finch's minders. The hulking inmates keep their distance, unwilling to come any closer.

I stumble across the yard to where the prisoners have gathered. They have the look of a crowd that's gathered for a lynching, or to see a heretic get burned. They part before me, those with torches holding them out as though to ward off the evil I have brought into their midst. I lower my head as I pass among them. It hurts to look directly at the flames now.

Finch stands to one side of a newly excavated hole. I shuffle up to the edge and peer down at the hotbox. There's little more to it than a rectangle cut into the frozen dirt, no wider than a grave, and not quite as long. A wooden trapdoor sits back against the snow. The timber is rough, gapped, but the hinges and bolt look sturdy. Tully gestures with the pistol for me to get in. I glance over at Finch, but he just spreads his hands in an expression of apology.

'I am sorry, Gabriel. I'm afraid it's the best I can offer.'

I ease myself to the ground, sit on the edge and lower myself down. It's not quite deep enough for my height; I have to hunker low as they close the door until all that remains of the light from their torches is what seeps through the gaps in the timber, barely enough to let in the air a man might need to breath.

The wood creaks as someone steps on it to slide the bolt into place, and then one by one the prisoners leave for their cells, taking what remains of the light with them.

I press my hands to the sides in the darkness. I'm glad there's little more than the memory of Claus left inside me. I don't think he would have cared much for this.

I find if I scrunch myself up I can just about sit, and so I settle to the bottom, my back flat to the rough planks behind me, knees pressed to my chest. Finch said the hotbox had been put there to punish inmates, back when Starkly was first built. Its location was chosen with that purpose in mind: slap bang in the middle of the yard, where for most of the day not even the prison's high stone walls would have offered any respite from the Carolina sun. A man left in here for a day would literally bake to death, he said. Right now that doesn't sound so bad.

I close my eyes and press my mittens to my temples, trying to drive out the pain in my head. I think about where Mags might be tonight. The note she left me is in the inside pocket of my parka, but I don't need to take it out. I've read it over in my head so many times I know every word by heart.

Gabe

Peck is here, with Kurt and the other Guardians. He just killed Angus, right in front of me. Whatever it was he used, it was quick; there was nothing I could do to stop it. Peck said they had canisters of it. They're going to dump it into the vents unless I go with them. Gilbey thinks I'm the key to the cure she's been working on, so Kane's done a deal with her: if Peck brings me back she'll let him go.

I'm not going to let that happen. Truck told me a little of what Gilbey does in that other room, when I was in the cage. I won't be something for her to experiment on.

When you read this you might think of coming for me,

but you need to be smart now. There's too many of them.
And there's something else. I think you've begun to
suspect, but you can't know the extent of it. I'm not sure
I know it myself. I'm not the person I was before. I can
do things now. So you see, I stand a better chance by
myself.

Besides, you have another job, you and Jake. Once I
get free Peck will come back; he has no other choice.
You can't still be in Fearrington when that happens. You
need to get the Juvies somewhere else, somewhere safe.

I know you can do it.

M

I want to believe it, that she'll find a way to escape
before they get her back to The Greenbrier. But that's
not the way it's going to go. Those were Jax's prints I
saw; there was no mistaking them. They mean to bind
her tight, like they would a fury, carry her back.

The tracks were headed south, but that road curves
west soon after. My guess is they'll follow it as far as
Greensboro. From there they can pick up 220 and then
it's a straight shot all the way up to I-64. They might be
on it already; it's been two days since Peck arrived at
Fearrington. He'll push hard to get back, to set Kane
free. He should be able to make good time, too. It's
mostly flat country, at least until they're past
Blacksburg. Carrying Mags won't slow them down. I
doubt Jax will even notice her weight.

I start to feel the panic rise. I need to get there before
them; if I let them take her back inside it's over. I take a
deep breath, push it back down. Finch said he needed to
sleep on it, but he'll go for it, I know he will. I saw the
look on his face when I told him about Mags and
Johnny, and what the scanner did for them. I figure by
sometime tomorrow I can be on my way again. Peck has
a head start on me, but Starkly's almost a day closer to

The Greenbrier than Fearrington. I saw how fast Mags was, after. Whatever time I've lost coming here I can make it up on the road.

Assuming you survive what comes before?

A fit of shivering hits me, rattling my teeth together. When it finally subsides the voice is quiet again.

I can't let myself dwell on that. What it might be like. Whether it will even work.

I tell myself it just has to.

*

HE WAITS UNTIL THE REST OF THEM HAVE GONE THROUGH, then steps into the airlock. The outer door is open; he can see the snow beyond, littered with cans. He holds his breath and hurries out, picking his way among them. The wind carries most of the smell away, but it is still pretty bad. He finds a spot away from the others and sits to strap on his snowshoes, keeping his head down. The sky is gray, brooding, but after the darkness of the plant room it seems impossibly bright.

The girl with the blond hair pulls up her hood, hoists her pack onto her back and starts making her way towards the gate. The three bodies that lie in front of the entrance are mostly covered over now, only their outlines visible. She takes a wide path around them all the same. One by one the others follow until there's only him and the boy with the curly hair left. The boy heaves the blast door closed and turns the handle to lock it. He tightens the bindings on his snowshoes and then they both set off through the clearing after the rest of them.

At the guard shack they stop, waiting for those ahead to climb over the barrier. Nobody speaks; there's only the crunch of snow as one by one they shuck off their packs and clamber over. When it's his turn the boy with the curly hair reaches down for him. The others are already shuffling into the woods so he lets himself be picked up. The boy climbs over after him, then tells him to wait. He disappears in among the blackened trunks and when he returns he's holding the green plastic case the tall boy carried with him on the way down. They set off into the woods. Before long the trees end and they make their way out into open fields. The others are strung out in a raggedy line ahead of them, lifting their snowshoes high as they trudge through the deeper powder.

When she reaches the road the girl with the blond hair waits for them to catch up. The others gather around, hands gripping the straps of their packs tight as they lean into them, their breath smoking in the cold. The boy with the curly hair stops, sets the container down. He pushes his goggles onto his forehead, turns his gaze south. There's little to see that way; the wind has already scrubbed the snow of the tracks they made. He bends down, his fingers tracing the crusted outline of what might once have been a snowshoe print.

'They need our help.'

The boy's voice is low, barely a whisper, as if he's talking to himself. He shuffles a little closer.

'Do you have a plan?'

A troubled look crosses the boy's face. He shakes his head.

'Plans were more Gabe's thing.'

He says nothing for a while.

'Perhaps if we follow them something will come to us.'

The boy's eyes don't leave the tracks, but he nods his head, like he's reached a decision. He calls the girl over. The others start shuffling their snowshoes around, anxious to know what's happening.

'Lauren, I'm going after Peck. We can't leave Gabe to do this by himself.'

She lifts her goggles onto her forehead and stares at him in disbelief.

'You're crazy, Jake. You know what he meant to do. You can't help him now, either of them. You'll just get yourself killed as well.'

The boy reaches into his pocket, like he hasn't heard. He pulls out a map, holds it out to her.

'I marked the route Gabe told me to take. It shouldn't

373

be hard to follow; mostly it's the way we came down. Can you get them back?'

The girl takes the map, opens it out. She pretends to study it, but her eyes are elsewhere. She points down.

'And what about him?'

The boy with the curly hair looks undecided.

'I don't…'

He doesn't wait for him to finish whatever he was about to say. He tells him he'll need him. He's the only one who's been there. Inside. He knows it's sort of a lie, even as he says it. He doesn't remember much from that place, mostly just the cage. But as frightened as he is of going back, he is certain he does not wish to stay with the others.

The boy stays quiet for a long moment, considering. Eventually he reaches a decision.

'I'm taking him with me, Lauren.'

The girl folds up the map, slips it inside her parka. She says *Alright*. It's hard to tell behind the mask she wears, but he thinks she might be smiling.

I HUDDLE AT THE BOTTOM OF THE PIT, my knees tucked up to my chest, shivering like a beaten dog. It doesn't seem like sleep will ever come, but at some point I must drift off.

I'm not sure how long I'm out, only that when I wake it's still dark outside. The wind's picked up again. It blows ashen flakes through the gaps in the timber that settle on my parka. I slide off one of my mittens and reach inside my thermals for the dog tags. I poke my finger through the slit in the liner (*I wonder when that happened. I keep my gear pretty good*) feeling for any changes in the metal. But the only imperfections I can feel are ones I think I recognize.

I pull the mitten back on and just sit there, counting out the seconds as they tick into minutes and those slowly become hours. The cracks in the trapdoor grow visible again, as somewhere off to the east the first lifeless grays of dawn break over the horizon.

It won't be long now. I pull my hood back, making an effort to stop my teeth from chattering so that I'll be able to hear whoever Fitch sends to let me out. But there's nothing other than the wind. I press my back to the plank sides. The cold has crept into my muscles, stiffening them; they cry out in protest as I shuffle myself upwards. I stay like that for a little while, one ear pressed to the timber, just listening. It's not long until the muscles in my legs are trembling, however. I slump back down to the bottom of the box before they give out.

An hour passes, two. Far above the clouds the sun continues its slow pass over Starkly's stone walls, its crumbling watchtowers. The gaps between the planks are narrow, but somehow inside the hotbox it gets uncomfortably bright. I shuffle my head as far back into the parka's hood as I can and close my eyes.

Finch said he needed to sleep on it, but it's been light for hours now. I don't understand. Has something caused him to change his mind? Maybe he thinks it's too dangerous to let me into the prison. There are things he could do, to make it safer. I try to remember whether I made that clear, last night, in the holding pen. But when I search for the details of what I told him they're muddled, fragmented, like a conversation held years before and not revisited since.

I feel an uneasiness growing inside me.

That was only a few hours ago.

Mags had forgotten all about Watership Down.

The kid can't remember a thing from before he got infected.

I tell myself it was because I was sick, exhausted, but what the voice said has me worried. I close my eyes, trying to ignore the pounding in my head while I call up the map Marv gave me. I can picture it. Blue and red. It had a logo across the front. But when I try and picture it I can't remember what it said. *Something Oil. Shell?* There were fourteen facilities in total; seven on the map itself, another seven listed in his neat hand at the bottom. Thirteen codes between them; we never had one for Eden, I'm sure of it. But when I try and list them off I manage no better than ten. The codes are wrong, too. I used to be able to just close my eyes and they'd appear, but now the letters and numbers are fuzzy, indistinct, and when I read them out it seems like parts are jumbled up.

All winter I studied that map. I knew it like the back of my hand.

What else might be slipping away?

The Juvies. I list their names, girls first, then boys.

Mags, Ruth, Angela, Beth, Fran, Amy, Jen, Beverley,

Lucy, Stephanie, Alice. Jake, Tyler, Eric, Kyle, Michael, Ryan, Carl, Nate, Leonard, Kali.

That's twenty-one. Including me, twenty-two.

Somehow that doesn't seem right. But when I run through the names again the number doesn't increase.

There were thirty of us in Miss Kimble's class.

Six of the Guardians stayed behind when we fled Eden. Kurt, Angus, Hamish, Zack, Jason, Seth.

Twenty-four.

There was a girl that died. I can picture her face. She was pretty; she made me nervous. She asked me to get her something once, from the outside. Her name is on the tip of my tongue but I can't remember. I'm almost positive it was Lauren, but it might have been Laura.

Twenty-four less Lauren would leave twenty-three. Twenty-three sounds right. I'm almost positive that's how many we were over the winter.

So who am I missing?

I go back over the names again, but no matter how many times I list them out the count remains at twenty-two.

I've known each of the Juvies for almost as long as I can remember. How can I have forgotten one of them? But the answer is obvious; I don't need the voice to tell me. The thought of it suddenly fills me with dread, a terror I have not felt since Claus. I need to get out of here, before I lose anything else to whatever is coursing through my veins.

I struggle to my feet, my knees popping like dud firecrackers. I brace my shoulder against the trapdoor and push for all I'm worth. The old timber creaks, but the hinges and bolt are stout, designed to resist attempts like this. I slam my shoulder into the wood, over and over, until at last a coughing fit takes me and I have to stop.

I slide back down to the bottom of the box and pull

my parka tight around me. I start to make lists of everything I remember. Not just the Juvies, or what was written on Marv's map, but everyone and everything I have ever known. Books I have read, the characters in each. Articles I found about the virus. Places I have been, before the Last Day, and since. Things I would carry in my scavenging kit. Flavors of MRE. I recite each out loud, one item after the other. When I get to the end of a list I come up with another. When I can think of no more things to list I go back to the first one and start over.

The light coming through the trapdoor grows steadily brighter. I shrink back inside my hood, pull the drawstrings tight and continue on, stopping only to holler at Finch from the bottom of the hotbox. But the rest of that day I don't hear from him.

Dusk settles slowly over the yard. Little by little the pain behind my eyes abates, enough that I might even sleep. I don't allow it; I'm afraid of what I might lose to the darkness if I let it take me again. So instead I sit there, rocking backwards and forwards as I work my way through my lists.

As the last of the light slips from the sky I shuffle my way up to the trap door and call out to Finch, but a coughing fit forces me back down before I can get very far into it. I continue hacking until I can taste the blood in my throat and when I slump back down it feels like something inside me has broken.

I reach for the dog tags, probing the slivers of pressed metal with my fingers. They feel rough now, grainy. We're coming to the end of the third day since I infected myself. Whether Finch ever intended to let me out of this box, soon it won't matter. Because the same thing that's eating away at the tags is gnawing away at me now, too, hollowing me out from the inside. I can feel it, stripping away what's there so it can rebuild me, rewire me, make me the way it wants me to be. Not just flesh and bone, muscle and sinew, but the important stuff, the things I know, the memories I have.

The things that make me who I am.

*

I WAKE TO A LOUD THUD as someone jumps down onto the trapdoor. I open my eyes to scorching brightness. I squeeze them shut again, yank my hood forward.

Where am I?

I reach a hand out uncertainly. Rough planks beneath me, on all sides.

A shuffling noise from above and I feel flakes drifting down through the gaps in the timber. The muscles along my jaw ache, like I've been grinding my teeth, and when I run my tongue along the roof of my mouth there are ulcers there. I cough painfully, spitting to clear the blood from my throat.

There's the scratch of bolts being drawn and then whoever is up there steps away again. I remember where I am just as the door swings up and a flood of searing white light fills the box. I raise my arms above my head, trying to get away from it. Strong hands reach down, grab me. From somewhere behind them I hear a voice I think I recognize.

'Easy now. Finch said we was to be gentle with him.'

The voice giggles, like this might be funny.

My hood slips back as I'm dragged from the hotbox. I screw my eyes tight against the blinding glare, but not before I glimpse a man with golden teeth. The grin he's wearing dissolves; his eyes go wide as he sees my face.

Then I'm being hauled across the yard. I try to straighten my legs, but they've seized and won't unbind; I can manage only the small, mewling steps of a newborn, unaccustomed to the business of walking. I give up, allow myself to be carried. The toes of my boots drag through the snow, leaving shallow furrows in the gray powder. I let my head hang down. The parka's hood falls forward, mercifully returning me to the shadow of its cowl.

We pass through a door and beneath me snow gives way to stone. It feels no warmer inside, or maybe I have stopped noticing the cold, but at least I'm out of the merciless light. I'm dragged through the cellblock, into a dark passageway, past kitchens and laundry. I lift my head a fraction. The smells are stronger here, a complicated raft of odors. Concrete replaces stone and the corridor narrows, forcing whoever is carrying me to press closer. Their smell is tight-packed, overpowering; a pungent blend of breath and sweat and clothes long unwashed.

And something else, underneath all of those things.

I lift my head a fraction, wrinkling my nose at it. A sweet, coppery aroma fills my nostrils and I feel something flicker inside me. Ahead the man with the gold teeth continues to jabber away, but I can barely pay attention to what he's saying. I am suddenly aware that I have not eaten in days. An image flashes before my eyes, of an earlier visit to this place. The thing I had glimpsed, back in the shadows, dangling from an old hook, as I had passed the kitchens.

And for a second something flares, writhes inside me, a compulsion so fierce, so complete, that it might bend my very bones if I do not obey. Inside the hood my jaw clamps shut and the muscles there clench in a long, shuddering spasm.

The men carrying me are breathing hard. They walk with the quick, shuffling steps of those hefting a difficult load; every now and then I hear one or other of them grunt with the effort. My weight's not enough to trouble men like that. I tilt my head to one side, slowly, so they don't notice, and then I see why: they hold me awkwardly between them, out at arm's length, like I'm a hundred and fifty pounds of sweating nitro on a bumpy road.

I let my head fall back down. Inside my mittens my fingers curl into claws.

They are right to fear me.

I am weak now, and they are strong.

But soon that will change.

We pass through a metal gate. To one side a guard booth, the glass reinforced with safety wire. Another corridor. The bars of cell doors, each ajar.

I'm dragged into a large, candlelit room. Thick drapes line one wall, as though we are on a stage. In the center on a raised plinth there's a heavy wooden chair, almost like a throne. I don't think I've been in this room before, but the chair is familiar.

Next to it a small man, kneeling by an old diesel generator, tools scattered around him. My boot catches on a thick rubber cable that snakes across the dusty floor and then I'm being hauled up onto the platform, lowered into the seat. I'm stripped of my parka. Thick leather cuffs fold themselves over my forearms.

The men who have been carrying me each take a side. They work quickly. Fingers cased in thick rubber hold my head to the back of the chair. The one with the beard leans in and there's that smell again, slick in the back of my throat, so strong I can almost taste it. He reaches under my arms, pulls a thick strap across my chest, feeds the end through a heavy buckle.

From behind me I hear a *tut-tut* at the big man's handiwork.

'I think that will need to be a little more secure Mr. Knox'.

A pause and the one called Knox steps forward again. My spine is pressed into the back of the chair and I feel the air squeezed from my lungs as he pulls it tight. He steps away smartly, but the smell of him lingers.

I lift my head. A small, neat man stands by the wall, clutching something to his chest.

Him I know.

Finch.

He hobbles forward.

'You must forgive the delay, Gabriel. Rest assured, Mr. Culver here has been working around the clock since we last spoke.'

He holds up the thin volume, offering me a better look. The pages are dog-eared, tattered but I can read what it says on the cover: *North Carolina Department of Corrections*, and underneath, *Modular Electrocution System Operating Manual*.

My boots and socks are being removed. I look down. The top of a large, domed head, glistening with sweat. I feel the leather around my shins being tightened.

Finch leans forward on his cane.

'Yes, Mr. Culver has been quite the wonder; we would have been lost without him. Inverters; capacitors; regulators; I had no idea this could be so complicated. We've had to improvise a little, of course. The chair has not seen use in decades; it was in need of considerable repair. And then there's the matter of the voltage. Too low and I fear this simply may not work; too high and the body will simply combust.'

He splays his fingers, demonstrating that effect, then sets the manual down and pulls on a pair of rubber gloves. He takes my head in his hands, more gently than the other men did. His brow knots with concern.

'I have to say you're not looking very well, Gabriel. I do wish you could have given us more notice, so that we might have been ready for you.'

He turns to the man bent over the generator.

'Mr. Culver, are you almost done? I really think we should proceed without delay.'

He turns back to me, reaches for my neck. The one he

called Knox steps forward to restrain me, but Finch sends him away with a flutter of his hand. He grasps the chain there, lifts it gently over my head. He holds the dog tags out, examines them for a moment. As the dull metal catches the light I can see it's pitted and pocked, like something's been eating away at it.

The other man, the one with the beard, holds out a thick garbage bag and Finch drops them in.

He turns around and Knox passes him a set of hair clippers, the kind you work by hand. The metal is cold where he presses it to my scalp. He works his way gently from front to back. The clumps of hair that fall to my lap are shot through with white. When he's done he carefully brushes the last of it away, dropping the clippers into the bag with the dog tags. Then he reaches above my head for the metal headpiece that hangs there. There's a dull creak as it swings forward on its bracket.

He turns around and points to a bucket on the floor.

'Mr. Tully, if you would be so kind.'

The man with the beard whose name is Tully dips his hand into the bucket and hands him a sponge. He places it on my head and lowers the metal cap. Another strap goes under my chin. He tightens it. Water streams down my face, stinging my eyes. It runs down my neck, inside my thermals.

Finch pulls a handkerchief from pocket of his suit and mops my brow.

'I am sorry, Gabriel.'

Another sponge wets my shin and I feel something cold, metallic, close around my ankle, the hard nub of an electrode pressing into the bone there. Tully sops up the excess water with a rag. When he's done he dumps it into the bucket.

Culver makes some final adjustments to the generator and then hurries up onto the platform clutching a thick rubber cable. More water runs down my forehead, wetting my cheeks, as he attaches it to the headpiece.

Finch steps off the platform.

'Are we ready, Mr. Culver?'

He looks back at me.

'Would you care for a blindfold?'

I shake my head.

Culver returns to the generator, bends over it, grasps something there, pulls. It takes several goes before the motors catches, then it sputters to life and settles into a lumpy idle. He retreats to the far side of the room, like he may not have as much faith in his handiwork as Finch made out. The two large men join him.

Finch steps over to the wall and flicks a switch on a large console. A moment later there's the whir of an exhaust fan somewhere above my head. His hand moves to a large lever. He looks at me for a long moment and then pulls it down. There's a loud bang. A sharp, acrid smell fills the room, like burning metal.

The hair on the back of my neck stands straight up and suddenly every muscle in my body tenses all at once and it feels like I'm on fire. I try to scream, but my jaw has clamped shut and won't open. I can think of nothing save the pain and in that instant I know there may be nothing I would not sacrifice, no one I would not give up, to make it stop.

And then, mercifully, I'm gone, carried off into oblivion on a bolt of white lightning.

HE WALKS DOWN THE HALLWAY. The floor is dusty, littered with debris. Once-colorful posters hang from the walls, the edges lifting, curling with damp. Here and there withered pieces of rubber that might once have been balloons dangle from faded ribbons.

The boy with the curly hair said this place was a school, once. When they climbed the steps out front he had shone his flashlight up above the entrance and read the words there out loud, slow, like he was uncertain of them. *Stoneville Elementary*.

They hiked all day, until it got dark and it was too cold for the boy to continue. He lit a fire with branches he had gathered from outside while the boy warmed a couple of the cans with the little blue squares that sting your eyes. The boy wolfed his down, but he had only picked at his before setting it aside. When the boy was done with his own tin he had looked over and asked if he meant to finish it. He was worried the boy might think he was sick, but he only seemed interested in what was left of his ration, so he handed it over. He watched hopefully in case there might be a candy bar in return, but there wasn't. The boy took to his sleeping bag as soon as he was done eating.

The boy is sleeping now. It will be hours before he wakes and they can set off after the girl again. The boy says they are making good progress, but he's not so sure. They have been on the road for two days already, and they have yet to see any sign of the dangerous man. They have a map the boy found in a gas station. He takes it out and studies it whenever they come to a sign. He spells each word, checking them carefully against what's written there, as though he doesn't trust the directions he gives himself. At night he traces the route they have taken with his finger. It has been mostly flat so far and the snow has settled, so he can go quickly. The boy tries to keep up, but he has to wait for him a lot. Tomorrow they are going to cross into another place the boy says is called *Vir-gin-ya*. He asked the boy if that is where the doctor and the soldiers live. The boy said it wasn't, but they are closer.

He wanders into one of the classrooms. In the center of the room rows of tiny desks, facing a large chalkboard. A couple of crudely-drawn pictures still cling to the walls, but for most the tape that held them up has long since failed and they lie scattered across the floor. He makes his way in, pulls back one of the small chairs, takes a seat. A piece of plastic is peeling from the edge of the desk he has chosen. He pulls at it and it lifts easily, revealing the board underneath.

He's not sure what they will do if they ever catch up to the dangerous man. There has been no more talk of that since they left the others. At night the boy takes out the gun the girl gave him. He turns it over in his hands, studying it, but it doesn't look like he knows how to use it.

It is good they are going after the girl, though, even if they don't have a plan yet for what they will do if they find her. The boy explained to him what the tall boy intended to do. He doesn't think that is a very good idea at all.

He sits there for a while, just staring up at the row of letters written across the top of the chalkboard. When the boy studies the road signs they pass the names that are written there are foreign to him, alien. But there is something about the way these letters have been arranged that is familiar, pleasing even. He looks up at them from the desk for a long time.

Eventually he gets up, makes his way out of the

classroom. And for a second as he steps back into the hallway the colors return and he hears sounds: laughter; voices; the squeak of sneakers on polished floor. Somewhere in the distance a bell is ringing. At the end of the corridor a woman stands, waving to him. Her lips move and although he can't hear what she is saying he knows she is calling to him. He stares at her for a moment. Her hair is long and brown, except where the sun catches it and it turns gold. Her eyes are dark, smiling. But in spite of all these differences he recognizes her immediately.

He starts to run towards her but in a blink the colors are gone again, replaced with silent shades of gray. He stands in the middle of the empty, trash-strewn hallway and looks around, confused.

Has he been in this place before?

He tries to bring the woman back, but all he can see now is 98, as she was when he knew her, crouched in the cage opposite his: her head shaved, her cheeks hollow, her eyes dark and sunken, except when the doctor would shine the flashlight on her and they would flash silver.

The woman he just saw at the end of the corridor, it was her, though; he is sure of it. She had been calling his name. His real name. He couldn't hear her above the other sounds, so doesn't know yet what it might be.

Only that it isn't Johnny.

I COME TO SUDDENLY, like someone's just flicked a switch inside me. The experience is abrupt, jarring, and for a few seconds I just lay there, blinking in the gray half-light, awake but empty, unsure of what I am now, or who I might have been before.

There's a strange taste in my mouth, like metal. A smell, too: charred, sulfurous. I look around. The room I'm in is small. Concrete on three sides, the fourth, bars. The narrow cot I'm lying on takes up most of the floor. At the foot of the bed a toilet, without seat or lid. Above it a steel mirror, bolted to the concrete. Otherwise the walls are bare. Something's wrong, though, not with the room, but...

It takes me a moment to work it out. There's no color, just gritty, ashen tones. Everywhere I look it's the same, just grainy shadows, shades of gray and black.

Is this how I see things now?

A helpful voice inside my head suggests that's the wrong question. It wonders how I'm seeing anything at all. I look around the cell again. The voice has a point. There are no windows. The corridor beyond the bars is dark.

I sit up slowly, noticing for the first time that my ankle is bandaged. There's a sensation there I recognize as pain, but somehow it's distant, unimportant. For a moment another memory – *the creak of a hinge closing; something hard, metallic pressing there* – threatens to break the surface, but then slips under again.

From somewhere outside my cell, the fitful chug of a generator. A different memory shifts, slowly uncoiling itself. But when I reach for it it retreats, just like the first.

I stare down at my ankle again. I wonder if I am

injured anywhere else. I roll my shoulders. The smell becomes momentarily stronger. I tilt my head to one side, testing the air, trying to work out where it's coming from. It's heavy, cloying. It clings to my nostrils, so thick and rich it's almost a taste.

The generator grumbles away in the background, its lumpy clatter muted by the concrete between us. I probe for a little while longer and then all of a sudden it hits me.

A heavy wooden chair. Leather straps, tight across my arms, chest.

Something bad. I was afraid.

A metal cap for my head.

A tumble of memories now, each more vivid than the one before.

Cold water streaming down my cheeks, the briny taste of it in my mouth.

A small man with pale eyes and a cane, his hand on a lever.

The hairs on the back of my neck rising on a wave of gooseflesh.

A loud bang and an instant of unbearable pain.

Suddenly I'm standing. It happens so fast I put a hand out to steady myself. But it's unnecessary. There's no dizziness, no disorientation. I stare down at the thin mattress, at the shallow indentation where I was just lying.

What just happened?

I don't remember deciding to get up. I was thinking about it, and the next thing…

I bring the back of my wrist to my nose.

I know what the smell is, now.

I hold out my hand, flex my fingers.

Have you ever smelled burning flesh?

Have you smelled your own?

It's not just the smell, though; I realize I can feel

every singed hair, every inch of bruised, charred skin. My mind isn't ready for this; it baulks at the sheer volume of information, the absence of control. There's another part of me, however, an older, animal part, the part that never cared to trade tooth and claw for reason and intellect.

That part is already rejoicing.

I return my gaze to the bars, just as the last of the memories slot into place.

Mags.

I can't be here.

Next thing I know I'm standing at the front of the cell, barely aware of the sequence of actions that brought me here. I grasp the thick steel, but it won't budge. A voice inside my head, familiar, but somehow calmer, quieter, tells me I should pay attention to that. The rest of me's already busy shouting. At first my cries come incoherent, wordless, but soon they settle around a name:

Finch.

I keep it up for what seems like an eternity. At last from somewhere off in the darkness I hear the soft *click-tap* of heels and cane on concrete. As they get closer I can make out the heavier footsteps of two others behind him. I can smell them now too, the faint odor of their sweat. From the end of the corridor there's the sound of a gate opening, and then a flicker of candlelight. It grows steadily brighter, bringing with it traces of color.

At last Finch appears in front of my cell. The men take up positions on either side of him. I know their names. Tully and Knox.

Finch leans forward on his cane, regarding me through the bars.

'And how is the patient feeling?'

'How long was I out?'

He waves the question away, as if it is unimportant.

391

'*How long?*'

'A matter of hours.'

'You need to let me go.'

'All in good time, Gabriel. All in good time.'

'No, *now*. I've shown you it works. That was the deal.'

He shakes his head.

'You are back with us, and that is indeed encouraging. A proof of concept, so to speak. But you offered *me* a transformation, not merely the right to preside over yours. Rest assured, once your part of the bargain has been satisfied I will release you.'

'She doesn't have that time.'

His pale eyes grow brighter, but he just shakes his head again, more slowly this time.

'I'm sorry, Gabriel. We had a deal. A man's word is his bond, and I mean to hold you to yours.'

I feel a rage then, sudden and terrible, rising up inside me. I grip the bars tight, press my face to the cold steel. The quiet voice warns me that this will do no good, but the fury in me drowns it out. My lip curls upwards in a snarl.

'Let me out, you son of a bitch.'

Finch's face hardens, his features twisting with appalling suddenness. He raises a hand and the one called Knox steps forward, shoulders tight, his muscle-bound body following a simple program his much smaller brain has not yet thought to re-evaluate. He raises his hands, cracks his knuckles, signaling the ease with which he could snap my bones.

The quiet voice speaks again, telling me it is still not too late. There is another game to play here, a smarter one.

Just step away from the bars.

The other part of me is in no mood to heed that advice, however. I tilt my head to one side, watching the big man's approach with disdain. He moves so slowly.

The voice sighs. For now it cannot compete with the anger. Instead it puts itself to better use, measuring distance against the reach of my arm.

Not yet.

Wait.

Wait.

I relax my grip on the bars. He's still coming forward, as yet unaware of the mistake he's made. I allow him one more step before I reach through - *very fast, oh, so very fast* - and slip my hands behind his head. His eyes widen, only now beginning to sense the trouble he's in. I feel the first hint of his resistance, but he's left it far too late. I grasp tightly, bracing my feet against the steel, then yank him towards me. There's a soft crunch as his face slams into the bars and he goes limp. I hold him there for a second then release my grip, letting him slump to the floor.

Tully takes a quick step back with the candle, showing more intelligence than I had earlier allowed him. Finch's expression doesn't change, but his eyes seem to shine. I jab a finger at him.

'You let me out. You let me out *now*.'

For a long moment he doesn't budge. Then without warning he lifts the cane and takes a step closer. He glares back at me through the bars, and now those pale eyes seem hot enough to strike sparks from the steel. When he speaks again his voice has lost all of its softness.

'You should take care not to offend me, Gabriel. If you do you will have to stay in there until I feel better towards you.'

He holds my gaze for a long moment. Then without warning he steps back. His voice softens again.

'Well, I believe it is time. Mr. Tully, if you please.'

Tully sets the candle down. When he turns back

towards me he's holding a familiar metal flask, a length of fraying cord looped around the handle. He sets it on the ground, pushes it forward with the toe of his boot. Finch taps it with his cane.

'To sustain you.'

Tully slips his hands under Knox's shoulders and starts dragging his limp form down the corridor. Finch continues to examine me through the bars. The flickering candle casts ugly shadows over his face.

'I have to say, Gabriel, I don't much care for your new look.'

He lifts the cane, points it through the bars.

'I fear we may have left you out there in the yard a little too long.'

*

AFTER FINCH HAS GONE I retrieve the candle from where Tully left it and bring it to the back of the cell. Above the toilet there's a small square of stainless steel, bolted to the concrete. I hesitate for a second, then step in front of it. Years of neglect have left the metal dull, but it shows me enough.

The eyes that stare back at me from the mirror have sunken deep into shadow. The virus has taken a knife to the rest of my face, too, carving away my cheeks, sharpening my jaw, thinning my nose. I run my hand over my newly-shorn scalp. It's done its work there as well; my fingers can trace every curve and angle of the bone beneath.

Finch was right. I've definitely looked better.

I lean a little closer, holding the candle up. It takes a few seconds to find it, but when I tilt my head just the right way I catch a flash of something behind, like a fish, knifing through water. I was expecting it, but it's a shock nonetheless.

I return to the cot, but I can't settle. I'm not tired, and even if I were I couldn't sleep now, assuming that's still a thing I do. If Finch was telling the truth about how long I was out it'll be four days since Peck took Mags from Fearrington. By now they'll be well into Virginia, more than half way back to The Greenbrier.

I can't be here.

I return to the bars and start shouting. That does little except rile up the fury in the cell next to me, but I keep it up for a while regardless. Eventually I grow tired of listening to my voice just echo off into darkness. I don't have it in me to sit still, so instead I take to pacing the thin strip of concrete between bed and wall. The generator continues to chug, marking indifferent time with its lumpy idle. I return to the bars every now and then to call out to Finch, but I don't hear from him. The candle burns low. At some point I start to feel a scratchiness behind my eyes. When I rub them it doesn't ease it, and before long an overwhelming tiredness comes over me. I lie down on the cot.

Seconds later I'm out.

I come to some unknowable time later, eyes blinking wide. For a while I just lie there, staring up into grainy darkness, heart pounding, while my brain reboots. When at last the memories return I look around. The candle's little more than a guttering flame in a puddle of wax, but it's still lit. I can't have been out for that long. I jump off the bed and start hollering for Finch again, but I get no more response than I did earlier. I return to pacing, back and forth between cot and wall, even though there's barely a couple of strides to it. Soon after the candle burns down, flickers out.

After that it grows hard to keep time straight.

Sometime in what I judge to be evening of the following day, but which could in reality be earlier or later, I finally hear a sound. I stop to listen. A metallic squeak, listless, languid, like a wheel in need of grease; faint with distance, but growing louder. I rush to the front of the cell and press my face to the bars.

It reaches the end of the corridor, stops. The gate creaks open and it resumes, accompanied now by footsteps. A glimmer of light and moments later Culver appears, a candle in one hand, a jerry can in the other. Seconds later Finch follows in an old wheelchair, his cane across his lap. He doesn't look well. His head's been shaved; shadows deepen his eyes and his already narrow features look stretched, gaunt. Knox stands behind, a strip of tape stretched across his busted nose. He glares back at me from the raccoon eyes that go with it, but keeps both himself and his charge to the far wall, well out of reach. There's no sign of Tully.

I beg with Finch to let me out, but he has just the one word for me:

Patience.

He delivers it without looking in my direction and then his wheelchair passes beyond the stretch of corridor visible from my cell and is gone. I hear their procession come to a halt at the end. The noise from the generator builds as the door is opened, then drops again as it closes behind them.

I grip the bars, straining to hear. It seems like they're in there for a long time.

Suddenly the pitch from the motor increases, like someone's goosed the throttle, and I think I hear the whir of a fan. Seconds later there's a deafening bang, and I start, even though I'm expecting it. The diesel engine drops back to an idle for a few minutes and then suddenly picks up again. There's a second bang. Was that part of the plan? Did they have to jolt me more than once? I have no way of knowing.

A little while later the door at the other end of the corridor opens. A burning smell fills the air.

Culver appears in the corridor outside my cell. I call out to him to release me but he scurries on by, his head down. Finch follows a few moments later, slumped forward in the squeaking wheelchair. Knox pushes him past my cell without stopping. I plead with him to let me out, but he ignores me too.

I keep shouting after them to come back, long after they've gone.

But none of them ever do.

It won't be much longer now, that's what I tell myself.

At least at first.

A man's word is his bond, those were Finch's very words. I repeat them over and over as I pace the narrow stretch of floor between cot and wall. People lie, I know it, but Mac said that was one of the few rules Finch abided by. As soon as he comes to he'll release me. It can't be much longer. I was only out for a couple of hours, and I'm sure I was sicker than he looked, going in.

I try and work out where Mags will be by now. Far as I can tell we're coming to the end of the fifth day, which should put them north of Boones Mill, maybe even as far up as Roanoake. Peck will take them the long way around, to avoid going over the mountains, I'm sure of it. That'll add time to their journey. It'll be three days yet before they're back at The Greenbrier.

I can still make it.

As the hours slip by I start to doubt myself, however.

I return to the bars to listen for any sign of my release. But all there is is the listless chugging from the generator.

What if something went wrong and Finch didn't survive? He certainly didn't look well when they wheeled him out. Maybe Culver and Knox took the opportunity to be rid of him? But if that was their intention surely they could have done it easier than with the chair? And where was Tully during all this? Is he gone for good? Is it only Knox, now? I begin to wonder if what I did to him wasn't a mistake. If Finch doesn't survive I could be relying on his kindness to let me out of here.

The voice inside my head says *I told you so*.

I return to the front of my cell and take to hollering again. It does me little good. My cries echo down the corridor, but nothing ever comes back. All that's left in their wake is the distant drone of the generator.

A night passes, then, as best I can tell, another day. I take to reciting the lists I made in the hotbox. My recollection of Marv's map does not improve, and the number of Juvies' names I can remember never gets higher than twenty-two, but I do not seem to have lost anything more as a result of my time in the chair.

I think.

Truth is I have no way to be sure.

I still shout for Finch, but less frequently now; nothing ever comes of it. Peck will already be in the foothills of the Alleghenies; the day after tomorrow they'll be back at The Greenbrier. Whatever Gilbey has planned for her after that, I'm going to be the best part of a hundred and fifty miles away when it happens, with the whole of the state of Virginia between us.

And these bars.

I have failed. The certainty of it settles beneath my ribcage, a gnawing hole in my gut that has little to do with the hunger that has now started to plague my waking moments. I feel the anger building inside me, that I will be powerless to stop it.

The voice inside my head tells me to stay calm, that no good will come of letting that other part of me back in charge. But sometimes the feelings of rage and despair grow too strong to be resisted. When that happens it's like a barrier descending, inside my head, and that part of me capable of directing my actions is trapped behind it. The barrier's not a solid thing, like a blast door or the roadblock that rises out of the ground at the entrance to Fearrington. It feels more like the wire that braces Eden and Mount Weather's tunnels. It allows me to see through well enough, but while its down it's like my hands are off the controls, my role reduced to that of passenger, spectator, while the other side of me does what it must to vent its fury.

To my surprise that part proceeds mostly in silence. There are no howls of rage, no wordless, incoherent cries. Mostly I grit my teeth and take to testing my strength against the steel. That bears no more fruit than my hollering does, however. The cell has been designed not just for those who were content with their captivity. It meets each of my assaults with its own patient resolve, happy to wait until the last of them has been spent.

The creature in the next cell stays quiet for the most part, but when I take to shouting or to wrestling with the bars it stirs, and for a while after my anger has been spent and I have returned to my cot I hear it, scuffling backwards and forwards on the other side of the wall that separates us.

The hours slip by; I give up on keeping them straight. When my eyes grow scratchy I sleep, or whatever absence of consciousness now passes for that. I can't say I care for it much. I don't think it lasts for long, but without the candle I have no way of knowing. Only one thing I'm certain of now: no one's coming to let me out. Dead or alive, Finch won't be keeping his side of the bargain. I eye the flask he left, sitting outside my cell. I tell myself I won't drink from it, but the truth is I could have rolled it further along the corridor, put it out of my reach, once and for all, if that really was my last word on the subject. I remember what Mac said, that night in the print shop. I might have skipped a meal here and there, but I hadn't yet come to understand hunger. I stare at the flask a moment longer, then go back to pacing.

That time might not be far off now, however.

*

THEY FINALLY CATCH UP to the soldiers three nights later. Or at least two of them.

They enter a town with dusk upon them. All day they have hiked in the shadow of mountains that seemed to grow no closer, but now in the fading light they suddenly loom high over them. The boy with the curly hair checks a road sign against the map he carries. He says this place is called Salem, and beyond it lies the interstate. That way is easier, but longer. Or they can continue north, into the mountains. Tomorrow they will have to decide.

The boy chooses a small church for shelter. He knows there is something wrong as soon as he steps inside. A smell packs the air: thick, sweet, and for a moment he feels something inside him stir. The boy dumps the branches they have gathered on the floor and shucks off his backpack, seemingly unaware.

He glances down at the bundle of moldering sticks. It is his job to light the fire. He is good at it, and so the boy lets him. That task will have to wait, however. He peers into the grainy shadows, trying to locate the source of the smell, but there is nothing. There is no mistaking it, though; it is strong; almost overpowering. It makes him think of another church and the soldier with the patch over his eye, opening a flask, sliding it towards him. The thing inside him clenches again at the memory, and this time he has to work harder to force it back down.

He tilts his head, testing the air. It seems to be coming from somewhere in the back. He crouches down, making his slowly way between the scattered pews, checking each as he goes.

He finds the first of them lying on the floor at the end

of one of the long wooden benches. It is one of the men from the night they arrived at the first place inside the mountain. Not the dangerous man, with the gray eyes and the gun, but the other, the one who had been standing by the lake while the others had held the boy with the curly hair down and poured water on him. He lies propped against the wall. His cheeks were red before, but all the color has drained from them now. His parka is open and a large bandage has been taped to one side of his neck. The material is dark, sodden with his blood. His eyes are closed, but now and then his chest rises and a fresh bead of it breaks free from underneath the gauze, trickles down his neck.

The thing inside him struggles, and for a moment all he can do is stare while he wrestles with it. At last he calls out. The boy must sense something is wrong from the tone of his voice. He drops the kindling he is gathering and comes running. When he sees the man lying on the ground he bends down next to him.

'Sergeant Scudder.'

For a moment there is nothing, but then the man's eyes flutter open. He sees the boy and then his eyes shift to him, grow wide. He tries to get up, but he is too weak.

'It's okay. He won't hurt you.'

The man's eyes suggest he doesn't believe it. He stares like that a moment longer, then croaks for water.

The boy fetches his canteen and holds it to his lips. The man sips greedily, but most of it runs down his chin, mixing with the blood on his neck. When it seems like he is done drinking the boy lifts the canteen.

'What happened?'

The man's eyes flick to the boy, then return to him. He takes a shallow breath, whispers a single word: *Waiting*.

'Someone was waiting for you?'

The man nods.

'Here?'

The man points over in the direction of altar. The boy reaches for his flashlight, but he has already seen them. Two more bodies. The nearest is one of the boys from the lake. The other he doesn't think he recognizes, but it takes him a moment to be certain. The sunken eyes and hollowed cheeks make it seem familiar, but then everyone looked like that when he was in the cage.

The boy cranks the flashlight's handle. As the beam settles on the nearest body he mouths the word *Seth*. He lets it linger there for a moment, then moves it along. When it finds the second one the boy jumps to his feet. He drops the flashlight and starts fumbling in his pocket for the gun the girl gave him.

The man shakes his head.

'Already dead. Peck. Shot it.'

The boy picks up the flashlight. He stares at the creature lying on the floor for a long moment, like he might not trust what the man has told him. After a few seconds he slowly returns the gun to the pocket of his parka. His eyes return to the man.

'Mags? Was Mags okay?'

The man closes his eyes, nods. He raises a finger, points to an old metal radiator mounted to the wall.

'Tied up, right there.'

He holds his hand there for a while, like it's important. Then he lets it fall to his side, as though the effort has exhausted him. He shakes his head.

'Showed no interest in her. Would've...had to step right over her to get by.'

THE FLASK FINCH LEFT ME remains untouched, but I find myself eyeing it each time I reach the bars now, so I give up on pacing and take to the cot. I stare up at the ceiling, listening to the sound of the generator. The last few hours it's been running ragged. The motor will hunt for a while, up and down, like someone's tweaking the throttle, or it'll take to sputtering, like something's caught in the pipes. It always seems to right itself, however. Even as I listen it coughs, once, twice, like it's clearing its throat, then returns to its languid drone.

I close my eyes. Peck will be on the home straight by now; tomorrow evening they'll be back at The Greenbrier. My fingers grip the side of the cot as I imagine Truck dragging her into that other room. The curtain inside my head starts to descend as the anger builds, pushing aside the feelings of helplessness and despair. The voice speaks, telling me to breath. I prefer its measured tones to the craven whispers of whatever it has replaced, but I can't help but think it's being far too relaxed about this. I wonder if whatever lives inside my head has gone native. Hicks said the furies put themselves into some sort of hibernation when they ran out of food. Maybe it's looking forward to that.

No.

The generator takes to coughing again, for longer this time. Eventually it settles, but the chugging drone has become lumpier, more erratic.

Are you ready?

I sit up slowly.

Ready for what?

The motor catches, and for a second revs, like it's been goosed. Then without warning it simply dies.

There's a moment's silence, followed by a loud click from the front of my cell as the lock releases. I watch for a second in disbelief as the door slowly swings back on its hinges, and then I'm on my feet.

But as I step out into the corridor I freeze. A little further along I can see my parka, draped over the back of the chair Finch had placed in front of the fury's cell. The rest of my clothes are resting on the seat, neatly folded, my boots side-by-side underneath. None of those things are what's giving me pause, however. The door to the cell next to mine: there's no sign of the chain that once held it fast, and now it hangs open, too. I guess my lock wasn't the only one to release when the generator died.

I stare at it for a moment. Has the creature Finch kept there already escaped? But even as I think it I catch movement from the shadows behind. I watch as it slips through.

It looks up as it sees me, and for long seconds we both just stand there, no more than a half-dozen paces apart, each waiting to see what the other will do.

My eyes flick past it, to the corridor beyond.

I don't have time for this. I take a deep breath, getting ready to run at it.

Wait.

On the floor; look.

I glance down, not daring to take my eye off the creature in front of me for more than a second. The flask Finch left is right at my feet. When I look up again I see the fury's gaze has shifted there too.

I slide it forward with my foot. As soon as it's within reach the creature snatches the flask up, then hurries back into its cell. It pushes itself into the corner and busies itself with the lid. Its eyes dart to me one last time, then it lifts the battered metal container to its lips, tilts its head back and starts to drink. Drops of something dark trickle from its lips, falling from its chin to spatter the concrete.

I'm already reaching for my parka when the smell hits me. My head snaps back to the cell, and for a moment I'm rooted to the spot, transfixed; all I can do is stand there and stare. Something inside me awakens, uncoils itself. I know what it would have me do. The creature in the cell senses it; its lip curls and it snarls back at me from the shadows. It is a puny thing, though, pathetic; it will be no match for me. I take a step towards it. Inside my head the brace wire shutter starts to descend.

No.

I grip the bars, wrestling for control. But the smell is maddening; it takes everything I have not to rush into the cell, rip the flask from the creature's hands.

You have somewhere else to be now.

It shows me an image: Mags, forced onto her toes, her feet scrabbling for purchase as the noose tightens around her neck. The muscles along Truck's arms bunching as he hoists her up.

And now the rage has a different focus.

I take a step backwards, then another. I grab my parka and boots from the chair and set off along the passageway at a run.

At the top of the stairs concrete gives way to stone and I stop to pull on my boots. I take a couple of deep breaths as I tighten the laces, still trying to clear my head. I'm not sure what almost happened back there but whatever it was I can't allow it again, least not till I'm clear of Starkly's walls. I shuck on my parka and make my way down the hall, past laundry, kitchens, pantry, straining for sounds ahead.

When I reach the cellblock I stop again. My luck seems to be holding; Starkly's quiet as a morgue.

Too quiet.

The voice is right. It might still be dark outside, but there's nothing; no snores, no dream-laden grunts, none of the other night sounds the prisoners would make. Only the tinny silence of emptiness, the occasional gust of wind against stone outside.

If this is a game Finch is playing with me I don't understand it. He either means to let me leave or he doesn't. I take a deep breath and step through the door, making my way across the open expanse of cellblock quick as I can. I hold my breath, expecting at any moment to be challenged. But there's nothing, and then I'm out in the yard, crunching through snow. Ahead lies the holding pen. I pull back the gate and step inside. The pockmarked booth is dark, empty. I make my way towards the access door set into the towering main gate and slide back the bolt. The hinges creak as I heave it open. I don't bother to close it behind me. My snowshoes are waiting where I left them, propped against the wall outside. I step into them, ratchet the straps tight and then I'm gone.

I stop on the ridge overlooking the valley long enough to dig up Mags' backpack from where I buried it on my way in. I strap on the gun belt, sling her crucifix around my neck, and then I'm off again, bounding down to the highway with a pace I can scarcely believe.

I take the straightest route I can figure, cutting cross-country where I figure it might save me a quarter mile, less. I'm a five-day hike from The Greenbrier with at best two days to cover that distance. I don't trouble myself with whether it can be done. I just point myself north and make my strides as long and fast as my legs will allow.

One by one the miles fall under my snowshoes. I pass through places with names like Prospect, Blanch, Vandola, but don't stop in any of them. The day grows uncomfortably bright. I keep my head down, cupping my hands to my goggles when I need to raise it to study the road ahead. At last, somewhere far behind the clouds, the sun starts tracking for the horizon. As dusk settles I quit North Carolina and continue on into Virginia.

Neither darkness nor cold will stop me now.

Just before dawn I get that scratchiness behind my eyes that tells me I'll soon need to sleep. I fight it for as long as I can, but soon my vision starts to narrow and things that cannot be there appear in what remains, making me think what I see now might not be trusted. Up ahead a shotgun shack sits just off the highway, gray snow banked against its dilapidated sides, more pressing down on its corrugated roof. A padlocked gate hangs rusting between two crumbling posts, but I don't trouble myself with it; only a few broken staves remain of the fence that once completed its sad perimeter.

The front door's already busted open, so there's no need to unsling Mags' pack for the pry bar. I snap off my snowshoes and climb the steps. The boards were waterbuckled, sprung; they creak under my boots as I yank the screen door back. Ahead there's a narrow hallway, the wallpaper mildewed, peeling; the ceiling cracked, crumbling, the laths poking through behind.

I don't bother with a fire, just find a spot on the floor and lay my head down. My eyes close and seconds later I'm gone.

By evening of the second day I'm most of the way through Virginia. The flatlands are behind me now, and in front the Appalachians rise up, their snow-capped peaks scraping the underbellies of the clouds that hang ominous and low over them. I arrive at a place called Salem with dusk falling and hurry through it, looking for the interstate beyond. Peck will have cut east from here in search of one of the low passes that wind their way through the valley floor. But the quickest way's north, into the mountains.

I make my way across the overpass and continue on, what little color there is leaching away as darkness settles around me. Beyond the road climbs steeply, switching back on itself as it twists ever higher, each ridge gained merely a foretaste of the one to come. For the first time I begin to sense the limits of my newfound endurance, but it's alright. My legs only need to hold a little longer. I am closer now than I could have hoped.

Just as night's getting ready to be done the road finally levels and I arrive at a place called Crows, where I stopped with the soldiers on our way to the hospital in Blacksburg. My eyes have been feeling gritty since Catawba, and for the last hour the darkness has had a dreamlike quality to it. I find a gas station and curl up behind the counter. I figure I'll close my eyes for twenty minutes, be on my way again before sunup.

*

HE SITS IN THE DARKNESS, staring out. Beyond the station house's candy cane pillars the parking lot is mostly empty. The boy with the curly hair huddles in the corner, bundled up in his parka. They cannot have a fire and inside the crumbling station house it is cold.

It has been two days since they found the other two, in the church. The man called Scudder didn't last the night. He listened from across the room as his breathing grew ragged, then just before dawn he hitched in a final gasp, something inside his chest rattled, and it settled for the last time.

Before he died the man told the boy which way they had taken the girl. They picked up their tracks later that day and have been following them ever since, always staying out of sight, occasionally catching a glimpse as they crested some distant hill, but mostly just following their prints in the snow. Yesterday evening, as the last of the light was leaving the sky, they saw them ahead in the distance, trudging up an off-ramp as they exited the highway. He hurried to catch up, leaving the boy with the curly hair behind. But then he had been forced to watch, helpless, as they had marched through the crumbling gates and up towards the big house.

He looks out into the parking lot. It is still dark, but already he can sense the approaching dawn. The girl will be back in the cage by now. How long will it be before the Doctor takes her to the other room?

'We have to go inside.'

He says it mostly to himself, but across the room the boy lifts his head from his knees.

'H-how? We c-can't get in. You saw yourself. Those were s-soldiers up at the entrance to the bunker. They

410

had rifles.' He holds the pistol up. 'I d-don't even know how to shoot this!'

He goes back to staring out the window. The boy is close to giving up; he can hear it in his voice. He is afraid too. He tells himself the tall boy will know what to do, when he gets here. Except he should have been here already, and now they are out of time.

He looks out at the parking lot. His eyes fall on a long-abandoned car, waiting patiently under a blanket of snow right in front of the station house. He gets up, crosses the floor. He clears a spot on dusty, trash-strewn floor with his mitten then sits next to the boy.

'There's one more thing we can try.'

They hurry through The Greenbrier's gates and start up the long driveway. The tracks they are making will be fresh, but that cannot be helped; if they stick to the churned up snow no one should notice. Behind him the boy stumbles uncertainly, feeling his way through the darkness. They cannot have the flashlights and dawn is still some time away; it is not light enough yet for his eyes.

The road curves around, finally revealing the massive building. He makes for a dark shape that squats on the lawn in front of the entrance's towering columns. As they draw close he leaves the tracks they have been following and hurries towards it. The huge rotors hang down under their own weight, the tips almost touching the powder. They creak and groan as they flex in the wind.

He makes his way along the fuselage, all the way to the back. The loading ramp is down and snow has drifted up into the darkened interior, settling deep in the gaps between the cargo bay's ribs. Webbing adorns the bellied walls; thick ratchet straps hang from the riveted ceiling, twisting in the wind.

411

He unsnaps his snowshoes and makes his way inside, heading for the front. For a machine so large the cockpit is surprisingly cramped. Two high-backed seats side by side, only a narrow space between, busy with controls. He clambers over the frame, using the straps of the harness to swing himself into one of the seats. A console sweeps around in front of him, crammed with dials, gauges, their surfaces white with frost. More levers sprout from the floor between his feet. Snow darkens the canopy, but here and there a section remains clear. He presses his face to the closest one.

He hears footsteps staggering up the ramp, and seconds later the boy appears at his shoulder, shivering. He looks down into the crowded cockpit, eyes the narrow space between the seats, then decides against it.

'This is c-crazy. It won't work.'

He ignores him, continuing his search. Stress patterns craze the curving perspex, making it hard to see, but outside dawn is finally breaking; a reluctant light slowly congeals over the ashen snow. Without warning the wind catches one of the huge rotor blades, dips it down in front of them. He shifts in his seat so he can see around it, then stops, points. Behind him the boy leans forward, following his outstretched hand. A puzzled look troubles his face.

He points again, jabbing at a spot all the way back in the shadows.

And then the boy sees it too.

On the far side of the massive columns a red light blinks once, then goes dark again.

*

I WAKE WITH A JOLT, blinking furiously at unfamiliar surroundings while my brain reboots. Then the memories load and I jump up, rush outside. My legs have stiffened while I slept, but I have no time for that now; dawn's already spreading itself over the spiny ridges to the east. They'll loosen on the road.

I pick up the Kanawha Trail, beginning a hurried descent into West Virginia. I haven't been on the road more than half an hour when up ahead I spot a weather-beaten sign for the interstate. The switchback mountain trail I'm following crests and at last I can see it below me, snaking its way through the valley floor. I quit the track for the steeper but more direct route through what would once have been forest, my snowshoes sending small avalanches of powder tumbling down the slope ahead of me as I bound between the blackened trunks, Hicks' pistol bouncing against my leg with each stride.

The trees come to an abrupt end and I stop and scan the highway below for any sign of them. The road's clear in both directions, but it doesn't take me long to spot where they've passed through: a wide swathe of tracks out of the east, at least seven or eight abreast. They've beaten me here.

I hurry down the embankment and join the highway, searching the snow for the deeper indentations Jax will have left, but it's so badly chewed I can't pick them out. I bend down, tracing the outline of the nearest one with my fingers. The edges are crisp, well-defined; the wind can't have had more than an hour to smooth them out. They must have come through here earlier this morning. There's still a chance I can head them off.

I pick up the pace. The wake of freshly-churned snow

413

leaves the interstate a mile later, at an exit marked 60, but I stay on, searching for the quicker route Hicks took when he first brought us this way. Soon after the turnoff the road fishhooks and then passes over a railway line, just as it exits a tunnel. I throw my leg over the guardrail and drop down the embankment on the other side. I hit the bottom in a cloud of powder and take off along the narrow ravine, pounding through the deeper drifts with as much speed as I can muster. The track curves around for a half-mile or so and then finally straightens. Ahead there's a short siding, a corroded railcar sitting idle against snow-covered bumpers, and beyond in the distance a long shelter, roof timbers swaybacked under the weight of snow. I hurry towards it. A faded Amtrak sign, the words barely visible under a crust of ice and snow, tells me I've arrived.

I leave the tracks behind and hurry through the parking lot. But as I come to the station house I stop. A set of fresh prints exit from between the candy cane pillars that mark the entrance.

What was someone doing in there?

I follow the prints out to the road. On the other side two sections of wall curve inward to a pair of crumbling gateposts. The tracks head in that direction, but the mystery of who made them is already forgotten; something else has caught my eye.

The snow between the gates has been disturbed. A swathe of tracks, wide, just like the ones I ran into up on the highway less than an hour ago. I hurry across the road, thinking there might still be time to head them off before they reach the house. But as I get closer I can see the prints here are faint, the edges smoothed by wind, the hollows already mostly filled in by the driven snow.

These tracks are old; whoever made them came through a while ago. I stare at them for a long moment, not understanding. And then my heart fills with dread as off to one side I spot the deeper set I have been looking for.

I'm too late.

They already have her inside.

I STARE DOWN AT JAX'S PRINTS, not understanding. The tracks I picked up out on the interstate were fresh. But these are a day old, maybe more.

I point my snowshoes around and start heading west on 60, away from The Greenbrier's gates. My legs are tiring, but I force them on, pounding the snow harder than ever. The road slowly curves around. A huge gray structure rises up on my left, its breached roof and disintegrating bell tower familiar from the time I spent there with Hicks. I barely notice. The thought of what Gilbey might have done with the time she's already had fills me with rage.

When I reach the trail I cut off the road and switch back, making my way in among the blackened trunks. The path starts to incline as it skirts it way around the hill that sits behind The Greenbrier. The muscles in my legs send a warning that they might not be expected to keep this pace up much longer, but I pay it no attention. I strain for any sounds from the trail ahead, but there's only my breathing and the crunch of my snowshoes through the ice-slicked powder.

The track widens and a low concrete structure slowly separates itself from the trees. Snow drifts high against its featureless sides; more of it rests in heavy layers on its flat roof. The woods seem still but I stop, forcing myself to listen. And that's when I hear it: from somewhere up ahead, the low murmur of conversation.

I slip off my mittens and slowly unzip my parka.

I start forward again, forcing myself to go slow. The track curves around and now I see them, in front of the entrance to the bunker: two figures, bundled up in parkas, their breath smoking in the cold. A fire burns between them. They stand close, holding their hands out to the flames. One has a rifle slung over his shoulder; the other doesn't appear armed. Neither has seen me yet, but that won't last. My hand drops to the pistol on my hip. I start to draw it from its holster.

No.

The voice shows me an image: a small clearing; a can nestling in the crook of a branch, untroubled by the bullet I had just fired at it.

It's too far.

You can't let them raise the alarm.

I let the pistol slide back into its holster. I raise my arms out from my sides and start making my way up towards them.

It's Boots who spots me first. He looks up from the fire and calls out to his companion, who turns to face me. My head's down, my face hidden in the shadow of the hood's cowl, but Weasel seems to have little trouble working out who it is. He slings the rifle off his shoulder, but keeps it low.

'Well, there he is. Hicks said you'd show up.'

I keep trudging up the path towards him, my arms outstretched. He takes a step away from the fire, unconcerned by my approach.

'You're too late, though. Doc's already begun.'

He smiles, revealing a gap where the stock of Mags' rifle dislodged the teeth there. There's a cruelty to the expression that seems to infect the whole of his face and I feel something harden inside me, that he would take pleasure from this. I feel an overwhelming urge to break into a run, to launch myself at him, to claw the grin from his face.

The voice inside my head tells me to wait. It starts to measure out the distance between us. The count helps calm me down.

Good.

Weasel turns to his companion. Private Kavanagh is at least showing the good sense to look nervous.

'Just look at him come, Boots. Must be keen to get himself into one of those cages.'

He turns back to face me.

'Is that right, Huckleberry? You been missing us?'

I keep walking towards them. My hands are still held out from my sides, but now I slowly start to flex my fingers. Behind the soldiers the entrance to the bunker slides into view. A section of the huge metal gate at the end is already visible; the outline of a smaller door set into the steel. A rusting sign above, a faded symbol of a lightning bolt.

They have no idea.

'What's the rush, Huckleberry?'

The smile's still there, but for the first time I hear nervousness in Weasel's voice. His thumb reaches for the safety, even as his finger slips through the trigger guard. With his other hand he reaches down for the charging handle.

Just a few steps more.

'Hey! You just hold it right there, now.'

Alright. That'll do.

I exhale slowly, forcing my heart to slow. In the skip between beats my hand reaches for the pistol. I lift my head and the hood falls back, for the first time revealing my face.

Weasel's smile vanishes like a breath in the wind. His eyebrows reach for his hairline and he starts to bring the barrel up. The rifle's still at half-mast, but in his panic he squeezes the trigger anyway. Flame bursts from the muzzle, the snow between us erupting in an arc of exploding powder that tracks its way ever so slowly towards me.

I slide the pistol from its holster, my thumb already reaching for the hammer. I feel the tension in the

418

mechanism, the click as it locks in place, and then the barrel appears before me and there's nothing to do but squeeze. There's a loud bang and the pistol jumps with the recoil, sending my first shot high and wide. A puff of snow behind and to the left tells me where the bullet lands and I see now how right Hicks was to tell me to watch for it; that part *is* important. Adjusting for it is child's play, and then it's just a matter of waiting for the cylinder to rotate, placing the next round under the hammer. It seems to take forever, but at last I hear it click into place.

The second bullet catches him in the neck, snapping his head back. His legs give out from under him and he slumps to the ground.

I swing the pistol around, searching for Boots, but he hasn't moved. He stands, rooted to the spot. He stares back at me, eyes wide with fear.

I keep the pistol on him as I draw level with Weasel. There's a ragged hole where his throat once was. He holds a hand there, trying to stanch the flow. He opens his mouth, but nothing comes out except a low gurgle and a pink cord of saliva. He looks up at me a moment longer, like he doesn't yet believe it, then a dull blankness slides over his eyes and he just flickers out like a candle.

I stand over him for a second, watching the blood slip from between his fingers to stain the snow beneath. Something twists inside me at the sight of it, but the voice repeats the message it gave me in Starkly: *there's no time for this; I have things to do*; and this time I heed it quicker. I turn to face Boots.

'What he said about Gilbey, is it true?'

He stares at me blankly, like he's having trouble processing the question. He seems more scared of me than the pistol I have on him, so I grip the throat of his parka and draw him close.

I ask again, and this time he bobs his head, quick.
'You'd best not be here when I come back out.'

*

I HOLSTER THE PISTOL and bend down to unsnap my snowshoes, then hurry inside. Behind me I hear the crunch of snow as Boots stumbles off into the woods, but I don't bother to check which direction he's taking. The blast door's open, resting all the way back against the wall on its huge, buttressed hinges. Beyond it the tunnel stretches off into grainy gloom.

High in the corner the red light of a camera blinks once, then goes dark. The voice wants me to wait, to think this through. Hicks is expecting me, and there's no cover that way, nowhere to hide.

But I'm already sprinting. With each step I expect to hear the first crack of gunfire, but somehow it never comes. I make it to the door marked *Decontamination* unharmed and pass under another camera bolted to the wall above, entering the showers. Rusting nozzles protrude from the tiles, narrowing my path, and then I'm through, stepping into a long corridor. Safety lights hum, adding shades of green to the gray. From somewhere off in the distance there's the low drone of a generator.

I run towards it, past dormitories, a cafeteria, infirmary, drab halls filled with chairs. The thrum from the generator increases as I open the door to the power plant. I make my way up onto a narrow gangway, my boots clanging on the metal grating. I push through another door at the end; the noise from the plant recedes as it closes behind me. I hurry down the stair beyond, taking the steps two and three at a time, but the descent seems to take forever in spite of it. At last I reach the bottom. A single door leads out of the shaft, a keypad to one side blinking out its silent guard.

I try it, but it won't budge, so I shuck off my

421

backpack, reach inside for the pry bar, and start to attack the lock. It has been designed to resist such attempts, however: the gap between door and frame is narrow, the edges reinforced with steel. There's nowhere for the bar to get purchase.

My efforts grow increasingly frantic, as I imagine what Gilbey might be doing right now to Mags in that other room. Inside my head I feel the brace wire starting to come down. I drop the pry bar and draw the pistol, level it at the lock.

No! They'll hear.

I squeeze the trigger. There's a bang, loud in such a confined space, and the gun bucks in my hand. Sparks fly from the lock and there's the whine of a ricochet. The shaft fills with the smell of gunpowder.

I take a step back and aim my boot at the lock. There's the sound of wood splintering, and this time I feel it give. It yields on the third kick and I burst through into a familiar room: long, low-ceilinged, plastic cages lining the walls on either side.

I leave everything behind me and set off at a run, the cages little more than a blur on either side. Halfway along I think I catch the briefest glimpse of something, a shape, drawing back into the shadows behind, but I don't stop. Whatever might be there isn't my concern now.

The room ends at another door. I brace myself, getting ready to charge it. The voice inside my head pleads with me to slow down; it tells me I can be quiet and still go quickly. But it is small now; it struggles to make itself heard. It goes silent for a moment, then it says the one thing that might cut through the maelstrom: her name.

You'll be no good to her if you get yourself caught.

I manage to reassert some semblance of control just as I arrive at the last cage. I skid to a halt in front of the door and reach for the handle. To my surprise there's no resistance; it isn't locked. I push down, more gently than I would have thought possible only seconds before.

The door opens with a soft groan and I step through into a smaller room, its only feature a row of black metal chambers set into the wall at waist height. Each has a large latch handle, the words *Crematex Incinerator Corp.* stamped in raised letters above. I pass quickly between them. Most of the chambers are closed, but near the end one of the doors hangs outward on its hinges. I catch a glimpse of charred concrete behind as I hurry past.

The next room's like the first, long, low-ceilinged, rows of plastic cages stretching off into gloom on either side. The ones closest the door are empty, unremarkable, but as I make my way deeper among them that changes.

The first one I come to has the number 98 stenciled along the top. Inside a gray shape crouches. A scar circles the top of its shaved scalp, the tissue puckered and rucked around the edges. Its shadowed eyes are open, but it just stares out, unblinking, giving no indication it knows I'm there. On a shelf above rests a large glass jar. Inside, something gray and folded, cut in cross-section, hangs suspended in clear liquid.

The cages beyond are all the same; I make my way quickly among them. A sound drifts towards me out of the darkness now, faint, muffled. I can't be certain if it was there earlier, or if it just started up.

I hold my breath for a moment, listening. It's high-pitched, like the whine of a mosquito, only regular, mechanical. And then I feel my throat constrict as I realize what it is.

HE STANDS AT THE TOP of the loading ramp, peering out. The wind gusts around him, sending flurries of gray snow dancing up into the helicopter's darkened cargo bay. He tilts his head to one side, scenting the air, listening for any sound. But there's nothing. The sun has been up a while now. They can't wait any longer.

On the other side of the helicopter a path has been cleared through the snow. He makes his way down the ramp and scurries along it, making sure to keep his head low. He does not want to be seen. Not yet.

As he approaches the front of the massive building he slows. Peeling flagpoles jut from the second floor balustrade, the tattered flags that hang there snapping and fluttering in the wind. Ahead, recessed in shadow, the wide entrance door, and above, mounted high on the wall, a single camera. Its red light blinks once, then goes out.

He glances back at the helicopter. The boy with the curly hair stands by the cargo door, watching his progress. A worried look troubles his face. He does not think this is a very good plan; he only agreed to it because he could not think of another.

He returns his gaze to the entrance. The lobby's dark windows stare down menacingly. His heart races, fluttering inside his small ribcage like a trapped moth. He does not want to go back in the cage. He looks at the helicopter again. It is not too late; he could still turn around. He and the boy could hide there for the hours of daylight that remain, and then escape together under cover of darkness.

But that would mean leaving her in there.

He closes his eyes and takes a deep breath,

summoning his courage. There is not as much of it as he had hoped; already far less than there was when he left the helicopter, just moments ago. Before even that has the chance to desert him he stands, takes several quick steps into the shadow of the portico.

The colossal columns tower over him. He makes his way between them, continuing up the steps to the entrance. He stands on tiptoe and peers through the door, but beyond the lobby is dark, empty. Above the light on the camera blinks, then goes out again.

His heart is pounding; he can hear it now, hammering away inside his chest; it is all he can do not to run. He closes his eyes, tries to push the fear back down, like he saw the girl do in the airlock.

He takes a deep breath and steps under the oblong box mounted to the wall. He lifts his goggles onto his forehead and looks up. The camera's single mechanical eye stares down at him impassively. He raises his hands above his head, waves them hesitantly. The light blinks and he almost bolts, but then it goes out again.

He keeps his arms above his head while he watches through the glass for any sign of their approach. The doctor wants him back; the dangerous man said so, when he came to take the girl away. As soon as they see he's here they'll come out for him. He needs to lead them away, to give the boy time to go inside and find her.

He looks up into the camera. But how much longer should he wait? Surely they've seen him by now. He imagines them, sprinting along whatever corridors and passageways lay beyond, only seconds from bursting into the lobby. The muscles in his legs tense at the thought. He mustn't let them catch him.

A soft whirring from above, barely audible above the sound of the wind. His eyes flick upwards, just in time to see the camera's iris narrow as it focuses on him.

His hands reach up for his goggles even as he bolts

for the path that's been cleared through the snow. He takes the steps in short, urgent strides and then his feet are crunching powder. For a second he thinks he hears something behind him, a sound that might be the thud of boots on stone, but he forces himself not to look back – surely they can't be here already?

The thought of it spurs him on; he tucks his elbows tight to his sides and runs for all he is worth. When he reaches the spot where he left his snowshoes he steps into them and drops to a crouch, fighting the impulse to look over his shoulder while his fingers works the straps. As he tightens the last one he hears the clunk of a handle and the unmistakable clatter of a door being thrown back on its hinges. There's a harsh shout and then he is on his feet, mittens bouncing on their tethers, arms and legs pumping as he scrambles up the embankment and takes off into deeper snow.

I DRAW HICKS' PISTOL and break into a run, ignoring the vacant stares from the cages on either side as I sprint towards the source of the sound. The room seems to stretch out, like I might never reach the end, but eventually a door separates itself from the gloom ahead. The voice begs me to be careful, but it is small now, drowned out by the shrill whine that grows louder, the rage that builds with each step.

I reach the door, crash through it without slowing. I find myself in dazzling brightness; instinctively raise a hand to shield my eyes. The sound is coming from somewhere in front of me, but the light is so intense I can't stand to look directly at it. My entrance seems to do the trick, however; the pitch drops as whatever's causing it is switched off.

A complicated raft of smells pack the air. The sharp tang of disinfectant, the coppery aroma of blood, the burn of an electric motor. And underneath it something else, stale, familiar. The voice inside my head really wants me to pay attention to that but I can't, not till I've found her.

The light's too bright to look at so I squint into the corners, trying to gather details. The room is square, wider and higher than the one I've just left. Counters run most of the way around the walls. A sink, a microscope, other equipment I don't recognize. Above, shelves, stacked with bottles, jars, other containers, an array of glass and ceramic, all gleaming in the brilliance. To my right a doorway, or maybe a large alcove, a dark curtain hiding whatever's behind.

I force my gaze back to the center. What looks like an operating table, its angular surfaces ablaze under a huge

427

domed light hanging down from above. I catch a glimpse of movement on the other side of it and I step forward, narrowing my eyes against the glare. I point the pistol in the direction I thought I saw it.

'The light; turn it off.'

'It bothers you?'

A long pause and then the light is cut, leaving only the soft glow from a handful of bulkhead lamps bolted to the walls. Pinwheels and starbursts swirl and explode across my vision, but if I squint past them I can make out shapes.

She's lying in front of me, wearing only a surgical gown. A thick Velcro strap circles her waist; cuffs bind her wrists and ankles to the table. Her head has been shaved and a dotted line that looks like it might have been drawn there with a sharpie circles her scalp. A metal clamp holds it in place. A trickle of blood where the screws have pierced her skin.

I call her name but she doesn't respond. I search her face for any sign she knows I'm there, but her eyes have been taped shut.

I look up, for the first time seeing Gilbey. She studies me over her glasses, the rest of her face hidden behind a surgical cap and mask. In her hand some type of electric saw, the jagged-toothed disc still spinning as it grinds slowly to a halt.

'What have you done to her?'

She pulls the mask down.

'Nothing, yet. I was just about to begin.'

I step forward, touch her shoulder.

'Mags.'

'She can't hear you.'

I point the pistol across the table, still struggling to keep the rage from bringing down the brace wire.

She holds up her hand, says *Wait*. My vision is still swimming with color, but it's almost like the instruction isn't meant for me. The voice inside my head concurs; something is wrong.

She should be afraid of you, but she's not.

She sets the saw down.

'You've infected yourself.' She tilts her head, as though considering her own statement. 'You saw what it did to her; thought it might give you a chance against the soldiers. Reckless, given how little you could possibly understand of the pathology, but there's a certain logic to it. It is what the virus was designed for, after all.'

She takes a step around the table, then stops. She looks down at Mags and then back to me, as though another thought has just occurred to her.

'You're no longer contagious; you wouldn't have touched her like that if you were. How did you manage it?' She looks up, not waiting for my answer. 'I'm guessing an electrical shock of some sort?' She leans closer, studying me over her glasses. 'It looks like you may have overdone the voltage.'

'Wake her up, now.'

'I can't.'

She points at a metal stand beside the table. A plastic drip bag hangs from a hook. A tube snakes down from it, entering her arm just below the elbow.

'She'll be out for a while yet. I had to give her quite a large dose. The changes to her physiology were...profound.'

I point the pistol at the straps.

'Then untie her. I'll carry her.'

She just ignores me.

'And how do *you* feel, Gabriel?' She studies me over the rims of her spectacles. 'You seem lucid, but perhaps not entirely...in control?' She pinches the bridge of her nose, shakes her head. 'The delivery mechanism: that was always the problem. The virus was supposed to shut itself down, once the remap had been completed, once the subject's central nervous system had been optimized. We could never get it to do that, however. It always seemed to want to keep on going.'

I raise the pistol, thumb back the hammer.

'I said untie her.'

Gilbey's eyes flick to the gun, then for an instant they cut right and narrow. She gives the briefest shake of her head, but something's wrong; the gesture is far too calm.

That's because it's not meant for you.

I hear a sound from behind me and suddenly there's that smell again, stronger than before. Too late I recognize what it is. Stale sweat, and underneath it, tobacco.

I turn around, just as Truck steps from the shadows behind me, a baton in one hand. He lunges forward with it, an arc of blue light dancing between the metal prongs.

I TRY TO BACK UP, but the operating table's in my way, blocking my retreat, so instead I swing the pistol around. The speed of it takes him by surprise, and for an instant I see the shock re-arranging his features. But even as my finger tightens around the trigger, I know it won't be enough. I feel the prongs of the baton pierce the thin material of my thermals, jabbing hard into my ribs, just as the last of the slack comes out of the mechanism. The pistol bucks in my hand and in the same moment there's an instant of pain, quickly cut off as some internal circuit breaker I didn't know I had gets tripped.

Darkness rushes in from the corners of my vision and the ground beneath my feet lurches alarmingly. I hear the gun clatter to the floor and then my legs give way and I'm falling in some indescribable, slantwise direction. I expect to hit wall, but instead I feel something soft give way behind me. I reach for it with the hand that still seems to work and for a second thick material passes between my fingers, but I can't get a grip on it. I feel something sharp slam into my back, and then the floor comes rushing up to hit me.

I lay there for a moment, uncertain whether I am still conscious. I think I might be. Afterimages of the light from the other room swirl across my vision, but the darkness beyond is not complete; it has texture, grain. From somewhere on the other side of it I hear voices, furry, indistinct.

'…have to do that, Corporal?'

'…bastard shot me.'

I shake my head, trying to clear it, but   it's   like someone's ripped out a bunch of the wires inside me, and now nothing works like it should. The right side of my body seems to have switched off completely. I try to push myself up, but the arm there is limp, useless; it ignores whatever messages my brain tries to send it. My other side's better; I can still feel things there, enough to tell me I'm trapped against something hard, with ridges, presumably whatever I fell against on my way to the floor. I reach out with my hand. My fingers close around plastic.

I turn my head in that direction. The bars of a cage. When I look down I can see a section of the floor has been marked off with tape. I stare at the striped perimeter for a moment. It reminds me of another place. There was tape on the floor there, too, but the bars were metal, not plastic. I'm still trying to make the connection when I hear a shuffling sound behind me and then a single click, low and guttural. The hairs on the nape of my neck raise like hackles.

A face presses itself to the bars, only inches from mine. What once might have been a girl, not much older than I am now. The furies that occupied the cages in the other room seemed unaware of my presence, but this one knows I'm here. It stares back at me from deep, shadowed eyes, its nostrils flaring. I lie there, not even daring to breathe. After a few seconds it retreats.

The curtain I fell through is pulled back and Truck stands over me, the baton loose in one hand. The shot I fired before he zapped me has torn a gash in his fatigues and the material there is already dark with his blood. More of it runs down inside his sleeve and drips from his fingers. I feel something flicker inside me at the sight of it, but weaker then before, like the jolt I took from the baton has disabled it, too.

Truck takes a step closer. Unfortunately my bullet doesn't seem to have impaired him significantly. He wipes his hand on his pants leg, then tightens his grip on the baton, flicking the switch with his thumb. I watch as blue-white electricity sizzles between the prongs. Gilbey appears at his shoulder.

'He's no use to me dead, Corporal.'

'Don't worry, ma'am, I ain't going to kill him. Just going to mess him up a little. You can have him when I'm done.'

He smiles down at me, his face a mask of dull, lazy violence.

There's a soft, scrabbling sound beside me and I glance over. On the other side of the bars the fury has stiffened like a dog on point. It stares out, the muscles along its jaw clenching and unclenching, its fingers slowly raking the floor of the cage.

Truck doesn't seem to have noticed; it's dark in the alcove, and right now he seems more preoccupied with the vengeance he's about to extract from me. He takes another step towards me, thumbing the switch on the baton's handle again. I slide my good hand along the top of the cage, like I mean to pull myself up.

'That's it, Huck, you try that. Just make it that much more fun for me when I put you down again.'

I grasp the front, like I mean to do just as he says, but at the last second I shift my hand over. For a second Truck's brow knits together as he tries to work out what I'm doing, then he raises the baton, brings it down hard. There's a sickening crunch and I hear myself scream as the bone in my finger snaps like a twig. I pull my hand back, but he's too late; I've already released the catch. The gate springs open and the fury bounds out, teeth bared. Truck staggers backward, surprisingly fast for a man of his size. He raises the baton to ward off the attack, but Gilbey steps between them and grabs it, trying to wrest it from him.

'Don't! You'll hurt her!'

The fury's on her in an instant. I hear something clatter to the floor and then all three of them disappear from view.

I lie there for a moment, cradling my busted hand to my chest as I wait for the pain there to subside. To my surprise it quickly settles to a dull throb. I haul myself slowly to my feet. My right arm's still useless, but a measure of feeling seems to have returned to the leg on that side. I grab hold of the curtain and peer through. The fury has dragged its kill into the shadows underneath the operating table. It looks over at me, its jaw dark with blood, then returns to its meal. I watch to make sure it's settled, then turn my attention to the rest of the room. On the other side of the table, pressed up against the counter, stands Truck, one hand held to his injured arm. He shifts his gaze to me for a second, then his eyes dart back to the fury.

The pistol I dropped lies on the floor. I bend down to recover it. Mags is lying on the operating table, still unconscious. I'll need to get a lot closer to the fury if I'm to free her. I tell myself it'll be alright. It had the chance to attack me, when I fell against its cage, and it didn't. The one in the basement of Starkly was just the same; it paid more attention to the flask Finch left than it did me. Maybe whatever I am now isn't of interest to them.

I'm not sure I'm ready to trust everything to that theory, however, so I grip the pistol with the fingers I have that still work and pry the hammer back. It's awkward work getting the middle one through the trigger guard, but it gives me the courage I need to shuffle closer. The fury glances up as I start to advance and I freeze, but after a few seconds it returns to feasting on Gilbey. I hold the pistol on it a little longer, then take a deep breath and step up to the table.

I set the gun down, trying to ignore the grunts and snaps coming from by my feet. I start with the needle on her arm, removing the tape that holds it in place, sliding it out as carefully as I can. Then I turn to the clamp that's holding her head. I have to feel with my fingers for the screws, but one by one they come free. A trickle of her blood wets my fingertips as I withdraw the last one.

Truck watches me close, his eyes darting between the pistol and what's going on under the table. As I move on to the straps at her ankles he takes a step away from the counter. I shift my hand to the gun.

'You don't want to test me, Truck, not today.'

I can't be sure if it's me or the fury at my feet that's keeping him back, but he returns to the wall, glares at me for a while, then hitches his pants up and starts pacing, a slow shuffle back and forth along the length of the counter, like a wounded bear. There's a crunch and a wet sucking sound as beneath the table the fury takes another bite out of Gilbey. Truck's gaze flicks to the floor and back again, but he comes no closer.

I go back to Mags' restraints. The Velcro's tricky to manage one-handed, with the digits I still have at my disposal, and every now and then Truck gets a look in his eye and I have to pick up the pistol and show it to him again, but eventually I get the last cuff open. There's a couple of sensors stuck to her skin, but they come off easy.

I spot a roll of tape on the counter, like the kind Gilbey's used on Mags' eyes, sitting on top of a spiral bound notebook. I slip the tape into my pocket, adding the notebook for good measure. Then I slide my good arm underneath her and hoist her onto my shoulder. Truck shuffles forward, but I'm ready for him; I snatch the pistol up before he gets close enough to rush me. I back up slowly, watching as he starts to inch his way around the table.

He doesn't get very far before the fury lifts its head, flicks it in his direction. A single click, low and menacing, emanates from somewhere deep in its throat. I grip the pistol, getting ready to switch aim if I have to, but it's not me that's caught its attention. Truck freezes, unwilling to come any closer.

I take the opportunity to make our exit. The heel of my boot clips the baton he dropped, sending it clattering against the baseboard, but the fury pays it little mind; it returns to its meal, like I'm not even there. I put my shoulder to the door and then I'm out, letting it swing shut behind me. I set the pistol on the ground, lay Mags down as gently as I can and return to the door. I push it open with the toe of my boot, checking that the fury's still busy chowing down on Gilbey, then I bend down to retrieve the stick. On the far side of the operating table Truck hitches up his pants and hisses across the room at me.

'Hey! So that's it? You're just going to leave me here?'

I nod.

'I haven't killed you, which is more than you deserve.' I glance down at the fury, then point the baton at the alcove. 'If I were you I'd think about finding myself somewhere to hole up. Might want to do it quick, while it still lets you.'

I hold his gaze for a second longer then back out. Last I see of Truck he's taken my advice and is shuffling along the wall in the direction of the curtain and the plastic cage behind.

The door closes and I look over my shoulder. Mags hasn't stirred from where I set her down. I wonder how much longer she'll be out of it. Behind her rows of cages stretch off into the gloom. I think of how I found her, the first time I rescued her from this place; the dark, ugly welts Truck had inflicted with the same baton, branding her from hip to shoulder. And for a second the anger flares again, only this time I'm not sure it's the thing the virus put inside me that twists with it. This feels familiar; something that was there all along.

I pick the baton up, turn back to the door, slide it through the handles.

I make sure to wedge it in tight.

*

I SIT ON THE FLOOR next to Mags and reach for the pistol. The finger Truck broke is already starting to swell, but as long as I don't ask too much of it it doesn't hurt that bad. I wonder if that's the virus's doing too.

It doesn't change the fact that my chances of hitting anything that doesn't oblige by positioning itself at the end of the barrel and holding still are slim, however, so I use the tape to bind my busted finger to the middle one, just like I remember reading in the first aid book I used to keep under the bed in the farmhouse outside Eden. When I'm done I return the pistol to its holster. My right arm's starting to tingle, but that appears to be as much as it can be relied upon to do. The leg on that side feels rubbery, unreliable, too, but for now at least it seems to be obeying the messages my brain's sending it.

I hoist Mags onto my shoulder and start retracing my steps. I make my way between the cages, ignoring the vacant stares from those hunched on the other side of the bars. Then we're past them, hurrying through the crematorium, and finally back in the first room. I hobble towards the door at the end, my thoughts already on the stair beyond. But halfway along something catches my eye and I stop.

On the floor of one of the cages, a plastic food tray. I balance Mags on my shoulder and bend down for a better look, making sure to keep a respectful distance from the bars. A large shape crouches on the other side of the tray, too big for the dimensions of his confinement. His head's been shaved and when he looks up his eyes are sunken, dark. The face that used to soft, round, has angles to it now, and there are deep hollows where his cheeks used to be. It is familiar, nonetheless.

'Hamish?'

He shifts uncertainly at the mention of his name.

'Angus?'

I shake my head.

'No Hamish. It's Gabe.'

He says my name a few times, as though testing it. I think there's a glimmer of recognition there, but it's hard to tell. He shuffles forward, looks up at me hopefully.

'Is Angus coming?'

'Angus is dead, Hamish. I'm sorry.'

As soon as the words are out I wish I could take them back. It's as if his face is held together by a number of unseen bolts and each of them has suddenly been loosened a turn. His head drops.

I feel the need to say something, to explain.

'It was Peck who killed him, but it was my fault. I should have known, when I sent you both back to him…'

He looks up. The face that was slack a moment ago has tightened again. He whispers a single word.

'Peck.'

'Yes, Peck, but it was me...'

'Peck.'

I try again, but there's no point. The name seems to be all he's capable of now; he just keeps repeating it over and over, like it's the only thing he cares to hold on to.

I glance along the aisle, towards the broken door. Hicks is still up there, somewhere, together with Jax and whoever else remains of the soldiers. Kane, Peck, and the Guardians, too. By now they must realize something's wrong; they're probably already looking for us. I hesitate for a moment and then get to my feet. I take a step toward the exit and then stop, turn around and press down on the latch. The spring releases and the gate opens a fraction, but Hamish doesn't come out. I make my way between the cages. When I reach the door I check behind me again, but the aisle remains empty.

I lay Mags on the floor and step into the storage room. All her stuff's there, in a plastic crate just inside the door. For a second I consider trying to dress her, but it'd take too long with my hands they way they are; I'm not even sure I'd be able to manage it. I'll worry about it when I get us outside. Her backpack's where I left it, against the wall. I stuff her things into it, then lift her onto my shoulder again, grab the pack and start up the stair.

It takes longer on the way up than coming down, but at last I can hear the thrum of machinery above, growing louder with each step. As we near the plant room she stirs on my shoulder, starts to struggle. I whisper to her to stay still.

'Gabe?' Her voice is thick with the anesthetic. 'Where are we?'

'Still in The Greenbrier. We'll soon be out.'

'I feel weird.' She shifts her head. 'I can't see.'

'There's tape on your eyes, that's all. Just hold on to me and as soon as we get to the top I'll take care of it.'

'Okay.'

At last the stair ends. I push the door open a crack. The clatter from the generator increases, but when I peer through our luck seems to be holding; the gangway ahead is still empty. I carry her up onto it, set her down on the metal grating. She reaches up to her face but her movements are clumsy, uncoordinated.

'Here, let me.'

I kneel down in front of her. It takes a while, but I finally get an edge of the tape between the thumb and third finger of my good hand and gently lift the tape from one eye, then the other.

She looks up at me, blinking. It takes her a moment to focus and then she breathes in sharply and recoils, pressing herself back against the railing.

I turn away quickly; I had forgotten what I look like now. I grab the backpack and start pulling out her clothes, anxious for something that will keep me from seeing that look on her face again. I feel her hand on my arm. She reaches up, touches my cheek.

'I'm sorry. I...I was just surprised. What happened?'

I clear my throat, not sure I trust myself to speak.

'I'll tell you later. Right now we need to get out of here.' I hand her her clothes. 'Put these on.'

She looks down, for the first time realizing what she's wearing. Her fingers fly to her scalp.

'It's okay. She didn't get a chance to do anything.'

She probes the skin there a moment longer, like she may not believe me, then she picks up her thermals and starts putting them on. Her movements are still awkward. I try to help, but the best I can manage is to hand her stuff. She pulls on a boot while I reach for the other.

'What's wrong with your arm?'

'Truck. He zapped me with the baton.'

I look down at it, hanging useless by my side. It used to be numb, but now if I concentrate I think I can feel a prickling sensation, like pins and needles, in my fingertips. I tell myself that has to be a good sign.

She finishes tying the laces while I close the pack and heft it onto my shoulder

'Do you think you can walk?'

'I'm not sure.'

I hold out my good arm. She grabs my wrist and I pull her to her feet. But when she tries to take a step her legs buckle and she has to reach for the railing behind her.

'It's alright, I got you.'

I slip my arm around her waist and we make our way slowly across the gangway and down the steps on the other side. I open the door a fraction and peer through.

The safety lights still hum, bathing the walls in their green glow, but the corridor that was empty when I came through earlier now has a body in it. Or to be more precise, a pair of legs; the rest of whoever it is has been dragged into one of the dorms. The boots are missing, but the fatigues tell me it's one of the soldiers. I stare at them for a moment, trying to work out who it might be. It's not big enough for Jax, but it could be any of the others, except maybe Weasel, unless someone's bothered to haul him in from outside. It might even be Hicks, although I can't see how we'd ever be that lucky.

I whisper to Mags that we need to go. She holds on to me and together we step into the corridor. The noise from the plant room recedes as the door closes behind us.

As we get closer more of the torso becomes visible. I can read the name above the breast pocket of his fatigues now, but I no longer need it. This is the man the other soldiers called Pops. The deep lines that bracketed his mouth and grooved themselves across his forehead have softened in death, but his eyes are wide with surprise, like whatever it was he last saw, he wasn't expecting it. A single bullet hole punctures the middle of his forehead, a trickle of darkening blood snaking its way into the gray stubble at his temple.

Mags looks up at me.

'What happened to him?'

'I don't know.'

I dip the toe of my boot in the dark puddle of blood that surrounds the back of his head. It's still tacky.

'Whatever it was, it wasn't long ago.'

WE LEAVE THE CORRIDOR and enter the decontamination chamber. The nozzles that protrude from the tiles make it hard to walk side by side. Mags says she's okay, but when I let go of her she sways alarmingly and has to reach for the wall to steady herself. I slip my arm back around her waist and we continue on, shuffling sideways between the pipes. Behind us the door to the bunker closes, robbing the cramped passageway of color. When we make it to the end I tell her to hold on to something; I need my hand to work the handle. I push down; the door creaks softly as it swings out into the tunnel.

I put my arm around her again and we step through. But when I look up I stop. Ahead of us in the tunnel, a pair of flashlights, quivering in the darkness. I glance back the way we've come, but there's no light that way that might reveal us to whoever it might be. I stare at the beams for a moment, trying to work it out. They don't seem to moving away. It's like they're just standing there, waiting.

'What is it?'

'Someone in the tunnel.'

'Can you see who?'

I shake my head.

'Probably the ones who did for Pops.' I look up at the pipes that hang down from the roof, running straight out into darkness. It's the same all the way to the blast door; there's no cover in there. 'Maybe we should find another way out.'

I say it mostly to myself, but I hear her whisper back to me.

'Who had to quit so you could be in charge of smart decisions?'

I open my mouth to respond, but before I get the chance I sense movement behind us. I feel Mags tense at my side. Without warning a light flicks on, momentarily blinding me, and I have to turn my head away. My brain sends a message to my reaching hand, but it just twitches uselessly. I squint into the glare, trying to see who's behind the flashlight, but all I can make out is the muzzle of the pistol it's pressed up against.

'Cute.'

I may not be able to see his face, but that voice I know.

Peck.

He points the beam at Mags for a second and then returns it to me.

'Hell, Gabriel, what have you done to yourself?' He holds the flashlight on me a second longer, then whistles into the tunnel. From off in the darkness a voice answers, faint with distance, but immediately familiar.

'Who is it, Randall?'

'Someone here you might want to see, Mr. President.'

I force myself to look into flashlight, trying to gauge the distance to his gun. I have one mostly good hand, and I'm fast now, fast enough that I might even be able to surprise someone like Peck. He's standing just far enough away to make the outcome uncertain, however. And then there's Mags. She can barely stand, let alone be counted on to step aside from a bullet.

The lights in the tunnel grow brighter as Kane and whoever's with him make their way back towards us. I glance into the decontamination chamber, searching for another way out. Colors are still swirling across my vision from the flashlight, but for an instant I think I see a sliver of green.

'I warned you not to underestimate me, Gabriel.'

I ignore him and instead screw my eyes shut, trying

to clear the comet tails and starbursts. The light I thought I saw at the end has gone, if it was ever there.

Peck shifts the gun a little closer; I feel Mags grip me tighter.

'Hey, do I not have your attention?'

'Sure. I heard you. Underestimate.'

My eyes flick back to the showers, but now there's only darkness. For a second I could have sworn I saw the door at the other end open, though.

Kane's getting closer, his footsteps growing louder as they echo towards us out of the tunnel. I peer into the gloom, trying to make out who's with him, but I can't see beyond their flashlights.

I risk another glance into the decontamination chamber. This time I think I see movement. One of the soldiers? I only glimpsed it for a second, but the shape I saw didn't look big enough for Jax, and that only leaves Hicks. I'm not sure how his arrival will play out any better for us. And then I catch a sound. I glance over at Peck. I don't think he's heard it yet. I squeeze Mags' waist and shuffle backwards.

'Hey, where do you think you're going?'

'Nowhere, Peck.'

I say it loud. My voice echoes back at me from the chamber. I take another step away from the Secret Service agent.

'Hold it right there, Gabriel.'

The flashlights coming down the tunnel are almost on us, and for a second one of the beams slips into the narrow chamber. The light shifts over tiles, nozzles, for an instant lands on a pair of silver eyes, moves on.

I back up again. Peck moves forward, and now he's the one standing in front of the doorway.

'Godammit Gabriel, I'm serious. Move again and I'll shoot you where you stand.'

'Okay, Peck.'

This time when his name comes back from the showers the echo isn't right. His brow furrows and he looks at me, momentarily puzzled.

'Sorry, Randall.'

The pistol drops a fraction and his eyes flick into the chamber, then widen.

'You son of a…'

If he gets another word out I never hear it. I grab Mags tight and drag her backwards even as Hamish appears in the doorway. He sees Peck and lunges forward, hands outstretched, reaching for the Secret Service agent's throat.

*

PECK RECOVERS SURPRISINGLY QUICKLY. He takes a step backwards, wheeling around to face the new threat. His gun comes up, his finger already curling around the trigger, even as Hamish slams into him. They stumble backwards together then both go over, hitting the ground with a dull thud. Hamish is the bigger of the two, even now, but there's no finesse to his attack, only frenzy, fury. His teeth snap, his fingers clawing at the Secret Service agent's neck. At last he finds purchase there, lifts his head in both hands, slams it back down. There's a sickening crunch, then a muffled bang as the pistol goes off.

Hamish grunts once and slumps forward, the last of the life already going out of him. Peck makes no move to push him off. His eyes are open, but they stare up sightlessly. A pool of blood spreads from the back of his head, darkening the dusty concrete.

I look up to see Kane, striding out of the tunnel, a camouflage parka flapping around him. The tag on the breast says it once belonged to Pops, and I'm guessing that's where he got the boots he's wearing too. They look out of place on him, but then I realize this is the first time I've seen him out of a suit. He comes to a halt a few feet away. Kurt appears beside him a moment later, a rifle clutched to his chest.

Kane studies his Secret Service agent for a moment then slowly turns his gaze to Mags and me. Last I saw of him was in Eden's chapel, when we left him with the soldiers. He hadn't been himself then, as though the wind had been knocked out of him by the events of the day. He looks like the President we always knew now,

447

though. He brings himself up to his full height.

'Gabriel.' His lip curls in distaste, like the mention of my name causes him displeasure.

I slip my arm out from around Mags and step in front of her. Feeling's starting to return to my fingers, but I still can't rely on them do my bidding. I don't think Kurt notices. He stares at me, slack-jawed, his mouth open, like he's not sure he believes what he's seeing.

Kane glances down at the pistol.

'Unwise of you to keep that sidearm holstered, son.'

I take a step closer, my eyes still on Kurt. His finger hovers over the trigger, but he hasn't yet swung the rifle in my direction.

'There's no rush, Mr. President. I'll draw it when I'm good and ready.'

I shift my shoulder back a fraction so my fingers rest over Hicks' pistol, trying to make it seem natural.

Kane studies me for a moment, like he's making his mind up about something, then he turns to the Guardian.

'Shoot him, Kurt, and let's get out of here.'

I ignore him, addressing myself instead to Kurt. I raise my good hand and point my taped fingers behind him, into the tunnel.

'You and Peck must have come in the same way I did, earlier.' I don't wait for him to confirm it. 'You'll have seen Private Wiesmann on your way in, then. You remember Weasel, don't you, Kurt? Small, kinda ratty-looking? Has a big hole where his throat used to be? He tried to shoot me earlier, too. Didn't work out so well for him.'

I wait a second for that to sink in.

'Did Kane ever tell you what the virus was designed for, Kurt? I just found out, from Dr. Gilbey. It wasn't meant as a weapon, least not the way the world got to experience it. They were trying to create a better soldier; someone faster, stronger. More resilient.' I hold up the hand that still works, slowly curl it into a fist. For a second the pain from my busted finger is excruciating, but then something inside me shuts it down.

'And that's exactly what it does; it rewires you, makes you all those things.' I stare at my hand a moment longer, then let it fall to my side. 'You could ask Gilbey yourself, she'd tell you. If I hadn't killed her, that is. Her and Corporal Truckle.'

I leave him a moment to digest those details, then I glance down at the gun on my hip.

'See, Kurt, if I wanted I could draw this pistol, put a bullet right between your eyes, have it back in its holster before you even knew you'd been hit. I'm new to the killing business, though, and it's been a busy day. So I reckon I'll wait till you swing that rifle in my direction. I figure that way I'll sleep a little easier tonight.'

Kane's eyes narrow, like he's not buying it. He turns to Kurt, his tone impatient.

'If he was going to do something he would have done it already. Finish them both and let's go.'

I ignore him, keeping my eyes on the rifle Kurt has clutched to his chest.

'Ready whenever you are, Kurt.'

I try to flex the fingers of my right hand, and this time I think I feel them wiggle. Kurt's gaze drops there.

'Maybe we should just get out of here, Mr. President.'

Kane lets out an exasperated sigh, and for a second I think he might take the weapon and do this himself. But he doesn't. He simply shakes his head and then turns and walks off into the tunnel.

Kurt calls over his shoulder.

'What about Randall, Mr. President? I-I think he's still breathing.'

Kane doesn't stop. His voice drifts back up to us through the tunnel, already growing hollow with distance.

'He's beyond saving. That other one was infected, so he'll have it now too. Come along.'

Kurt looks down at Peck, then his eyes return to me.

The voice inside my head warns me against it, but I can't resist. I wave my good hand in his direction, like he's dismissed.

'Listen to your master, Kurt. Best you run along now.'

He starts to follow, then his face twists and he jabs a finger at me.

'Freak.'

I lean forward, offering him a smile. My features the way they are now I'm guessing that brings him no more comfort than I intend it to. He takes a quick step backwards, and when he speaks again there's fear in his voice.

'I'm warning you, both of you: you'd better not follow us.'

He holds up the rifle as if to make his point, but I notice he takes care not to point it at me. I spread my good hand, a gesture of supplication. To my surprise the other manages something vaguely similar.

He takes another step backwards, then without warning he turns and runs off after Kane.

I watch their flashlights until they're little more than pinpricks in the darkness.

*

WE MAKE OUR WAY through the decontamination chamber, back into the bunker. The safety lights are still burning, but other than Pops the corridor remains empty. Mags squeezes my side and points to the left, to a door with a push bar marked *Emergency Exit*.

'That's the way we came, the first time Gilbey brought me down here.'

I push on the bar, half-expecting an alarm to sound, but it just creaks open. We step through into a concrete stairwell and start climbing. Mags seems a little steadier on her feet now, but it's slow work all the same. When we reach the first landing I stop and try to splay my fingers. They twitch, like they want to do my bidding, but the messages my brain's sending still aren't getting through right. Mags watches, then her gaze shifts to the pistol, nestled in its holster.

'Is it true, everything you said back there?' She studies the floor a moment. 'It's not that they didn't deserve it, after all they've done. And I know what it feels like, to be so mad...'

Her voice trails off and she looks up at me, waiting for an answer.

'I shot Weasel, just like I said. It was that or he was going to shoot me. Gilbey's dead, too. I didn't kill her, but I did release the thing that did. I meant it for Truck, but she got in the way. As for Corporal Truckle, as far as I know he's still alive, most likely holed up in one of those cages they put you and Johnny in, hiding from it. So, no, I didn't kill him either. I just didn't save him when I had the opportunity.'

I look away as I say the last bit, because there's more to it than I've let on, and I don't want her to see it in my face. I wonder what she'd think if I told her about the baton I slipped through the door handles, or why I might have chosen to do something like that.

We continue up the stairs. At the top there's another door and then a long, low-ceilinged corridor. A single fluorescent tube hangs from the ceiling, the light it throws barely sufficient for its length. Beyond, set back in the shadows, a familiar vault door, a large latch handle at its center.

We make our way towards it. I press down on the handle and the door creaks back into darkness. I reach out with my hand, feeling for the join, and then push. The section of fake wall pops out, concertinas, allowing me to slide it sideways. We step into the Exhibition Hall.

An emergency lamp flickers above my head. Shadows from the concrete pillars that brace the high ceiling shift against the walls. The garish wallpaper does well to hide the fact that we haven't yet left the bunker, a fact I mean to remedy without delay. On the far side of the room stairs lead up to the Colonial Lounge. Beyond there's a long passageway and then the lobby, all that now stands between us and getting out of this place.

We're halfway across when I hear a sound. Mags must have caught it too; she freezes at my side.

Something appears at the bottom of the stairs. A dark shape, the contours unfamiliar, until I realize it's not a single person but two: one lean, rangy, the other of much heavier build. The larger one reaches the foot of the stairs, stumbles into the flickering light and now I recognize him. He's bent forward, an arm twisted high behind his back. The thinner man stands behind, shoving him on.

Hicks.

It's less of a shock than I was expecting; I guess deep down I knew the chances of us getting out of here without running into him were slim. His prisoner's more of a surprise, however. By now Jake should be somewhere in Virginia, leading the Juvies back to Mount Weather.

Hicks pushes him forward a few more steps, then stops and looks at me.

'You shouldn't have come back.'

I feel the anger bubbling up again, that he would say something like that.

'You didn't leave me that choice.'

He nods, like he understands.

'I figured.' He squints at me, shifts his jaw from side to side. 'You've been busy.'

He says it without an explanation of what he means. Could be the way I look now, or that Mags is free. Maybe he found Weasel outside. It might be all of it.

I slide my arm behind my back and try to flex my fingers again. This time they tighten, like they want to do my bidding, but the signal my brain's sending's still getting jumbled somewhere before if reaches them.

Mags looks over at Jake.

'Are you okay?'

Jake looks scared, but he nods.

She turns to Hicks.

'So what do we do now, Sergeant?'

The voice warns me against saying anything rash, but its influence is already waning as the anger builds inside me. I don't wait for him to respond.

'He'll let Jake go and step out of our way, if he knows what's good for him.'

I don't need the voice to tell me that's not going to happen, though. That's just not who he is; I doubt there's ever been a single thing in his life he wouldn't have sacrificed on the blessed altar of getting the job done. I think of Mags, and Johnny, all the others he helped put in cages. And for what? To comply with an order he'd been given, years ago, by some politician or general long since dead.

The thought of it makes me even angrier.

'I'm warning you, Hicks. Get out of our way now. I haven't come this far to die in the trying.'

Mags squeezes me, letting me know she needs me to be quiet now. I hear her say the one thing that might change his mind.

'Gilbey's dead, Sergeant. Whatever you thought you were doing here, it's over. There's no point anymore.'

Hicks stares at her for a moment, then looks at me for confirmation. I feel Mags squeeze my side again. I'm not sure I can be trusted to speak, so I just nod. And for a moment it seems like it might work. He sags, like the weight of the world has just settled on his shoulders; like there may be nothing holding him up anymore but the clothes he's wearing. But then he shakes his head.

'Godammit son, do you know what you've done?'

And with that whatever hope there was for us all to walk out of the room evaporates. The anger returns, and this time there's no hope of holding it back.

What *I've* done?

I spit the words out, with as much venom as I can muster.

'Something you should've, a long time ago.'

He rocks back on his heels, like I've just slapped him. Whatever strength had abandoned him a moment ago, something else takes its place now: a cold indifference, as though he cares little about what happens next, only that there is business yet to finish.

He lets go of Jake.

I slip my arm out from around Mags, hiss at her to get out.

She opens her mouth to protest, but I tell Jake to take her. He hesitates, then hurries over. I push her towards him, not daring to take my eyes off Hicks.

'Gabe, wait…'

I don't want to hear what she has to say. I bark at them both to leave. She starts to struggle, but Jake picks her up easily, starts carrying her towards the stair.

Hicks shifts his arm and the parka falls back, exposing a pistol, just like Marv's. He works his jaw from side to side.

'Whenever you're ready, kid.'

And just like that it hits me, sudden and absolute. This is it; I have embarked on the final seconds of my life. And for a moment the shock of it displaces even the rage. I look past Hicks to where Jake is dragging Mags up the stairs. The sight of it triggers a final burst of memories: the first time I saw her, in the dayroom of the Sacred Heart Home for Children, a tattered paperback cradled in her lap; sneaking up to the roof of Eden's mess before the curfew buzzer sounded, to tell her the stories I had found on the outside; the first time we kissed. And with them an instant of unbearable sadness. Because these are things I want so much.

Hicks' hand hangs loose at his side, his fingers still hovering over the steel on his hip, the instrument that will take this away from me. And just like that the anger returns, hardening my will. The calm voice lets go, ceding control to the older part of me, the part that takes care of heartbeat and breath, tooth and claw. The part nature built first to keep my ass alive.

Behind me the emergency light flickers. My nerves are already jumping like bowstrings; it's all it takes. The muscles in my hand twitch, and then it begins.

Time slows, is replaced by something else. Hicks' fingers are already closing around his weapon. When I saw him, in the basement of the hospital in Blacksburg, after Ortiz got surprised by the fury, I could scarcely believe how fast he was. *Shrapnel*-fast. One instant his hand had been empty and the next there had been a pistol there. I told Mags afterwards I didn't think even Peck would have been a match for him, and now I see the truth in that.

It wouldn't have been close.

My brain's sending furious messages to my own hand, but it still hasn't moved, and yet I know with cold certainty that even now I could beat him, if I weren't for what Truck had done to my arm.

The anger grows, becomes a rage, a fury.

And at last I feel something there.

Purpose.

My hands dips for the holster.

Too late.

Hicks has already drawn the Beretta. He brings it up in one smooth motion, sudden and terribly deadly. I can see the barrel now, wide, like a tunnel. He can't miss, not from this distance.

And then my own pistol is in front of me. I feel its weight, the coldness of the steel, the contours of the grip, the subtle give in the trigger, the punch of the recoil. There's the pepper-smell of gunpowder and then I'm stepping through it and it's gone, even as I squeezc again.

I stride forward, keeping my finger tight on the trigger, my off hand fanning the hammer back, over and over. The bullets shake him, like a sapling in a blizzard, and then I'm standing over him, the last round fired and all there is the dry click of the hammer hitting an empty chamber. The pistol slips from my fingers and I let out a howl, wordless and incoherent, of relief, or rage, or sadness, I can't be sure.

I feel something touch my arm and I spin around, still struggling to drag my brain out of the torrent of adrenalin.

Mags.

She bends down and collects the Beretta from where Hicks has dropped it. Her brow furrows and she looks up, like she's deciding whether to show me. She hesitates a moment then holds it out.

I take it from her, not understanding. She points to a spot at the back, between the grip and the rear sight, and then I see.

The safety.

It was never off.

I RELOAD THE PISTOL with the last of the bullets from the gun belt while Jake explains how he's come to be here. His skills don't lie in storytelling; he's done before I've dropped the final cartridge into its chamber. I snap the gate shut and return the pistol to its holster.

We're not done yet.

The kid's plan to empty out The Greenbrier worked, at least as well as could be expected; Jake said he took off with Jax and a couple of the Guardians on his tail. I can't see how that will have gone well for him. The kid's quick, but his legs are short; no way he'd be able to outpace The Viking, not in the snow. I need to go find them. First we need to get clear of this place, though; if there's anyone still left inside they'll have heard the gunfire.

But when we reach the lobby there's just a single figure waiting. He stands in the center of the checkerboard marble, hands clasped behind his back, staring up at the chandelier that hangs from the high ceiling. He looks over as we enter.

'Ah, Gabriel.'

'Mr. Finch?'

He's wearing the overcoat with the fur-trimmed collar he had on that night in the holding pen. The hem is splashed with dirt, like he has travelled a distance in it.

He turns to Mags.

'And this must be Mags.' He holds out a hand. 'I am delighted to meet you, my dear. Gabriel has told me so much about you. My name is Garland Finch.'

Mags eyes him suspiciously, then takes his hand. He offers Jake a smile, then gestures to a pair of armchairs that sit either side of a tall wooden clock.

I look around uncertainly, still not sure what's going on. Through the lobby's tall windows I see a handful of dark shapes, bundled up in rags, making their way towards the entrance.

'I'm sorry Mr. Finch, but we have business to attend to. There's a friend of ours still unaccounted for.'

He flutters his fingers, like this should not be a concern.

'Oh, don't fret on his account, Gabriel. I expect he'll be with us presently.'

I'm not sure what he means by that, but now more men are gathering outside and I have yet to figure out how to get us by them, so I follow him over to the chairs. His heels click on the marble. There's no sign of the cane and only the merest hint of a drag in his stride. He stands in front of the clock, taking a moment to admire the carvings on its golden face, then bends to the nearest chair and lifts the drop sheet that covers it. The upholstery is patterned like the feathers of some colorful bird. He brushes the dust from it and motions for Mags to sit. She hesitates then takes a seat. He points me towards the other one.

'I'll stand, if it's all the same to you, Mr. Finch.'

'As you wish, Gabriel, as you wish.'

He chooses a spot on the sofa opposite, carefully placing one knee over the other, then looks up at me. The spectacles are gone. Without them his eyes seem an even paler shade of blue.

I glance back towards the entrance. What looks like the entire population of Starkly Correctional Institution now seems to be waiting outside. I realize it must have been their tracks I saw this morning, out on the interstate, not Peck's.

'When did you send them out?'

Finch's lips crease in a smile.

'The morning after you showed up.'

'You were always going to go for it.'

He nods.

'I do hope you will excuse the subterfuge.' He spreads his hands. 'Only when I heard you speak of this place, it seemed like an opportunity too great to pass up.'

He leans forward and his expression changes, as though an unpleasant thought has just occurred to him.

'You didn't have any designs on it yourself, did you?'

I shake my head. I can't imagine anything worse than spending another night here.

'Good, good. I would hate for us to fall out over it.'

'You held me in that cell, though.'

He spreads his hands by way of apology.

'Yes, but your incarceration was only temporary. I assumed you would need our help, and I needed time to get these fellows here. You will forgive me Gabriel, but your plan did seem a little...threadbare.' He looks over at Mags, then back to me again. 'Although I have to say, you seem to have managed admirably.' He gestures in the direction of the Exhibition Hall. 'What will we find back there?'

'Just bodies, for the most part. There's a level beneath the plant room; you might want to be careful when you go check it out. One of the furies got free. It has a soldier trapped down there.'

He stares at me a moment, like he's trying to work out whether there's a part of it I'm not telling him, but then he just says, *I see.*

There's a commotion from outside and I look over in time to see Jax being dragged forward. His arms have been bound, but nevertheless it's taking Tully and three of the other inmates to hold him. Behind him I see Zack and Jason. It looks like they've found Boots, too. There's no sign of Kurt or the President.

Goldie appears at the entrance, presses his face to the

glass. Finch waves him in and he enters the lobby, pushing the kid in front of him. The kid sees Mags and makes to run over to her, but Goldie grabs him by the shoulder, holding him back. Mags gets to her feet; there's an expression on her face that suggest Goldie had best take care what he does next.

The fingers of my reaching hand flex involuntarily. There's still a few pins and needles there, but my arm seems like it might finally be ready to do my bidding. It doesn't change the fact I only have five bullets to my name, though.

I look over at the kid.

'You okay?'

He nods.

'That one's our friend, Mr. Finch. We'll be needing him back.'

Finch leans back on the sofa. His fingers brush the knot of his tie.

'You know it's not wise to get between a predator and its meal, Gabriel.'

Mags' expression hardens at his words. I catch her eye.

Let me take care of this.

'I know, Mr. Finch. But this time I'm afraid I'm going to have to insist.'

My hand settles on the haft of the pistol, but I make no move to draw it. The voice speaks softly.

'I'll trade you for him, though.'

Good.

'And what is it that you have to offer me, Gabriel? More books?'

I shake my head.

'Something much better than that, Mr. Finch.'

I lean forward, whisper it into his ear.

He sits still for a moment, then turns his head to look at me.

'I'm not sure, Gabriel. You know what they say: a bird in the hand. And that one looks tasty.'

But his eyes are sparkling as he says it; I know I have him.

'Oh, you wouldn't find him palatable, Mr. Finch. Trust me on that.'

He lifts a finger, starts tapping the arm of the sofa with it.

'You're not putting me on are you, Gabriel?'

I shake my head.

'I know better than to lie to you, Mr. Finch.'

He beckons Goldie forward. I take him off to one side, tell him which way Kane was headed. He looks at Finch for confirmation then hurries back outside. Moments later he leaves, taking half a dozen of the prisoners with him.

Finch gets to his feet, smoothes the front of his overcoat.

'Well then, it appears our business is concluded. Will you be joining us for dinner? It appears we have plenty to go around.'

'I don't think so, Mr. Finch. We'll be on our way, if it's all the same to you.'

He nods, ushers us toward the entrance. At the door he stops and turns to Mags.

'Well my dear, it was a pleasure to make your acquaintance.'

The smile doesn't waver, but as he says it he grabs her by the wrist, so fast it surprises me. His other hand darts inside his coat. Mags' eyes narrow and she starts to pull away, but it's clear whatever Finch is up to he's caught her off guard too.

My fingers don't wait for an instruction from my brain. I have the pistol clear of its holster and pointed at his head with the hammer cocked before his hand has a chance to re-emerge. He pauses, then slowly pulls out a small package wrapped in brown paper, tied up with string. He places it in her hand.

'Something Gabriel would have wanted you to have.'

She hesitates a moment and then pulls the string. The paper falls away and inside is a book. On the cover a dark rabbit, hunched in silhouette, its ears folded back, its teeth bared. The copy of *Watership Down* he gave me on my first visit to Starkly.

I return the gun to its holster.

'That wasn't smart, Mr. Finch. I could have killed you.'

He spreads his hands.

'It was a risk, but I had to know.'

I'm not sure I understand. A smile creases his lips.

'You do remember our discussion, Gabriel? The totem pole; where we each stand on it.' He leans a little closer and the smile becomes wistful. 'I think I could have been a little braver, with that gift you gave me. Held out just a little longer.'

Mags wraps the book back up in the paper and slides it into the pocket of her parka. Jake holds the door open for her and the kid and they step outside. I'm about to follow them, but then Finch rests a hand on my arm.

'I have enjoyed our time together Gabriel, I really have. Probably best that our paths don't cross again, though, wouldn't you agree?

'I would, Mr. Finch.'

He nods.

I push the door back and step into the shadow of The Greenbrier's massive portico.

'Gabriel.'

I turn around.

Finch is standing in the doorway, his hands clasped behind his back. I remember what I thought, the first time I laid eyes on him, in the cellblock of the Starkly Correctional Institution: that he was other, exotic; that he

463

did not belong in a place like that. Perhaps it's The Greenbrier's outward splendor: the towering columns; the sweeping staircases; the paintings that hang from its gaily-colored walls. Or maybe it's the darkness that for so long has lurked just beneath that polished veneer. Either way, Garland Finch no longer seems out of place. It seems like he is home.

'What is it, Mr. Finch?'

'That flask I left you; did you happen to try any of it?'

'No, Mr. Finch, I did not.'

He smiles, then turns to go back inside.

'Good for you, Gabriel. Good for you.'

*

OFF IN THE DISTANCE a lowering cloud gives sudden birth to a sliver of blue-white light; seconds later the low boom of thunder rumbles through the valley. I look up into the darkening sky. To the east thunderheads the color of charcoal, heavy with the snow they carry, drag their swollen bellies along the peaks. Storms are coming; it won't be long now until the first of them are upon us.

I pause to let Jake catch up while Mags continues on ahead, the kid following close in her tracks. It's been ten days since we quit The Greenbrier and she's yet to ask me what it was I offered Finch to let him go. I guess she doesn't need to. There was only the one thing I had to trade, and she knows it. When we had Kane and Hicks and the other soldiers all tied up in the chapel in Eden, after she'd come through the scanner, I told her I was ready to shoot them, and be done with it. And looking back at how things have turned out, I can't say as that would have altogether been a bad thing. Those we spared then are dead now, or worse, and there are a few, like Tyler and Eric, and Angus and Hamish, who might still be alive if I had. But she stopped me. She said that wasn't how we were going to do things now.

This time she didn't raise a finger.

Still, though, I can't help but wonder if she'd have done it any different, in my shoes. I can't see how she could. Sometimes there just aren't any good choices, even if you see the world the way Mags does.

I turn back to Jake, watching as he struggles towards me through the drifts. I doubt he has much left in him now. I can't fault him for it. He doesn't have the pace we do and I've been pushing hard, hoping to get us most of the way back before our rations ran out.

Tell the truth I never thought we'd manage to stretch them out as long as we have; the MREs I brought with me from Fearrington weren't ever intended for four. But something's changed since Starkly. I can get by on much less than I used to need, even pounding the snow all day long. Mags and the kid, too. Jake's been getting the lion's share of what we have.

I've been reading Gilbey's notebook at night, searching for clues as to how the virus works, what it's done to make us the way we are now. Most of what's she written I just don't get, and I doubt any dictionary I might find down the road will help with that. But occasionally there's something, a paragraph, a sentence, even just a single word, I can make sense of.

On one page she'd scribbled *Fuel* above a bunch of equations, underlining it several times for good measure. The rest of what followed looked like so much gobbledygook and I was about to flip the page, when among the jumble of symbols I spotted a word I recognized from years of studying the backs of MRE cartons: *calories*. It appeared more than once in the pages that followed.

Food is like fuel, same as diesel for the generator or branches for the fire, only for our bodies; that much I already knew. I always figured it got used up when you did stuff, like running around, or hiking through the snow. Turns out I had that bit wrong, however. According to what followed in Gilbey's notes for the most part it goes to regulating your body temperature, keeping you warm. And if I've understood her right, Mags, the kid and me, we don't need that anymore.

MRE doesn't stand for *Magically Replenishing Eats*, all the same, and I've yet to figure out the workings of that loaves and fishes trick Kane would sometimes sermonize about, when he was trying to convince us what was left in Eden's stores would be enough to see us through the winters that lay ahead. We split the last of the cartons yesterday morning. Ever since there's been nothing but the snowmelt in our canteens.

I'm not worried, though. An hour ago we quit the John S Mosby highway for the Blue Ridge Mountain Road. There can't be more than a couple of miles left between us and Mount Weather now. By nightfall we'll be there.

Jake's still struggling up the incline. I look behind him. All along the horizon lightning flashes inside the clouds, occasionally breaking free to stab down at the peaks below. I count the seconds until the thunder reaches us. Still distant, but getting closer. Back in Eden I used to dread the winters, the long months spent locked up inside a mountain. But this one I'm looking forward to. I've had enough of the world outside to last me a good long while. I'm ready to be home now.

Jake finally draws level then pulls down his mask and bends over, hands on his knees. When he's got his breath back he reaches for his canteen. He unscrews the cap, raises it to his lips, but there's little left. He tilts his head back and upends it, shaking the last few drops into his mouth. I dig mine from the side pocket of my pack and hold it out to him. He stares at it a moment, then he says he's okay.

I take a swig. I can't say as I blame him. I'm not sure I'd accept a drink from someone who looks the way I do, either. Things are a little better than when I first caught my reflection, in the cell, back in Starkly: the dark circles around my eyes are beginning to fade and I think I've gained back a little of the weight I lost to the virus, in spite of the short rations we've been on. My hair's yet to start growing back, however, and the deep grooves where my cheeks used to be persist. Mags says she likes them – she reckons they lend my face character - but I'm not so sure about that. All in all there's a little too much of the night about me.

I screw the cap back on, return the canteen to my pack.

'Good to go?'

He nods once, pulls his mask up and we set off again.

For the next mile the road continues to climb, but then it finally flattens and, true to its name, starts to snake its way along the ridge. Withered trunks poke through the snow on either side, stretching off down the slopes into the valley below. The gap between them narrows until there's little to tell where our path might be, but if Mags is uncertain of our path she doesn't show it; she leads us on without slowing.

As dusk settles we come to a large sign, almost buried in a drift. The lights above are hooded under black metal cowls, the kind you'd see at a railroad crossing, the lenses rimed with ice. It says we're entering a restricted area and should turn back. Beyond the road curves to the right. We follow it around and then it straightens and crests, revealing a large clearing straddling the mountain's spine.

We've made it; we're home.

The main gate rises up from the snow in front of us, a high chain-link fence topped with razor wire stretching off into the distance on either side. Mags has already found the section I opened with bolt cutters the day I first arrived. The kid follows her in. I bend down to squeeze myself through, then hold the wire back for Jake.

We make our way into the compound. Up ahead the control tower juts from the highest point of the ridge. A flash of lightning illuminates the sky behind, briefly silhouetting the antennae that bristle from its roof, the awkward gray shapes of the microwave transmitters. On the far side of it is the portal. When I first came here part of me had hoped that I would find it bathed in light; that survivors, people who had spent the last decade eking out an existence inside a hollowed out mountain, would be waiting to welcome me in. But as I look up what I see is a thousand times better.

Behind the tower's tall, angled windows, the soft glow of firelight.

Mags has seen it too. She turns to look at me.

'The Juvies; they made it back.'

Jake pushes his goggles onto his forehead. He's exhausted, starving, but I hear the smile in his voice.

'They've been posting a watch.'

We hurry up towards it, calling out as we go. As we get closer I can see the door's been left open; it creaks back and forth on its hinges in the wind. I keep my eyes on it, waiting for a familiar face to appear there. But no one comes down to greet us. As I get closer I see a single set of tracks, leading off in the direction of the tunnel.

We make our way past the tower, down to the helicopter landing pad. The tattered windsock snaps and flutters on its tether. Beyond it the path curves around one final time and at last I see it.

The gate that Peck blasted open has been repaired, returned to its runners. Where the bars couldn't be bent back into shape strands of razor wire have been strung across them, covering the gaps. A heavy chain and sturdy padlock secure it to the frame. Behind the tunnel stretches off into grainy shadow.

Mags stares into the darkness while I call out to whoever might be there. When there's no answer she turns around, makes her way back up to the control tower. The kid watches uncertainly, like he can't decide whether he should follow. She returns a few moments later.

'A fire's been lit, but there's nobody up there.'

I turn back to the gate and resume shouting. After a

few seconds Jake joins in. The last of the light's leaving the sky and the temperature's starting to fall, but for a long while there's nothing except our own voices and the wind. And then at last the sound of footsteps, drifting up through the tunnel. Jake keeps hollering; he hasn't heard them yet. I hold a hand up and he falls quiet.

Moments later a single flashlight appears around the corner, making its way slowly towards us. The beam is brighter than a windup has any business being; I can't make out who's behind it. As they draw closer I raise a hand to ward it off. For once Jake's eyes serve him better.

'It's Lauren.'

She stops, still some distance back from the gate. Jake takes a step towards the bars.

'Lauren, thank God. We were beginning to think we'd have to spend the night in the control tower.'

She keeps the flashlight on me.

'We didn't think you'd be back.'

'I know. We have a lot to tell you. Let us in.'

Jake's voice is trembling with the cold now, but she makes no move to come closer. She holds the light on me a little longer then just shakes her head.

'I can't do that.'

I join Jake at the bars.

'What do you mean?'

'I'm sorry. We all decided. The way you are now. We can't take the chance.'

'But we're no danger to you.' I'm not sure what else to say so I reach inside my thermals for the crucifix, hold it up to the light. 'See?'

'I'm sorry.'

Something about the way she says it makes me think she's not though, not really. Beside me Jake clutches his arms to his sides.

'You can't do this, Lauren! You can't! We have no

470

food, nowhere to go.'

This time her answer comes quickly, like she's had time to think about it. The walk through the tunnel, maybe. My guess is probably longer than that.

'There are rations in the control tower. You can take whatever's there.'

I feel myself growing angry, that they would do this; that a handful of MREs is the best they would offer. *I* found this place. They're here because of me. I lower my hand and stare through the bars, wanting her to see my eyes. Her face is hidden behind the light, so I can't see her reaction. But I can smell her fear, a bitter, acrid thing, not unlike the Sterno tabs we would burn to warm our food.

I reach for the bars. Inside my head the voice calls out a warning.

Careful.

Look.

I shift my gaze from the beam, back into the shadows. Afterimages from the light are still swirling across my vision, but I see a pair of cables, snaking up from the snow to the elevated walkway that runs down one side of the tunnel. They end at the terminals of a large battery that sits there.

Lauren must have followed my gaze.

'We've electrified it, just like the blast door in Eden. We don't want any trouble. It'd be best if you all just went on your way.'

I unzip my parka, start to reach inside for the pistol. Before I get to it Mags steps between us.

'You'll let Jake in. He was never infected.'

Lauren glances over at Jake, but she's already shaking her head, like that decision might have been made some time ago, too.

'No. We can't be certain.'

Mags slips off one of her mittens.

'You misunderstand me, Lauren. I'm not asking.'

I see what she means to do, but when I try to warn her she just turns to me, shakes her head. She reaches for a strand of the razor wire, runs a finger along it, as though testing it. Then she chooses a spot between the barbs, grasps it, and slowly twists. There's a jangling sound as the wire goes taut, and then it snaps with a *ping*. She pulls the strand from the bars, holds it up.

'Is that it? You really think what you've done here will keep us out?'

She lets the wire fall to the snow. Lauren stares at it for a moment and now when her eyes return to Mags they're wide with fear.

'So this is what's going to happen, Lauren. We're going up to the control tower to get those rations. You're going to let Jake in, and then you're going to *run* and fetch us Marv's map. When we come back if Jake's still out here, or if that map's not waiting for us, I'm coming in, and you're the one I'll be looking to for an explanation.'

Lauren nods quickly.

'Okay. Okay.'

Jake stumbles forward, shaking his head.

'No. They have to let us all in. Otherwise I'm coming with you.'

Mags turns to face him.

'No, you're not, Jake. Winter's almost here. Gabe, Johnny and me, we can survive on the outside now, but you can't. Besides, they need you in there.' She glances through the bars. 'Even if they don't realize it yet.'

We make our way up to the control tower and fill our packs with the MREs. When there's no more space left we strip the HOOAH!s from the cartons that remain and start stuffing them into the pockets of our parkas, as many as will fit. As we open the last of them I catch

Mags flexing her fingers.

'Is your hand okay?'

She nods.

'It's fine, just a little numb. The battery was old, probably lifted from the fire truck. Between that and the cold I figured what little charge it still held wouldn't be enough to do me serious harm.'

I close the snaps on my pack.

'They have no right to banish us. We should go back, make them let us in.'

She doesn't say anything for a moment, but then she reaches over, grabs my hand.

'I've had longer to think about this than you, Gabe.' She looks over at the kid, then back to me again. 'The truth is the Juvies aren't going to get used to the way we are now, no matter how much time we give them. I wish it were different, but it's not. So you can go back inside if you want to. But I'm not sure it's for me, or Johnny. We just don't care to go on living with people who don't want us there.'

When we return to the portal the tunnel's deserted. Marv's map's waiting at the foot of the guillotine gate, wrapped in a Ziploc bag. I pick it up, transfer it to the inside pocket of my parka. Mags and the kid start back up the path, but for a few moments I just stand in front of the bars, staring into the darkness.

There's a crack of thunder, louder than the ones that have gone before, and I glance up. Lightning shudders through the thunderheads above, a warning of the wrath to come. Mags told Jake we could survive out here, but I have less confidence in that than she does. She and the kid are the only things left in this cold, broken world I care about, however, so I take one last look into the tunnel then turn around and follow them.

By the time I reach the gate they're already waiting

for me on the other side. Mags holds the wire back and I squeeze through to join them. She pulls her hood up, turns to look at me.

'So where are we going to go?'

The remains of the tracks we made coming up stretch off into the trees. We could go back, but what lies that way is already known to us. None of it is any good.

I let my gaze follow the ridge in the opposite direction, the road I came up when I first arrived here. There are places on Marv's map that way, places I never thought I'd have to visit. I know little of them, but I'm not sure what other options we have.

I reach up for my goggles, slide them down.

'North.'

I hope you enjoyed Gabe and Mags' latest adventure. I'm currently working on the fourth book in the series. If you'd like to be notified when it will be available, or indeed if you'd just like to say hi, please get in touch through the contact page at www.rahakok.com. I love getting emails from readers.

And if you'd like to read the newspaper clippings Gabriel collects to try and figure out what happened to the world, or follow his progress on the map Marv gave him, you can download each free at www.rahakok.com.

But before you go…

It's hard to overstate how important reviews are to an indie author, so if you enjoyed *Lightning Child* and you have a moment to spare, could I ask you to visit wherever you go to get your books and post one? A sentence or even a couple of words will do just fine!

Thank you!.

LIFE IS TOO SHORT.

AT LEAST FOR SOME...

A brilliant young geneticist, desperately seeking a cure
for the disease that took her father. A Nevada sheriff,
charged with solving a crime that threatens the very
existence of his small desert town. But when an
unmarked van crashes in sleepy Hawthorne, Alison
Stone and Lars Henrikssen find themselves looking for
the same man.

Only Carl Gant is not what he seems. And they are not the only ones looking for him.

Available on Amazon.

AMONG WOLVES RECAP

THE WORLD LIES IN RUIN.

Outside a thick layer of ash-filled snow shrouds the frozen ground, and through the long winters violent storms rage. A nanovirus that devours metal has wreaked havoc. Bridges and interstate exchanges lie collapsed in rubble; buildings list and crumble under their own weight. The virus attacked people too, leaching the metal from their bodies, turning them into bloodthirsty furies. Nobody knows where it came from.

Only a handful survived. When Washington was attacked, the President, Kane, and a Secret Service agent, Peck, fled with a visiting class of first graders to a mothballed mountain bunker they now know as Eden. Kane tells the children they are the Chosen Ones. Soon the last of them will turn sixteen and he will reveal their matches. Then it will be their job to repopulate the planet.

But after so long inside the mountain supplies are running low. One of the children, Gabriel, and the troubled soldier, Marv, are sent outside to scavenge for things they need. They carry steel crucifixes that allow Peck, and the handful of children he has appointed Guardians, to check whether they've been contaminated when they return.

Gabriel searches the places he scavenges for books. Most of the children can't read, but he and the rebellious Mags remember how. Books aren't allowed in Eden, so Gabriel relays the stories he finds on the outside to Mags when he returns.

One day while Gabriel's outside scavenging he comes across the body of Benjamin, a soldier who was in Eden when they first arrived, together with a bloodstained map that shows the way to a place called

Mount Weather. When Kane learns of the map he sends Gabriel and Marv out to find Mount Weather, even though winter is close and the storms are coming. On the way Marv becomes infected with the virus and starts to change into a fury. Before he kills himself he explains to Gabriel everything that's wrong with Eden. Benjamin had been trying to get the children out, but Kane uncovered his plan and sent Peck to kill him.

Gabriel continues to Mount Weather where he finds another bunker, stocked with supplies. He returns to Eden, only to discover that Kane had never intended either he or Marv to return. He sneaks back in through one of the vent shafts, intending to free the Juvies without Kane realizing. But Kane has brought forward the ceremony where the children will be matched, forcing Gabriel to rethink his plans.

While searching for a way to get the children out of the mountain Gabriel discovers stockpiles of the virus, proving that it was Kane who was responsible for releasing it in the first place. Gabriel interrupts the ceremony and confronts Kane, threatening to contaminate Eden if he won't let them leave. The children are scared to go outside, but Gabriel convinces them. He holds Peck and the Guardians at bay while Mags and the others escape into the tunnel that leads to the outside. As he's running after them Gabriel is shot, but Mags and one of the others, Jake, come back for him and drag him out. Together they seal the tunnel and Gabriel leads the children to Mount Weather.

THE DEVIL YOU KNOW RECAP

The Juvies have spent the winter in Mount Weather, but Gabriel knows they're not safe there. Soon the storms will clear and Kane will send Peck for them.

The Juvies are reluctant to leave without a destination, however, so Gabriel sets out with Mags, looking for another home for them. He has the map Marv gave him, with all the bunkers that once were part of the Federal Relocation Arc marked on it. The closest is in West Virginia, a place called The Greenbrier.

On the way Gabriel and Mags run into a group of soldiers from The Greenbrier led by the wiry gunslinger Hicks. They follow them back to a once-luxurious resort where they meet the detached Dr. Gilbey. Gilbey is a scientist; the resort conceals a huge underground bunker she has been using as a lab while she works on a cure for the virus.

When two of the soldiers, Truck and Weasel, attempt to sneak into Mags' room that night Hicks suggests she would be safer in the bunker with Gilbey, but she ends up becoming infected by the virus. Hicks explains that Mags' only chance is for Gabriel to help Gilbey in her quest for a cure. Gilbey needs furies that are still active on which to test her work. Hicks and the other soldiers search hospitals, looking for specimens hiding in areas that might have been shielded from the effects of the pulse released when Kane scorched the skies.

Gabriel joins Hicks and the other soldiers on a visit to a hospital in Blackburg. They find a fury, but Gabriel freezes when it attacks Ortiz, one of the soldiers, and Hicks has to kill it, along with his comrade.

When they return to The Greenbrier Gabriel insists on seeing Mags. Unbeknownst to Gabriel it was Gilbey who infected Mags; she has been kept in a cage in the basement with a young fury, Johnny 99, since. Gilbey threatens a similar fate for Gabriel if Mags reveals this, but when they bring her out Mags manages to warn Gabriel that he has to flee.

That night Gabriel escapes The Greenbrier. He knows that Gilbey will send the soldiers after him; he intends to lead them away so he can double back and rescue Mags. His plan is to bring her back to Eden and put her in the scanner, to remove the virus from her system, but a storm blows in and he ends up collapsing in the snow outside The Greenbrier's gates. Hicks rescues him and brings him to a nearby church. He reveals that he was infected when the furies overran the last of humanity a decade before and has been surviving on medicine Gilbey gives him. The medicine slows down the virus, but its effects are dwindling. He agrees to help Gabriel free Mags and bring her back to Eden if he can come along.

Gabriel and Hicks break Mags out of her cages. When Mags refuses to leave without Johnny 99 Hicks stays behind to try and get more of Gilbey's medicine. The three set off but Gabriel and Mags are both injured and Johnny 99 is too small to move quickly. In an attempt to evade the soldiers Gilbey sends after them, Gabriel leads them into the Appalachians.

Mags insists on sharing the medicine Hicks gave her with Johnny 99 and it quickly runs out. She and the kid both become sick. Hicks catches up with them, but when he sees Mags he explains to Gabriel she doesn't have long now, even with the medicine he's brought. Hicks convinces Johnny 99 he's holding them up, so the kid leaves. When Mags finds out she grows angry. Gabriel goes off to try and find him while Hicks takes her on.

Gabriel finds Johnny but then they run into Truck and the other soldiers. They manage to evade them and catch up with Hicks, but Mags and the kid are very sick now. They make it back to Eden with the soldiers hot on their heels. Gabriel gets them inside, where he learns that Peck has taken most of the Guardians to Mount Weather. He brings Mags and the kid to the scanner, leaving Hicks to close up the blast door, but Hicks double-crosses him, letting the soldiers in.

When he finds out Gabriel aborts the scan, but the scanner has fried Mags' and the kid's circuits, rendering them both unconscious. Gabriel hides Mags in the armory and goes back out to confront the soldiers, hoping to bargain with Hicks' for his help saving Mags' life. Hicks offers to let him go if he'll give up the Juvies at Mount Weather. Hicks wants to take them back for Gilbey to experiment on. But then Mags bursts out of the tunnel and overpowers the soldiers. She, Gabriel and Johnny 99 make their escape, leaving them tied up in the chapel with Kane.

They set out for Mount Weather, hoping to get there ahead of Peck. Mags seems better but Gabriel has doubts about her sudden transformation, worried that the work of the virus is not yet done.

Ready to begin?

Made in the USA
San Bernardino, CA
11 July 2018